IREHIDE

DeAndrea Pete

DEDICATION

For the women who hold tightly to control yet dream of the freedom found in trust. For the romantics who crave destiny's hand but fear giving theirs away. For those who doubt people but never doubt love itself. This book is for you—a proof that your heart can be both guarded and open, strong and tender, all at once.

Irehide: (*Noun*) The quiet restraint of
generational resentment, carried by
Black people to survive in an unequal world,
until it's released and reclaimed as power

TABLE OF CONTENTS

Part I: Lighting

Chapter 1: Cries of the Soul   1
Chapter 2: Soul Ties Never Leave   25
Chapter 3: Leave Me at the Alter   43
Chapter 4: Alter the World   63
Chapter 5: Worlds Colliding   77
Chapter 6: Colliding Frame of Mind   89
Chapter 7: Mind Games   99
Chapter 8: Games, Games, and Less Gains   111
Chapter 9: Gains and Unrequited Affection   127
Chapter 10: Affections Causing Infection   137
Chapter 11: Infection of the Heart   145

Part II: Thunderstrike

Chapter 12: Newfangled Love   157
Chapter 13: Love Can Be Poisonous   167
Chapter 14: Poison Seeps into Us All   175
Chapter 15: All the More   185
Chapter 16: More Stirring   199
Chapter 17: Stirring the Cauldron   209
Chapter 18: Cauldron of Witches Brew   225
Chapter 19: Brew the Test   239

Part III: Clear Skies

Chapter 20: Serendipitous Meeting   253
Chapter 21: Meeting the Month of May   265

Chapter 22: May Your Flowers Bloom 283
Chapter 23: Bloom the Colors of Your Soul 295

Epilogue 315
Acknowledgments 323

Part I:
Lighting

CHAPTER 1:
CRIES OF THE SOUL

Detroit, 1968

The only thing white people loved more than money was superiority. It was etched on the boardroom walls and woven into polite talk. Even those with little money clung to it while looking down on people of color. Whiteness alone gave them an edge, or so they believed. It was a phenomenon Florence couldn't ignore.

Women weren't exempt either. Society deemed them lesser, yet white women rarely seemed to see themselves that way. Even when treated with cruelty, they clung to the illusion of privilege that came with their skin. It was a false comfort, but Florence had no time to resent them for it.

This was why she'd chosen law: to wipe the smug looks off their faces, to prove them wrong, to rise no matter the cost. If her job had taught her anything, it was that the law could change, and she would be the one to change it. Once they saw that she was smarter, more prepared, and just as capable, they wouldn't have a leg to stand on.

A loud thud broke her train of thought. She blinked, then bent down to pick up the papers that had fallen from her hands. She straightened her blazer and continued walking around the long, polished table, its surface gleaming under the overhead lights, reflecting nothing but empty chairs and unspoken tension. The room felt silent and heavy around her.

She gathered the last of the papers as the room emptied, not a single person offering so much as a glance. Invisible, as always. It reminded her of her childhood, where she felt mute and overlooked. Growing up colored in Tulsa, Oklahoma, felt like being seen as less than human. Florence had never forgotten that feeling. It surfaced now and then, especially in moments like this, when silence spoke louder than words.

It was the Friday before the Fourth of July weekend. The men from the law firm went to the bar next door to celebrate. That wasn't unusual—it happened every Friday. The women, never invited to join, had their own tradition: going out dancing. Florence wasn't part of their plans. They gathered at a dance hall meant for white people. Even if that wasn't the case, she didn't feel close to any women at work. They stayed away from her unless they needed her help with their tasks.

Florence stood by the open window on the third floor. She looked down at the bar across the west side of the parking lot, the same side where the colored employees were supposed to park their vehicles. She rested one hand on the sill, the metal cool beneath her fingertips. It was already dark outside, and though it was only six o'clock, the employees had deserted the office. Most of the firm left by four, especially before a holiday weekend.

The silence gave Florence time to prepare. She compiled a list of tasks for the following week, determined to start Monday morning ahead of schedule. After organizing her files, she savored the quiet. Since she hadn't become a junior associate, her only way to move up was to review the work of other associates. She used this to refine her skills.

When Florence started at Mayfield & Associates, also known as Mayfield Law, she didn't expect to find fairness. She'd never been under any illusion that the firm would give her a fair shot. Like everything else in her life, she knew she'd have to work for it. Her assumption proved true. Despite completing graduate school and passing the bar, the only positions "available" to her were entry-level roles like file clerk or secretary—an unspoken result of the discrimination and systemic bias that kept women, especially women like her, out of higher ranks. It wasn't ideal, but it was better than staying in Oklahoma. She accepted the job, telling herself it was just a foot in the door, and began planning her rise to the top. She would succeed based on merit, not favoritism or nepotism.

***

Her first weeks were brutal. Tasks came not with instruction but with assumption, tossed at her like scraps, as if she were supposed to know what to do with them simply because she was there. No one mentored her. No one paused to help. They said, "You learn by doing," as though confusion were a rite of passage, not a wound.

She floundered—redid what should have been right the first time, lost time, lost face. Kept her head above water by instinct alone.

To keep from drowning, she began arriving before dawn. The building was always serene at that hour, the air not yet heavy with breath and blame. She made small lists, tackling the tasks that would later be buried in noise. But even then, there was no room to stretch, no time to grow— just enough space to survive the day without breaking.

That was when she started reviewing old case files. A good lawyer, she believed, should work across all key areas of law: criminal, civil, pro bono, and more. Studying precedents helped her prepare for anything. No case was ever the same, but the lessons were valuable. She imagined herself in a courtroom—confident, capable, commanding respect. The vision made her smile.

***

But it was getting late. Florence cleaned her workspace,

gathered her notes from the typewriter, and put the case files back where they belonged. She grabbed her purse, switched off the lights on her floor, and made her way to the elevator. No one noticed when she worked late. The office doors locked automatically at 9 p.m., which gave her a faint sense of relief.

The old elevator groaned as it descended. On the first floor, she stepped out and headed to the basement. There was no refrigerator for colored employees on her floor, so she had to keep her lunch pail in an old fridge downstairs. No one worked down there anymore, and the space was dusty and neglected.

The clicking of her heels echoed in the silence, creating an unsettling atmosphere. A line from George Berkeley popped into her head: *"If a tree falls in a forest and no one hears it, does it make a sound?"* She dismissed it. *It's just nerves,* she told herself. Still, the flickering light overhead didn't help.

She grabbed her pail and climbed the stairs to the west exit, hurrying as unease crept into her chest. Outside, the muggy July air wrapped around her like a heavy blanket. She opened her car door, leaned in to place her purse and lunch pail on the passenger seat—and froze. Footsteps.

Florence stiffened as droplets hit her face. She looked up. The clouds had gathered fast, and a storm was moving in. Rain fell steadily, blurring her glasses and turning the parking lot silver.

Then she saw them. Two men. Close. Too close. The stench of whiskey and cigars reached her before anything else, making her stomach churn. Their shirts clung to their skin, soaked through, exposing pale flesh. Their laughter echoed—low, cruel. One had yellowed teeth stained with tobacco; the other bore a scar above his cheekbone.

They were drunk. Florence took a breath. "Gentlemen," she said evenly.

They didn't respond; they just stepped closer. Recognition hit her at once. They worked on the fourth floor—for the litigation team. She didn't know their names, but she'd seen them in passing.

In the dim light and pouring rain, their faces blurred into shadows—unrecognizable, almost inhuman. She felt like prey: cornered, hunted. They were so close now she could nearly feel their breath against her skin. Every instinct screamed, but Florence clung to reason like a fraying rope. *They're lawyers*, she told herself. *They wouldn't dare do something like this—not right outside their own workplace… would they?*

She tried to believe it, to swallow the panic rising in her chest, to hold on to something that still felt like reason. But as she stepped back, her escape ended in cold metal—her spine pressed flush against the car. There was nowhere left to go.

The taller man exhaled through his nose, slicked his rain-soaked hair back with one slow sweep of his hand, and slurred, "Nice car…"

"She must've stolen it," the other sneered. "Only way niggers get anything this nice."

"Eric, Eric," the tall one said, slapping his friend on the shoulder with mock disapproval. "They're not niggers anymore. They're colored people, remember?" He shook his head as though correcting a minor mistake.

"You're right, Jeffrey. My mistake," Eric said with syrupy mockery. Then they laughed—sharp, joyless, and cruel.

Florence said nothing. Her fear surged, tightening her throat like a fist.

Then Eric reached out and took her chin between his fingers, firm and deliberate. Tears welled in her eyes as she clung to a single, fragile mantra: *This isn't real. This isn't real.*

"How'd a woman like you land a job working with people like us, huh?" Eric asked, his voice thick with alcohol and contempt.

"She must be someone's whore," Jeffrey answered. "Gregory's? Anderson's? Ben's? Eh—doesn't matter… how 'bout you be mine next?"

Then, without warning, Eric pressed his cold, booze-laced lips to hers. She froze, horrified, as his tongue forced its way into her mouth. The violation jolted her into action—she bit down hard.

He yelped, stumbling back and clutching his bleeding tongue. "You stupid bitch!" he shouted, spitting on the ground. He grabbed the bottle from Jeffrey and took a long drink, then threw it on the pavement, shattering it with a loud crash.

"Aw, man! Why'd you go and do that?" Jeffrey whined. "I was going to drink that!"

Eric didn't answer. He motioned toward Florence. "You think biting me is going to stop us?"

Jeffrey stepped forward—slowly, predatory. He leaned in close, inhaling at the nape of her neck. "I hate everything about you," he whispered. "The way you walk with your head up. Like you've got something we don't. Like you're not property."

"Please," she whispered—so softly she wasn't sure it had left her lips.

"Please… stop." Her voice cracked.

She tried again, stronger this time. "Stop touching me!"

She shoved him back and brushed herself off, trying to collect what little strength she had left.

The response was immediate. Eric struck her hard across the face.

"You shouldn't get smart," he hissed. "It's not very polite."

He grabbed her face with both hands, his fingers digging into her skin, making her wince. "Don't you know your place? Or should we remind you?"

His smile was sharp as he squeezed her cheeks, leaving marks from his nails. Jeffrey kissed her skin. Eric, still spitting blood from where Florence had bitten his tongue, said, "Let's take her for a spin." He leaned in, reeking of whiskey, his hands tracing her legs from her ankles upward.

Florence trembled. A cold sweat mingled with the rain soaking her back. Eric began unbuckling his belt. Jeffrey, now towering over her, gave her a look darker than before.

He grabbed her blouse and ripped it open, buttons scattering across the ground. She couldn't even hear them land— her heartbeat thundered in her ears.

The rain poured harder. Warm tears burned tracks down her cheeks as the stench of alcohol and foul breath turned her stomach. Jeffrey shoved her forward, and she collided with Eric's shoulder. He moved behind her, gripping her wet hair in one hand and twisting until her scalp screamed. With the other, he bound her wrists, pinning them behind her back.

Eric's fingers grazed the edge of her light-blue brassiere. Florence squirmed, but the more she resisted, the rougher they became. He dropped to his knees and tugged her pencil skirt and stockings higher. She tried to close her legs, but Eric wedged his between hers, forcing them apart.

By now, she had stopped pleading. What good would it do? Florence closed her eyes and retreated inward, to that mental place where pain couldn't reach her. *So this is what the tree felt like,* she thought. *It wasn't that no one heard it fall. It's that no one cared if it did.* She stood there, silent and desperate.

Then, she heard something new: keys jingling, footsteps approaching. A third figure stepped into view. Florence opened her eyes, dazed. Water smeared her glasses, her arms still bound. A new man loomed larger than the others, his shadow stretching long across the pavement—a giant in the rain.

"Gentlemen," he said, calm and commanding, "please remove your hands from this young lady." His tone was deep, smooth, unnervingly composed. It made Florence tense. She wasn't alone in her fear. She trembled, wondering if she had traded two small monsters for one giant one.

Jeffrey turned, and for a moment, Florence saw true fear on his face. Eric still held her wrists, unaware of the stranger.

"And who the hell do you think you are, giving us a— " Eric started, but stopped cold when he turned around. Stunned recognition crossed his face. He released her arms and stepped back.

"I'm... I'm sorry, sir," he stammered, head lowered. "It wasn't what it looked like. We were just having a little fun."

"Rape in Michigan," the stranger said coldly, "can get you life in prison." His words cut deeper than screams. He sounded like a man familiar with the law—maybe even one from their own firm. "Is this what you call fun?" he asked.

Florence jumped as something warm settled over her shoulders. The new scent—sandalwood and rain—replaced the bitter tang of alcohol and smoke. The warmth felt foreign, almost soothing. The mysterious new stranger stepped closer with his chest brushing against her back as he stood protectively. She could feel the tension in his body, coiled tightly but contained.

Florence was still stunned. What kind of man could make Eric and Jeffrey tremble with only a few words? He was right: By law, their actions warranted a life sentence. But she knew how the world worked. Justice rarely came for colored women. At best, they would get a slap on the wrist.

"I assume you both have somewhere else to be," the stranger said. The two men muttered clumsy apologies.

He stepped forward, towering over them, and placed a firm hand on each shoulder. He leaned in and whispered something Florence couldn't hear over the rain. Whatever it was, it made Eric and Jeffrey retreat. They lowered their heads and slunk off into the shadowy lot.

The man turned, his face still hidden under the brim of his hat. An umbrella shielded him, shadows masking his features. Yet his presence was undeniable. Florence's body stayed locked in place, unsure whether to run or collapse. He had saved her. But what if it wasn't real? What if it was a trap, a false sense of security? Her body quaked, mind racing. She tried to convince herself it was a dream—a nightmare she would soon wake from. But her skin still stung. Her heart still raced. Her lips still burned. And she feared this man might be her next threat.

The stranger turned to her. "Are you okay?" he asked,

his voice deep and smooth, like velvet laced with thunder.

Florence hadn't expected that voice. It curled around her, stirring something in her chest she couldn't name. She looked up through fogged, rain-splattered glasses and wiped them. The image that emerged was... distracting. He stood close enough to feel his presence without startling her.

When she didn't answer, he took a careful step closer. "Do you need help?" His words snapped her out of the fog.

"No, thank you," she said sharply. "And I don't need this either."

She yanked the blazer from her shoulders—the one he must have placed there—and shoved it toward him. Her fingers brushed his by accident. A jolt sparked through her, making her stiffen. He felt it too. He cleared his throat, averting his eyes. "Please, I insist," he said, his voice lower now, almost a command.

Florence glanced down at herself. Her ripped blouse clung to her skin, transparent in the rain. She shivered, feeling exposed. She hesitated, then pulled the jacket back around her body. It smelled like him: sandalwood, clean cotton, and a hint of expensive cologne. Her senses felt overwhelmed.

"You must be in shock," he said, tilting his head, eyes hidden beneath the brim of his soaked hat.

"I'm fine," she replied. "I've suffered worse fates."

She didn't understand why she was so curt. He wasn't doing anything wrong. Still, the calm he radiated and his protective energy unsettled her. How could a white man make her feel calm? Her senses were clearly scattered from what had occurred. That, and his shirt—drenched and clinging to his broad frame—didn't help. His jaw was sharp, shadowed with stubble, and the hat cast just enough darkness to give him an air of mystery. It was too much.

Florence narrowed her eyes. "You didn't save me from anything," she muttered, unlocking her car door. "And I don't need your help."

"It looked like you did," he said evenly. His voice

followed her, curling under her skin. Then he lifted his chin. Florence's eyes met his for the first time. She turned her head, her heart racing.

"Would you rather I had left you with those drunken savages?" he asked.

Her smile was all teeth, sharp and humorless. "Funny," she said. "I've found the savages usually wear better suits."

"File a complaint with HR," he offered, as if it were that simple.

She rolled her eyes. "Move," she demanded, shutting her car door and shifting into reverse. She backed out of the space and saw him one last time in her mirror.

That night, the bruises on her wrists pulsed with heat. Her cheek still stung where the slap had landed.

Once home, Florence didn't speak. She didn't cry—not yet. She stepped into the shower and scrubbed hard, but the smell of sweat, alcohol, and fear lingered on her skin. It clung to her mind.

She stared at herself in the mirror. Her dark skin, which usually radiated beauty, displayed mottled purple bruises. Her hair, once curled and elegant, was now frizzy, tangled, and matted. Her shoulders sagged. Her head hung low.

She poured a cup of tea with trembling hands. The warmth helped slightly.

Mooni, her black-and-white long-haired cat, paced by her side. He meowed as if he sensed something was very wrong.

She curled into bed, wrapping herself in blankets like armor. Only then did she let herself cry.

The next morning, Florence awoke late, surprised that sleep had come without nightmares. The dreams had been gentle, peaceful—a mercy.

She moved through her morning routine on autopilot: teeth, shower, ponytail. She dabbed concealer on the worst of the bruises. It wasn't much, but it would do. Buttered toast was all she could stomach. Her appetite had left with the night.

As she fed Mooni, he twisted around her legs, impatient. She watched him eat with tender eyes. He was the only friend she had in the city—the only being who had never judged or ignored her.

She found him that first winter after the move, curled beside a dumpster, half-frozen and too weary to run when she approached. His fur was matted, his eyes wary, but what caught her was the crescent-shaped birthmark beneath his chin. It looked like a sliver of moonlight pressed into his skin. She named him Mooni. He was like her: cold, tired, and alone.

Now, years later, she gave him one last gentle pat on the head before leaving the house. "Be good," she whispered. "I'm going to the market."

She grabbed her keys and headed out to pick up Denise—the only person who truly knew her.

Denise had a different upbringing from Florence. She grew up in a warm home filled with people. She had both her parents, many siblings, and memories full of laughter. Florence envied that. But Denise's life hadn't been without hardship. Chronic medical issues had kept her in the hospital for much of her childhood. Colored hospitals had low funding and few resources, so her journey was hard. Still, Denise maintained a bright demeanor, an optimistic outlook, and boundless kindness. Florence admired her for that.

As Florence approached her friend's house, Denise welcomed her with a warm smile. She was already on the porch, looking fresh and radiant, but Florence could see the strain beneath it: late nights, mounting coursework, and the exhaustion of a sophomore year that was wearing her down.

The drive to the farmers' market was silent.

Denise glanced sideways. "How are you doing?"

"I'm fine," Florence said, keeping her eyes fixed ahead.

Denise didn't press.

Florence saw some familiar faces at the market. She noticed neighbors, the mailman, and Mrs. Verna from church. But she hardly paid attention to the conversation. The vibrant smells of ripe fruit, fresh herbs, and smoked meats filled the air, but she felt dull and far away.

She grabbed hot dogs and hamburger meat for the cookout. Denise added drinks and ice cream to the basket. Florence was set to host Saturday dinner this weekend, as they did every week. It wasn't glamorous, but it was theirs—two women, some food, and peace.

Florence glanced at her friend out of the corner of her eye. Denise hadn't noticed the tension in the car. But why would she? Florence had worked hard to seem composed.

At the checkout, Mabel from their NAACP group greeted them with a wide smile.

"Florence! Denise! So good to see you girls. What are y'all up to this weekend?"

Florence offered a polite smile. "Barbecuing at the house. Taking it easy."

Mable tsked. "You young girls ought to be out and about! The church is having a cookout too. You should come meet some folks. Some nice fellas."

Florence forced a laugh. "Ha! No need. Work keeps me too busy."

Mable turned her attention to Denise. "What about you?"

Denise chuckled. "No, thank you. I've got a mountain of homework."

They paid and left, relieved to escape the small talk. Florence knew what people whispered: she and Denise were too close, too sheltered, too unmarried. Folks assumed things. Florence didn't care. She knew what she wanted—someday, a tall, confident man who respected her mind and didn't flinch at her ambitions. The hardest part was telling men she didn't want children. That truth usually sent them running. She didn't want to bring kids into a world that wouldn't accept them because of their skin or gender. Florence knew the cruelty of the world and had no intention of making her children suffer as she had.

Back at the house, Denise cracked open a beer while Florence put away the groceries.

"What's wrong with you?" Denise asked.

Florence turned, pausing mid-shelf. "Nothing is wrong."

"Don't lie to me." Denise stepped over, moved the bags aside, and looked her in the face. "You've been in your head all day. And you're wearing a sweater in this heat."

The pressure finally broke. Florence burst into tears, her whole body trembling.

"I was so scared," she choked. "They… they tried to rape me."

Denise pulled her into a hug, stroking her hair as Florence wept. Once she calmed down, she told Denise everything: the alley, the men, and the stranger who scared them off.

"So… the guy who saved you?" Denise asked.

Florence sniffed, wiping her face. "I don't know who he was. He wore a hat over his face and looked completely ordinary."

"Except for this," she added. Florence went to the bottom drawer. She hesitated, then took out the cream blazer.

Florence hadn't been able to look at it since the night before. It was still damp and carried the scent of the man who had put it on her shoulders. She stared at it as if it might reach out and grab her. The memory of his body next to hers lingered longer than she wished. It felt tense and restrained but also protective. She shook her head and scoffed. She hated the feelings the blazer stirred—one part safety, two parts submission, and an edge of fear she didn't understand. She hadn't opened that drawer until now.

Denise's eyes widened. "What?"

"What?" Florence panicked. "What's wrong?"

"Do you know how expensive this jacket is?"

"Not really. I didn't look at it. I just thought it was… unremarkable. I almost threw it into my donation pile."

"Girl, don't you dare!" Denise exclaimed. "This is a

Brioni. My cousin's a tailor—he's only seen a few of these in his life. This is Italian. Luxury. Whoever owns this is not just anybody."

"Oh God," Florence muttered. "I hope he doesn't come looking for it. I hope I never see that man again." She paused, her voice low. "But for some reason... I haven't been able to get him out of my head."

Denise tilted her head. "Why?"

Florence looked down at the coat, fingers brushing the collar. "His scent. His voice. That heat. It was like I... submitted to him without a second thought. It wasn't romantic. It was just... instinct. And that's what scared me most."

Denise grinned. "So what I'm hearing is: you two should meet again."

Florence gave her a look, but inside she was shaken. The man hadn't only protected her—he'd unraveled her.

They finished putting the groceries away. Denise grilled while Florence chopped vegetables. Mooni leapt onto the counter and snatched a hot dog.

"Mooni!" Florence yelped. "Get back here, you little thief!"

Denise laughed. "I told you, cats are bad luck."

"Don't talk about my baby like that!" Florence said with mock anger.

"I'm just saying," Denise cackled, "your baby ate part of our dinner."

"I'll make muffins to make it up to you," Florence conceded.

"Deal," Denise said with a snort. "But only if they're the ones with the cinnamon crumble on top."

That night, they danced barefoot in the living room, twirling until the world tilted. They belted out karaoke to "My Girl," laughing so hard their stomachs ached. Florence dozed off with her head in Denise's lap while Mooni curled against them—warm, small, and safe, at least for tonight.

When Florence woke the next morning, it was to Mooni's yowling and the throb of a splitting headache.

Some things never changed.

****

Ben Mayfield stood outside the old tailor's shop on Jefferson and Main, his hands deep in his pockets. The summer humidity and the lingering storm made his shirt cling to his back. He stared at his reflection in the dark glass window, but he could barely recognize himself.

He was still thinking about her—the woman in the parking lot. He hadn't meant to stop. In fact, he had tried to talk himself out of it. The moment he saw the two junior associates cornering a woman, his instincts took over. It wasn't her vulnerability that stopped him; it was her presence. Even in fear, even trembling, even drenched in rain and raw with tension, she looked regal.

He hadn't seen her face at first. He noticed the set of her shoulders, the tilt of her chin, and the strength in her stance. She refused to collapse, even when outnumbered. Then she turned to him. When her eyes met his, wide behind rain-soaked glasses, they burned with a stubborn fire. He felt it—a current that lit his chest and tightened his jaw. She wasn't just beautiful; she was alive. Elegant. Dignified. She stood there, vulnerable yet unbroken, her body stiff with contempt. And she had rejected his help as if it were poison.

Ben let out a bitter laugh at himself and finally pushed off the brick wall of the shop. "She didn't even say thank you," he murmured.

The truth was, it didn't matter. Because she didn't need saving; he had seen that in her eyes the second she turned away. She didn't want a knight in shining armor. She wanted power, autonomy, control. And that stirred something in him.

Her voice still echoed in his ears, sharp and cold: *"I've found the savages usually wear better suits."* The way she shoved his blazer back at him had been dismissive. Yet, when she felt exposed, she held onto it again. That moment stayed with him. It was a tension he couldn't name. She hated the help, but she needed the protection. And he wanted to be the one to give it. God help him, the way she looked at him—wide-eyed and wounded, yet fierce—had knocked the wind from his lungs.

Now, he wanted to know who she was.

The blazer. He hadn't even considered asking for it back. It was a thousand-dollar Brioni, but that didn't matter. He wanted her to keep it.

Something about her lingered in his mind like a story missing its final page. Ben looked up at the night sky. The storm had passed, but heavy clouds still hung low, unwilling to leave. He didn't know her name, or where she lived, or if he would ever see her again. But deep in his chest, something coiled—a quiet certainty, steady and unshakable, like a warning: He would.

***

Afterward, Florence got up and changed into fresh clothes. It was Sunday. She dreaded Sundays, not because of church or chores, but because her mother would always call that afternoon without fail. The conversation would be long; winding; and, more often than not, uncomfortable.

Denise, now dressed in borrowed clothes, joined Florence for a quick breakfast of grits, eggs, and toast. When they finished, she thanked Florence and promised to return the outfit soon.

"Don't worry about it," Florence said, waving her off. "I borrow yours all the time."

"I love you," Denise called as she headed toward the door.

Florence gave a slight nod, already retreating into her thoughts.

Denise popped her head back in. "I said, I love you!"

Florence rolled her eyes and mumbled, "Okay, okay… I love you too."

Denise grinned, satisfied. She always made Florence

say it out loud, knowing full well how much she hated any-thing "mushy."

After the door shut, the apartment grew still. Florence settled into her usual spot on the couch, already bracing her-self. Sure enough, at exactly 1:30 p.m., the phone rang. She sighed, took a deep breath, and picked it up.

"Hello, Mama. How are you?" Florence asked, her jaw tightening against the irritation creeping in.

"I'm good, Francesca," her mother, Elane, snapped, her voice as sharp as ever.

"My name is Florence. You named me," Florence said, rolling her eyes until it nearly hurt.

"Yeah, but it was supposed to be Francesca," Elane murmured, the edge in her voice dull but deliberate.

"Well, it's not. So please call me by my name," Flor-ence replied, her voice clipped.

"Well, anyway," her mother said, waving the correc-tion off like a fly. "I'm sitting here with your auntie, telling her how you still haven't moved up at that job yet. Not sur-prised, with all those white folks in charge. When I was your age, I already had a good man and was getting married."

"You were working as a maid," Florence muttered, barely audible. She could recite this whole monologue in her sleep.

"Mama, my job is more important to me than finding a man right now," Florence said, trying—and failing—to keep her tone even.

"Remember what I told you… without a man, you ain't a woman," Elane said, as if it were gospel.

Florence mouthed the line under her breath, a bitter litany she'd grown up repeating.

"Well," Elane sniffed, "I heard you've been spending all your time with that girl… What's her name?"

"Her name is Denise," Florence replied flatly. "And if you already know what's going on in my life, why call at all?"

"I'm checking that you're not having any impure thoughts over there. I'm not sure that being friends with her is good for your image."

"Mama!" Florence snapped. "What image?! Denise is my only friend in this whole city. And no, I'm not having any 'weird thoughts.' I'm busy!"

"You always were too much like your daddy," Elane said with a sigh. "Think you're better than everyone just because you got a degree and passed the bar. Back in my day, all it took was a smile and some manners to land a man."

"I'm happy with my job, Mama. Any progress is still progress." Florence rolled her eyes.

"A step in the right direction to what?" her mother asked. "Those people aren't ever going to let you rise. You'd do better finding a man and settling down. Which brings me to my point. Now, don't get mad—I went ahead and reached out to Sister Shirley's mama, the one from our old church. Her nephew lives up there by you. Nice boy. You should meet him."

Florence nearly laughed, but the sound never made it past her throat. "If I can't be honest about who I am, then the relationship is doomed from the start."

"Well," her mother sighed, the weight of expectation slipping between them, "he'll call you in a day or two. Let me know how it goes. Hopefully, you'll be married by the end of the year."

"Yeah," Florence murmured. "Bye, Mama."

"Do this for your mother," Elane pleaded. "It will be worth it."

Florence hung up, her fingers tightening around the receiver. She sat for a moment as the silence filled the room. Finally, she exhaled, her jaw tight. She had lost count of how many men her mother had "found" for her over the years. Not one of them had been able to look past their own egos or handle a woman like her. She had never told her mother she was looking for anyone. She wasn't. She had a career. She had dreams. And she was surviving, thriving even, in a world that had never made room for her.

Her mother's obsession with marriage felt like a relic

from another time. Florence knew that fear—of poverty, of loneliness, of survival—rooted it, but it still stung. It was the late 1960s. Things weren't perfect, but women had options now. Florence had options. She wished her mother could see that.

Desperate for a distraction, she drifted toward the bookshelf. Her fingers hovered over the spines of familiar titles: torn, well-loved, faded by time. She hesitated between *Pride and Prejudice* and *To Kill a Mockingbird*. The former was soft and familiar; the latter was stiff and unread. With a tired sigh, she chose comfort. Curling up on the couch, she tucked her feet beneath her and opened the book. The first few pages came to her mind like muscle memory, calming and slow. But this time, something felt different.

The tension between Elizabeth and Darcy was palpable. Their glances and heavy silences spoke volumes. It was a quiet battle between restraint and desire that made her chest tighten. Darcy admired Elizabeth's spirit. He tried to resist his attraction, but it consumed him. Florence felt that same energy ripple through her—something warm and electric stirring low in her belly.

She shifted on the couch, trying to shake it off. Then the memory surfaced. That night. That man. The weight of his blazer draped over her bare shoulders. His scent lingering in the air. The way his voice rolled over her skin like velvet—steady, grounding, maddening. A shiver traced her spine.

She remembered how close he had stood, how safe she had felt despite everything. That was what frightened her most. She didn't know his name—didn't even want to. Yet even now, the ghost of his presence clung to her, woven into her bones.

Florence closed the book. The words on the page blurred. Deep down, she knew—she hadn't seen the last of him. She shook her head, her thoughts knotted and restless. It had been too long since someone had touched her. Not the casual brushes in passing or the stiff, polite hugs of acquaintances. She wanted more. The kind of touch that made her breath catch, that made her feel seen. Fingers tracing the curve of her spine. Lips brushing the hollow of her throat. A body leaning into hers with a promise—not just desire but reverence.

She held the book to her chest, as though it could quiet the ache inside her. She wanted someone to look at her the way Darcy looked at Elizabeth. To be desired, not merely acknowledged. To be cherished. To be undone by a man's touch—a man who spoke in whispers and poetry, who loved with patience and devotion. Someone who would leave her breathless and unguarded. Someone who would make her forget to hold back. To be wanted—deeply, unapologetically.

The book slipped from her hands, and she exhaled, scolding herself. She had always been a romantic, but tonight, the longing felt sharper, edged with something real. This wasn't fantasy. It was hunger. It was hope. A tender hope that somewhere, someone out there ached for her too.

As the thought settled, Mooni leapt into her lap, curling into a warm ball. Florence stroked the cat's back, grateful for its soft, steady weight. For a moment, the ache dulled. When she glanced at the clock, it was half past four.

Her eyes fell on the laundry hamper. A torn shirt with missing buttons, a ripped skirt—both unwearable. She decided to throw them out, unwilling to keep the reminder. Yet something in her hesitated. With a weary sigh, she shoved them into the bottom drawer—alongside the blazer she hadn't dared to touch in weeks.

***

Florence ran as if her life depended on it, wet grass slicing between her toes. "Help me! Help me!" she screamed. The rain kept pouring down, drowning her cries as thunder rolled overhead. Blood choked her throat, the metallic taste filling her mouth and nostrils. Something grabbed her leg, dragging her through the woods. Branches tore at her hair while she scraped over wet grass and sticks. A hand clamped around her ankle, trapping her as she tried to shake it off. Florence hurled rocks in desperation, trying to free her bloodied leg. "Please, don't do this," she whispered. "Please... don't."

Her alarm blared, pulling her from the nightmare. She jolted upright, and her heart pounded like a drum. The sound deafened in the silence of her bedroom. The day had begun. She had set her alarm early again to cover the bruises before work. Standing in front of the mirror, Florence inspected every mark. The reflection staring back felt foreign: blue, purple, and black bruises mottled her wrists, her thighs, and even her neck. Her heart thudded in her ears.

***

The copier beeped repeatedly, snapping her back to reality. Her supervisor, Charlotte, glared at her and barked for not paying attention. Florence shook her head, grabbed the papers, and hurried over to hand them in. She was, for lack of a better term, Charlotte's assistant. Though in truth, she was more of an errand runner—printing copies, fetching files from other buildings, doing whatever Charlotte required.

"Get those papers, girl. I want to finish on time today!" Charlotte snapped.

"Yes, ma'am," Florence replied, handing her the stack of papers.

It was two in the afternoon. Charlotte was eager to leave early, and Florence hoped to get home before dark as well. Last Friday had left her especially wary. She'd been given coffee from the "colored" coffee pot—a so-called gift from Charlotte. The only colored woman on her floor, she was told she "deserved" it.

Florence had long grown used to being singled out, and it hardly fazed her anymore. Still, the coffee pot gave her an excuse to go downstairs. There, she overheard a few legal counselors discussing an upcoming workplace discrimination case. Ironic, she thought, clutching a stack of books she was about to deliver to the law library.

Technically, she was a secretary, but the errands kept her in the loop on office gossip. Florence held a bachelor's degree in political science and had passed the bar on her first try. She had taken this job to help women and girls like her. So far, all she had changed was how people liked their coffee.

Mayfield Law was a legal powerhouse, known for handling high-profile cases and setting major precedents. The firm specialized in high-stakes litigation for major corporations. Its practice encompassed every facet of corporate law—from employment and HR disputes to pro bono matters, corporate volunteering, and corporate malpractice—leaving no area untouched.". Florence had heard that Mr. Mayfield was rarely in the office, always away on business trips, giving presentations, or meeting with clients—something she had noticed because Charlotte's absences often coincided with his. Not that it mattered much; she had little interaction with the partners anyway. She had never even laid eyes on Ben Mayfield.

Back upstairs, Florence watched as people filtered out of the office. The last to leave, unsurprisingly, was Charlotte, despite her earlier complaints about wanting to go home early. Now, she lingered at her desk, hoping for a chance to gossip about their boss's supposed charm.

Florence stayed quiet. She saw no reason to join in, especially since she had never met Mr. Mayfield.

Partners worked on the top floor, behind closed doors and frosted glass. People like her were neither expected nor invited to interact with them. She had passed his name on memos, maybe overheard it in the break room, but that was all. She assumed he was an older white man.

When the office finally emptied, Florence followed Charlotte out. The parking lot was nearly deserted except for her baby blue 1959 Galaxie Sunliner. She drove home with the top down, the cool night air a small relief. To avoid the police, she took the back route by the railroad tracks.

Living in Detroit in 1968 was dangerous for colored women. Police often rounded up anyone they spotted, especially during protests or riots. Since Florence lived on the white side of town, she had to be extra cautious. It was a small price for the luxury of driving her own car instead of taking the bus.

The only requirement was that she wear a set of pearls to work. Florence didn't own any, but they had made an exception—saying they couldn't expect a colored woman to have them. She appreciated the job, even if it was largely to help the company avoid discrimination claims. Florence had yet to see another colored woman in her building, but she still hoped change would come. For now, she chose patience, believing that one day she could move up and use her knowledge for good.

As she drove home through the twilight, Florence's thoughts drifted to her father. She glanced at the passenger seat, and for a moment, it felt as though he were sitting there beside her. The familiar scent of sandalwood and oil filled her senses. A soft smile crossed her face as memories of him returned. Contentment washed over her, easing the weight of the day as she pulled into her driveway.

CHAPTER 2:
SOUL TIES NEVER LEAVE
1948

At four years old, Florence found joy in her father's warm laughter and comforting hugs. He would kneel by her side and listen closely. His eyes shone with understanding as he cheered on her dreams. In blanket forts beneath the living room lamps or under constellations whispered with secrets, she felt seen, treasured. Her father wasn't just present; he was her safe place, her unwavering anchor in a world she was still learning to navigate.

One morning, determined to start the day with love, Florence decided she would make breakfast all by herself.

"Daddy, I made breakfast!" she beamed, tugging on his hand and leading him proudly into the kitchen. Pride danced on her face like morning light.

The pancakes were pale and doughy, the eggs barely set, the grits stubborn with lumps. But to Florence, it was a five-star feast plated with heart.

"Mommy, here's yours," she said sweetly, setting a dish in front of Elane.

Her mother, always more ice than warmth, barely looked at the plate.

"I'm not eating that mess," Elane snapped, curling her lip. "And neither should you," she added sharply, reaching to snatch Harold's plate instead.

Tears welled in Florence's eyes. "You don't like it?" she whimpered.

But Harold caught Elane's wrist before she could touch his food. "I'll eat it," he said firmly, turning to his daughter with a smile. "My little star cooked it for me."

He took a big, theatrical bite and grinned. "Mmm, mhmm! Your cooking is so good," he said. He pulled Florence onto his lap and playfully nibbled her chin, making her giggle.

Elane rose from the table in disgust, tossing her plate into the trash. "Stop all that giggling and put her down. I'm going to my bedroom. I have a headache."

Florence watched her go. "Is Mommy sick?" she asked. "Should I bring her something to help?"

Her father stroked her hair with a soft touch. "Don't worry, sweetheart. I'll take care of her."

And just like that, the rest of their day continued as if nothing had happened. They read together, played pretend court in the living room, and ended the evening with a story and a lullaby.

But later that night, Florence awoke needing the bathroom. As she rubbed her eyes and dragged her blanket down the hallway, she paused by her parents' bedroom. The door was open, spilling soft yellow light into the hall. Voices floated out.

"Would it have killed you to pretend?" Harold asked, his voice low but tight. "She's a child who wants her mother's approval."

"You need to stop coddling her," Elane snapped. "The world is harsh. Better that she learns now. If I made you a plate of slop, you wouldn't eat it. So why pretend for her?"

"That's because I'm not four years old, Elane," Harold shot back, raising his voice.

"What do I have to do to get your approval?" she nearly screamed.

"Lower your voice," Harold warned. "Florence is asleep. And I'm going to say this once: You're going to respect her. You're going to treat her like the child she is. I don't know why you're jealous of your own daughter, but the next time you hurt her, I'll take her, and we'll leave."

"With what money?" Elane scoffed. "You're close to being broke."

Florence stood frozen in the hallway. She held her blanket and stuffed animal close. Then, she tiptoed back to her room. Her heart was pounding. She didn't understand why Mommy was so angry. *If I cook better,* she thought, *Mommy won't be mad anymore, and they won't argue.*

The next morning, Elane was up early. She greeted them with a tight smile and two warm plates.

"Here," she said, placing them down. "I made breakfast."

Florence beamed. "It's good, Mommy! Really good."

"Aww, thank you, baby," Elane replied, patting her head. But when she looked at Harold, he had barely touched his food.

"It's fine," he grumbled, not meeting her gaze.

From that day on, Harold carved out time for Florence each morning, no matter how tired he was.

"What do you want to learn today?" he'd ask, his voice still rough from the night shift at the factory.

By day, he became her teacher; by night, her provider. Florence's questions were endless: "Why?" and "How?" tumbled from her lips like breath, and not once did he lose patience. When he didn't know an answer, he didn't fake it. He'd stop by the library on his way home, thumbing through books with grease-stained hands, determined to give her the truth, even if the library shelves offered little.

They started with history—slavery, the Great Depression, the Black Cabinet, Mary McLeod Bethune. He taught her not just dates and facts but also how to see the threads of injustice woven into every system around her.

One morning, he looked her straight in the eye and said, "You're a colored girl with a sharp mind. This world won't always be kind about that. But if you stay curious and stay ready, it won't ever stop you."

"Men and women alike will envy you," he told her. "They'll try to silence you, dim your light. Don't let them. Speak louder."

He made sure she knew, deep in her bones, that a woman's strength could shape the world just as powerfully as any man's. As she grew, their lessons expanded: conflict resolution, elocution, the art of speaking up with purpose. Those kitchen-table talks, modest as they seemed, would later nudge her toward the NAACP and the movement rising all around her.

Florence's obsessions came in waves, but one lingered: the stars. She became enchanted by constellations—Perseus, Hercules, Draco—until her bedroom ceiling was papered with their forms. Each night, they stood sentinel above her as she drifted off, wrapped in wonder beneath a sky of her own making.

But no matter what fascinated her that week or month; there were a couple of loves that always lingered: history and math. Numbers didn't flinch at her questions. They never asked her to sit still, smile more, or lower her voice. In a world that too often tried to shrink her, equations made room. They offered clarity when everything else felt too loud, too cruel, or too complicated.

Her father taught her life skills he believed every woman needed: how to change a tire, check oil, weld, and saw wood. "Don't wait on anyone," he'd say, "especially not a man. Save yourself."

Florence had a sharp mind and an even sharper tongue. One evening at dinner, when she was about ten, she presented her case to stay up past bedtime.

"But Dad," she said, leaning forward, "I've done the math. If I read just thirty more minutes tonight, that's fifteen extra pages. Multiply that by five nights a week—that's seventy-five pages I'd miss if I went to bed right now. That's like giving up a whole book every week!"

Her father paused, fork in hand, watching her with

amusement and awe.

"You know, Florence," he said, shaking his head, "with that kind of logic and delivery, you'd make one hell of a lawyer. You don't just argue; you build a case."

She paused, blinking. "A lawyer? Like the people on TV who always have the last word?"

"Something like that," he said. "But being a lawyer is about helping people—finding truth, making a difference."

Her father winked and added, "Keep working on those debating skills. The courtroom had better watch out!"

Florence was not interested in becoming a lawyer; she liked working with her hands. She responded, "No, I'll become an engineer. That way I can always work with you in your shop." She smiled.

Harold stood six-foot-five with arms like tree trunks. Despite his size, he had a gentle heart. Florence often thought of him as a giant made of kindness. Her mother, Elane, was more complicated.

If Florence could have shared anything with her mother, it might have been a love of cooking. But Elane never stayed with anything long. When Florence was around eight, her mother folded her apron, tucked away recipe cards she'd never finish, and left the kitchen. Her focus shifted rapidly from one new hobby to another: painting, sewing, gardening. Each was a bright spark that faded before Florence could catch her breath.

By the time Florence worked up the courage to ask if they could cook together, it was too late. Elane had moved on, leaving the pots cold and silent and the recipe cards gathering dust.

In the kitchen, Florence sometimes stood still, imagining the life she never got to live. She pictured the rhythm of two hands moving in sync—chopping, seasoning, laughing by the stove. She ached for those whispered, tender moments that never came to be. But those memories weren't hers to have. Instead, she turned to the only person who had never let her down.

"Daddy," she asked one afternoon, tentative but hopeful, "do you think you could teach me how to cook?"

He laughed, a warm, sheepish sound that made his eyes crinkle at the corners. "Me? Florence, I can't even boil water without setting off the smoke alarm."

She giggled, nudging his arm. "We'll figure it out together, then."

And they did. She thought he was joking, until he proved it. Fumbling with the stove, the pot, and even the simplest of ingredients, he felt completely lost. Watching him struggle made her heart ache. He had always seemed strong and steady, but now he was awkward. The stovetop knob turned too far, clicking loudly. Soon, the kitchen filled with the smell of burning butter. In that moment, as she saw him vulnerable, she faced a harsh truth: her father was a flawed person doing his best.

The realization was bittersweet, tinged with both disappointment and understanding. It was the first time she realized the people she loved weren't the heroes she had always pictured. They were human, imperfect, sometimes unreliable. But even in their failings, they were hers.

After dinner, her father would sit with her, asking how she felt, always knowing just the right thing to say.

"I don't know what I want to be when I grow up, Daddy. I used to think I wanted to be an engineer, but I don't think I do anymore," Florence admitted one evening, her brow furrowed with uncertainty.

He settled into the corner armchair, his voice soft and thoughtful. "Hmm..." he mused. "I don't think you have to choose now. By the time you grow up, I'm sure you'll be able to be anything you want, Little Star."

Florence smiled at the thought. She'd imagined herself as everything from an engineer, an astronomer, and even a writer. The choices overwhelmed her. Before bed, her father would go over every constellation with her, his voice warm and steady.

"Out of all the constellations in the sky, you are the

only one I'm connected to, which makes you my favorite. And one day," he said, brushing her hair behind her ear, "you'll find your Perseus. But always remember, you don't have to become Andromeda to receive love."

She didn't grasp the reference at that moment, but she nodded and tucked it away for later.

***

When it was time to learn to ride a bike, Florence assumed her dad would be the one to teach her. He always was. But to her surprise, it was her mother who stepped up. Overjoyed, Florence ran to grab her bike.

Their neighborhood was tranquil on Sundays, and the weather was mild. Her father crouched beside her, removed the training wheels, and gave the handlebars a quick check. "You'll do great," he said, brushing her cheek with a calloused thumb. "Mama's got you." Then he kissed her forehead, grabbed his keys, and left for his shift at the plant.

Florence, decked out in a helmet and knee pads, turned to her mother. "I'm ready."

Elane gave her a tight nod. As they exited the garage, she held the back of the bike steady.

"Don't let me fall!" Florence squealed.

"You'll be fine," Elane said flatly. "Just pedal like normal. I'll guide you."

Feeling her mother's grip on the seat gave her courage. She pushed forward with a grin, until she glanced back.

Elane had let go.

Florence's stomach dropped. Her balance faltered, the bike wobbled, and then she crashed into the grass. Her mother rushed over.

"Florence, baby, are you okay?" she asked, checking her arms for scrapes.

"You said you wouldn't let go!" Florence wailed. "You lied to me!"

"It's okay, Darling," Elane said in a soft tone. "Let's stop here for today."

But the warmth didn't last. Once they got home, the mask cracked.

"How dare you embarrass me like that?" Elane snapped, yanking her by the arm. "I was nice enough to take you out, and this is how I'm repaid? Ugh! This is why I didn't want to take you in the first place."

Tears spilled down Florence's cheeks as she ran to her bedroom and slammed the door.

That evening, the floorboards creaked as her father made his way down the hallway. The door eased open, and warm light from the hallway spilled across her bed.

"Hey, Baby Doll," he said, his voice low and kind. "I heard you fell today. Are you okay?"

Florence tucked her head deeper into the pillow.

"Don't worry about Mama," he said, scratching the back of his neck. "Maybe she just had a rough day. I'll take you next time."

"I don't want to ride bikes anymore," she mumbled.

"I know," he replied gently. "But we don't give up that easily. We'll try again. And if you still hate it, we'll stop. Maybe next time, we'll bring your cousins to help."

Her father, noticing her boundless energy, introduced her to baseball. She felt unsure about the dirt and sweat, but his excited commentary, like a cheering crowd, won her over. She played for years, developing a deep love for the sport. She admired legends like Jackie Robinson, Ernie Banks, and Willie Mays. This passion stayed with her into adulthood.

Despite these happy memories, her mother's distance always loomed. Elane accused Florence of stealing Harold's affection, which Harold told her was ridiculous. Harold took on both roles of mother and father. He combed her hair, helped her bathe, and packed her lunches. He blamed Elane's coldness on her abusive upbringing.

Florence remembered the one time her mother tucked a note into her lunchbox that read, "I love you." It felt like a mistake, an accidental softness. But she kept it anyway.

Over time, though, even small gestures like that wore thin. She started noticing a pattern: her mother only packed her school bag or made breakfast when Harold was home to see it. Florence learned not to expect affection unless it served a purpose.

Her brilliance didn't go unnoticed at school. Teachers quickly picked up on her drive, her curiosity, the way she lit up when discussing ideas that stretched beyond the textbook. By age nine, her lessons couldn't keep up. One teacher gently suggested the library. Florence went and never stopped going.

She devoured *The Odyssey* as if it were a secret map, each page leading her closer to something buried and powerful. *True Grit* felt like it had been written for a girl just like her: tough, determined, and aching to be seen. But it was history that truly captured her heart, maybe even more than math. There, she discovered stories of resistance and resilience, of women who refused to shrink, who carved out space in a world determined to keep them small.

Then when she turned twelve, everything changed. The floorboards creaked under the weight of her father's heavy steps as he entered her room one last time. Florence stirred but didn't fully wake. Moonlight slipped through the thin curtains, casting silver lines on the worn wood floor. Harold watched his little girl curled up beneath the blankets, her face peaceful, slack with sleep, one arm flung across her stuffed rabbit. A gentle breeze rustled the curtains, brushing cool air against her cheek. Harold knelt by her bed, careful not to wake her. He rested one large hand on her back, feeling the steady rise and fall of her breath.

He closed his eyes. "Lord," he began in a low murmur, barely above a whisper, "thank you for this child. Thank you for her light, for her laughter, for her wild and curious mind. Watch over her when I can't. Let her know she's never alone, even when it feels like it."

His voice caught, but he pushed on. "Let her grow strong, not just in body, but in heart. Let no bitterness take root in her. Let her rise above the storms. And when the world is unkind, let her remember she was made from love. From hope. From me."

He leaned in and kissed her forehead, his lips lingering a second longer than usual. "Goodnight, Little Star," he whispered, echoing the name he always called her. She shifted, murmured something incoherent, then stilled again.

"I'll see you again." he whispered. "But if I don't… just know, you were my greatest joy, my reason, and my everything. I'll carry you with me until my last breath."

Harold stood, pulling the rough wool coat from the foot of the bed. As he stepped into the hallway, he glanced back once, his figure half-shadowed in the doorway. A long breath escaped him, and then he was gone.

****

Florence woke to the sound of sobbing seeping through the thin wall, sharp, wet, and ragged, as though something vital had cracked wide open. She pulled the blanket over her head, thinking it was just another fight. Then Elane stormed into the room. Her makeup was smeared, her eyes swollen, her breath jagged with fury. "He left," she snapped, her voice raw. "Walked out on us in the middle of the night, like a coward. Left you. Left me. Just a weak bastard. He was never worth anything."

Florence stared at her, stunned. Her chest tightened, her knees gave way. She reached for the doorframe to keep herself steady.

The house felt unfamiliar—too cold, too still. She searched every room in silence, the floor creaking beneath her bare feet as though it, too, was in mourning.

In the kitchen, she found it: a single envelope, heavy with goodbye, resting beside a neat stack of money. Her hand trembled as she picked it up. The paper was warm from the sun but cold in meaning.

Her thumb hovered at the edge of the flap. She didn't want to know what it said, but she had to.

She opened it.

Dear Florence,

By the time you read this, I'll be gone. Even writing those words breaks something in me. You are, and will always be, the most important person in my life. There is nothing in this world I love more than you and nothing harder than walking away from your light.

I wish I could explain this in person, but I'm not sure I'd be able to get the words out. The truth is, in this day and age, the law almost never gives a father custody, no matter how hard he fights for it. If I stayed and pushed for it, the courts would still leave you with your mother, and my fight could make her even more bitter toward you. I've seen what her anger can do, and I couldn't risk making you the target of it every day.

Your mother and I have become strangers. We tried, Florence. We really did. But some things, once broken, don't mend right. Staying in this house has been like trying to breathe through a closed door. I haven't felt like myself in a long time—not the man who danced with you in the living room, taught you constellations, or cheered you on like you hung the moon. That's the man I want you to remember, not the ghost I was becoming.

I've met someone. That may be hard to understand and even harder to forgive, but it's part of why I had to go. I couldn't keep living a lie—not to your mother, not to myself, and certainly not to you. I need to live a life that feels honest, even if it means loving you from a distance.

I am so sorry for the pain this will cause you. None of this is your fault. You are good, Florence—bright, bold, and full of fire. Whether you become a lawyer, an engineer, an astronomer, or something the world hasn't imagined yet, I know you'll leave your mark. You have the kind of mind and heart that changes things. Don't ever let anyone dim that light.

You are my little star. My compass. My greatest joy. No matter where I am, know this: I will always be proud of you.

With all my love,
Dad

***

That letter turned Florence's world upside down. She had always taken care of herself, relying on her mother only for rides. Her father had taught her everything she needed to know. After he left, Florence watched her mother find a new mission: securing another man to support them, despite Florence's reassurance that they would manage on their own.

The months passed in a blur, and before long, Florence's birthday arrived. She didn't expect her mother to plan anything, so when Elane asked if she wanted a small party with family and friends, she was genuinely surprised. For a moment, she wondered what had sparked the sudden warmth. It didn't matter much—she felt grateful for the effort.

She was about to turn thirteen. She wished for new history books and baseball cards but didn't dare ask, knowing how hard those things were to come by. Whatever she received, she would accept with gratitude.

Her mom and cousins planned the party together, inviting neighbors and church friends. It was a cheerful day—there were games and cake, and everyone sang "Happy Birthday" to Florence. For a moment, she almost forgot her father's absence. When it came time for presents, she received clothes and practical gifts: makeup, a leatherette journal with a lock, a Jet Magazine subscription, a small pink clutch, and typing lessons book and typewriter. But her face lit up when her cousins handed her a brand-new baseball bat and glove. She hugged them, her smile wide and genuine.

Her mother asked everyone to keep their receipts, just in case items didn't fit or were broken. Then she raised a toast to Florence, thanking everyone for coming. It had been a good day.

That evening, Florence left her gifts in the living room, planning to organize them after school the next day. When she got home from class, the house felt strangely still. Dust hung in the air. She set down her bag, made herself a snack, and sat at the table, her hands moving through the motions of routine. The hum of the refrigerator and the soft creak of the floorboards felt almost comforting. She opened her homework and began.

Her mother wasn't home yet. A quick glance around the living room revealed no gifts. Her brow furrowed. Maybe Elane had moved them to her bedroom? She padded down the hall, opened the door, and looked inside. The room was spotless. No presents. No cards. Nothing. A small unease crept in, but she shook it off, deciding to shower and ask later.

Three hours passed. Dusk stretched long shadows across the floor when the front door finally opened. Her mother stepped in, wearing a satin coat and clicking across the floor in sharp heels. Her hair was pinned into a sleek twist.

"Hey, Mom. You look… nice," Florence said, trying to sound casual though her curiosity slipped through. "Did you have a good day?"

"I did, baby. Thanks for asking," Elane replied, setting down three glossy shopping bags.

Florence hesitated, watching her unpack a new pair of heels. "Um… I was wondering—where are the gifts from my birthday?"

Elane didn't look up. "I returned them."

Florence blinked. "Wait… what? Why would you do that?"

"You didn't need any of that," her mother said, her tone flat. "I needed to look presentable. I have to find us a man who can take care of things. Isn't that more important?"

"You used my birthday money to go shopping?" Florence asked, her voice rising.

"For us," Elane corrected, her annoyance slipping through. "Got my hair done, bought a few things. I need to look like a woman worth investing in."

"What about the money Dad left?" Florence pressed, her voice shaking.

Elane rolled her eyes. "That's for bills. You're being selfish, Florence. Once I reel in that man who's been eyeing me, you'll have more than enough. You can buy whatever you want—with his money."

Florence stood frozen, staring at the woman who called herself her mother. Then, without a word, she turned, stormed down the hall, and slammed her bedroom door.

She collapsed onto the bed, face buried in her pillow as betrayal burned through her chest. Sobs came in waves, sharp and hot. *Was he thinking about me? Does he even miss me?*

Eventually, the tears stopped. She sat up, wiped her face, and glanced toward the baseball bat in the corner—the one thing her mother hadn't taken. *That's enough,* she told herself. *I don't need more.*

But that night, the silence pressed down on her, heavy and unrelenting. She cried herself to sleep, clutching the bat like a lifeline.

***

Her mother, desperate to avoid being alone, eventually landed the man she had mentioned. But he turned out to be cold and brutish: rude to Elane, harsh with his words, and at times physically aggressive. When Florence expressed concern, her mother brushed it off. "Don't worry. He pays for everything. He just gets grouchy sometimes."

When the man was around, Florence stayed in her room. When Elane was out, she spent time at her cousin's house nearby. She loved it there; the air was warm with the smell of real cooking, and laughter lingered late into the night. They giggled under the covers until her aunt scolded them, then whispered themselves to sleep.

Elane was striking—tall and graceful, like Florence. Her long limbs and flowing hair only added to her beauty. Her eyes were deep and magnetic—a charm that hid her true nature. To strangers, she appeared shy and enigmatic, but beneath that smile lay a sharp mind—used not for kindness, but for control. Elane bent others to her will with charm and calculation.

***

In 1954, schools were ordered to integrate after *Brown v. Board of Education*. In Tulsa, resistance was swift and fierce. Though desegregation began in 1955, it moved slowly and faced constant pushback. The White Citizens' Council applied pressure through protests and economic threats. The shadow of the 1921 Tulsa Race Massacre still loomed, and fear clung to the colored community like a second skin. Few dared venture out after dark.

Florence remained in a segregated school through high school, studying with determination, her gaze fixed northward. She dreamed of Chicago, where things might be freer. Her father had written that she would make a great lawyer, and she held those words close, like a promise.

Every Wednesday, she reminded her mother that she needed a ride after tutoring. The bus didn't run that late, and her cousins would already be home. One Wednesday evening, Florence waited at the stop. Her friend offered her a ride, but she declined. "My mother will be here soon."

The sky dimmed from orange to deep purple. A light rain began to fall. She brushed at her cheek—was it rain, or a tear? She glanced down the street again. That was when she heard the slow, heavy footsteps. A sharp, sour scent clung to the air, like the liquor her mother favored. On a park bench nearby, two white men sat watching her, their eyes sharp and mean. As thunder rolled in the distance, they stood and began to approach.

"You waitin' on someone?" one asked, his tone almost casual.

Florence stiffened under the streetlamp's glow and nodded. "Yes. I'm waiting for my mother."

The taller man chuckled. "Storm's coming. We could give you a ride."

She shook her head. "No, thank you."

But they kept closing in. Her stomach tightened. One of them sneered. "Not safe out here for a young girl, especially one like you. You never know what could happen if you end up in the wrong hands."

Their laughter was short and sharp, scraping the quiet like broken glass. Florence stepped back.

"Don't touch me!" she snapped when one reached out to touch her hair. But the other lunged first, his arm locking around her waist like a trap snapping shut.

"I'm sick of you niggers thinking you can talk back," he hissed into her ear. "The Supreme Court throws you a bone, and now you think you're equal?"

She twisted, trying to break free. "Please—I just want to go home. My mom's waiting for me."

His nails dug into her cheek, leaving deep crescents. "Doesn't look like she's coming. Looks like she forgot you."

The reek of alcohol burned her nose. They knocked her backpack to the ground. Papers, books, and a pencil case scattered across the wet sidewalk. One man stomped on her notebook, grinding it into the concrete. The other spat on her belongings.

"Stop trying to be like us," one barked, his face twisted with rage. "Your kind will never be smart enough to do anything but cook, clean, and serve us."

She tried to scream, but the taller man shoved her hard. Her head struck the pavement with a sickening crack that seemed to echo louder than the thunder. The world spun. Warm blood trickled into her eyes. Her limbs refused to move.

Her mind drifted away from the pain, clawing toward someplace safe. She was back in the open field behind her childhood home. The sun had once shone there, her father tossing her baseballs under a bright sky. But now the rain soaked that field, turning it dark and empty. The storm followed her even there.

"Daddy, please," she cried, spinning in the downpour.

"Where are you?"

Only the wind answered. Lightning split the sky, and the rain fell harder, washing over her skin and her memory.

She was alone.

CHAPTER 3:
LEAVE ME AT THE ALTAR

Ben's day dragged on, and irritation simmered beneath his calm exterior. His car was in for maintenance, so he had to rely on a temporary driver, Tim. He owned other vehicles, but they were antiques—flashy showpieces, not practical for daily use.

The frustration deepened as he recalled the long board meeting. Hours spent persuading partners to approve new positions. Mayfield Law was doing well, yet rivals like Kirkland & Ellis, Latham & Watkins, and Baker McKenzie made the team anxious. Ben wasn't worried. Even if those firms hired fresh talent, it would take time for the impact to show. He valued innovation and knew fresh ideas could bring growth if the door stayed open.

Charlotte, his assistant, had kept everyone late since the board was still in-house. Now Ben was the last to leave. He told Tim to meet him out back at six to avoid the usual rush-hour chaos. Night had fallen, and still no sign of his driver.

Ben sighed, shifting on a bench beneath a flickering streetlamp. The dim light cast uneven shadows on the wet pavement. The air smelled of coming rain. He picked up a few loose stones and tossed them toward the curb. That's when the first droplets began to fall.

A sound cut through the patter of rain—a voice. A cry for help. Ben froze. The rain muted it, but the urgency was unmistakable. He stood, rain seeping into his collar. Tilting his face to the sky, he let the cold drops hit his skin—sharp, grounding. Then he moved toward the sound.

Around the corner, he saw them: two men, clearly drunk, looming over a woman with torn clothes. The hem of her blouse hung loose at her waist. The sight sharpened his anger. He recognized them—low-level clerks from his own legal team.

Ben lowered his head, letting his hat shadow his face. He approached silently, standing behind one of the men like a figure emerging from the rain. A low grunt escaped him, halting them in place. His fists itched to swing, to crush their hands beneath a hammer. He restrained himself—barely.

They turned, their bravado faltering. Ben leaned in, his voice cold and deliberate.

"Touch a woman without her consent again—on my property or anywhere—and I'll have your faces in every paper from here to Kansas. Every lawyer I know will blacklist you for life."

He smiled slightly, the threat delivered with chilling calm. A pat on the shoulder sealed it. Then he turned to the woman. She was trembling. He removed his jacket and placed it over her shoulders. Instead of gratitude, her eyes burned with defiance.

"Are you hurt?" he asked carefully.

"I didn't need your help," she snapped, clutching the jacket as if to shield herself while avoiding his eyes.

He blinked. Her reaction didn't anger him—it intrigued him. He wanted to press, to know what fueled that fire. But this wasn't the time. Moments later, she left, her tires cutting through shallow puddles with a sharp hiss.

When Tim finally arrived, his eyes flicked to Ben's soaked suit and missing jacket.

"You good, boss?"

"Don't ask," Ben muttered, sliding into the car. The smell of rain clung to his skin and the leather seats, cold and damp beneath him.

When he entered his penthouse, the lights were low, and dinner was already set.

"Mama Benard, I'm home," he called.

No answer. He found her bent over in the study, organizing the piles of books he'd left scattered.

"Ma," he said softly, touching her shoulder. She jumped.

"Boy! You trying to give me a heart attack creeping up like that?"

"I called you," he said, raising a brow. "And you're cleaning my study again. I told you, you don't have to—"

A picture slipped from her hand. Ben picked it up, smiling at the photo of himself and a little boy.

"I can't believe you had this. Isn't this Elijah? The boy from the park?" he asked.

Mama Benard cleared her throat and quickly returned to the earlier topic.

"If I waited for you to clean up, this place would turn into a landfill," she said sharply.

Ben chuckled and kissed her cheek. "Have you eaten?"

She nodded. He hesitated, then asked, "Would you... eat with me?"

She gave him a knowing look. "You wouldn't ask if you'd found a woman already."

They sat at the kitchen bar, falling into their familiar rhythm. She sliced his food without asking, and he poured drinks for them both.

"I'm a grown man. I can cut my own food," he grumbled.

"Yeah, a grown man with no girlfriend, still sleeping with a nightlight," she replied with a wink.

Ben let out a breath. "Hurtful."

She shrugged. "Truth hurts."

He leaned over and kissed her cheek again. "It's fine. I have you."

"And I have you, making messes," she fired back. "You should clean up before you get a wife. No woman wants a man-child."

Ben shared what had happened earlier. She listened, setting her fork down.

"So... are you upset by how she responded," she asked, "or by how you wanted her to respond?"

He sat back, considering. *I didn't expect praise... but the way she looked at me—like I was another problem....*

"I don't know," he admitted.

She raised a brow. "Mhmm. I'll leave you with that."

He blinked. "What? That's it?"

"You said you're a grown man. Solve it like one," she said, smiling as she stood. "I'm old. I'm going to bed."

Ben watched her shuffle away, muttering under his breath, "I really need to get a dog."

After dinner, he cleared the dishes. The soft clatter of ceramic mixed with the low hum of the sink, breaking the silence in the penthouse. When he finished, he went to the master suite, unbuttoning his shirt as he walked and tossing it over the back of a chair. The shower groaned when he turned the knobs, steam quickly curling around the mirror's edges.

He stepped beneath the stream, water beating down on him in a steady rhythm. Yet it did little to soothe the tightness in his chest. Why had her reaction unsettled him? He scrubbed a hand over his face, trying to pinpoint it. *I didn't expect a thank you,* he thought, rinsing shampoo from his hair.

Compared to others, Ben considered himself different. He never ignored the unrest boiling in the country—that was why he became a lawyer. But lately, he questioned whether being different meant anything at all. The world around him felt like it was unraveling: riots, protests, pushback. For what? So his people could cling to the illusion of superiority?

The tension in 1968 hung thick in the air, especially in Detroit. A year after the riots, the city was still raw: charred storefronts, broken windows, and neighborhoods held together by grit and fear. Across the country, civil rights protesters faced batons, tear gas, and rage.

For men like Ben—white, Harvard-educated, living in a house with more rooms than people—it would have been easy to look away. To retreat behind privilege. To stay untouched by the struggle. But he couldn't. Not when the very system that padded his life seemed built to suffocate everyone else's.

In the working-class neighborhoods of Detroit, resentment simmered. White families felt threatened as policies shifted and integration efforts grew. They sensed their familiar world slipping away: affirmative action, job quotas, desegregated schools. It didn't matter that the changes were overdue—many resisted them like a personal attack.

Ben's law firm felt those shifts too. An institution built on his father's reputation now faced pressure to change. Some of the older staff resisted, murmuring about the dangers of "alienating clients." They didn't want diversity. They wanted things to stay as they were: safe, familiar, exclusionary.

But Ben pushed back, hard. "Bringing in new voices won't destroy us," he had told the board. "It'll save us."

He believed that, especially as the local economy bled jobs from every industry. Automation replaced workers, both Black and white. Instead of blaming corporations, many turned against one another. Still, women faced the steepest uphill climb. Colored women, in particular, bore the brunt of the city's chaos. They worked the longest hours, earned the least, and endured the worst of both racism and sexism. As white men fretted over their status, women focused on survival. The women's liberation movement was growing, but it hadn't yet reached their doorsteps.

In Detroit, colored women supported their families and became scapegoats for a society that feared their strength. Ben saw it every day, even if others refused to. Steam rose around him as he tilted his head back, letting the water run down his face. His temples throbbed with a slow ache. A sharp memory surfaced—his first meeting with someone from outside his circle. A colored boy.

He wore the title of partner like armor. But it hadn't protected him from a cold childhood, shaped more by silence than love. The Mayfield name brought power and status, yes, but only if you were deemed worthy by his father. For Ben, affection always came with conditions. They placed him in every high-class activity imaginable—piano, golf, French, fencing—as if success could fill the void where warmth should have been.

The first time he brought home straight As, he sprinted into his father's study, chest heaving with hope.

"Dad, look! I got As in all my classes!"

His father didn't look up. "Didn't I tell you not to bother me when I'm on a call, Boy? Show your mother."

So, he did. She was on the phone too. "That's great, Son," she said absently, twirling the cord. "Now, go play. I'm busy."

The light in his chest flickered. He found himself in the kitchen, feeling small and empty. Hope clung to him, thin enough to slip through his fingers.

"I got all As," he mumbled, placing the paper on the counter in front of Ms. Benard.

She didn't hesitate. "Oh my goodness, that's wonderful!" she exclaimed, gathering him into her arms and lifting him off the floor. "That calls for something special. Want your favorite dessert tonight?"

His grin returned, bright and full. "Deal!"

***

Ms. Benard celebrated him in a way that felt whole, real. But as Ben grew, so did the weight of his father's shadow. He remembered the grand piano in the living room, its black finish shining like polished stone. Eight-year-old Ben sat before it, back straight, fingers trembling.

"Again," his father ordered.

Ben played the piece once more, stumbling over a note. His chest tightened. His father's presence loomed, sharp and unyielding.

"Wrong," came the cold voice. "Again."

Another mistake. Another silence. Then the creak of wood as his father lifted the heavy lid of the piano. Ben's breath caught.

"You see this lid?" his father asked, his hand poised as if to strike. "You know what it can do to your fingers?"

Ben's fingers hovered over the keys, knuckles white. His heart pounded so hard it drowned out the ticking clock. The lid never fell, but the threat hung in the air like smoke. That day, Ben learned something essential: Not all attention was good attention, and not all fear came from strangers.

"You want to make mistakes, Ben? You think life lets you get away with that?" His father lowered the lid, the weight inching closer to Ben's trembling fingers. "Someone can take away everything, easily."

The lid stopped short of his hands. Ben flinched, tears welling in his eyes. His jaw locked, a small tremor betraying his effort to stay composed. His father leaned in, his breath cold against Ben's ear. "That's why you have to be the best," he growled. With a thunderous crack, the lid slammed down. Ben jerked back, heart hammering, snatching his hands away a split second before they were crushed. "Because if you're not, the world will crush you without a second thought. Do you understand me?"

Ben nodded frantically, his small head jerking like a marionette on frayed strings. His vision blurred, but he refused to let the tears fall. Crying only made it worse.

"Good." His father straightened, the weight of his presence receding but never gone. With a flick of his wrist, he gestured to the keys. "Start over."

With trembling hands, Ben obeyed. But the lid wasn't the heaviest thing in the room. It was his father's expectations. His father's eyes held no compassion, only disdain. The man wore his pride like a medal, one that only adorned those who met his impossible standards and shared his ideals. His cruelty struck with harsh words and rough hands, the pain lingering long after the bruises faded.

***

Long before the weight of the Mayfield name pressed down on Ben's father, he had known tenderness. He was just a boy then, reckless with love. Ms. Benard had been the sun in his shadowed world: soft laughter in the kitchen, eyes that met his without judgment. They had stolen moments, whispers pressed into quiet hours. For a season, he believed the rules of blood and name could be broken.

Then Ms. Benard told him there was going to be a child. His child. Their child. His heart soared, but hers trembled. "We can't," she whispered. "You're you, and I'm me." The world will never let us be. Yet instead of walking away, she pretended to surrender, agreeing to have the baby. For a moment, he believed love had won. But later, she shattered him with a lie—telling him she had ended the pregnancy. From that day on, his heart hardened, growing heavy with bitterness and hate.

What he never knew—what no one told him—was that his own father had paid for her silence. Money exchanged hands, along with promises of a pregnancy ended. But Ms. Benard carried the baby in secret, raising him quietly and alone.

Ben's father never knew. He believed the lie: that she had abandoned him, betrayed him, traded his love for a life without him. From that wound, bitterness took root. And from that bitterness grew the hatred he passed down like inheritance.

***

Ben wasn't allowed to have friends. His schedule left no room for companionship. He would sit in the car, watching boys laugh in the sandboxes at playgrounds, the ache in his chest almost unbearable.

"I wish I could make friends like them," he once whispered to Ms. Benard.

Moved by his loneliness, Ms. Benard did something she knew she shouldn't—she broke the rules. One afternoon, while Ben's father worked and his mother hosted a ladies' luncheon, she took him to the park. His mother had insisted he be gone, claiming he disrupted her image of perfection.

The sun rested gently over the grass, warm and sure, like a hand on a child's back. Ben ran, arms stretched wide, his laughter skipping ahead of him. For a little while, he looked like a boy who belonged in the world.

Another boy, one Ms. Benard had picked up from her house, joined them. Watching the two play together made her heart clench. They chased each other, kicked a ball until their shins ached, then collapsed in the grass, dirt streaking their knees as they laughed.

When Ben returned home, his eyes shone with a life his father rarely saw.

"Father," Ben blurted, breathless. "I met a boy today—he had blue eyes, just like mine! He runs fast like me, too. We—we even look kind of the same."

His father's smile faltered. Slowly, he turned toward Ms. Benard, his face carved from stone. "A word," he said sharply, pulling her aside.

In the shadow of the hallway, his voice dropped, cold and sharp. "That boy Ben spoke of—who is he? Tell me the truth."

Ms. Benard's lips trembled. Tears welled before her words escaped. "Yes. He's yours. Your son. I wanted to tell you, but your father paid me to stay silent. I thought hiding him was the only way."

The color drained from his face. Fury surged in his chest—not only at her but also at his own father's betrayal.

Before he could speak, before he could claim or reject the boy, his father stepped from the next room. He had heard everything.

Without hesitation, without even granting the boy a chance to simply be a child, the old man silenced him forever. A life ended like it was nothing more than a secret to be buried.

Ben never saw Elijah again. Whatever warmth remained in his father's heart froze to ice that day.

***

Ben raved for days about his friend until his father finally snapped. "You won't be seeing that boy again, so stop mentioning him."

Ben's voice cracked. "What do you mean? Why can't I see him?"

His father wiped his mouth with a napkin. "Eat your dinner. Then go upstairs and study until your eyes bleed."

He left the room, and the silence lingered like a shadow. Ben stared at his plate as the world tilted beneath him, the food turning to ash in his mouth. When he returned to the park, Elijah was gone—no warning, no explanation, no goodbye. Days passed, then weeks.

Once, Ben gathered the courage to ask Ms. Benard what had happened. Her lips pressed tight, and her eyes filled with tears she refused to name. She shook her head, tears streaming, then untied her apron and fled the room before he could comfort her.

He didn't ask again.

After that, he stopped trying to make friends. The cost was too high. The scar was too deep. It wasn't until adulthood, far from his father's shadow, that Ben dared to let anyone in again. But Elijah's memory never left him. Even now, in quiet moments between meetings and cases, Ben could hear Elijah's laughter in the wind and wonder what had become of him.

In the years that followed, Ms. Benard thought she would be dismissed, but instead, she suffered a far worse fate. Ben's father made her life a living hell, blaming her for keeping his son from him. The pain of that loss only deepened his cruelty. Despite everything, she could not bring herself to leave, especially after Ben was born. Tragically, she was forced to watch as the man she once knew withered into a hollow shell of himself.

***

Ben had never understood the hatred. He hadn't grown up avoiding colored people, not until he was forced to. Even though she was the family maid, Ms. Benard had practically raised him. Her love was the only warmth he had known in childhood. Colored or not, why was it wrong to love her? That question never left him.

Years later, he stumbled upon a name that stirred something familiar, something defiant: Thurgood Marshall, the first Black Supreme Court Justice. A man who had carved his legacy in courtrooms, dismantling the same system Ben's father once wielded to maintain control. Ben first found him in a torn newspaper article buried in his father's study, the top half missing, as though someone had tried to erase part of the truth.

That night, Ben dug deeper. He read everything he could—*Brown v. Board of Education, Chambers v. Florida*. Legal briefs, biographies, speeches. Marshall became his inspiration. If Ben could speak like that, fight like that, his father would finally be proud. But when his father found out, it was worse than he imagined. He stormed into Ben's room, eyes wild.

"This is garbage," he shouted, tearing the pages from Ben's book and flinging them across the floor. "You should be idolizing me! Look what I've done for this firm, for this family!"

Then came the slap, hard and fast. Ben hit the floor. The book sailed across the room, its corner catching him in the temple.

"You don't have a lick of good judgment," his father hissed, looming over him. "That's why your grandfather had to take care of that little colored boy… You won't be seeing him again."

"What do you mean?" Ben gasped, eyes wide. "What

did Grandpa do to him?"

His father only sneered.

"I hate you!" Ben shouted. "I wish you weren't my dad!"

But the words meant nothing. His father had already walked away. That day marked a turning point for Ben. As he entered his early teens, resentment grew inside him. It turned into a cold, dangerous resolve. He couldn't face his father head-on—no fists, no words. So he chose another way to fight.

His parents were often away, attending conferences to support the Mayfield name and attract high-end clients. While they were gone, his father's meticulously curated office sat unguarded. It was his sanctum, a shrine to ego and order. Ben decided to desecrate it. He didn't move recklessly. He was precise. He mixed up important case files, placed key documents in the wrong folders, and jumbled notes. He created just enough confusion to avoid being noticed right away. It wasn't enough to shout. He wanted his father to feel the disruption in both his work and his personal life.

Defiling his father's sacred space offered a fleeting sense of justice—a small, burning taste of vengeance. From that moment on, Ben learned to bury his true self. What began as forced study transformed into something more: a sincere love for law and justice. But in his father's house, even passion had to be disguised. Joy, curiosity, empathy— these were luxuries he could only afford in silence.

Ben's mother was a woman of contradictions. She could brighten a room with her presence, then vanish just as quickly, like a ghost gliding through velvet curtains. Sometimes, she held him close and called him her darling boy, pressing kisses on his forehead, treating him as though he were the greatest treasure in the world. Other times, she wandered through the house with her gaze far away, her fingers playing with the hem of her silk blouse.

"Why are you sulking?" she snapped once, after hours

of ignoring him. "I've been nothing but kind to you."

When she had company over, she was a completely different person—kind and loving. But kindness, for her, was currency. She gave it only when it suited her, always with conditions attached. One afternoon, Ben presented her with a crayon drawing of a castle, proud of every spire and colored stone.

"Oh, how lovely," she cooed, placing a kiss on his cheek. "You're my little artist."

But the next day, after he spilled juice on the carpet, her warmth vanished.

"You're so careless, Ben! I have guests arriving. Why would you do this? Why do you have to be so clumsy?"

She would not look at him for the rest of the night. He sat in the corner, cheeks burning, waiting for her affection to return. To him, her love felt like a break in the clouds— bright and beautiful but always temporary.

She had never chosen this life. Born into privilege, her future was charted long before she knew how to speak her own mind. Her family groomed her to marry well, to uphold the name, to smile in pearls and stay in line. They arranged her marriage to Ben's father when she was still a teenager, clutching paperbacks filled with starlit promises and slow-dance dreams. What she got was a man who saw her as a trophy—admired when polished, ignored when not. Ben didn't blame her; he even forgave her. But forgiveness couldn't erase the consequences her indifference had carved into him.

By the time Ben arrived, loneliness had already settled in like wallpaper. She had Ben's father, but he was rarely home, and when he was, he offered little beyond a paycheck. She was practically alone. She loved Ben fiercely when he played the role she imagined for him—well-mannered, brilliant, beautiful. But if he faltered, if he failed to reflect the fantasy, her warmth disappeared. Not out of malice but out of self-preservation. Her selfishness wasn't cruelty; it was the only power she had left in a life that had never truly belonged to her.

One afternoon, she ran her fingers through his hair and said, "You'll understand when you're older," with a hint of longing. "Being a parent isn't easy. Sometimes, I feel like I wasn't ready."

Ben only nodded. He didn't understand, but he wanted to comfort her anyway. Her sadness lingered like a still ocean behind her eyes, always on the verge of spilling over but never quite doing so.

In his younger years, she offered him tenderness, shopping trips, and stolen moments of laughter. But as he grew older, her attention drifted. Friends and designer purses took priority over her son. Still, Ben noticed the bruises—the same kind that marked his own skin. She never explained them. She didn't need to. Speaking up for his mother had always been considered insolence in his father's eyes. The night Ben stepped between them, refusing to back down, his father threw him out without hesitation.

He didn't expect anyone to defend him, and no one did. Each responsibility laid upon him felt like another stone pressing on his back. For others, childhood meant laughter and freedom. For Ben, it was silence, duty, and restraint. His maternal grandparents, who adored him and visited often, eventually took him and Ms. Benard in. At sixteen, he found safety in their home, far from his father's oppressive rules. This was when Ms. Benard became more than a caretaker. She became a true maternal figure. She often said Ben felt almost like her own son. From then on he referred to her as Mama Benard.

Living with them gave Ben his first taste of real freedom. But freedom didn't erase the scars. He struggled to connect with peers, never quite knowing how to talk or laugh the way they did. His quiet nature made others question his sexuality—not with cruelty but confusion. He wasn't interested in chasing girls like the others. To him, most seemed shallow or opportunistic, eager to exploit the Mayfield name—a name he no longer valued.

Yet guilt gnawed at him. He had left his mother behind. But he consoled himself, knowing his father rarely left his office. She would manage, he told himself. By his junior year, Ben had a plan. He would not follow in his father's footsteps. Instead, he would build his own firm and carve his own path. College was his stepping stone. Even though his scholarship came from his father's alma mater, he refused to ask for help.

He would not be indebted to a man who treated generosity as leverage. Then came the news. Months before graduation, his grandparents sat him down, their faces drawn and grave. His mother was sick. He knew it was serious—if it weren't, she would have told him herself. From that day on, Ben started returning home after school. When his mother asked, he blamed homesickness. Deep down, he believed she knew the truth. She never said it aloud. Instead, she let the silence grow between them.

Her health deteriorated rapidly. She became frail, often too weak to bathe herself. Sore spots bloomed across her skin, and she was always cold, always aching. Ben did what he could, but between caring for her and keeping up with school, he was drowning. At last, he did what he hated most—he asked his father for help.

They met in the dimly lit study, the room heavy with the scent of tobacco and leather. His father's gaze was sharp, unyielding.

"She's dying," Ben said, his voice breaking. "She doesn't have anyone else. I can't do this alone. Could you help?"

His father didn't look up from his paperwork. "Help?" he echoed, almost amused.

"Yes," Ben pressed. "She's still your wife."

"She stopped being my wife the day she stopped being useful," his father replied, leaning back. "I don't owe her anything. And neither do you. Let her family handle it. That's what they're there for."

Ben's throat tightened. "She's not a burden to pass off.

She's my mother," he said, fighting to keep his voice steady. "And she has been your wife for decades."

His father's lips curved into something that might have been a smile, though it was cold and hollow.

"Life isn't fair, Ben. People make choices, and they live with them. She made hers."

Ben understood the venom behind those words. His father had despised his mother from the start, resenting the arranged marriage their families had forced upon him. In his eyes, she had been an anchor dragging him into a life he never wanted, and he punished her for it in every way short of leaving.

Ben stared at him, fury rising like bile. "So, that's it?" he asked. "You won't even see her?"

"That's it," his father said flatly. Then, almost as an afterthought, he opened a drawer, pulled out a manila envelope, and slid it across the desk.

"Actually… you can hand her these."

Divorce papers.

Ben blinked, stunned. "You're serving her papers now?"

"I don't want anything passed to her people when she's gone," his father said. His tone was casual, but the words landed like blows. "This way, there's no confusion."

Ben's hands shook as he picked up the envelope, then dropped it onto the desk as though it burned. "She's on her deathbed," he said, his voice low and trembling, "and this is what you care about? Money?"

His father didn't flinch. "It's about what's mine, staying mine."

Something in Ben snapped. This was the breaking point, the last straw after years of cruelty, prejudice, and cold detachment. "You're a coward," he said, venom dripping from every word. "And I'll never forgive you for this. Ever."

His father said nothing, only watched as Ben stormed out, the door slamming behind him.

Left with no other choice, Ben turned to his

grandparents. When he asked for help hiring a nurse, they didn't hesitate. With their support, he arranged for a kind, capable nurse named Retina to care for his mother while he was at school.

Ben didn't think twice about Retina's race; most of the nurses he'd encountered were colored. But he forgot to consider his father's deep, ingrained prejudice.

One afternoon, his father stormed into the house.

"Why is there a colored woman in my home?" he shouted. "I thought you took that Benard woman with you when you left!"

Ben's jaw tightened. The sound of his father's voice scraped against his already frayed nerves.

"Keep your voice down," he said. "Mother has a headache."

"I don't care if she's got thirty seconds to live," his father snapped. "Get that woman out of my house. And don't you dare come back unless you're ready to take over the firm and stop this foolishness!"

Ben stood tall, his voice flat and unwavering. "Don't worry—I wasn't planning on staying long. I'll take her to Grandma's."

He packed his mother's belongings without a word, ignoring his father's tantrums, and took her to his grandparents' home. There, she could spend her last days surrounded by love—something she had known little of in her life.

The days that followed were long and filled with slow-burning heartbreak. Ben stayed by his mother's side, holding her hand as her body weakened. In her lucid moments, she whispered apologies. He forgave her, though the weight of their shared pain lingered.

His father never visited—not once. When the end came, Ben sat beside her, his grandparents nearby, their grief a silent bond. He gazed at her peaceful face. Anger simmered in him—not only because of his father's absence but also because of the years of neglect that had led to this lonely end.

From that day on, Ben carried two burdens: the memory of his mother and a bitterness toward his father. One, he vowed to honor; the other, he would never release.

In the end, his father's heartless prediction wasn't far off. Thirty seconds? No, thirty days. At seventeen, Ben felt orphaned. Losing his mother didn't change his life much; it had been falling apart for years. Still, it left a void nothing could fill.

The autopsy revealed she had died from complications of measles, a disease that claimed millions of lives. Her death came weeks before Ben's high school graduation. At the ceremony, only his grandparents attended. That didn't stop his father from playing the heartstricken widower.

Looking out over the unfamiliar crowd, Ben realized he had no ties to Michigan anymore. He still loved it, but a fresh start felt necessary.

He abandoned the idea of university. When the military draft notice arrived, he didn't resist. Two weeks after graduation, he boarded a plane to California for training. It was the first time Ben had ever left Michigan.

His grandparents had made his life comfortable, but the military hit him with harsh reality. It was a melting pot of backgrounds and nationalities. His eight weeks of boot camp were grueling. Days began before dawn. Everything, from bunk corners to uniform creases, was checked with strict precision. Screaming was the only language the commanders spoke.

By the end of training, Ben began to question his decision, but it was too late to turn back. Most of his squad was white, with only a few colored soldiers. Racial tension simmered beneath the surface, especially during off-hours. Ben, shaped by his past, bore no prejudice, but not everyone shared that mindset.

When he sprained his ankle, a colored nurse treated him. She was warm and kind, chatting with him during treatment. Yet outside her duty, she avoided him completely. The coldness stung, but Ben understood. For both their safety, distance was the better choice. Still, it left behind an ache he couldn't shake.

After "hell training," the recruits got a short break before their assignments. Ben returned to his grandparents, spending most of it catching up on sleep—a luxury he hadn't enjoyed in weeks.

Deployment brought a shift. In the field, segregation faded. Everyone depended on each other to survive. Ben bonded with his unit, especially with the other outcasts. He became friends with a man named James Smith. They shared easy humor, a love for basketball, and an appreciation for the pretty nurses at camp.

One night, drunk on cheap beer and homesickness, James confided something to Ben. At the time, Ben thought little of it, assuming it was the alcohol talking. The men often spoke of home—meals, family, warmth. Ben remained silent. He missed his grandparents but kept his thoughts guarded.

When they received news of another brief leave, Ben invited James to join him in Michigan. James accepted, as he, too, was from there. Ben asked him to wait in the car while he warned his grandparents. Even though they had always been kind, he never expected them to welcome a colored man into their home.

To his surprise, his grandmother ran outside, hugging James, her eyes filled with tears.

"You can't go hugging strangers like that, Ruth," his grandfather muttered.

But she turned to James and said, "Thank you for taking care of my boy."

James smiled. "It was nothing, ma'am. He took care of me."

That night, they prayed, ate a warm meal, and shared stories late into the evening. Their welcome stunned Ben. For once, he felt there might be room for kindness in the world he'd come from.

Three days later, they redeployed—this time, to

Vietnam. The war was worse than Ben had imagined. Anti-war propaganda in the States had soured public opinion. When the men came home on leave, they faced not parades but insults, spit, and hate.

"Baby burners," they were called.

The welcome was brutal and disorienting. Still, through it all, James remained a steadfast friend. One weekend, during a rare break, Ben and James visited the city. Most bars remained segregated, but they stumbled upon one that welcomed both of them. It felt like a small miracle. Women flirted with Ben, but he barely noticed—his thoughts were elsewhere.

Later that night, Ben realized James had slipped away. The crowd had grown loud, and the whiskey made everything feel hazy around the edges. Needing air—and curious—Ben went to find him.

Behind the restrooms, he heard muffled sounds. A groan. A low voice. He opened the door without thinking.

And there it was.

James.

On his knees.

A man standing before him.

The moment cracked like glass. James looked up, eyes wide, shame and defiance flickering across his face. The other man froze. Ben did too.

No words passed between them.

Ben closed the door, his hand trembling on the knob. He stood in the hallway for what felt like hours, the pulse of the bar now a distant hum beneath the weight of what he'd seen.

They never spoke of it.

But after that night, something between them shifted. Their friendship held, but not without caution. There was a new silence between them, shaped like a secret—one Ben didn't fully understand but would never forget.

CHAPTER 4:
ALTER THE WORLD

Ben was on the brink of the most pivotal case of his career. His client, a whistleblower armed with evidence of corporate misconduct, had come to him just days earlier. They'd spent hours unraveling the details: an intricate web of lies, money, and manipulation. The case had the potential to catapult Ben's reputation, to finally prove he was more than a partner riding his father's name. This wasn't just strategy; it was vindication.

The morning of their next meeting, Ben chose to park in the back lot. It was peaceful, less crowded, and tucked just enough out of sight to calm the unease that had been growing in him all week. He told himself it was practical, but something deeper stirred—an instinct that this case was going to change everything.

The next few months would be crucial for the firm. They were preparing for a major legal summit and planning strategies for their cases. He also had to prepare for the upcoming board meeting. He didn't enjoy meeting the board; they were a group of wealthy old men with more money than they knew how to spend. His mind needed to be completely focused on the tasks ahead.

Yet the more he tried to focus, the more his thoughts fogged with the image of the woman he had seen last week. She clearly worked for the firm, yet he had never seen her before. There was something in the way she looked at him—like she knew a secret he hadn't discovered yet, and wasn't in any rush to tell him.

Ben had never been one to get stuck on a person. He was good at separating personal feelings from work—maybe too good. Growing up, he was often ostracized; he was never interested in what his peers found fascinating.

In high school, it was teenage girls. Ben was far from uninterested in women, but he never found one who truly intrigued him. Most of the girls he encountered were shallow or simply drawn to his family's name. Once he got to college—a few years later than most, due to his service—he tried dating and even had a few one-night stands. Each time, he left unsatisfied, never pursuing anything serious.

***

The dining room table was laid out like something from a magazine spread: china polished, crystal glasses catching the light, the roast steaming in the center.

"The Andersons are good people. A union between our families will set you on the right path. Enough of this running around."

Ben's fork clattered against the plate. "A union?" he repeated, heat crawling up his neck. "You mean a marriage I never asked for."

"Don't raise your voice at this table," his father snapped, jaw tightening. "You'll thank me one day. You've been nothing but reckless, and this girl will straighten you out."

Ben pushed his chair back so hard it scraped the hardwood. "No. I'm not some horse you can trade off for breeding stock. I don't love her. I don't even know her."

"Love?" his father scoffed, his face darkening. "Love doesn't put food on the table. Love doesn't build a legacy. We're talking about family, about the future. You will do as you're told. Your mother's dead. You'll come back home and do as I say."

Before Ben was nineteen years old, he had lived

without his father for a while. He had no intention of following his demands now. That was the breaking point. Ben's fist came down on the table, rattling the silverware.

"No, I won't!" His voice cracked with fury. "You can't buy me a life I don't want. I won't marry your idea of a future. I'll make my own."

"Don't be a child, and watch your mouth," Ben's father said in an indifferent tone. "You'll marry who I tell you. When I say jump, you'll say how high—or you'll get out of my house."

If his father wanted control, Ben would spend every ounce of himself proving he couldn't be tamed.

Snapping out of his thoughts, he began working again. Ben's office sat on the very top floor of the firm's building, giving him a commanding view of the city. He often arrived before anyone else. He appreciated the tranquility before the phone started ringing nonstop. He paused, rubbing his hands through his hair. There was a knock at the office door, and Charlotte walked in.

"Mr. Mayfield," she said in a soft, timid voice.

"Yes, Charlotte, please join me," he said, knowing his day had officially begun.

Charlotte had been his secretary for about eight months. His last secretary left because she was pregnant. Charlotte paid special attention to him. At first, this was quite annoying, especially considering she did not hide her interest in him. But she was a hard worker, so he endured it. Ben never held her in any romantic regard, though that didn't stop her from trying. She was the dream of every typical guy—long legs, green eyes, a killer smile, and a figure that could stop traffic. But she wasn't his type. Still, given his lifelong bachelorhood, perhaps he should reconsider.

"Do you have a moment to speak about the quarterly employee evaluations?" she asked.

"Honestly, I forgot. I apologize," he responded. "I've been so busy that I haven't gotten any work done. I'll review them today," he promised.

She continued standing in front of him, staring. "Is there something else I can assist you with, Mr. Mayfield? You seem out of focus today. Is something wrong? I can bring you a hot tea," Charlotte offered.

"Yes, that would be great. Thank you," he said. She scurried out the door.

Ben turned his attention back to the employee evaluations. Her name must be in this stack of packets. All he had to do was find her and determine what section of the building she worked in. Three hours later, Ben found three names that might be hers. Funny, he thought, any of these names would sound good with Mayfields. As he searched, he came across one packet that was completely blank.

"Charlotte," he called from his office.

"Yes, sir," she answered, running in.

"Have all the hires not finished their packets?" Ben asked, a little irritated.

"Yes, they have," she responded.

"So why is this one blank, then?" he held up the packet for her to see.

She stopped and flipped through it. "Oh yes, she is a colored hire, and she's nothing more than my assistant. I figured she didn't need a serious review like the others."

Ben's jaw tightened at that comment. "It doesn't matter if you see her as only your assistant. She's my employee. I want her work history and the questionnaire to go with it," he said, his tone sharper now. Charlotte flinched.

"I—I apologize, sir. I will get it for you immediately," she stammered.

"Send the rest out," Ben said as he rose from his chair. "I have finished reviewing them. I will deliver this one in person. What section does she work in?"

"Don't trouble yourself, sir," she tried to interject. "I can deliver it, as it was my mistake."

"It's fine, Charlotte. Since hers will be late, I'd like to apologize on my behalf. I don't want my employee thinking I've discriminated against her," he said, brushing off her concerns. He handed Charlotte the rest of the packets. As she sauntered out the door, he couldn't help but chuckle. He knew he had her.

Charlotte raced down the stairs to find Florence. Florence was changing the printer ink.

"Florence, please complete this employee evaluation. It's late, so hurry up and finish it," she barked, thrusting the packet at her.

Florence was puzzled. How could something she never received be late? She shook her head and focused on finishing the ink change before lunch. Only Charlotte in the office ever disturbed her, which was a relief. It allowed her to complete her tasks quietly and efficiently. Only one person in the whole building seemed to notice her—Henry Anderson, a sixty-five-year-old Korean War veteran, long retired yet still clocking in each day to clean the building. He claimed he got bored at home, and Florence considered him a trusted confidant whenever she needed advice. Even though he was an old white man, he treated her with respect, just as he did everyone else.

Unlike the older white men she had known—men who carried their power like rusted armor and looked at her with eyes full of dust—Henry was different. There was no leer, no malice dressed as charm. He was tender, almost quaint, like something forgotten on a windowsill that still caught the light. A widower, yes, with the gentle sadness of one who had outlived love. He had children, grandchildren, and a smile framed by false teeth he swore were real, as though the lie stitched him closer to something vital.

The building, heavy with silence and the soft rot of class, kept its distance from him. People passed by without truly seeing him, though he kept their halls swept, their trash gone, their air almost holy in its stillness. Florence guessed it was the uniform that made them turn away: janitor, custodian, a worker of things no one wanted to touch. Anger rose in her throat when they ignored him, but he, with a stillness older than pain, would wave it off.

"People who lack sight will always be in the dark," he would say, his voice moving like water through stone.

She did not fully understand the words. It sounded like a riddle meant for someone else, meant for a world where metaphors still mattered. But she nodded, the way one does when reverence stands in for comprehension. She had her own battles to fight, and not enough hands to carry anyone else's sword.

When they had downtime—usually two hours after lunch—they would sneak to the cafeteria while it was closed and share Pringles, their guilty pleasure. She spent about forty minutes in the café before realizing she had lingered too long. If she wanted to leave before dark, she needed to finish her evaluation. She thanked Mr. Anderson and made her exit.

Florence decided to complete the employee evaluation before leaving. Since she rarely did anything significant, there should not have been many questions. She checked her list, making sure it was complete before taking the elevator back to her floor. For today, her luck held. She sat down at her cubicle and flipped through the papers on her desk. The packet began simply: first and last name, address, home phone number (if any), and an emergency contact. She wrote down Denise—pretty much the only person she had to call if something happened.

Do you wish to move to a different position in the company? What motivates you to come to work each day? Do you like your job? If you had to rate your performance this quarter on a scale of one to five, what would it be? These were basic questions she had expected. But as she moved farther down the packet, the questions became oddly personal.

What hobbies or activities do you enjoy? What made you the person you are today? How do you unwind after a long day? How would you describe your personality? Are you married? Do you have or want children? Florence assumed the questions were meant to gauge how her personal life affected her work. She answered the basics, mentioning how her father motivated her. Thinking of him always brought out her best self.

Then she reached a harder one. She wanted to be honest, but what if they disliked her answers and let her go? Florence began writing: Law has always excited me. My father's commitment to justice inspired this dream, and university strengthened it. I have always loved advocacy, analysis, and standing up for what is right. I appreciate my current role, but it does not align with my goal of practicing law and making a difference. I would find joy in being more involved in legal discussions and shaping strategies. I often linger in the firm's legal library, pretending to organize paperwork. I like to imagine I am part of their case preparations. I dream of a day when my arguments and insights might shape the firm's legacy. My legacy.

Charlotte began packing her things, and that was Florence's cue. It was time for her to wrap up as well. Florence gathered her belongings and headed downstairs. For the first time in months, she left work on time. The daylight greeted her and lifted her spirits. The warmth of the sun made her feel lighter, as though she might actually pamper herself when she got home. As she crossed the parking lot, she noticed an Aston Martin parked on the edge. It was sleek, intriguing, and beautiful. She wondered who owned it and wished for a closer look. She tossed her things in the back of her car, slid into the driver's seat, and turned off the radio. The silence helped clear her head.

The drive reminded her why she rarely left work at that hour. Traffic dragged for what felt like ages, until she finally broke free by turning onto a back road toward the colored side of town. When she arrived home, daylight still lingered, so she decided to visit Denise next door. Denise opened the door with a playful smile.

"What are you doing home so early?" she teased.

"I got off early to see you," Florence joked, earning an eye roll as Denise stepped aside.

Denise shared that she had spent the day doing home-work, since she did not work. They chatted about the strange questions Florence's job had asked. "It's weird, right? A job asking such questions?" Florence said.

Denise shrugged. "Maybe they're trying to make you feel included. I doubt they'll do anything with the answers—it seems like general knowledge."

Reassured, Florence nodded. "You're probably right."

Florence loved fashion but could rarely afford to shop. So she often rummaged through Denise's closet, and Denise did not mind. Florence tried on several dresses, twirling as she imagined where she might go and who she might go with. Once Denise made dinner, Florence stopped day-dreaming. It was late, and she had to return home to feed Mooni.

As she opened the door, Mooni was already waiting, his wide eyes full of anticipation. She scratched his head, filled his bowl, and watched him eat. It gave her a comfort-ing sense of purpose. His need for her reminded her she was not alone. Even on hard days, feeling needed gave her strength to keep going. Florence had just started her night routine when the phone rang in the kitchen.

"Hello, this is Florence speaking."

The deep voice on the other end made her pause.

"Hello, this is Mr. Smith. My mother gave me your contact information and mentioned that we should go on a date," he said.

Florence replied, "Ah, yes. My mother mentioned this as well."

"I see you're busy. I've had trouble reaching you. What day and time works best? We could meet at Johnson's Chicken House, unless you have another place in mind."

"Any time next week after 5:00 p.m. works for me. That's around when I finish work."

"Alright, how about Friday at 8:00 p.m.?" Mr. Smith asked.

"Yes, that sounds great," she said. "I look forward to

meeting you. Have a blessed night."

"You as well."

As Florence hung up, she let out a small sigh. Overthinking was her superpower. Her mind buzzed with thoughts about the date ahead. The nagging voice in her head would not let her forget—dates like these rarely went well. Still, she resolved to stay optimistic, even as doubt lingered. Maybe this man would become her partner and, at last, her mother would stop pestering her.

Early Saturday morning, Denise burst into Florence's house and headed straight to her bedroom. "It's time to get up!" she yelled.

Florence groaned, tugging the blanket as Denise pulled from the other side. "Please, I don't want to. It's my day off. Let me sleep in," she pleaded.

"All the good stuff will be gone if we wait all day," Denise countered. She finally stopped pulling and leaned in close, her face inches from Florence's. "If I make you breakfast with coffee, will you get up?"

Florence nodded. Satisfied, Denise bustled into the bathroom, handing her the morning vitamins and a glass of water before leaving to prepare breakfast. Florence gratefully drifted back to sleep for another hour.

When Denise returned, she carried a tray with eggs, grits, sausage, and toast, each prepared just as Florence liked it. She even brought both coffee and orange juice. Florence couldn't help but feel thankful as she sat up to eat.

After breakfast, Florence got ready for her usual Saturday trip to the farmer's market. This time, she had a goal: to find a dress for her date. After cuddling Mooni and reluctantly leaving, she headed out.

The farmer's market bustled with life, as always. It was the heart of the community, a place to shop, eat, and socialize. Food stalls offered a variety of comforting dishes that warmed the heart at any hour. Florence often admired her mother's generation, many of whom had grown up cooking and cleaning for white families. But times were changing.

As they browsed, Florence heard Denise's excited "oohs" and "ahhs." Denise pointed out dresses she thought would look stunning on her friend, but each time, Florence found a reason to dismiss them.

Although she hadn't been on many dates, Florence considered herself stylish. Her tall frame helped her stand out, and she often chose pieces that highlighted her long neck and legs. In her younger years, she had worn flats because many men preferred shorter women. But as she grew older, she decided she would rather be loved as she was. She glanced at the heels she hadn't worn since college and smiled. Who knows? Her special someone might be taller than her.

"I'll wear something from my closet," she mumbled.

Denise gasped dramatically. "Oh, absolutely not! You are not going on a date wearing your regular clothes. Not that you don't look gorgeous every day, dear, but this is your first date in how many years? We have to go all out! Hair is next, so let's focus and pick a dress!"

Florence rolled her eyes, but Denise's determination was unrelenting. Eventually, Florence found a dress she liked, though it was far out of her price range. Denise insisted on helping her pay for it despite Florence's protests. Florence vowed to pay her back, but Denise waved it off with a casual, "Don't worry about it."

The dress was perfect—a pale pink piece so soft it almost looked white. It had a low-cut V neckline that highlighted her long neck and delicate bows on each shoulder. The skirt flared at the waist and fell to her calves, leaving space to show off her heels while maintaining an air of mystery.

Next, they went to the salon for her hair. Florence's thick, long hair needed special care, so they chose a roller set with soft curls and a side part that framed her face neatly.

When they were finally done, Florence looked at herself in the mirror. The dress, the hair—it all came together. She was ready.

***

After a long night with Mr. Smith and aching feet, Florence thought she would sleep through Sunday. But once again, Denise pounded on her door. Before Florence could reach it, Denise burst in.

Florence muttered, "We must stop doing this."

Denise smiled with relief. "I'm so glad you're okay!"

Still sleepy, Florence gave her a confused, slightly irritated look. "Why wouldn't I be okay?"

Denise's expression turned grave. "Did you not hear? Last night, the police shot Mr. Nelson's son in front of the movie theater. A crowd started running, and the cops sent dogs after them. Everyone went home early, afraid of running into white folks on a rampage."

That explained why the restaurant had been so empty during her date, Florence thought. "Oh no, I didn't know. Is his son okay?"

"No," Denise said quietly. "He died right there in the street. No one even tried to take him to the hospital. He lay in his own blood until he passed."

Florence's chest tightened. She pressed a hand to her mouth, stunned into silence for a moment. The weight of Denise's words lingered in the air, heavy and unshakable. Finally, she shook her head. "It feels like everything has been getting worse since they shot Dr. King. These riots are out of control. It's getting really bad out there."

Once Denise was reassured that Florence was safe, her tone shifted. "So, how did your date go?" A mischievous grin crept across her face.

It was eight in the morning. Florence rubbed her eyes, feeling both annoyed and amused. Denise was used to her grumpy mornings, so it didn't faze her. Florence trudged back to bed, kicked off her slippers, and pulled the blanket over her. "Can we discuss this later?" she asked. "Preferably three hours later, when it's not so early."

"Nope," Denise said with a grin. "I want all the details now."

Florence sat up reluctantly as the questions began.

"What did he look like? Was he handsome? What does he do for work? What did he say about your job?"

Florence held up a hand. "One question at a time, please." She leaned back against her pillow. "The date was… good," she said, drawing out the word as Denise leaned forward expectantly.

"Good? That's all you're giving me?" Denise raised an eyebrow.

"No, I mean it was good," Florence said. "He's polite, charming even. He arrived on time, held the door for me, and complimented my dress. It looked amazing with the heels!" She smiled, though her tone carried a hint of hesitation.

"Okay, okay, keep going. What did you eat? Where did you go?" Denise pressed, practically on the edge of her seat.

"We went to that fancy French place downtown—the one with the live jazz band. It was lovely. For appetizers, we had shrimp cocktail—you know, those big, glossy prawns that look like they belong in a magazine. And let me tell you, he clearly had money. Not the showy kind, but the kind that whispers with custom tailoring and table-side steak service."

"Then we shared this incredible châteaubriand. They carved it right at the table. So classy! It came with asparagus and a creamy potato dish I'll be dreaming about for days."

"Fancy!" Denise said, grinning. "And dessert?"

"Cherries Jubilee," Florence replied with a small laugh. "They set it on fire at the table. It was dramatic, but kind of impressive. The ice cream melted just enough to soak up the sauce—it was perfect."

Denise nodded approvingly. "Okay, sounds like a dream. And Mr. Smith? What's the verdict on him?"

Florence hesitated, chewing on her bottom lip. "He's… nice. Really nice. He asked about my work, my favorite books, even classic movies—turns out he's a fan of Audrey Hepburn too. And he listened, Denise. Really listened—not that fake nodding-while-zoning-out nonsense. I felt comfortable with him."

"Comfortable, good," Denise said cautiously, sensing there was more. "But?"

"But," Florence sighed, "there was no spark. He's everything you'd want on paper—handsome, thoughtful, respectful—but it didn't click, you know? I wasn't sitting there imagining a second date or wondering what it would be like to kiss him. I was just there, eating steak, having a perfectly fine time."

Denise tilted her head. "So, what are you saying? You're not into him?"

"I don't know," Florence admitted. "I could see myself settling for someone like him. He's solid, stable. The kind of man who wouldn't let you down. But is that enough? Am I being too picky? I thought there'd be fireworks—or at least a few butterflies."

Denise studied her for a moment before shrugging. "I'm not going to push you either way," she said, "but it was only the first date. You may be judging him too quickly. Give it another chance, go on a couple more dates, and then decide. Things could change once you get to know him better."

"Oh, there's one thing I forgot to mention," Florence added. "I've met him before."

"What!" Denise exclaimed. "You've met him before? How is that possible?"

Florence turned to face her friend. Denise looked genuinely shocked. Florence sighed, setting down her coffee cup. "It's a long story. I was stranded on the side of the road, and I had no idea who he was at the time."

CHAPTER 5:
WORLDS COLLIDING

These were turbulent times in America. The air crackled with unrest, grief, and a hunger for change. Leaders like Martin Luther King Jr. and Malcolm X had stirred a nation awake, only to be violently silenced, leaving a generation grappling with the weight of unfinished revolution. The civil rights struggle pressed on, raw and urgent, especially for those fighting on more than one front.

Florence was one of them—young, brilliant, and walking into Detroit with ambition in her spine and law in her heart. She didn't just want to practice law; she wanted to rise, to lead, to carve her name onto the door of a firm that had never imagined someone like her in power. But as her dreams climbed higher, reality tightened its grip. Being who she was meant that every door came with a lock and a warning.

And still, she dared to knock.

On a scorching summer day, Florence ran out of gas. That afternoon, she stopped at a gas station on the outskirts of Detroit. As she approached the counter, the white man behind it scowled.

"Hello," she said carefully. "I'd like to pay for gas."

He crossed his arms, his glare unwavering. "Not from me you won't."

Florence blinked, unsure if she had misheard. "Excuse me?"

"You heard me," he growled. "We don't serve your kind here. Best you get going before sundown, or you'll regret it."

"Please, I don't need much, sir," she said, her voice trembling.

The man's smile turned cruel. "You'll find out soon enough if you stick around. There's a tree out back waiting for a girl like you."

His words struck like a punch to the gut. Florence turned and walked out, her hands shaking. She drove as far as she could until the car sputtered to a stop, the fuel tank empty. With no options, she parked in a grove of trees and spent the night in her car, terrified and unable to sleep.

By morning, Florence was exhausted and thirsty. She began walking along the roadside, searching for help. The heat pressed down like a weight. After a few miles, she collapsed, her palms scraping against burweed thorns. As she lay there, a sleek white Lincoln Continental pulled over, and a man stepped out.

"Miss, are you all right?" he called as he approached.

Florence looked up to see a well-dressed colored man, his expression filled with concern.

"I saw a car abandoned a few miles back. Is it yours?"

She nodded. "Yes, I ran out of gas."

"Let me help you up," he said, offering his hand with a soft smile.

As he lifted her to her feet, he noticed her injured hand. "Looks like you got caught on some burweed. Let me take care of that."

Florence watched as he removed the thorns with surprising care. "Thank you," she murmured.

"There's a gas station a couple of miles ahead. I can give you a ride if you'd like."

After some hesitation, Florence agreed. During the drive, the man introduced himself.

"I'm James Smith," he said warmly. "Partner at Davis & Smith Law—an all-colored firm."

Florence's brows rose. "You're a lawyer?"

"Yes, ma'am. And what about you? What brings you out here?"

"I'm trying to start my career in law," she admitted. "But opportunities have been… limited."

James nodded knowingly. "Detroit's not an easy place for folks like us, but things are changing. Here." He pulled a business card from his pocket and handed it to her. "If you're serious about law, come by our office. We're always looking for determined people."

Florence stared at the card, unsure what to say. "Thank you," she murmured.

At the gas station, James paid for her fuel despite her protests. The memory of that encounter lingered with her.

***

Denise's eyes sparkled. "It's fate!" she exclaimed, bouncing in her seat. "Both of you are lawyers! What are the odds? And this was right before you met me! Why didn't you ever contact him about the job?"

Florence smiled, a hint of guilt in her expression. "I lost his card, or I forgot to call him. I ended up where I'm supposed to be anyway."

Denise wasn't letting it go. "Girl, listen, it's meant to be! Don't you think it's crazy that you two crossed paths like that?"

Florence shook her head. "He doesn't have the qualities I find appealing. Something about him felt… off. I can't explain it."

Denise groaned, throwing up her hands. "Sis! At least give the man a chance! You haven't been with anyone for five years."

She wasn't wrong. Florence had kept her heart guarded after too many heartbreaks. Too many men had been selfish or unkind, and she'd promised herself not to settle for less than she deserved. She hadn't dated in years, waiting for someone who sparked a genuine connection. James didn't feel like that person.

"I want more than a 'good enough' guy," Florence said quietly. "I want something real. It's like he's reading from a script. I don't feel any real romance with him. It's more like spending time with a dear friend than someone who's courting me. I can't quite put my finger on it, but something's missing."

Denise rolled her eyes. "You always say that! But how are you supposed to feel sparks if you don't give anyone a chance?"

The two friends agreed to disagree. Florence chose to trust her instincts. The next day, she returned to work, her thoughts still swirling from the night before—and from Mr. Smith. Maybe she was being too picky. She didn't need perfection, just someone kind and consistent.

***

Her head throbbed with a dull ache as she stepped into the basement breakroom, clutching her mug like a lifeline. She brewed a stronger pot of coffee and groaned when she saw the creamer was gone. With a heavy sigh, she made her way upstairs to the cafeteria, silently swearing never to go out on a weekday again.

The cafeteria buzzed with early risers: mugs clinking, coffee hissing. She scanned the fridge. No creamer.

"Looking for this?"

Florence turned. A tall, broad-shouldered man in a crisp shirt with a loosened tie held out a bottle of hazelnut creamer. His hair was still damp at the temples, his face distractingly handsome—the kind that made her forget what she was doing. Something about him felt familiar.

"Yes, thank you," she said, startled by both the interruption and his intensity. Their fingers brushed as she took the bottle, a small jolt sparking up her arm. Of course, it was hazelnut—her least favorite.

"There's only a little left," she murmured. "I'll leave some for you."

"It's yours," he said simply, his voice calm and assured. "I don't think I've seen you around before," he added.

"I work upstairs. Just came down for coffee." Florence added.

"Lucky timing," he said with a faint smile.

She hesitated, then nodded toward the exit. "I should get back."

"See you around," he replied, and it sounded almost like a promise.

Back at her desk, she had barely set her mug down before Charlotte's heels clicked up.

"Have you finished those papers?" Charlotte's tone was clipped.

Florence slid them across the desk. Charlotte snatched them, then set down a fresh list of tasks. At the bottom, something caught Florence's eye: Meeting – 3 pm, Team-led Meeting.

"Ms. Charlotte?" Florence called, catching her at the elevator. "This last item—what does it mean?"

"You'll be filling in for one of Mr. Hargrove's assistants. Two people are out sick. Take notes. Keep your head down. Don't speak unless spoken to. You're a placeholder."

Still, it was something. A foot in the door.

Later, over lunch, she found Mr. Anderson in his usual spot. "This is my first real team assignment," she said, trying to contain her excitement.

"I told you things would start to shift," he said warmly. "The road may be bumpy, but you're on it now. Smile back at adversity."

At 2:45, she triple-checked her notes. At 3:00 sharp, Florence stepped into the conference room. Mr. Hargrove sat near the head of the table, radiating cold authority. She slid into a seat along the wall, notebook ready. The room hummed with the low, nervous energy of junior associates and paralegals.

Stories about Ben Mayfield were legendary: cold, brilliant, and ruthless. He had no patience for mediocrity and didn't waste words. He didn't guide; he demanded. Power ran in rigid lines at the law firm, and Ben stood firmly at the top.

The door opened. Ben Mayfield entered, taller than she expected, his presence like gravity. His tailored suit fit with unnerving precision. He scanned the room, then his eyes landed on her.

It was him. Florence's breath caught. The man from the parking lot. The one who had placed his jacket over her in the rain. The man who had handed her hazelnut creamer less than two hours ago.

The room seemed to tighten. His gaze didn't just land—it searched, held, and tugged at something deep inside her. And then he smirked. Ben Mayfield didn't smirk. Not in meetings.

Her stomach dropped. She gripped her pen, forcing her attention forward.

"Each of you will submit a strategy proposal," Ben began, his voice clear and commanding. "Anonymous. The best proposal wins, and the winner will shadow me throughout trial prep." Gasps and murmurs fluttered across the room.

"I'm not giving you a checklist," he continued, pacing slowly. "No handholding. Think critically. Anticipate challenges. Create something bold. These packets outline the facts. You have forty-eight hours. Drop your proposal in the locked box outside my office by Friday. No names. No excuses."

His voice hit like a gavel.

"Am I boring you, Mr. Green?" Ben's tone cut across the room toward a young man whose head had been down, scribbling furiously.

The man froze. "No, sir. I was taking notes."

"I've given you everything you need," Ben said evenly. "There's no need for notes. Just pay attention."

Mr. Green stammered an apology, which Ben dismissed with a flick of his hand, as though swatting away a fly. "This isn't about winning a case. It's about setting a new standard. If you can't rise to that, don't bother submitting."

He ended the meeting with a single nod. The silence he left behind was electric.

Florence stayed seated a moment longer. She had been waiting for an opportunity like this for years but never imagined it would come from the same man who had handed her hazelnut creamer—and once shielded her from a storm... literally saving her life.

Back at her desk, she stared at her bulletin board, usually cluttered with flyers and internship announcements. Normally, she shared opportunities with others. Not this time. This one was hers. She had something to prove now. And for the first time, she wanted to be seen—especially by him.

***

Perched at her desk, her hand cramping from so much writing, Florence was jolted by the kitchen phone's sharp ring. She hurried in, smoothing her skirt as she lifted the receiver.

"Hello? This is Florence."

"How did your date go? I hear you went to a fancy restaurant!" her mother said, her voice bright with excitement. Florence couldn't even get a hello first. She sighed.

"Hello, Mama," Florence said, bracing herself. "It wasn't a fancy restaurant, just a regular one in town, and the date went okay."

"Just okay?" her mother exclaimed, her tone shifting into immediate disapproval. "Well, what did you tell him? You told him you work with all white folks, didn't you? Did you tell him you have that made-up depression stuff? Or your cat? Ugh, I told you not to say any of that."

Florence took a deep breath, clutching the phone tightly. Arguing would get her nowhere.

"No, Mama. It was okay because I don't know him that well yet."

"Could you give it more than one date, please?" Elane

asked.

Florence didn't want to say she had met this man before. Her mother would take that chance to push even more.

"It didn't take many dates for me and your daddy to be together. We knew almost instantly," her mother retorted.

"And how did that work out?" Florence snapped. "You knew Daddy for eight years before marriage. Since you're not together now, that's not a great example."

Her mother scoffed, the sound grating in her ear. "Thank you for the reminder. Take my advice," she said, her voice dripping with condescension. "Good men rarely come along. Settling is your best option; you can learn to love him. Consider this: He can pay for those clothes you can't afford. Or maybe you just enjoy looking great, even if you hardly go out. Hence why we're setting you up on dates now."

Florence clenched her jaw, the words stinging more than she wanted to admit.

"That's not the kind of love I want, Mama. But I'll go on more dates with him, and we'll see what happens."

"Be sure to keep me informed. I'm trying to get you married off before Josie's daughter."

Anger flared in Florence, sharp and sudden.

"My life is not something for you to gamble with your friends about! I'll choose the right guy when I feel like he's the one, regardless of Josie's soon-to-be marriage or not. Goodbye, Mother. I hope you have a good week."

She hung up before her mother could say another word. Her mother's remarks weighed on her chest. For a moment, she let herself feel the full burden of frustration and insecurity. Life felt unbearably heavy, and for once, she allowed herself to acknowledge it.

That night, she snuggled up to Mooni tighter than usual. As she slept, her eyebrows pinched together and she mumbled incoherent words as she drifted off.

Florence found herself back in the field where she used

to play baseball. But now she stood in the middle of an endless expanse of cotton roses. These flowers usually shifted to bright pinks and reds in the sunlight, their petals shining like little flames against the green. But here, they stayed muted: charcoal gray, as if all their vibrancy had been drained away.

The air was thick and oppressive, and the only sound was the faint rustling of the roses in an unseen wind.

She bent down and cradled a bloom in her hand, willing it to change. But the petals stayed cold and lifeless, crumbling a little under her touch.

Overhead, the sky began to churn. Dark clouds rolled in, heavy and menacing, like smoke billowing across the heavens. The storm carried no rain, only a deep, resonant boom that shook the earth beneath her feet.

Florence's heart pounded as she turned in every direction, searching for an escape. Then, in the distance, she saw it: a small gap in the storm. A thin, golden ray of sunlight pierced through the chaos, touching the field far ahead. For a moment, it felt like the flowers were waking up. Their colors warmed and glowed, as if they were alive.

She began to run, her feet sinking into the soft, damp earth with every step. The air grew colder. The storm rumbled louder, as if taunting her. The closer she got to the light, the narrower the gap became.

"A little further," she whispered, her voice trembling. "I can make it."

But as she reached out, the clouds closed with a deafening roar. The sunlight vanished, swallowed whole. The field plunged into a darker abyss. The flowers around her shivered. Their petals curled inward, retreating like hope slipping away.

The storm howled, wind whipping through her hair and stinging her skin. Florence fell to her knees, overwhelmed by the weight of it all. She clutched at the roses nearby, but they were brittle, breaking apart in her fingers like ash.

"Why can't I fix this?" she cried, her voice barely audible over the wind. The storm didn't answer. It only grew louder, fiercer, mocking her.

In the heavy darkness, Florence could only sit, surrounded by lifeless roses and the storm's relentless void.

Then, with a jolt, she woke up, gasping for air. Her sheets were damp with sweat, her heart pounding against her ribs. She fought to steady her breath. She had tossed and turned so much in her sleep that her bonnet slipped off.

She stared at the ceiling, the remnants of the nightmare clinging to her like cobwebs.

In the silence of her room, she whispered, "It's a dream." But deep down, she felt the field and the storm were more than that. They mirrored her life, her struggles, and the faint hope she feared might never return.

She glanced at the clock. A few hours remained before she had to be at work. She laid back down but couldn't sleep, so she got up early, made herself a proper breakfast, and wrote in her journal.

Mayfield Law had made public its intention to include more colored employees in its programs. It was a bold step, and one not met with universal applause. The decision unsettled certain townspeople and stirred sharp criticism from reactionary groups whose vision of progress ended where equality began.

Driving through the city's industrial area, the air felt still, as if it were holding its breath. Her old car rumbled along the uneven streets, the radio softly playing Sam Cooke's "A Change Is Gonna Come." She turned a corner onto 47th Street, and that's when she saw them: a group of protesters, consisting primarily of white men, filled the street. They shouted and waved signs, blocking her way. Florence's heart skipped a beat. Her first thought was to back up and take a different route to work. But cars had already lined up behind her, trapping her in.

"Stay calm," she whispered to herself, gripping the steering wheel tighter.

As she inched forward, trying to avoid making a scene, someone from the crowd turned toward her car. A man yelled something she couldn't understand. Others soon joined in, turning their anger toward her.

"Hey, hey! Get out of here!" one of them yelled, slamming his fist against the hood of her car.

Florence froze, her breath caught in her throat. Another man hurled something at the windshield—a crumpled soda can, by the look of it. It clanged off the glass, leaving a faint streak behind.

"Please, no," she whispered, her voice shaking.

The crowd surged closer, chanting louder. A signpost struck the driver's side window. Florence ducked instinctively, tears filling her eyes. She fumbled with the gear shift, trying to reverse, but the line of cars behind her made it impossible.

The scene grew tense. The crowd shifted and moved further down the street in a sudden wave. A police cruiser arrived, its siren slicing through the air, drawn by the protest. The officers didn't stop to help; they pushed the protesters aside to clear the road.

Florence restarted her car with trembling hands. She moved with caution, her knuckles white on the steering wheel. Her heart pounded with such intensity that she was sure it could be heard outside her body.

When she finally reached the office parking lot, she parked in her usual spot. Her hands shook violently, refusing to let go of the wheel. For a long moment, she sat there, staring at the chipped paint on the edge of the hood where the signpost had struck.

Everything seemed to come crashing down at once. The protests and violence weighed heavily on her, as did her colleagues' disapproval over hiring more colored employees. It was part of the growing national debate on workplace inequality for colored women, reminiscent of the famous *Griggs v. Duke Power* case. But this time, it was personal. A group of white employees openly opposed the hiring and promotion of colored women, and her case sat squarely at the center of the controversy. She felt trapped in a storm, unable to escape the chaos swirling around her.

But no tears came. Not now. She took a deep breath, adjusted her rearview mirror, and dabbed at her face with a tissue. By the time she walked into the office, her mask was secure; no one would know what had happened on her way there.

She didn't notice who drove the car that had blocked her earlier. That incident had sparked the chaos, yet she pushed the thought aside as quickly as she always did.

Florence glanced over at the car that had recently parked in the back lot with her—a rare sight, since hardly anyone else arrived this early. She was eager to see who it belonged to. This person had beaten her to work, and she wondered if they'd endured the same dreadful morning. But more than that, the car caught her eye for a personal reason. It was an Aston Martin, her father's dream car, the one he used to talk about in almost reverent tones, knowing deep down he'd never be able to afford it. Seeing its sleek lines and polished chrome in the pale morning light felt like stumbling upon one of his daydreams made real.

She made a mental note to leave home earlier tomorrow, not just to avoid the crowds but to finally catch a glimpse of the mystery driver.

CHAPTER 6:
COLLIDING FRAME OF MIND

Ben felt a twinge of guilt as he adjusted a few answers on the employee evaluation packet. He wanted to know more about Florence. Instead of leaving the packet with Charlotte, he decided to deliver it himself. He made his way to the fourth floor, where Charlotte said Florence would be, but when he arrived, she was nowhere in sight.

He lingered for a few minutes, frustration simmering as he asked around. No one seemed to know who or what he was talking about. Feeling foolish for chasing someone he barely knew, Ben turned back toward the elevator. Just as the doors opened, Charlotte appeared.

Great. Just my luck.

"Hello, sir. What are you doing here?" she asked, surprise in her voice.

"Oh, just trying to deliver this paper," he said, holding up the packet casually.

Why was he going to such lengths for this woman? This wasn't him. He had always been nonchalant, composed, never the type to fuss over anything. But with her… something shifted. She stirred in him a wildness he hadn't felt in years, something restless and unsteady. Around her, he felt like his teenage self—careless, impulsive, doing foolish things just to catch a glimpse of her. The worst part was, she wasn't even his.

"You haven't found her yet? That's strange. She's usually here by now," Charlotte said, glancing down the hall.

"It's fine. I'll take it back to the office," Ben offered.

"No, I can deliver it to her," Charlotte insisted.

Ben hesitated. If he kept it, she might suspect something. If he handed it over, she might glance through and notice the discrepancies. In the end, letting her take it seemed safer.

"I won't trouble you," he said, though the words felt hollow.

Charlotte took the paper anyway. Ben nodded politely and walked away, unsettled. Regret tugged at him as the elevator doors closed. Why was he letting this woman rattle him? The thought irritated him—and yet, his heart beat a little faster.

Back at his desk, he turned to preparations for a legal compliance meeting set for the next morning. Later, the revised evaluation packet slipped under his door. The sight of it stirred something—an excitement he didn't care to name. He worked quickly, eager to get home and read it.

It wasn't Florence's full lips, glowing skin, or striking hair that held him—it was her indifference. Her lack of reaction bruised his ego more than he wanted to admit. Shaking his head, Ben pushed the thought aside. He needed to focus.

He knew the unspoken rules about office decorum, especially when it came to women like Florence. A relationship—or even the hint of one—could unravel a career. But something about her conviction chipped at his restraint. She wasn't like the women he'd met in polished corridors or at charity galas. Florence moved with purpose, not pretense. And for once, Ben wanted something that wasn't about legacy or image. He told himself it wasn't romance—just respect, admiration, curiosity. But deep down, he knew better.

Still, what harm could there be in simply watching her brilliance unfold? Admiring from a distance didn't break any rules. At least, not yet.

That evening, his penthouse was as quiet as ever. Mama Benard had already retired, leaving him alone with his thoughts. He kept no pets; he couldn't bear the idea of losing them, not after everything else he'd lost. His circle was small—Mama Benard and a few distant acquaintances.

His routine rarely changed: shower, dinner, legal briefs. But tonight, the packet called to him. He read it carefully, looking for insight into the woman who unsettled him. By the end, he had a plan—he would begin his pursuit in earnest.

Buzzing with energy, he couldn't sit still. He headed to his private gym and pushed himself harder than he had in years. Sweat slicked his skin, his shirt clung to his chest, and he gasped for breath. Running a hand through his damp hair, he finally stopped. His muscles still thrummed, but the tension had eased.

The next morning, he woke early and trained again. Lately, it had been harder to stay still, his body alive with a restless charge. He hadn't felt release in months—something he would need to address soon.

After his workout, he dressed in a bespoke Giovanni Vacca suit, the kind of tailoring that announced power before he said a word, and fastened his grandfather's watch—a reminder of the weight he carried.

He parked at the back of the firm's lot, a new habit since the day before. Florence had already been gone when he left, the lot empty and echoing. He liked arriving early; the silence gave him space to think.

Ben had decided to propose something bold—a new direction for the firm, one rooted in inclusivity. The meeting began with light chatter and catered dishes he had arranged himself. He'd remembered everyone's preferences, even ordering lemon chicken for Stafford, who was allergic to seafood. One senior board member noticed Ben's plate of fried green tomatoes and ordered more for the group, earning a few laughs.

"Let's get started." His voice cut cleanly across the

room.

He set down the folders and lifted a stack of transparent sheets, sliding one onto the overhead projector. A soft whirr filled the room as the chart lit up on the wall behind him. "Over the past quarter, I've conducted client meetings, reviewed legal opinions from outside counsel, and prepared this presentation to map out where we stand and the direction we need to take."

The chart displayed neatly hand-drawn columns of case outcomes, pending litigation, and projected risks. Ben gestured toward it with controlled precision. "Several of our clients are entering high-risk phases of their contracts. We've flagged possible breaches that need addressing before they escalate into litigation. I've also outlined preemptive strategies—handled correctly, these could save months of courtroom battles and substantial costs."

He shifted to the next transparency, filled with figures and graphs painstakingly drawn in ink. "This isn't just about risk management; it's about positioning. I've coordinated with our corporate clients to align our legal strategies with their expansion plans. The opinions we've secured from external counsel confirm our approach is sound, but timing will be critical."

Ben leaned in slightly, eyes scanning the table. "There's another element—our growth is tied to inclusivity. Bringing more diverse clients into the firm isn't just ethical; it's strategic. More colored people working here means more people of color entrusting us with their business. It strengthens our network, enhances the firm's reputation, and ensures relevance in a changing market."

The room stayed quiet, all eyes trained on him. His delivery was clipped, precise—the cadence of a man used to presenting arguments under pressure. He wasn't just reporting; he was directing the firm's next moves.

Finally, he removed the last transparency and placed it back in the folder, sweeping his gaze across the table. "You've seen the framework. You've heard the opinions. If anyone has objections, state them now. If not—this is the strategy we're moving forward with."

The silence that followed wasn't hesitation. It was acknowledgment. And to his surprise, the firm didn't reject his proposal outright. Only three expected opponents resisted—his father's loyalists. The old guard.

Still, Ben stood firm. He spoke of progress and modern values, of shielding new hires from discrimination. He didn't expect immediate change, but he presented a case that was hard to dismiss.

By the end, he felt a quiet sense of achievement. Back in his office, he worked through the day, steady and focused. The landmark case he had taken on was gaining traction. It could prove why inclusivity mattered. Their firm had a chance to lead.

As evening approached, the thought of returning to his empty penthouse felt heavier than usual. The silence, once a comfort, pressed against him.

He went through the motions—another hard workout, a cold shower, dinner—but the restlessness lingered, coiling in his chest like smoke.

In an uncharacteristic moment of openness, Ben picked up the phone and called James, one of the few men who knew the sound of silence behind his polished voice.

James answered on the third ring, his tone bright.

"Mayfield, my man."

They traded the usual: work updates, women they weren't seeing, jokes only old friends could share. It was easy, familiar. But James heard it—the lag in his voice, the weight beneath his laugh.

"What's going on?" James asked. "And don't give me the usual song and dance. My retainer fee is expensive, but I'll give you the friends-and-family discount," he said jokingly.

Ben sighed, leaning back in his chair. "I've been thinking. About where I'm headed. What I'm really building. And whether any of it actually means something.

James didn't answer right away. The silence stretched, giving Ben room to say what he meant.

"I've got the job, the apartment, the suits… hell, even the last name that opens doors. But it still feels like I'm standing outside them."

"You're looking for something real," James said finally. "Something with your name on it, not your old man's."

"Exactly," Ben replied. "Something I can claim without feeling like it was handed to me."

James chuckled low. "You've built a fortress around yourself since the day we met, brick by brick. Now, suddenly you want to let someone in?"

Ben shook his head. "I don't know if I'm ready. I just know I'm tired of hearing my own footsteps echo off the walls every night."

James's voice softened. "Then maybe it's time to stop trying to outrun the silence."

Ben exhaled. "I keep hoping it'll just happen. That she'll show up, walk right through the front door, and make the place feel like home."

"Yeah?" James laughed. "And I'm hoping to hit the jackpot at the track."

Ben smiled. "Fair."

"Look," James continued, "you hate your father. I get it. But the man's name opened doors, and you walked through them. That's not nothing. But it doesn't mean you owe him your soul either. You want something of your own? Then build it. Don't wait for it to fall in your lap. But you know I'm right," James said. "And if you ever do find someone who gets past that wall of yours, I'd love to meet the woman who finally makes Benjamin Mayfield sit his ass down."

Ben leaned his head back, staring at the ceiling. "You and me both, brother."

The line went still for a few beats, but it wasn't heavy anymore—just honest.

James's words lifted Ben's spirits, but they lingered in

his mind. He had to stop avoiding connection. His loneliness wasn't about work; it stemmed from his guarded heart.

***

Across town, Florence needed to clear her head—but not from confusion. She was certain of her path as a lawyer. What she wasn't certain of was love, desire, and what kind of man—if any—fit into the life she was building. She had spent years grinding, sacrificing, shaping herself to fit into a world of white men in suits. Now, she wanted to taste something else. Something hers.

She made a decision: She would date. Often. Boldly. Many men, many nights. Not recklessly, but intentionally. How would she know what stirred her spirit if she never gave herself the room to explore?

Denise had just finished her summer courses and was eager for a new adventure. The night air was crisp as Florence and Denise stepped out onto the downtown streets of Detroit. The scent of fresh rain mingled with the smoky aroma of the city. They were free for the evening, dressed to impress in colorful dresses and bold accessories. Their style stood out against the gray backdrop of 1968's racial tensions. Tonight was a rare reprieve, a night to forget the weight of work and the world outside. They were looking for fun—companionship, even.

"We deserve this, Flo," Denise said with a grin. She linked her arm through Florence's as they walked. The click of their heels on the pavement created a rhythmic beat that matched their anticipation.

Florence sighed, a soft smile tugging at her lips. "I don't know... sometimes these nights blur together." She wasn't jaded—just cautious. But deep down, she hoped tonight might surprise her.

"Oh, please," Denise scoffed. "You've got that glow about you tonight. Men will be lining up."

The bar they entered was rare for the time: integrated, open, and somewhat welcoming. They could sit with white patrons without fear of being turned away. As they walked in, the noise dimmed to a murmur. There was no outright hostility, just a few curious looks. Florence felt it immediately. As one of the few women of color there, her stomach tightened, but she pushed the feeling aside.

They approached the bar. Denise ordered a whiskey sour, while Florence chose something sweeter. They clinked glasses, a silent agreement to enjoy the night.

As they sipped their drinks, Florence noticed a man— a white man—watching her. His gaze wasn't aggressive, but it lingered. She glanced away, unsure whether to be flattered or annoyed. When he stood and approached with an easy confidence, she straightened slightly.

"Mind if I join you?" he asked, his voice low and polite, even charming.

Florence hesitated, her hand wrapped around her glass. Denise arched an eyebrow, amused.

With a soft but firm smile, Florence replied, "I think we're good for now, thank you."

She turned back to her drink, more at ease than offended. It wasn't about him exactly—it was about the presumption. The way some men, particularly white men, assumed they belonged in every space, every conversation. She wasn't angry—just aware.

But the man wasn't deterred. He leaned closer, his eyes steady on hers. "I just wanted to say you're very beautiful."

Florence tensed. Denise leaned in and whispered, only for her to hear, "Girl, you don't get many chances like this. You're a free woman now; give the man a chance."

Florence shot her a look, curious more than sharp. "What's he doing over here, though? He's white. Why does he think he can just walk up to me like that?"

Before Denise could reply, the man offered his hand. "I'm Louis," he said, smiling.

Denise nudged her again. "Girl, he has an accent. He's not from here. If you don't grab him, I will."

"Have at it," Florence said flatly.

"No, thank you," she repeated, her voice firm. "I'm not interested."

Louis hesitated, then shrugged and backed away, returning to his seat. Florence exhaled, relief washing over her.

Denise huffed at her friend's stubbornness. "You know, when you end up single and alone, I'm not moving in with you," she teased, the thrill gone.

The mood shifted when a group of white women began whispering and glancing their way. Florence felt their judging eyes, the burn of their stares creeping across her back. Denise noticed too but ignored them, determined to enjoy the night.

"Girl, I told you," Florence murmured. "This is what white men attract: attention and trouble."

Denise shook her head with a mischievous grin. "You might be too stubborn for your own good."

Florence ignored her and took another sip of her drink, trying to focus on the buzz in her veins. The night was meant to be carefree, but now it felt heavy, pressing on them both. Every man who approached her felt wrong, no matter their color. Each one left her feeling more alone than before.

The night dragged on. Louis didn't come near them again, though Florence sensed his presence like a shadow in the background. It wasn't until another drink found its way to her hand that the alcohol began to blur the sharp edges of her thoughts.

By the time they were walking home, both women were tipsy, swaying slightly as they leaned into each other for balance. Denise was radiant, bubbling with laughter as she recounted every detail of the evening. Florence, however, had turned inward. Her gaze was distant, her steps slower, as though her body moved through the city while her mind lingered back at the bar. Something about the night clung to her, stirring questions she couldn't yet name.

When they reached Denise's house, they didn't bother

with the lights. They collapsed onto the couch, laughter spilling into the dim room. Scattered bottles of beer and wine covered the coffee table. Florence laughed with her, but her mind wandered, her thoughts tugging at the edges of the moment. She'd never had a wild phase; perhaps this counted as one.

After a few more drinks, Florence's walls began to crumble. Years of hurt and disappointment had made them strong, but now they gave way. She lay back, staring at the ceiling, tears welling in her eyes as she spoke, her voice thick with emotion.

"I'm tired, Denise. I'm tired of being strong. I'm tired of doing it all on my own, of always pretending everything's fine. I haven't had a man touch me or hold me in years."

Denise, still tipsy but tender, sat up and rubbed her friend's back. "Flo, you've been through a lot. You don't have to carry it all. You're allowed to let someone take care of you, too."

Florence turned her face into the pillow, her tears soaking the fabric. "But I'm not allowed to just be. I'm always the one who fights, the one who holds it all together. And I can't... I can't be alone like this anymore. I'm tired of being the strong one."

Denise stayed quiet, letting the words settle. She knew the world wasn't built for women like them—strong, colored, and expected to be both unshakable and invisible in a world that wanted them small.

"You can lean on me," Denise said softly. "And you can lean on someone else too. Don't let this world make you forget that you're worthy, Florence."

Florence lay there, the weight of her emotions finally spilling free. For the first time in a long time, she let herself cry. She let the exhaustion and longing move through her. She didn't have all the answers, but maybe—just maybe—she didn't need to.

CHAPTER 7:
MIND GAMES

Ben walked back to his office after the team meeting. Once behind his closed door, he let out a deep breath. His palms were sweaty as he leaned against the door. People knew Ben for being impenetrable, but who knew one woman could shake his confidence?

He pushed away from the door and sat at his desk. His plan was in motion now. Florence must have recognized him by this point. There was no more hiding. He would pursue her with determination.

Ben had already asked his private investigator to look into her background. He wondered why she was working as a secretary rather than as a junior associate. Given the times, he suspected it wasn't her choice. Discrimination was as common as cigarette smoke in an office like this. He made a mental note to investigate further, and, if he was right, to find a way to help her into a higher position without drawing attention.

Tension hung heavy across the building. If Ben wanted to stay ahead, he would have to work longer, push harder. He liked to think of himself as the one others measured themselves against, the one whose respect carried weight. But sooner or later, someone would surpass him. The thought tightened his jaw. And now, of all times, he had something to prove. He wanted Florence to see him—not just as competent but also formidable.

Charlotte knocked and stepped inside.

"Yes, Charlotte," he said, still distracted by his thoughts.

"Mr. Davis will be joining you for a meeting tomorrow."

"For what?" Ben asked, exasperated.

"There's a legal summit coming up in a couple of months, in New York. I've marked it on your calendar," Charlotte replied from the doorway. "Also, Mr. Davis would like to discuss potential networking opportunities with the firm."

Ben sighed. Of course he would.

"Fine. Schedule him for five, after the floor clears out."

"Will do, sir." She gave a tight nod and closed the door behind her.

Lance Davis. Even the name made Ben's jaw tighten. "Friend" was too generous; "colleague" too polite. In truth, he was a necessary nuisance—nothing more.

Lance had a way of making his presence felt the moment he entered a room—not through merit or charm but sheer legacy. The Davis name was etched into the architecture of American wealth: old money, inherited power, connections woven into every institution from the Ivy League to Capitol Hill. Lance had never earned a thing in his life, yet he moved through the world as though it belonged to him.

He treated introductions like auditions and women like decorations for a trophy case. Every conversation was an opportunity to dominate; every interaction a reminder of his family's reach. Ben had met him in law school, and from the first day, he had been insufferable. While most students wrestled with casebooks and caffeine, Lance coasted on pedigree and smugness. Professors bent over backward to accommodate him—some out of admiration, others out of fear. The Davis family name was carved into more than one building on campus.

Ben had spent those years avoiding him. But men like

Lance never disappeared; they lingered, inserted themselves, and found their way into rooms you hoped to keep clean.

Now, years later, Ben was tethered to him once again. Their fathers had been good friends, golfing at the country club and closing deals together. The Davis family remained the firm's top client, sending a steady stream of referrals. Losing Lance Davis could cost them far more than Ben was willing to risk.

Lance's presence was always grating. He strolled into offices without warning, flaunted his flashy suits, and filled the air with loud stories of his latest exploits. His most recent "adventure" involved chartering a yacht for his birthday, surrounded by models whose names he didn't care to learn. They were accessories to him—interchangeable and disposable.

Ben endured his wild stories and feigned interest, but irritation always simmered beneath the surface. Lance was a grown man who behaved like a spoiled teenager. He coasted on his father's connections, navigating a world he hadn't earned. To Ben, Lance was not a friend nor truly a colleague—just an annoyance he was forced to tolerate. Still, he kept his expression composed. Lance could twist even the smallest crack in his composure to his advantage.

Ben returned home that evening, dreading the storm Lance would bring tomorrow. Lance drained every room he entered, leaving fatigue in his wake. But once Ben pushed him from his thoughts, his mind returned to the morning's meeting—and to her.

***

He had watched Florence slip into the conference room before he entered. Her features carried an undeniable excitement. A faint blush colored her cheeks, and the memory nearly made him chuckle. She chewed on her full lips—nerves, perhaps, or anticipation. The light caught them softly, and he found himself wanting to make her smile for the rest of her life.

Now, with her image still vivid, he couldn't deny it: She was stunning. The memory of her being assaulted in the parking lot gnawed at him, and a low anger threatened to surface. Yet that terrible night had led her to him.

He wouldn't push too hard. The last thing he wanted was to make her uncomfortable. Besides, once she won this contest, they would be working closely together. Patience was essential.

He threw on his gym clothes and headed downstairs. Mama Benard had already gone to bed. Restlessness coiled in his chest, demanding release. Each lift of the weights felt like an attempt to purge her from his mind, but it was futile. Her presence lingered, sparking something deeper than attraction.

The attraction was familiar. This was not. His interest felt larger than a fleeting crush. Irony taunted him: the first woman to stir something real in him was beyond reach. Not just difficult—impossible. A thousand obstacles loomed, each one immovable.

He sighed as he stepped off the treadmill, wiping sweat from his brow. Thoughts wandered toward old patterns, unspoken truths. His history with women was complicated. He had dated, yes, but never with true intention. Even as a teenager, before his father passed, he hadn't been reckless—just curious. He'd sought connection, but it was always fleeting.

As an adult, the truth had crystallized: empty encounters weren't worth the effort. He missed physical intimacy, often, but without connection, it felt hollow. Abstinence had become his refuge, and for the most part, he hadn't regretted it. Better to live with frustration than settle for someone he didn't love fully.

Still, that didn't make it easy. Restraint was a daily battle, and now the stakes felt higher than ever. For her, he would wait—days, months, even years.

With a dry laugh, he muttered, "My left hand has been my closest ally for years. Guess that's not about to change." The self-deprecating joke fell flat, and his face sobered.

He should talk to Mama Benard. She always had a way of grounding him when life turned turbulent. One thing was certain—whatever this was, it wasn't fading anytime soon.

***

That same night, James picked up on the first ring. "Twice in one month? Damn, Ben, what is it—the end times?"

Ben chuckled and leaned back in his chair. "Figured I'd check in before the locusts arrived."

James laughed. "You're sweet. But I actually have a proposition."

Ben raised an eyebrow. "A proposition? What do I get for humoring you, Counselor Smith?"

"A front-row seat to greatness," James replied smoothly. "And the chance to mingle with folks who don't need name tags."

Smirking, Ben shook his head. "Look at you, talking slick. Alright, Mr. Soon-to-be Attorney General, I second your motion."

James sounded satisfied. "Good. I'll send the details later this week."

"Appreciate it," Ben said, already reaching for a pen.

They hung up without goodbyes, two men bound by ambition and history.

***

The next morning, Ben immersed himself in trial prep. The case involved workplace discrimination, a complex and evolving area of law. Determined to handle it with precision, he spent hours in the law library, poring over precedent with the discipline honed by years of litigation. He wasn't just looking for wins; he was studying judicial temperament, tracing patterns in how the bench had historically responded to discrimination claims.

The hum of fluorescent lights faded as he navigated through stacks of casebooks and annotated rulings. His workspace was a controlled mess of open volumes, handwritten notes, and dog-eared pages—each piece building toward a strategy he hadn't yet named but already trusted. Every citation had to earn its place. Every case had to work as hard as he did.

Ben adjusted his glasses, fingertips grazing the yellowed pages of *Phillips v. Martin Marietta Corp. (1966)*. The case was a cornerstone—one of the first to test the strength of Title VII. The Supreme Court ruled that employers could not bar women with young children unless the same standard applied to men. Narrow but powerful. Ben studied the briefing strategy, noting how the attorneys framed their argument around the Civil Rights Act of 1964. Every word had been placed with precision—meant to persuade and withstand scrutiny.

His eyes scanned *Griggs v. Duke Power Co. (1968)*. The Court ruled that job practices must not harm minorities if they were unrelated to job performance. Even though this decision came after his current case, Ben considered its potential implications. He wanted to show how systemic barriers often appeared neutral but were discriminatory in practice.

He flipped to *Tuggle v. Maryland Drydock Co. (1943)*, his jaw tightening. The plaintiff, a colored man, had sued after being demoted due to racial bias. The court ruled against him, citing insufficient evidence. Ben frowned. It was a stark reminder of how difficult it was for plaintiffs to meet the burden of proof.

"How can a worker be expected to gather enough proof?" Ben muttered, frustrated. The case arose in an era where racial bias was entrenched and rarely challenged, making intent hard to prove. He jotted a note: Focus on evidence. Tie policies to outcomes. Prove intent if possible, but emphasize disparate impact.

Next, he examined *Sweatt v. Painter (1950)*, which, though centered on education, influenced workplace law. Herman Sweatt challenged the "separate but equal" doctrine, arguing the law school for colored students was inferior to the one for white students. The Supreme Court agreed—a step toward dismantling segregation. Ben admired the case for its reliance on empirical evidence to expose systemic inequities.

This is the key, he thought. *Empirical evidence and a human narrative. I need both.*

He turned to *Plessy v. Ferguson (1896)*. Its precedent, "separate but equal," had long justified workplace segregation and unequal wages. Ben's pen hovered over his notebook. *I'm facing a history of rulings that justified injustice by pretending the field was level.*

More promising was *Mackenzie v. Miller Brewing Co. (1960)*, where a jury ruled in favor of a colored woman fired on false grounds after reporting racial harassment. The decision was narrow but signaled progress.

His approach was clear: focus on patterns, systemic gaps, and the human cost of workplace policies. Highlight real stories to make the court see the people behind the law.

The stack of books and papers grew taller, but so did his resolve. Ben sat back, rubbing his temples and glancing at the clock. The library was closing soon, but his work was far from over.

Each case, each story of triumph or defeat, sharpened his strategy. The law wasn't perfect, but it was a tool. Ben intended to wield it like a scalpel—cutting through bias to reveal the truth beneath.

As the day wound down, the meeting he had been dreading loomed closer. He closed his files, stacked them neatly, and returned each book to its shelf. Stomach growling from the long hours, he made his way back to the office.

When he opened the door, Lance was already there, sprawled in Ben's guest chair with his feet on the desk and arms folded behind his head. His shirt hung half unbuttoned, his tie loose like an afterthought.

The moment Ben entered, Lance spun the chair to face him with a crooked grin.

"How the hell are you?" Lance asked casually.

Ben drummed his fingers on the desk, holding back irritation. "I'd be better if you got your shoes off my desk." He knocked Lance's feet down, earning a chuckle.

"As uptight as ever," Lance said. "You know what will relax you?"

Ben raised an eyebrow. It was always the same with Lance.

"A week in Los Angeles, surrounded by women, cigars, and booze," Lance said, slapping him on the back.

Ben brushed his hand away, sat at his desk, and unwrapped the sandwich Charlotte had ordered. "Not my scene," he muttered, looking out the window as he took a bite.

Lance leaned forward, his tone shifting. "I see you've hired a pretty little colored woman."

"What about it?" Ben asked, tension creeping into his shoulders.

"I saw her going to her car earlier," Lance said. "How could you miss her in that skirt?"

Before he could finish, Ben turned his chair sharply and fixed him with a cold stare. Lance froze, sandwich halfway to his mouth. "What? Why are you looking at me like that? Not your type? Me, I think a woman is a woman."

Ben cut him off. "Did you come here for something, Lance?"

Lance blinked, as if remembering. "Oh, right. The legal summit in New York, a couple of months from now."

Ben raised an eyebrow. "Since when do you care about that?"

"My dad says I need to show responsibility if I want the family business," Lance said with a shrug. "So, I'll represent him."

Ben pinched the bridge of his nose. "Of course," he muttered.

"I haven't made any plans with Charlotte yet. We have time. I'll have her call you when I do," Ben added flatly.

He was lying. He didn't want Lance thinking he could

skip his share. Lance always pulled something.

The rest of the meeting dissolved into Lance's rambling—boasts about women, crude details Ben didn't care to hear. His thoughts drifted instead to Florence. Why did it bother him so much when Lance talked about her that way? It wasn't just about workplace safety. There was something else—a knot of protectiveness he couldn't quite name.

By the time the office emptied, Ben was alone with his paperwork. Charlotte had long gone. So had Florence—on time, which surprised him. She usually stayed late.

When Ben finally went home, he went straight to his Mama Benard. He needed her advice, though he wasn't ready to share the whole truth yet.

***

Florence left work early, not wanting to be out after dark. At that time of year, the evening descended quickly. It had been a couple of weeks since she and James had gone out, and she realized she hadn't set up a second date. She had been avoiding him, needing time to think. But now, she decided, she would call him as soon as she got home.

When she arrived, the phone rang. A man's voice answered on the other end.

"Hello?" he said, his voice laced with confusion. "May I ask who's calling?"

"Um, this is Florence," she began, momentarily flustered. "Is… is James available?" She hesitated, assuming it must be a family member.

"He's not available at the moment," the man said.

"Would you mind relaying a message to James? Please tell him I apologize for not being in touch. I was wondering if you could also ask him if he would like to go to Belle Isle Park for a picnic this week?"

***

As soon as she set the phone down, it rang again. Florence's heart skipped a beat. That was fast. Her voice lifted with unanticipated enthusiasm. "Hello!"

But instead of the deep voice she expected, she heard her mother's familiar, slightly grating tone.

"Hello, Mama," Florence said, her tone deflating at the sound.

"Well, you don't sound too happy to hear my voice," her mother chirped. "How are you doing? Good? Hope you're not getting fat. Men don't like fat girls."

Florence didn't bother correcting her. "I'm doing well, actually. I got to join—"

Her mother cut her off. "I've been working hard to find you a husband, you know, after your daddy. I found another man because I needed to keep us happy."

Florence pinched the bridge of her nose, knowing her mother wouldn't care about what she had to say anyway. "Mama, if you're worried about me being alone, you could visit," she said, trying to change the subject.

There was a long pause on the other end of the line. Then her mother replied, "Well, sweetheart, you know I'm needed up here. No time to stop at a place like that with all those folks. But how about you take that friend of yours—what's her name? Joyce?"

"Denise," Florence corrected, her voice flat.

"Denise. Well, whatever her name is, why don't you go shopping with her, so she can help you get ready for a second date with the James boy?"

Florence's teeth clenched as she braced herself. "I am a grown woman. I don't need anyone to take me—"

Her mother didn't let her finish. "Yeah, but you have the style of a prepubescent boy. You'll dress up for those white people but not for a man who actually wants—"

Florence cut her off, feeling the heat of frustration rising. "Mama, I need to make dinner. Is there something else you want?"

Her mother sighed on the other end. "Well, no. It was good to hear how you are doing. I'll talk to you later."

"Bye, Mama," Florence muttered, ending the call

before her mother could say anything more.

She sat still for a moment, the weight of the conversation pressing down on her. She refused to take her mother's opinions to heart. Florence would rather be by herself than be with someone who wasn't right for her.

After feeding Mooni, a wave of purpose washed over her. She reached for her journal, the one with the worn leather cover and pages that knew too much. This time, she didn't begin with memories of her mother. Instead, her pen moved instinctively to him—Mr. Mayfield.

She was still reeling from the shock of seeing him at the head of the meeting: commanding, composed, entirely unexpected. Even though he had shown her a brief kindness with the creamer that morning, something about him felt hauntingly familiar.

And then there were his eyes: sharp, assessing, as if they saw past her practiced poise. He had looked at her like he knew something she hadn't yet admitted to herself. That gaze left her unsettled, as though he had cracked open a door inside her she had long kept bolted shut.

CHAPTER 8:
GAMES, GAMES, AND LESS GAINS

The alarm betrayed her. Florence jolted awake, already behind. Her foot snagged the edge of the rug, her heart slamming against her ribs as she stumbled forward. She lunged into her morning routine, muttering rushed apologies to Mooni as she flung on clothes, brushed her teeth with one hand, and wrestled with her hair using the other.

Her keys nearly slipped through her fingers as she tore out the door, a blur of motion and expletives. She sped past her coworkers, catching their wide-eyed stares and muttered whispers, but had no breath or patience for pleasantries. "Sorry!" she called out, already halfway down the hall.

Her legs screamed with each step as she limped toward the elevator, silently praying the doors would wait just one second longer.

The elevator doors pinged open. Florence rushed out, scanning for Charlotte. She clenched her fists, jaw tight, neck prickling with sweat. She didn't see her right away. But when she walked to her cubicle, she spotted the list on her desk. She dropped her purse, ready to dive into her tasks. Then she froze. Charlotte stood over her, arms crossed.

"Where were you?" Charlotte's voice cut through the air.

"I'm sorry. My alarm didn't go off," Florence started, but Charlotte interrupted.

"Not my problem," Charlotte said, icy. "I expect my employees to be here on time. And your attire——" she paused, eyeing Florence up and down with disdain "——is not appropriate."

Florence nodded, gaze cast downward. "Yes, ma'am. I know." She felt a flush of embarrassment but didn't argue.

"If it happens again, I will fire you on the spot," Charlotte warned.

Florence nodded again, understanding. Charlotte turned on her heel and walked away, leaving Florence to slump into her chair with a deep sigh. *Way to go, Florence,* she chastised herself.

She stood again, forcing herself to push past the weight of her tardiness. The list awaited her, though there were no extra tasks today. Florence assumed, with a sinking feeling, that after this, there wouldn't be any for a while.

When lunch came around, Mr. Anderson offered Florence some of his food. She smiled—small, unspoken, edged with hunger—as her stomach gave her away. It took her back to school lunches her dad had packed: simple, caring, always what she needed. She explained she had no time to pack lunch. Florence accepted it with gratitude and sighed as she shared the rough start to her day.

"You know," Henry said, handing her a sandwich, "don't start overthinking. Everything happens for a reason—good or bad."

Florence rolled her eyes. He was right, but the last thing she wanted to hear on a bad day was a cliché. Henry chuckled, fully aware of her mood. "I didn't make it this far without a few mistakes. And I didn't make it without bad days either. You listen to my old man's wisdom, and you'll be all right. There's a reason I got these gray hairs." He winked, and Florence cracked a genuine smile.

She shook her head and sighed. "I was already under scrutiny, but now... I might as well be in hell."

"Well," Henry said, tipping his head, "you've got a real shot here. I'd hate to eat lunch alone while you're off hiding in the ladies' room."

Florence gave a dry chuckle. "Is that your idea of a guilt trip?"

He grinned. "Wouldn't dream of it. I'm just saying—stick it out."

She looked down, voice low. "I'm not quitting. I just… feel like I've got something to prove."

Henry raised a brow. "To who?"

She hesitated, picking at the edge of her napkin. "To them. To myself. That I can do more than fetch files and wait obediently."

He leaned forward, tone softening. "Florence, you didn't have to prove a thing. You belonged the moment you walked in."

Her cheeks flushed. She stood, brushing crumbs from her skirt. "Thanks. For the food. And for not letting me sulk."

Henry chuckled. "Next time, lunch is on you."

She smiled as she walked away. "Just don't order steak."

As she began walking, she paused. She felt someone looking at her, pulling her attention elsewhere. She shook her head. Who would be looking at me?

***

Ben was determined to talk to his mother but didn't know how to approach her. He walked in the front door, and the comforting smell of Mama Benard's cooking filled his nose. His stomach grumbled, reminding him he hadn't eaten all day. *Thank God for Mama Benard*, he thought, anticipating the warm meal awaiting him. He unwrapped the tin on his chicken pot pie, and the warmth of it seemed to wrap around him like a hug. He dug in, savoring each bite, when he heard footsteps descending the stairs.

"Hello, Ben," Mama Benard said, cheerful, a smile

playing on her lips. "I was about to head up to bed," she added, planting a kiss on his cheek.

"Okay, thank you," Ben replied, mouth full, stuffing in another bite. The food was almost too good to pause.

"I'm going to make you a stiff cocktail before I head to bed," she said, a knowing glint in her eyes. "It should help you sleep better. I heard your feet flopping around down-stairs when I got up in the middle of the night—you've been restless."

Ben's cheeks turned pink, and a smile tugged at his lips. *She knows me so well, he thought.* "Thanks, Ma," he mumbled, taking another bite.

Before he could explain, his mother cut him off with a playful look. "I don't know why you're so tired. No children to keep up with running around here," she said with a quick glance.

Ben almost choked on his food. "Ma!" he exclaimed, rolling his eyes. "I don't think kids are in my future anytime soon."

She waved her hand in disregard. "Pfft. Have a good night," she said, giving him a cheeky smile before heading upstairs.

Ben set the tin down and took a slow sip of the cock-tail. The drink was warm, but it did nothing to settle the unrest curling in his chest. Vulnerability had never come easy, but this moment felt too heavy to leave unspoken.

The kitchen sat in silence, broken only by the soft clink of his spoon against the glass. He stared ahead, eyes unfo-cused, wrestling with how to begin. After a long pause, he pushed back his chair and stood, the decision finally made. His heart thudded as he climbed the stairs.

His mother was in her room, preparing for bed. When he knocked, she called him in. She sat at the edge of her bed, wrapped in her nightclothes and scarf, already winding down.

"You better have a reason for coming in here," she said, sharp.

"Well, what a warm welcome for your son," Ben replied, trying to meet her edge with a hint of humor.

He hesitated before stepping further in, sitting on the edge of her bed. He stared at the floor, then looked up at her, face filled with uncertainty. "I… I've been thinking a lot lately. About something I'm not sure is right. And I don't know what to do about it."

She tilted her head. "Well, get on with it. My show is about to start." She smiled, shaking her head.

Ben took a deep breath. "Okay. Let's say there is a woman at the firm who I'm interested in."

"I'm listening," Mama Benard said.

"I'm concerned about a workplace romance with her because it could put both of us in jeopardy, especially if she's colored. How would you approach this?"

Mama Benard studied him, gaze sharp but not unkind. "I see," she said at last, narrowing her eyes. "Well, if we're speaking hypothetically, I'd tell you to understand just what you're stepping into with a colored woman. Folks out there won't make it easy for you. But I've known you since you were knee-high, and this is the first time I've seen you truly interested in someone. So, baby, I say follow your heart." She teased him with a smile. "Just make sure your head's coming along for the ride."

Ben rolled his eyes.

"Consider whether this is really what you want. If it is, are you ready to leave your comfort behind? I'd say give it your all, regardless of how hard it would be. You are no stranger to hard work, Ben. You have a tendency to obsess over things you like," she added. "Try not to scare her off." She pulled the covers up and turned onto her side.

Ben looked up, the question striking him harder than he'd anticipated. "I don't know," he admitted, low. "It's a bit scary to think about going after something that could cause harm, but at the same time… I can't walk away either."

Mama Benard smiled gently, face turned from him. "If

it's what you want, then that's the only thing that should matter."

There was a long silence as Ben processed her words. Finally, he let out a small, relieved sigh. "Thanks, Ma. I needed to hear that."

"Yeah, yeah, now get out of my room."

"I love you, too," he said with a smile, leaning over to give her a kiss, but she swatted him away.

"Goodnight, Ben," she called before the door shut.

He smiled, the warmth in her words a balm for his restless mind. Closing the door behind him, he returned to his room, the conversation still echoing in his thoughts. He didn't have all the answers, but now, at least, he had a clearer sense of what he needed to do. He would figure it out, step by step.

***

At twenty-eight, Ben had nearly everything a man was supposed to want: wealth, a thriving career, a condo in one of the city's most coveted neighborhoods. And still, an ache lingered, constant and unshakable. Even his gym visits, which he relied on to stay fit and maintain routine, couldn't fill the void. He wondered why, after all these years, he couldn't connect with any women that way. He'd had his share of casual flings, but these days, he had no interest in the women who came his way. They seemed more focused on his money than anything else. Their eyes sparkled with dreams of a cozy life and a family. Ben understood their interest, but that wasn't the life he wanted. He wanted someone ambitious—a partner who challenged him and stood by his side.

For a fleeting moment, he questioned his own sexuality—a private thought he never shared with anyone. One night, after a few drinks and a man flirting with him at a club, the thought simply faded away—not out of disgust but because he wasn't interested in men. Certainty about who he was soon settled in its place.

Ben lived a strange kind of life: comfortable, even privileged, but undeniably isolating. He didn't splurge on country club memberships, personal shoppers, or flashy extravagances. The only indulgence he allowed himself was Mama Benard. Not that she counted—if she ever asked, he'd spend his last dime on her without thinking twice. She had raised him, after all.

Cooking had always been a losing battle for him, and Mama Benard remained the only person in his world who could turn a kitchen into something that felt like love. Their arrangement—just the two of them—had worked for years. It was familiar. Safe.

But lately, even that comfort had begun to feel isolating. The horizon ahead seemed wide and hollow, and there was an ache growing inside him he couldn't quite name. Worse still, his physical desires—long dormant or, at least, manageable—had begun to surface with an intensity that unsettled him. Some nights, he felt embarrassed by how badly he wanted… something.

He pushed hard in his workout, aiming to tire himself out. His mind, however, never truly stopped. His calm intensity read as charisma to most—an elegant, chivalrous presence that made him a natural fit among the firm's top partners. If they truly knew him, they'd notice the brooding and antisocial side that filled his mind. The pressure to play the role of the perfect lawyer, one the public fawned over, was exhausting.

It wasn't until the day before, when he caught sight of her—the woman who had been haunting his thoughts. Ben watched from afar as she spoke with Mr. Anderson in the cafeteria. He wondered what their connection was. He knew Anderson well—not as an employee but as a mentor of sorts. The older man had once been a formidable attorney, well-respected and sharp. Years ago, he had been close friends with Ben's father. After retiring, Anderson had come to Ben—not out of necessity but for something to do, a way to keep his mind busy and his days from feeling empty.

As Florence turned to leave, Ben watched her hips sway, how her hair rested perfectly on her shoulders. Her long legs moved swiftly as she returned to work. He bumped into her, and her alluring scent sent a shiver down his spine.

The days that followed were spent observing Florence subtly, always at a careful distance. Ben lingered, waiting for the right moment to approach. He was patient, practiced at holding back, but when opportunity appeared, he knew better than to hesitate.

That morning, he stepped into the cafeteria with intention. His attire was more relaxed than usual: tailored slacks and an open-collar button-down—still professional but approachable. Calculated.

Mr. Anderson, always the one to break the silence, greeted him warmly. "What brings you down here with the regulars for lunch?"

"I was interested in some titillating conversation," Ben replied, his gaze shifting to the woman beside him. He tried not to be obvious as he studied her features.

Her reaction wasn't awe; it was annoyance. Not that Ben had expected anything else. She rolled her eyes, jaw tightening just enough to register her irritation. He noted it, amused. She didn't seem to care who he was, and that only piqued his interest further.

"May I ask why you're here?" Florence said, standing straighter now, lips pressed together in a polite but clipped smile. "And how do you know Mr. Anderson?"

"I could ask you the same thing," Ben replied, head tilting slightly. His tone was casual, with a hint of mischief.

Florence's expression shifted—still composed, but curious. Before Mr. Anderson could answer, Ben raised a hand, gently cutting him off.

"Mr. Anderson and I go way back," Ben said smoothly.

"Not that far back," Mr. Anderson chuckled, adjusting his glasses.

Florence nodded, ready to move on. "Well, if you'll

excuse me, I have to get back to work."

Ben stepped slightly closer, lowering his voice just enough. "Did I run you off?"

Florence rolled her eyes before gathering her things. "Enjoy your lunch."

And just like that, she was gone—walking away with a deliberate grace that made it hard not to look. Pencil skirt, heels, scarf tucked just so—she didn't have to try. She just was. Ben, still holding his tray, realized he wasn't as hungry as he'd thought

Turning back to Mr. Anderson, Ben casually asked, "How often do you two have lunch together?"

"Every day," Anderson replied. "Unless she's busy or decides to eat outside."

Ben mentally noted the information.

"Seems like Florence has piqued your interest," Mr. Anderson remarked.

Ben's face turned red. "I take an interest in all my employees, Anderson."

***

Over the next few days, Ben tried to catch her at lunch again, but Florence was nowhere in sight. The first time, Mr. Anderson mentioned she'd taken her lunch outside. The second time, Ben checked himself, only to find nothing. Later, Mr. Anderson told him she'd eaten alone that day. It began to feel like she was avoiding him, and the thought unsettled him more than he cared to admit. Still, he knew if he kept chasing her around the building, Mr. Anderson might think he was a stalker. So he abandoned the lunch strategy. Florence often came in early, and he decided those first moments before the workday began might give him the chance he was looking for.

It was a chilly morning. Ben sat in his car for a few minutes, watching her rub her hands together to warm them. She hugged her sweater tight against the cold. Intrigued by her posture and movement, Ben got out of his car and waited five minutes before heading inside, careful not to make her uncomfortable.

He walked into the cafeteria and spotted Florence at the counter. He assumed she was making coffee, but she had only grabbed the creamer. Ben moved next to her, planning to do the same. When he got close, she jumped, surprised by his presence.

"Good morning," Ben said casually, offering a smile. "Would you like some coffee with that creamer?"

"Good morning, sir," Florence replied with a forced smile, too polite to be genuine. "My coffee pot is downstairs, thank you."

He raised an eyebrow, confused, and didn't push further after hearing the discomfort in her voice.

"You're rather chipper this morning," Ben said.

"Well, you are my superior," Florence replied with another polite, strained smile.

"Treat me as you usually do," he said, a smile tugging at his lips.

"You mean with annoyance?" she asked.

Ben chuckled, flashing a grin that made her heart skip.

"If that's what you'd prefer, Madam," he said.

"Well, it would be inappropriate to treat my boss that way, don't you think? Especially as a colored woman," she said.

Ben's eyes flickered with regret but also understanding. "I prefer the real side of people rather than the fake corporate nonsense I'm fed daily. Your personality is refreshing," he said smoothly.

Florence looked away, gathering her things.

"Why are you here so early?" she asked, steering the conversation elsewhere.

He shrugged. "Paperwork and whatnot. Why are you here so early?"

She hesitated, stammering before answering. "I've been working on your case assignments."

Ben raised an eyebrow, surprised. "Oh? Really? I'm

impressed, Florence."

She looked up at him. "Why, because a woman of my color isn't usually smart enough to involve herself in such things?"

He raised an eyebrow.

"Nope. Just you. Most people aren't in this early unless they're forced to be. You coming in on your own? Says a lot."

"I don't work hard for recognition. I do it because I have to. You can save the flattery," she said, a little embarrassed.

Ben chuckled, taken aback by her boldness. "Is this a request or an order?"

She looked down at her hands, furrowing her brow, her voice almost a whisper. "A request," she said.

He smiled, amusement evident. "I'm not your enemy, I promise. I like learning more about you." He coughed, correcting himself. "I mean, about all my employees," he added, smoothing over his previous statement.

As Ben finished getting his coffee, he reached for Florence's lunch and started to place it in the fridge. She stopped him with a sudden movement, her voice tense. "Wait, my lunch can't go in here."

He looked at her, confused. "What do you mean? Where does it go?"

She shifted uncomfortably, frustration creeping into her tone. "I… I have to use the colored fridge," she said, agitated.

Ben blinked, feeling a brief flush of ignorance. "Ah, I see." He cleared his throat and nodded. "Apologies. I'll put it there."

"It's downstairs. I'll take care of it," she replied curtly, gripping the handle of her pail with a little too much force.

Florence turned and hurried away to place her lunch where it belonged. The encounter lingered with Ben as he chastised himself for the foolish mistake he had made. He had finally gotten her to talk only to put his foot in his mouth. And what did she mean by the basement? There was nothing down there. Ben made a mental note to check it out later.

He huffed a sigh and made his way up to his office to begin the day. He had a lot to do after work, and he was determined to leave on time.

****

Florence left work that day feeling confused about her conversation with Mr. Mayfield. When she looked into his eyes, they were green—so green they reminded her of the windows of enchanted forests, almost like the fields she had played in as a child. His presence annoyed her. She kept running into him, but this was her chance to return his jacket. Florence didn't want to hold on to something so expensive that wasn't hers. She decided to leave it in her car for the next time they met and would bring it up casually.

When she returned home, the phone was already ringing in the kitchen. It was James finally returning her call. She answered.

"Hello, this is Florence."

"Hello, ma'am, it's James. I'm sorry I missed your call. I've had a full schedule, but I want to make time for the lovely lady on the phone," James said.

Florence blushed. "Yes. How does Friday night at seven sound?"

"Sounds like a date. I'll see you then, Miss," he replied.

The week unfolded without issue, and before she knew it, Friday had arrived. Florence felt excited as she prepared for her second date with James. He told her to dress casually this time, so she paired jeans with an ivory shirt and a cozy fall sweater.

Florence stood on her porch as James's car eased up to the curb, the soft rumble of the engine breaking the stillness of the evening. In those days, a date at a burger stand could feel as fine as any night out. James stepped out with easy confidence, a bouquet of mixed flowers in hand. The gesture caught her off guard—thoughtful, unpretentious, and entirely James.

"I'm so sorry I'm late," he said, offering the bouquet. "I couldn't decide which flowers suited you best, so I brought one of each."

Florence smiled, the nervous flutter in her chest easing at his charm. "It's no problem. Thank you—they're lovely. We should get going."

James nodded and opened the passenger door for her. The drive to the burger place felt relaxed. They chatted and appreciated the comfortable silences. The small local spot had a warm, lively atmosphere with soft music playing and regulars at the counter.

Florence pulled the onions off her burger.

James chuckled. "Message received—no onions next time."

She smiled, taking a hearty bite of her burger. "This is really something," she said, her eyes bright.

"Told you," he replied with a grin. "Best joint in town, hands down."

The conversation drifted to their backgrounds. James spoke about his years in the military, while Florence shared stories of her family down South. "After I moved here, I earned my bachelor's in political science and passed the bar exam. But my job doesn't let me put those skills to use or grow, so I feel stuck," she admitted, though her pride still shone through, even in this difficult stretch.

Florence found herself studying James's features in the dim light as they ate. She wasn't sure what to make of him just yet. He was respectful, quick with a joke, and unfailingly thoughtful, yet there was a layer to him she couldn't quite read. Time, she knew, would tell. For now, she was content to let the evening unfold and savor the simple pleasure of a good burger.

When they finished eating, James admitted he had one more stop planned for their date. Outside, Florence took in the full view of him—tall, which she liked, and undeniably handsome. His build reflected his years in the military, and his dark skin had a smoothness that caught the light. His smile could knock the breath out of you, yet still, she felt no spark. She shook her head lightly and caught up to him as they headed for his car.

Their next stop was a drive-in movie. The ride there was easy and lighthearted; Florence teased James about his radio station choices, and he defended his love for classic Motown with playful conviction.

The lot buzzed with life as cars lined up, headlights cutting through the evening haze. The marquee announced a double feature: *The Odd Couple* and *Night of the Living Dead*. The mix of comedy and chills matched the evening's energy perfectly. James parked in a prime spot, grabbed the window speaker, and adjusted it before leaning back in his seat.

As the first film started, they laughed together. The antics of Jack Lemmon and Walter Matthau broke the ice. James stole glances at Florence, marveling at how relaxed she looked in the flickering light. They shared a box of buttery popcorn, their fingers brushing now and then. James enjoyed the moments when their laughter faded into quiet contentment.

During intermission, James caught Florence's attention. "I've got a friend with some pull—he could get you into a better position, one that actually uses your degree," he said, his tone easy. "He's one of the top lawyers at his firm—an incredible guy. If you're open to meeting him, I think he could help."

Florence arched a brow, curiosity piqued. "That actually sounds amazing," she said.

James smiled. "Just so you know, he's white, in case that makes you uncomfortable. But he owes me a favor, so I could set up a meeting."

Florence laughed lightly. "It's fine. I work with white folks all the time."

"Perfect. I'll give him a call tonight," James replied.

The second feature began, and the eerie tones of *Night*

of the Living Dead filled the air, adding a chill to the night. Florence shifted closer to James, and he draped his jacket over her shoulders. She appeared to watch the movie, but her mind was on his words. She wondered about the surprising door he might be opening.

As the final credits rolled, the drive-in fell silent. James pulled up to Florence's home and walked her to the door before heading back to his own place. Later, once he was settled in, he picked up the phone and called Ben.

"Hey, Ben," James began.

"What's on your mind, pal?" Ben asked.

"I have a favor to ask," James said. "There's someone you should meet. She's brilliant. She has a bachelor's in political science and passed the bar, but her current job isn't giving her a fair chance. Would you be willing to meet with her? She's looking to expand her network."

"Sure," Ben said. "When and where?"

"Saturday morning, nine at the park where we run," James suggested.

"Done," Ben confirmed. "But you owe me one, James."

"I owe you plenty," James admitted, laughing.

James phoned Florence right away and told her the day and time, assuring her everything was set. "You'll like him," he said. "One of the best men I know."

CHAPTER 9:
GAINS AND UNREQUITED AFFECTION

When James asked Ben to meet his friend, Ben felt a twinge of anxiety. Knowing James, he wouldn't announce they were dating, but he rarely went out of his way for people without a reason. Ben adjusted his cufflink, his skepticism mingling with curiosity. In truth, he wanted to see who this woman was. The law firm where she worked was discriminating against her, which could make her a valuable asset for his case. She had also passed the bar, and from what James had described, she seemed diligent and driven. If all went well, Ben might recruit her himself.

He arrived at the park early, claiming a bench within sight of the Grove Library. He made a mental note to stop in later. Libraries had always been his sanctuaries—the one place he could lose himself in books for hours. Today, he had traded his usual suit for jeans and a crisp white button-down—a quiet rebellion against his everyday formality. A simple watch on his wrist ticked steadily, a reminder that the ordered world he belonged to still waited.

At nine sharp, the crunch of leaves underfoot signaled their arrival. Ben rose to greet them, his breath catching when he saw Florence. She carried herself with a poised wariness—commanding, self-possessed, and more striking than he remembered. He would have recognized her legs anywhere. Her hair fell in soft curls, her luminous brown skin kissed by the morning sun, glowing almost angelically. She was everything. If she asked him now, he would hand over his trust fund and the deed to his condo without hesitation.

Florence wore a pink collared dress, white buttons running down the front, the skirt flaring just above her knees. White wedges completed her look, but it was her lips, soft, full, and the same hue as her dress—that captivated him. He forced himself to focus. This was a business meeting.

Florence, meanwhile, was shocked for an entirely different reason. From a distance, she had spotted the man on the bench—he was supposed to be their business contact. As they drew closer, his build became familiar. Too familiar. When she locked eyes with him, her breath stalled.

That same infuriating smile from their first meeting with Mr. Anderson. She smoothed her dress, forcing composure, and extended her hand.

"Hello, my name is Florence. It's a pleasure to officially meet you." Her tone was steady, her teeth bared in something that wasn't quite a smile. She would keep this professional and pretend she didn't know Mr. Mayfield.

Ben was more than willing to play along. He clasped her hand—firm, lingering—his gaze holding hers until she withdrew. He turned to greet James with a quick hug before they all sat. Florence across from him, still gathering her bearings.

As the men spoke, Florence allowed herself a fleeting glance at Ben. She had only seen him in tailored suits before; now, dressed down, he looked different. At ease. Irritatingly handsome. The sun caught in his dark blonde hair, softening the sharp planes of his face. His lips were fuller than she remembered, his frame lean and honed—a man disciplined in body as well as mind. And those green eyes, unflinching, as if they could strip a person bare without touching them.

Why am I analyzing him? she scolded herself, dragging her thoughts back to the present.

And then she realized he was watching her just as intently.

"Florence." James's voice snapped her out of it. "Ben was asking if you brought a portfolio."

"Oh, yes." She fumbled briefly before handing it over. Ben let a slow smile spread as she dug in her bag, knowing he had caught her staring.

James leaned back. "I told Ben you're very impressive."

Ben tilted his head slightly, his gaze steady. "What kind of lawyer do you want to be, Miss Florence?" His voice was measured, professional.

Florence straightened. "A civil rights attorney," she said. "To fight for those overlooked, denied, or dismissed. I believe in standing where the need is greatest—where people have no voice, and someone must speak for them."

Ben studied her closely. There was steel in her tone, a fire beneath each word. She was not only intelligent but passionate. From the way she spoke—precise, certain—he had no doubt she would command any courtroom. Yet, he couldn't ignore the slight pout she had worn since arriving. It made him want to kiss her just to see her smile.

"If you've passed the bar," he asked, "why were you hired for such a low position at your current firm?"

Florence's jaw tightened. "I can only assume discrimination. But wouldn't you know why?" Her smile was thin; her eyes, sharp.

James frowned. "Why would he know?"

Ben exhaled, rubbing his neck. "Because, according to this portfolio..." He sighed. "She works at my firm," he said, as though the fact surprised him too. "I apologize if that came off as rude, Florence. That wasn't my intention. I don't usually handle new hires, so I'm not sure of the process. But I do believe your talents deserve a higher position. Give me some time—I'll look into this."

James blinked between them. "So you two work at the same place? Well, that must be fate."

Florence wasn't sure she'd call it that.

Once the business ended, Ben's interest shifted. He needed to know—how had James met her? And were they… together?

"Can I treat you both to lunch?" he asked, careful to keep his tone neutral.

Florence opened her mouth to decline, but James accepted. She sighed, then fixed them both with a steady look.

"Is there a place where the three of us can actually eat together comfortably?" It was a fair question in 1968, especially for two colored professionals meeting a white colleague.

Ben understood. "My family owns a restaurant," he said. "They wouldn't dare turn me away—or my guests."

Florence allowed a small smile. "Well, that makes things easier."

Ben chuckled. She'd have to get used to this, he thought. Soon, he planned to give her everything she wanted. All of it. The thought settled like a promise as they headed to his car.

I am a horrible person, he mused. She might be seeing James, yet he couldn't stop wanting her. James had said they were just friends, and that made sense.

When they reached his car, Florence gasped. "Th-this is yours?" she asked.

"Yes. Do you like her?" Ben replied.

"I do," she said, feigning indifference. In truth, she now realized it had been him parking near her every morning.

"You can drive her if you'd like," he offered.

Florence glanced at James and shook her head. "No, thank you," she said, taking James's arm as they walked away.

Ben laughed. She was stubborn, and it made the pursuit all the more entertaining.

Florence couldn't deny a flicker of curiosity about what it might feel like to drive his car. Still, with James beside her, it seemed improper to accept. She kept her thoughts to herself, but the truth was, Ben commanded her attention. That calm confidence, that maddening smile—each one piqued her interest. Against her better judgment, she found herself wanting to know more.

"James," she asked as he drove, "how long have you and Mr. Mayfield been friends?"

"About eight years," James said. "He's a good man—a bit reserved, but down to earth."

Florence laced her fingers in her lap.

"Don't worry," James added with a small smile. "I'm sure you'll come to like him."

Unfortunately for Florence, he would soon be right.

When they arrived, the restaurant exuded quiet exclusivity, the sort of establishment frequented by top attorneys and the city's well-heeled elite. The polished mahogany doors gleamed in the late-afternoon light, their brass handles worn smooth by years of discreet clientele. From the slightly ajar door came the faint chime of silver on china, mingled with low, deliberate voices. It was a place where refinement wasn't declared; it was understood.

Ben was already out of his car, waiting. He moved with calculated ease, rounding to the passenger side and opening Florence's door. As they stood there, he gestured forward.

"Ladies first," he said evenly, allowing Florence to enter ahead of him.

He fought the urge to watch her too closely as she passed. If he let his eyes linger, it would only feed his desire. And desire was not what he wanted—at least, not openly. Instead, he noted her earrings: mismatched, slightly off from the rest of her ensemble. A string of pearls, he thought, would suit her better.

Inside, the maître d' gave Ben a fleeting look before leading them to their table. A few patrons glanced over with mild curiosity, but the staff said nothing.

When they reached their table, both Ben and James instinctively moved to pull out Florence's chair. Their eyes met in a brief, awkward standoff before Ben relented, letting James do the honors.

"Order whatever you'd like," Ben said. "It's on me today."

James chuckled. "Always the schmoozer."

Florence chose a classic: Chicken à la King—tender morsels of chicken and earthy mushrooms in a velvety cream sauce, ladled over crisp, buttered toast. Refined yet unpretentious. Ben filed that detail away. As she ate, he noted the faint, endearing puff of her cheeks with each bite. Her manners were flawless, each movement measured, each taste deliberately savored. There was a quiet satisfaction in watching her enjoy her meal. When dessert was mentioned, her eyes brightened with unguarded delight, nearly making him laugh. James caught it too, offering a knowing grin at her open enthusiasm.

After the plates were cleared, the atmosphere shifted. The air sharpened. Ben leaned forward, fingers steepled. "Let's test that quick mind of yours, Florence."

Her eyes narrowed. "I didn't realize this was an interview," she said lightly.

"Consider it an impromptu trial," Ben replied, his tone smooth but firm. "Say you're a junior associate on a case. A prosecutor accuses a wealthy client of embezzlement. The evidence is circumstantial—no direct proof, just a suspicious paper trail. A few disgruntled ex-employees are making claims. How do you build your defense?"

Florence didn't pause. "I'd start with the paper trail—check it for inconsistencies. If their case is weak, I'd discredit the witnesses. Why were they fired? Do they have a grudge? Motive matters."

Ben nodded, then pressed further. "What if a witness presents a handwritten ledger showing money funneled into private accounts?"

"Handwriting can be forged," she countered. "I'd call in an expert to verify it."

"And if it's authenticated?"

"Then I'd challenge access. Just because it's his ledger doesn't mean he wrote in it. Who else had access to his office?"

James gave a low whistle. "She's quick."

Ben didn't relent. "Alright. Flip sides. You're the prosecutor now—convince me he's guilty."

Florence straightened. "Financial documents don't lie. If every transaction is tied to his name, and the handwriting matches, the logical conclusion is that he orchestrated the scheme."

"But logic isn't proof," Ben said. "What if he was framed?"

She didn't flinch. "Then I'd prove motive. Did he benefit from the missing funds? Extravagant purchases during that period? That suggests guilt."

"And if his finances are spotless?"

Florence exhaled, eyes still steady. "Then I dig deeper. Who profits if he takes the fall? If it's not him, someone else is hiding in the shadows."

Silence followed. James glanced between them, impressed.

Ben leaned back, a slow smile tugging at his lips. "Not bad."

Florence sipped her water with studied indifference. "I know," she said, though she avoided his gaze.

Ben chuckled. This was the kind of sharp mind he admired—quick, relentless, unafraid of pressure. She didn't yet realize it, but he was going to enjoy this game.

As he and James exchanged lighter talk, Florence noticed how James seemed almost captivated. He hung on Ben's every word, eyes bright with respect. There was an unspoken trust between the two men, deeper than casual friendship. The dynamic intrigued her.

"How did you two meet?" she asked, her tone measured but curious.

Ben's lips curved with an easy smile. "Funny you should ask, Miss Florence. I was wondering the same about you and James." He leaned back, studying her.

Florence crossed her arms, lips twitching. "You're a lawyer through and through," she teased. "Always sizing up the competition."

"Are you my competition?" Ben asked, brow lifted.

Their gazes held until Ben broke into a low laugh. "Alright, I yield," he said, the words carrying an undercurrent she couldn't quite place.

James spoke then, his voice turning distant. "We met in the service. Both eighteen, green as spring grass, shipped off to Vietnam. It was chaos from the start, but we had each other's backs. That kind of thing… you never forget."

Florence glanced at Ben, whose expression remained composed, though something flickered in his eyes—a shadow of memories rarely spoken.

James added, "He saved my life more times than I can count. I wouldn't be here without him." His loyalty was plain.

Florence nodded, then offered, "James and I were set up by our parents. They thought we'd make a good match."

Ben arched his brow. "And are you?"

She hesitated. "Time will tell," she said smoothly.

Ben didn't press, but the faint twitch of his mouth told her he'd already formed his own opinion.

James finished his drink at that.

Ben paid the bill, and they stepped outside. He paused by his car, exchanging a few quiet words with James before turning to her.

"Be patient, Florence. Trust me," Ben said.

She smacked her lips. "Why should I?" Her brow arched, mocking.

"Because when I said I'd take care of you, I meant it."

Florence held his gaze a moment longer, something unreadable—half challenge, half curiosity—flickering in her eyes. Before she could answer, James cut in, his tone wry. "We best get going. I've got places to be after dropping Miss Florence home. Always a pleasure, Mr. Mayfield."

"Coming from the top dog at one of Detroit's finest law firms, Mr. Smith," Ben replied with a trace of humor.

Florence, however, was lost in her thoughts. Did he mean he'd handle the matter himself? Perhaps he'd misspoken. Yes, that must be it.

"Florence, shall we?" James prompted.

"Oh—yes. Thank you again, Mr. Mayfield," she said politely.

"Please, call me Ben," he replied, a faint smile touching his lips. "And I'll hold on to your portfolio. I'll return it at the office."

Inside, his thoughts ran darker: *Now I've got my reason to see her again.* The notion stirred something boyish in him—a quiet thrill he didn't name. He straightened his cuffs, the gesture hiding the flicker of satisfaction.

The ride home passed in silence, comfortable yet weighted. Florence sat back, biting the edge of her lip as her fingers traced the stitching on her purse.

Mr. Mayfield wasn't flirting with me. No, that can't be it. A man like him could have his pick of any white woman in Detroit, and he likely preferred it that way. Besides, he didn't strike her as reckless. Perhaps he was simply one of those men who carried easy charm into every conversation. Still, why did it seem as though he and James shared some unspoken secret whenever they spoke?

She shook her head, willing the notion away. *I wonder how much that bill came to. Probably nothing to him.*

Her thoughts circled back to Ben before she could stop them. What would it be like to know him beyond the tailored suits and polite introductions? To see the man behind the steady gaze and measured words? Was that magnetism something he offered to everyone, or was it meant for her? Did he belong to someone already, or was he the kind of man who never belonged to anyone for long?

Pull yourself together, Florence, she scolded herself. Turning her gaze to the passing streets, she tried to shake the thoughts loose, but they clung stubbornly, and to her irritation, her pulse quickened all the same.

CHAPTER 10: AFFECTIONS CAUSING INFECTION

In the weeks that followed, Florence kept her focus on the project for Mr. Mayfield. After that meeting with James and her boss, she confided in Denise. She admitted it felt strange knowing Mr. Mayfield and James were friends. Denise brushed it off. "Your career comes first," she had said. "If anything, their friendship might make things easier for you."

Florence knew Denise had a point. People leaned on connections all the time to get ahead, so why shouldn't she?

She stayed intent on presenting an unbiased view of the case. Still, Mr. Mayfield lingered in her thoughts. Ben. She felt odd calling him that, at least for now. He was intense, especially about the law, and she couldn't decide whether it unsettled or thrilled her more.

She hated to admit it, but each brief encounter with him left her strangely elated—electric even. He tested her in ways no one else dared. That steady confidence, that measured voice, stirred equal parts irritation and curiosity. He didn't merely challenge her; he compelled her to respond— to either rise to meet his intensity or step aside. And she couldn't explain why it fascinated her so. The way he looked at her was as if he could strip away every polite veneer. It made her want to yield and rebel in the same breath. That self-assured curl of his mouth was dangerous, and if she had any sense, she would steer clear of those deep green eyes.

Florence had nearly finished her submission, yet something gnawed at her—a sense that a key piece was missing. She was determined to win but just as eager to prove she could hold her own alongside a partner attorney. Frustration pricked at her as she flipped through the pages.

Her thoughts drifted to Mr. Mayfield—how he had pressed her, pushed her to think harder, sharper. He hadn't gone easy on her. At every turn, he met her head-on, dismantling her arguments with the precision of a surgeon's scalpel.

She recalled the scenario Ben had laid out for her during lunch with James.

"Consider it an impromptu trial," he had said.

His voice echoed in her head, sharp and smooth, as she remembered their battle of wits.

That was it. Florence straightened in her chair, her mind snapping back to the present. She had been so focused on proving discrimination that she forgot to flip the case. She needed to build both sides to make her argument stronger.

Ben had shown her that arguing wasn't just about proving a point. It was about bracing for the strike that came back. Her pulse quickened as she bent over her draft, clarity sweeping through her like a fresh wind.

She broke the case apart, just as she had during their impromptu trial. The plaintiff had weak support: no official complaints, no documented demotion, and no clear evidence. A pattern existed—a pattern of being passed over, of being spoken down to, of being paid less than men doing the same job. A pattern everyone saw but few would admit.

But Florence knew better. Patterns mattered. Circumstantial did not mean baseless. She had to be ready for the defense's tactics.

What if the company argued that hiring and promotions were at the employer's discretion? She drafted a counter. What if they claimed the plaintiff wasn't a good fit for advancement? Another counter. What if they ignored the concerns completely? What if the prosecutor said they were imagining things? Another counter.

Florence wasn't just making a case; she was dismantling every excuse before it could even be voiced. The realization struck so hard she almost laughed. Sitting back, she exhaled, finally feeling confident.

***

That night, after crawling into bed later than usual, her mind finally settled. Tomorrow, she would return to work and submit the proposal. Florence was eager to tell Mr. Anderson she had finally finished it. This time, she felt she had a real chance, and she knew he would be proud.

She laid her head down, Mooni curling up behind her. Every night before she drifted off to sleep, she prayed for dreamless rest. Tonight, there were no nightmares. Instead, Florence dreamt of something far more surprising. She dreamt of her boss, Ben Mayfield.

***

"Florence," Ben whispered in her ear, his breath warm against her skin as his hand slid up her thigh. *Prove to me you can handle this, sweet girl. I'll leave everything to you; this case can be yours,* "he murmured, his lips tracing the curve of her neck.

"*Ben, we can't,*" she began, trying to push him away, but he only pressed closer.

He lifted her onto his desk before she could protest. His hands gripped her wrists, holding her in place. His knee nudged between hers, parting them. Then his mouth captured hers, silencing her doubts. His kiss was hot, deliberate, sending a shiver down her spine.

His hands roamed higher, gripping her thighs through the fabric of her dress. When he finally released her wrists, she didn't resist. Instead, she wrapped her arms around his neck, giving in. His hips pressed against her, pushing her back. The motion knocked his nameplate off the desk, sending it clattering to the floor. His hand trailed to her knee, then slipped beneath her dress.

Ben's hands moved higher, until a sharp knock echoed through the room.

When Florence woke, her heart was pounding, and her skin was damp with sweat. A deep sense of embarrassment swept over her as she glanced at Mooni, still sleeping soundly. *Good Lord. Has it been that long?* She was losing her mind—or that man had infected it..

***

Florence went to work as if everything were normal. When she arrived, she noticed Mr. Mayfield's car parked outside. Curious, she walked closer. No one else came in this early, so he was likely already upstairs.

It was Mr. Mayfield's Aston Martin—the kind of car that could stop anyone in their tracks. The sleek body was a work of art, its deep British Racing Green paint catching the light with effortless elegance. Every curve looked expertly shaped; the front end, smooth and aerodynamic, flowed seamlessly into the sides and rear. Round taillights added a stylish touch at the back, and the chrome details gleamed against the dark green finish.

The car sat low to the ground, ready to spring into action. Its silver-rimmed wheels were pristine, a sharp contrast to the deep color. Florence couldn't help but be drawn to it. She imagined the engine's low purr as Mr. Mayfield steered it down an open road. A flicker of regret passed through her—she wished she had accepted his earlier offer to drive it.

Moving closer, she tried to peer through the darkly tinted windows, but they revealed nothing. In her mind, she could picture him inside: hands on the leather wheel, the interior exuding the same luxury as its exterior. The mystery of it all only deepened her curiosity.

Then, the door opened. She jumped, heat flooding her

cheeks.

Mr. Mayfield had been sitting there the whole time.

Florence's heart skipped. She had planned to avoid him ever since that dream, and now here he was.

"M-Mr. Mayfield, I—I'm so sorry. I didn't know you were inside," she stammered.

He stepped out, dressed in slacks, polished shoes, and a crisp button-up shirt. His jacket rested on the passenger seat. Towering over her, he wore a smirk that was half amusement, half satisfaction.

"At the risk of being rejected twice," he said lightly, "I'll ask again. Would you like to see the inside of this car, Florence?"

Her embarrassment lingered, but this time, pride wouldn't stop her. She nodded, avoiding his gaze. Part of her feared that if their eyes met, he might somehow know the dream she wished to forget.

She leaned into the car, her breath catching at the sight: plush dark-brown leather seats shaped to perfection, a gleaming dashboard with polished wood accents, and vintage dials that held a timeless charm.

The air smelled faintly of leather and something unmistakably him—a deep, earthy musk that wrapped around her senses. It was different from the rain-slicked scent she remembered before, but no less distracting. Her pulse quickened, and she pulled herself upright, unwilling to linger in that haze.

"Thank you," she murmured, bowing her head.

"You can sit in it if you like," he said with a faint smile. "I'd offer to let you drive again, but we'd both end up late—and she's my baby."

Florence raised a brow. "Afraid I'd crash your car?"

His eyes lingered a fraction too long on her lips. "Oh, I don't doubt you could handle it. But a car like this... it needs a certain kind of touch. The driver has to know when to be firm—and when to be gentle."

Heat rose in her cheeks at the suggestion. She cleared

her throat, lifting her chin.

"Trust me," she said, her voice steady though slightly breathless, "I can handle it—maybe even better than you."

"I don't doubt that, Miss Witkins."

Ben wanted to pull her closer, but instead, he chuckled. "For now, you can sit in it."

She moved to step in, and he stopped her. "Would you hand me my jacket first, ma'am?"

She leaned over the passenger seat, her long legs drawing his unwilling attention. He forced his eyes to the sky, but not before catching a glimpse. When she handed him the jacket, he took her purse and lunch to free her hands, then held the jacket up as a shield while she slid into the seat, her skirt demanding modesty neither of them dared compromise.

Her smile bloomed as she settled in—radiant, unguarded. Ben had never seen her look like that. It struck him more deeply than he expected.

"So," he asked, leaning against the door, "does this car suit you?"

She laughed softly. "Oh, absolutely."

Without thinking, he said, "Then I'll buy you one."

Her brows arched in surprise, then she laughed. "Now, you know folks don't just hand out cars to lady lawyers."

His grin deepened. "No—but keep working the way you do, and you won't need anyone to hand you a thing."

"That," she said, still smiling, "I could live with."

He offered his hand as she stepped out. For a moment, they stood closer than either intended, his pulse stumbling.

"Here are your things," he said, clearing his throat.

"Thank you. And your car… it's something else." Her tone lingered like perfume as she walked toward the building.

Ben trailed behind her, unwilling to let the moment end, but work awaited.

The day went on. Everyone was reminded to submit their proposals—Friday would reveal the winner.

Later, during lunch, Florence brought her memorandum to Mr. Anderson. She found him outside on a bench, enjoying the breeze.

"Mr. Anderson, I've submitted my entry," she said, her smile measured but warm. "I think it could be a strong contender."

"That's wonderful, Florence," he replied. "I expect nothing less from you. And remember—your position here doesn't define you. Whether you're starting out or running the place, you're more than a title on a door."

"I couldn't agree more," came a voice from behind.

Florence turned. "Mr. Mayfield," she said, rising instinctively.

"No need," Ben said smoothly. "Please, stay seated."

She hesitated, then cleared her throat. "Actually, I should get back. I'll see you later, Mr. Anderson."

Gathering her things, she walked away, her pulse quicker than she cared to admit. One slip that morning was enough—she couldn't risk crossing paths with Ben too often. It was dangerous even to think of a man like him: white, wealthy, powerful. And yet, all week, he seemed to appear wherever she went. Coincidence, she told herself. But avoiding him was becoming an exhausting effort.

By week's end, Mr. Mayfield called another meeting—one Florence was permitted to attend. The winning memorandum would be announced, its author working directly under his supervision. Each submission was anonymous. Hers was 274.

When the meeting began, his gaze found her immediately. She kept her eyes on her notepad, determined not to return it.

"Thank you all for coming," he said, his voice smooth but commanding. "The work ahead will demand even more from us, so consider this just the beginning."

He paused, letting his words settle.

"The memorandum I've chosen stood out for its clarity, organization, and depth of analysis. It demonstrated not only a precise understanding of the case but a strategy that aligns with our vision. Its attention to detail and persuasive reasoning made the choice plain." He glanced at the paper in his hand. "So—without further delay—the number I've selected is…"

CHAPTER 11:
INFECTION OF THE HEART

Florence had become the center of Ben's every thought. She lingered in his mind by day and slipped into his dreams by night. Each morning, he woke to her face in his mind. He found himself hoping she would win his competition; then he could work beside her from dawn to dusk, learning her every quirk, her likes and dislikes. At present, she seemed to dislike him, but that was something he intended to change. He wasn't arrogant, only determined. The contest would give him a reason to call on her beyond office hours. For now, he had to go through James, and that was a nuisance in itself. More than anything, Ben wanted to know exactly what she and James were to each other.

Ben stepped into the house, calling out, "Mama Benard! Where are you?" Silence.

He frowned. No dinner on the stove, no radio humming in the background. That wasn't like her. He took the stairs two at a time and pushed open her bedroom door.

She turned, startled. "Boy, why you bustin' in here like the police?"

"I thought something was wrong. No supper, no noise, just…"

She cut him off with a wave. "You're a grown man. You can fix your own plate one night," she said, covering a cough with her hand.

Ben stepped closer. "Sure, I can. That's not the point. Are you sick?"

"Of course not," she snapped, though another cough betrayed her. He reached for her forehead, but she swatted his hand away.

"Don't you fret over me. Go find yourself some dinner and let me get my rest."

Ben didn't argue. He grabbed his keys and drove to the corner pharmacy for aspirin, cough syrup, and whatever else might help. On the way back, he stopped for chicken soup—enough for them both—and a side salad for himself.

When he returned, she was already asleep. He set the bags on her nightstand and gently shook her shoulder.

"Mama, wake up and take this medicine."

She smacked her lips and rolled over. "Why'd you go spend money on all this? I told you…"

"Sure, you're healthy as an ox," he said dryly, pouring water into a glass. He helped her sit up and handed her the pills.

"You make too much fuss over me," she muttered. "Wouldn't have time for all this if you had a wife and some children."

"I'll always have time for you," he said softly. "You're all I've got left." He leaned in to kiss her cheek, but she turned away, settling back under the covers.

"Mm-hmm. Go on now, before I give you my germs."

Ben shook his head, smiling. "I love you, Mama. Goodnight."

"Thank you for the medicine," she murmured, almost too low to hear. "Love you." Then she closed her eyes, pretending sleep had already claimed her.

Ben left her bedroom and headed back to the kitchen, tucking her food into the icebox for later. When he'd first come home, he had planned to tell his mother about Florence. He had already decided to pursue her, no matter what, and he wanted his mother to hear it from him.

***

The day of the announcement came, and as much as Ben hated to admit it, he was nervous. Florence winning this contest was part of what could make or break his whole plan. He had the employees submit their memorandums anonymously. His professional integrity meant he could not be biased.

On her way to the boardroom, Florence passed a cluster of attorneys from their HR team whispering near the office corridor.

"I'm curious to see who survives a case with Ben Mayfield," one murmured, shaking her head. "Anyone who works with him is in for a world of hurt."

The other shrugged, a sly smile tugging at her lips. "True, but think of the status. Your reputation would skyrocket if you lasted."

"I'd hate for that to be me," the first replied, her tone wary. "I heard rookies don't last a month with him. He's impossible to work with."

Florence walked past them, shaking her head silently. Their warnings barely registered; she doubted it mattered what they said. Deep down, she wasn't even sure she could win.

***

When Ben stepped into the room, there was something different in Florence's eyes. Ordinarily, she greeted him with a hint of irritation or a well-mannered smile. But today, her gaze carried the weight of a brewing storm, steady, unyielding, and daring him to cross its path. It made him want to make her entire life full of sunshine. He wondered if she was unsure of her submission. Ben gave a short speech about everyone's work before it was time to call out the number. He took a breath.

"So, without further delay, the number I've selected is…"

Silence filled the air as the words left his lips. Everyone

looked around, trying to decipher whose number it was. When Florence rose to her feet, she said evenly, "I am number 274." Her voice carried confidence, yet a flicker of hesitation lingered in her eyes.

Ben stepped forward. He held back the urge to thank God for what had happened and shook her hand.

"Congratulations, ma'am. Your work speaks for itself. This is a fine accomplishment." He said it to keep his composure, though he had known all along just how capable she was. The prospect of learning more about her stirred something in him. Already, he noticed the sidelong glances from his colleagues, the tight smiles. It would not be long before the whispers started—claims that she had help or, worse, that she had cheated.

Luckily, Ben had already put plans in place for anything they would try to throw at her. In the end, they would want to discriminate, so this reaction would serve as a good experiment for his case. Ben did not want that, but if they were going to play dirty, then he would even the playing field for her. He called for the meeting to adjourn, and everyone left. He had Florence follow him to his floor to see where she would be working. Florence trailed behind him, hands clasped together as uncertainty crossed her face. He stopped, causing her to bump into his back.

"I'm sorry," she said quickly.

"Don't let yourself get rattled over what folks might say. I didn't choose your work as any favor to James, if that's crossed your mind. Yours was simply the best, and it was pure chance that your number came up. I don't bite, so there's no cause for you to be uneasy," Ben said, his tone measured, aiming to put her at ease.

Florence nodded. Though she wanted this opportunity more than anyone else, why did it have to be him of all people? Especially now that she knew James and Ben were friends it couldn't get much worse. She would seek Denise's advice immediately. Ben began to show Florence around his floor. He pointed out the different offices and explained who worked where. This helped her focus and remember who was who.

Ben's office sat squarely at the heart of the floor, its walls all glass with blinds ready to be drawn for privacy. He held the door for her, letting her step inside first. Florence took in the space—no family photographs, no trinkets, none of the clutter she had seen on other desks. His was stripped down to essentials: a polished surface, a nameplate, and the tools of his trade. She lingered while Mr. Mayfield took a call, her hand resting on the chair back. Just as she turned to leave, he lifted a finger, motioning for her to sit. She lowered herself into the chair, her mind drifting—could this ever be her life? To stand at the top of her field, to have people vying for the chance to work beside her. The thought warmed her ambition.

Ben finished his phone call, eyes narrowing as he slid a thick folder across the desk toward Florence. The air in the office shifted—gone was the playful mentor, the soft-spoken man she'd gotten glimpses of before. This was Ben, the attorney.

"The first task I'm assigning you," he said, his tone clipped and steady, "is a full field report. Now that you've got more information on Mr. Caldwell case, I want you caught up—completely. This is going to be a trial by evidence, and there's no room for sloppy work."

Florence straightened in her seat, the weight of the folder pressing against her palms.

"You'll start with the wrongful termination," Ben continued, his voice firm, deliberate. "Map out every detail. Dates, witnesses, patterns in management's behavior. After that, move into Briarstone Textiles breach of labor laws— minimum wage violations, unpaid overtime, anything you can dig up. And don't overlook the workplace accidents. There's a string of them tied to this company, not just Caldwell. I want names, statements, medical reports if you can find them. Everything."

His gaze locked on hers, stern and unflinching. "If

there's a crack in this case, we're going to find it. That's your job now. Don't miss anything. Not one detail, Florence. Because if you do, the defense will pick up on it, and they'll use it to bury us."

For a moment, the room was quiet except for the faint hum of the desk lamp. Then Ben leaned forward, his expression still sharp but touched with something else—expectation or maybe excitement.

"Show me you can handle this," he said, voice low, almost like a challenge. "This isn't practice anymore. You wanted the work—now you've got it." Ben was eager to see how well Florence held up against Ben's onslaught of work. He wanted to see what she was made of.

Suddenly, the door swung open, and there stood Charlotte. Florence rose at once. Charlotte's eyes widened, surprise written clear across her face.

"What are you doing in here?" Charlotte asked.

"Ms. Witkins will work for me now until further notice," he said firmly.

"If you need someone to get your coffee or run errands, we have plenty of—" Charlotte was cut short.

"If I needed that, Charlotte, I could always call you." He tilted his head to the side. "Please knock before entering next time," Mr. Mayfield said.

"Of course, sir. There's an emergency with your case. I thought you would want to see it before anyone else."

Charlotte handed him the paper. Ben's jaw tightened, and Florence found it strangely attractive. She wondered what he might look like when he was truly angry. She shook her head, trying to wipe the thought away.

"You're coming with me," Mr. Mayfield said suddenly to Florence.

This time, Charlotte and Florence both let out a drawn-out "uhhh…"

"Are you sure you want a rookie on a new, important case with you?" Charlotte asked. Florence wanted to fire back, but Charlotte's concern wasn't entirely unfounded.

"I don't like to repeat myself. Florence, you're coming with me. End of discussion," Ben said, his voice shifting back into lawyer mode.

Florence didn't argue. She fell in step behind him as he gathered his briefcase and, without a word, picked up her purse from the chair. They walked to the lot together.

When they reached his car, he opened the passenger door. Florence hesitated, glancing at him.

"I'm driving. Get in," Ben instructed.

"But my car is right there," she protested, pointing.

"We'll be gone a while," he replied evenly. "I'm not sure how long. My car gets us in and out without drawing attention. The press and regular folks won't recognize it, but the people I've already contacted will, and they'll wave me through so we can reach the client without trouble."

Florence let out a low laugh under her breath and slid into the seat. Even if he had not given her that whole explanation, she had no real reason to refuse the ride. She certainly couldn't say something like, "I can't, your presence makes my knees weak," without finding herself out of a job by morning. So, she pressed her lips together, steadying herself, and did what she had to do.

Still, she couldn't ignore the ripple of excitement running through her. More giddy than she would ever confess aloud, she settled into the seat's soft leather. She would have loved to get behind the wheel herself, but there was something just as satisfying about riding along, especially in a car like this, with him at the helm.

***

A moment later, they wove through traffic, Ben's hands locked firmly around the steering wheel. Florence noticed the tightening in his gaze, the telltale sign of a man bracing against something he didn't like.

Front-page news:

Briarstone Textiles: Discrimination Lawsuit Causes Public Anger; Mayfield Law Attorneys Under Fire

"They leaked it," he muttered under his breath, gripping the edges of the paper until they crumpled. Florence read the newspaper while he drove. The case was out. Thomas Caldwell, a colored man, was suing his former employer for racial discrimination. Now, he was a target, and so was the firm. But who had leaked it? The article mentioned an anonymous source; the company surely had a vendetta.

"We have to get to him," Ben said, his voice sharp with urgency.

As they neared the scene, the distant roar of a crowd reached their ears. When they turned onto the street where Tommy had been staying, the sight was chaotic. A riot had broken out. Protesters filled the streets. Some demanded justice for Tommy, while others—angry, white, and aggressive—shouted slurs and threats. Police were already present, struggling to keep the violence at bay. A rock had smashed the window where Tommy was staying, and thick smoke poured out from a small fire by the steps.

Ben parked a block away. "Stay close," he ordered, stepping out of the car.

Florence followed as they pushed through the crowd. A group of colored people had gathered at the entrance, trying to shield Tommy from the attack. As they moved forward, a sudden surge from the police line sent bodies crashing in all directions. In the commotion, an officer roughly grabbed Florence.

"Get back with the others!" he barked, twisting her arm behind her back.

"Let me go!" she protested, struggling.

Ben's pulse pounded in his ears as he surged forward, instincts overriding reason.

"She's with me!" His voice thundered, cutting through the chaos. Before he could think better of it, he seized the officer by the shirt, his fist poised in the air. Florence grabbed his arm, urging him to stop.

If the price of her safety was his freedom, he would

pay it without hesitation.

The officer's eyes widened as Ben's grip tightened, his knuckles white with restrained fury. But before he could strike, a voice cut through the moment.

"Ben!"

James's sharp call broke the spell. Everything around them seemed to still. The officer, tense and bracing for a blow, faltered. The crowd turned toward them, drawn by the sudden confrontation.

The officer's stance shifted from aggression to unease. He shoved Ben back roughly, his elbow catching him hard in the ribs. Ben staggered but did not flinch. His jaw locked, his breath controlled, but his rage simmered beneath the surface.

"Touch her again, and you'll regret it," he said, his voice low enough for only the officer to hear.

The officer took one look at him, saw the coiled stance barely containing fury, and did not press further. He ground his teeth, his lip curling with scorn at the sight of Ben protecting a colored woman. Ben dismissed him without another glance, his attention already elsewhere. In two strides, he reached for Florence's wrist. His fingers wrapped around it, his thumb brushing the red mark left by the officer. His hands, steady and firm, softened in contrast to his earlier fury.

"Are you hurt?" His voice was rough, laced with an urgency he could not temper.

Florence hesitated; his concern unsettled her in ways she had not expected. She withdrew her wrist.

"I'm okay," she reassured him, managing a small smile. Then her eyes shifted to his side. "But you—he elbowed you hard. Are you all right?"

For a moment, Ben said nothing. His expression was unreadable. Then, jaw clenched, he exhaled, rubbing his ribs. "I'll live."

Before she could ask more, her gaze caught something in the distance. She turned toward it, the thread of their exchange slipping away.

"What was going on here?" James asked.

Ben rubbed the back of his neck. "Nothing."

"James, Why are you here?" Florence asked.

James was shocked to see Ben and Florence together.

"I got called in," James explained. "One of my clients was arrested in all of this."

Ben exhaled, his anger shifting. "We need to get Tommy out of here before he's next."

James nodded. "Agreed. We'll talk later, when this isn't a war zone."

Florence glanced between them, feeling the weight of the situation settle over her. But before she could process it, Ben turned to her, his expression softer now.

"We need a plan to keep Tommy safe," he said, "and you." His voice dropped slightly, laced with something unspoken. For now, there was work to do.

Florence swallowed, her heart pounding—not from fear, but from something else entirely.

Part II:
Thunderstrike

CHAPTER 12: NEWFANGLED LOVE

The protest incident had shaken Florence. Ben's quick action to protect her left a lingering sense of comfort she couldn't quite explain. Weeks had passed, yet he still lingered in her thoughts.

Ben often called her into his office. They would review case law, analyze precedents, or discuss strategy. Each time, her composure faltered. It wasn't fear she felt, but an unsettling interest she resented.

"Florence," Ben's voice carried from his office.

She knocked before stepping in, her posture straight and composed. "Yes, Mr. Mayfield?"

"Have a seat," he said, gesturing to the couch beside him. A stack of legal volumes lay open on his desk.

"I pulled some materials from the law library. We'll go through these together, and I'll assign a few for you to review at home. I plan to hold a mock trial. I'll serve as the defense counsel, and you can act as either the jury or opposing counsel. I want to see how you build a case."

Florence paused, then selected a stack of books and sat across the room. Ben frowned slightly.

"Why all the way over there?" he asked. "This requires collaboration. I need to see what details you focus on in your analysis."

"So, I'm being scrutinized?" she countered.

"Not scrutinized," he corrected, amusement touching

his tone. "I need to understand how you think. A strong case depends on cohesion between attorneys. A well-matched legal team strengthens an argument before it even reaches a judge."

Florence regarded him for a moment before replying, "A compatible way of thinking."

"Precisely." He motioned again to the seat beside him. She hesitated, her usual assertiveness softened by something he couldn't quite name.

Finally, Florence sat next to him. His warmth was near, his hands moving as he flipped through pages.

Ben's heart pounded harder than it should have. They worked side by side for nearly three hours, yet his attention drifted more than once. Her legs seemed impossibly long, her hair soft as snow. He caught himself imagining how her skin might feel beneath his touch, how she might respond if his lips met hers—

"Ben... did you hear me?" Florence's voice cut through his thoughts.

He blinked, guilt prickling at the edges of his mind. It had been far too long since he'd felt the nearness of a woman, especially one with her quiet magnetism. Her scent—warm, sweet, with a trace of cinnamon—clung to the air between them. He cleared his throat.

"Hmm? My apologies, Miss Witkins. Could you repeat that? I got caught up in my reading."

"Yes, I was asking because I've never actually attended court. How will this work with me at your side?"

Two thoughts collided before he spoke. First, Witkins didn't seem a fitting last name for her—Mayfield did. The realization sent a quick heat crawling up the back of his neck.

"Well, first off, in this case, we're not defending anyone. I'm representing the plaintiff—the employee suing their employer. That makes me the prosecuting attorney, counsel for the plaintiff."

Florence nodded, following along.

"As for your role," he continued, "you'll observe, take notes, and assist with documents when needed. You won't be addressing the judge, but you'll help track evidence, organize case law, and monitor witness statements. It's hands-on learning, and you'll see how arguments evolve in real time."

She leaned in slightly, curious. "Will we meet the judge beforehand?"

"That depends," he said, regaining focus. "Before trial, there's often a pretrial conference where both sides meet with the judge to discuss evidence, witnesses, and motions. If settlement is possible, that's where it's considered."

"And you'll attend that?"

"Yes, and you will too. It's less formal than the trial but a critical step. After that, there may be motion hearings— debates over what evidence is allowed. Once that's set, we either move to jury selection or straight into opening arguments."

Florence's brow furrowed. "So, by the time the trial starts, everything's already decided?"

"In a way," Ben said, a faint note of approval in his voice. "By trial, the groundwork is done. The real battle is in how we argue, cross-examine, and tell the story."

Florence nodded slowly. "I see. I'll be taking a lot of notes."

Ben chuckled softly. "Yes, you will."

"Is it alright if I break for lunch now?" she asked.

"Why don't we have lunch together? I can bring something back," Ben offered.

Her heart quickened at the suggestion. *No, he's only being considerate.* "That's kind of you, Mr. Mayfield, but I have lunch downstairs."

***

A few days later, Ben discovered the "colored" fridge she'd been using. It was hidden down a creaking stairwell in a dim, unused room. The fridge buzzed weakly, leaking at the base, barely cool. His irritation grew at the thought of her eating here, isolated, vulnerable.

What if someone followed her down here? The idea tightened his chest. Ben slammed the door shut and strode back upstairs.

That week, he placed an order with Sears for new refrigerators, one for every floor. He knew Florence wouldn't work beside him forever. One day, she'd move on. But at least she'd have a decent place to store her food—wherever her office might be.

He shook his head at the thought. Ignorance had kept him from realizing she couldn't use the employee fridges. Florence didn't know yet, so for now, he kept quiet.

"Okay, ma'am, but at least once a week we should have lunch together." Florence's mouth fell open at the idea.

"This will give us time to catch up on our work and take the edge off this case. Sound fair?" Ben asked, tilting his head. "You won't need to pack lunch that day. Choose whichever day suits you." He lowered his eyes to the page, pretending to write as she lingered by the door.

"Yes, sir. Friday is fine with me." Florence's heart pounded in her chest.

"I'll mark it on my calendar. Have a good lunch, Miss Witkins."

"Likewise, sir," Florence replied.

At lunch, she chose a seat across from Mr. Anderson. That wasn't unusual, but today she had a reason: she needed his opinion. Lately, she'd been wondering if she was reading too much into things.

Mr. Anderson was halfway through his sandwich when she arrived. "Hello, Florence!" he greeted warmly, his face lighting up.

"Hello," she answered, her voice softer than usual.

He studied her for a moment. "What's with the long face? I figured you'd be riding high after winning that contest and working with Mr. Mayfield."

Florence hesitated, shifting in her chair. "Yes, about

that… How much do you know about Mr. Mayfield? I know you two are acquainted, but—" She stopped, unsure how to frame the question.

Mr. Anderson leaned back, rubbing his chin as though weighing his words. "Well, now… Ben's a fine fellow. Driven; smart; easy on the eyes; and, yes, he's got a streak of mischief in him. Reminds me of his father in certain ways," he said with a chuckle. "But in others, he's different. There's a compassion there most folks wouldn't expect."

Florence nodded, but he wasn't finished. "Never had much luck with the ladies, though. My guess? He's married to his work."

Her breath caught. No luck with women? That didn't add up. He was sharp, respected, and undeniably attractive. She'd assumed he was some kind of Romeo.

Mr. Anderson's eyes narrowed with curiosity. "Why do you ask?"

Heat crept up her neck. "Oh, it's… he's just… nice. It throws me a little, that's all."

"Nice?" he echoed, a trace of amusement in his tone. "Come now, Florence. You can do better than that."

She forced a smile, but her thoughts tangled. She had to be imagining things. Ben Mayfield wasn't interested in her. He was white, she was colored, and men like him didn't look twice at women like her.

Her fingers smoothed the fabric of her skirt as she tried to brush the thought away. Still, Mr. Anderson's knowing look suggested he wasn't convinced.

Back at the office, her confusion lingered. Ben sat at his desk, lunch in front of him, jacket draped over his chair. His sleeves were rolled neatly to the elbow, revealing strong forearms.

He looked up as she entered. "I can come back when you're finished eating," she offered from the doorway.

He leaned back slightly, a slow grin spreading across his face. "Don't be silly. I'd welcome the company."

Something in his tone sent a shiver up her spine. She

swallowed hard and took her seat, fingers tightening around the book she had grabbed as a distraction. She tried to focus, but her eyes kept drifting back to him. She noticed the deliberate movement of his jaw as he chewed, the way his lips parted slightly around the fork. Ridiculous, she told herself. Yet every stolen glance only made her pulse quicken.

Ben noticed. Of course, he noticed.

"Would you like to try my food, Florence?" His tone carried an edge of amusement, his eyes holding hers just a beat too long.

Her back straightened. "O-Of course not, sir. I just…"

He gestured for her to step closer. Before she could think better of it, she obeyed, moving to stand beside his desk.

One brow lifted, his voice dropping lower. "No? Then what were you looking at, sweetheart?"

The pet name sent heat flooding through her. He was teasing, but there was something dangerous in his gaze. She panicked, grasping at the safer option.

"Nevermind, I was looking at the food. Satisfied?"

Ben chuckled, slow and deep, as though he knew she was lying. He lifted a forkful toward her. She hesitated, then leaned forward to take the bite, but as she did, her hair fell into her face. Before she could react, his hand touched her cheek. He tucked a stray strand behind her ear. Florence froze.

His touch was brief, barely a whisper against her skin, but it set her entire body alight. She couldn't breathe. Couldn't move. She could only stare into his gaze as she chewed. What would his lips feel like? Would they be gentle? Firm? She had no business thinking about such things, but now she couldn't stop.

Ben's mind was nowhere near his lunch. The way her lips had closed over the fork—graceful, deliberate—lingered in his thoughts. She had accepted the bite to maintain her dignity, that much was clear, but the image stayed with him. Florence had a way of challenging a man simply by existing in the same room.

It was not the sort of thing a gentleman ought to dwell on, especially in the office, but Florence was no ordinary woman. She carried herself with the poise of someone who knew her worth, and yet there was a fire in her that could undo him if he let it. He found himself wondering, not for the first time, how far that fire might burn if the right match was struck.

His gaze darkened at the thought, drawn to the curve of her mouth. He leaned in without thinking, the air between them charged, the hum of the city beyond the windows fading into nothing. The moment seemed to hold still.

Then, three brisk knocks. Charlotte swept in, all light and chatter, and the current between them snapped like a wire cut clean.

Florence jumped back as if burned. She nearly tripped while scrambling away from his desk. She fell onto the couch, grabbing the nearest book and burying her face behind it to hide her flaming cheeks. Ben sighed deeply and pinched the bridge of his nose. He looked at Charlotte with pure exasperation.

"Yes, Charlotte?" he asked, his voice slightly strained.

Florence barely registered the conversation. Her heart was still hammering, her skin still tingling where he had touched her. She had come back to the office hoping to clear her head. Ben had practically undressed her with his eyes. She wondered if he had a fetish. Then, Charlotte called her out of the room while Mr. Mayfield took a call.

As Charlotte ushered her out, she handed Florence a stack of folders once the door was closed. A scowl darkened her face, as though Florence had wronged her somehow.

"Deliver these papers immediately," she demanded.

"Of course, ma'am."

Florence grabbed the folders and started her rounds. She delivered them to each floor, just as she had many times before. Usually, her presence went unnoticed—she was used to being invisible. But today was different. Today, they saw her. And they didn't like what they saw.

As she stepped off the elevator onto each floor, she felt it: the weight of their stares, the coldness in their eyes. They whispered softly, but loud enough for her to catch their sharp words. Their resentment hung in the air like smoke. She didn't belong. She didn't deserve this.

By the time she reached the fourth floor, her fingers ached from gripping the folders too tightly. The receptionist's desk was empty. She stood there, waiting, hoping someone would come and take the stack from her. No one moved.

The men lounged at their desks, glancing at her with disinterest—or perhaps something worse. Contempt. Still, she forced herself forward. *Do your job, Florence. That's all that matters.* She stepped toward one of the men, opening her mouth to ask where they wanted the papers. A foot shot out...

She had little time to react. She stumbled, and the folders slipped from her hands as she fell forward. The floor was unforgiving. Her palms burned as they caught her fall, and her knee slammed hard against the tile. One of her heels snapped, skidding across the floor with a sharp click.

For a moment, there was silence. Then came the laughter—low chuckles, muffled snickers.

Florence's throat tightened, and tears pricked the backs of her eyes. She swallowed hard.

This, I can endure. This, I will endure.

She forced herself to move, gathering the scattered papers with trembling hands. She stacked them neatly—because if nothing else, she could do that right—and set them on the front desk. She said nothing. Instead, she turned on her sore heel and walked away, refusing to show weakness.

Ben glanced at the clock, irritation twisting in his chest. Where had Florence gone? It had been fifteen minutes.

He exhaled sharply, cutting his call with Lance short. Where was she? He strode to his office door and yanked it open.

"Charlotte," he called, his voice tight.

She stood, smoothing her skirt. "Yes, sir?"

"Where is Florence?" His jaw tensed as he spoke.

Charlotte hesitated, then gave a casual shrug. "Oh, I had her deliver some papers since she wasn't doing anything."

Ben's expression darkened. Of course.

"Since she currently works for me, do not assign her tasks in the future," he said, his tone leaving no room for argument. "I have to step out, but inform Florence that in three weeks, she'll be accompanying me on a business trip."

Charlotte blinked. "Will I be attending as well, sir?"

"No. Just the two of us." He didn't wait for her to respond. The tension in Charlotte's forced smile lingered in the air as the elevator doors closed between them.

Charlotte stood frozen, her mouth slightly open, before her expression twisted with anger.

Meanwhile, Ben ran a hand through his hair, already dreading what came next—a visit to his father. But beneath that obligation, something else simmered: a weekend. Just him and Florence. No interruptions. A slow smile tugged at his lips. This would be his chance to draw her closer.

CHAPTER 13:
LOVE CAN BE POISONOUS

Ben had never liked visiting his father. Rarity didn't sweeten the task; it only meant their silences had longer to steep. They spoke when duty demanded it, and family gatherings forced Ben into the role of obedient son: the polished heir who smiled on cue. His father wore his public mask with ease, a man the world envied—charming, principled, untouchable. But Ben knew the man beneath the polish.

Crossing the threshold of the estate, Ben felt the weight settle in his chest. No greeting. No staff. His father had dismissed them years ago, after his mother's passing. Without her, the great house was nothing but a cavern: echoing, immaculate, lifeless. It reminded Ben of the man who owned it—wealthy, feared, and entirely alone.

He had not come to mend fences. He had not come to reminisce. He came because his father had summoned him, and summons were never without motive. Each step toward the study was heavier than the last. He already knew why he'd been called. It was not to talk. It was to be reminded of his place.

"Dad," he called, the word slipping out before he could stop it. His father barely looked up.

"I told you to call me Benjamin," he said flatly. "I am no longer your father."

Ben clenched his jaw. Right.

"Given that we share the same name, I didn't think you were serious." That was why his father was alone. Whatever shred of sympathy Ben had felt earlier evaporated. Running a hand through his hair, he exhaled. "Why the hell did you call me here if I'm not your son?"

His father leaned back in his chair, folding his hands. "We both know the law conference is coming up in New York next weekend," he said. "I expect us to stand as a unit for this event. We will represent the firm, and I don't want you embarrassing us with your civil rights nonsense. If you want the firm to be yours someday, I suggest you keep that in mind."

Ben's stomach tightened. "What… what do you mean?" he asked, his voice tense.

His father sneered. "You don't think I've noticed your people looking into my business? Fortunately for me, I have a clean slate." He tilted his head, watching Ben's reaction like a cat toying with a mouse. "You'll have to be better than that. Though… I suppose I could give the firm to you. After all, I did give you the position you have now."

Ben stiffened, anger burning in his chest. "You didn't give me anything," he said through his teeth. "I earned my position. My success as a lawyer has nothing to do with you." His voice sharpened. "The only thing we share is a last name."

He turned to leave, every line of his body rigid with anger, but his father had more to say.

"How dare you speak to me like this? I've made you who you are," his father bellowed, rising from his chair. His voice was pure fury, filling the room like a thunderclap. "You would be nothing without me! Nothing!"

Ben turned in time to see his father raise his hand. For a split second, it was like being a child again—small, power-less, and afraid. But Ben wasn't that little boy anymore. Be-fore Charles could strike, Ben's hand shot up, catching his father's wrist in midair. The room went still. Ben tightened his grip, staring his father down.

"You don't get to do that anymore," he said, his voice dangerously calm. "I'm not a child, and you don't scare me."

His father's face twisted with something unreadable—rage, shock, maybe even regret. But Ben didn't care. He released his father's wrist and stepped back. Without another word, he turned and walked out. Yet, as he left the house, doubt crept in uninvited. Had his father gotten him the position? Was there truth in what he said? The thought made his skin crawl. Shoving it aside, he stepped into his car and drove away.

He refused to let his father win. Not again. He had stormed out of the house, fists clenched so tight his knuckles ached. His father's words clattered in his mind, making him feel small. He hated that feeling. So, Ben called James—the one person who could help him work it off. Twenty minutes later, they were at their usual spot: the park where they raced.

"Alright, what's the plan?" James asked, already rolling up his sleeves.

"We race," Ben said. "Then push-ups, sit-ups—whatever it takes until one of us taps out."

James's lips curled. "I'm going to wipe the floor with you."

Ben let out a dry laugh. "We'll see." And with that, they were off. They raced each other like kids again, sprinting down the dirt path, their laughter carrying on the wind. Then came push-ups, each one grunting as they pushed their bodies to the limit. Then sit-ups. Then sprints again. Sweat clung to their skin, shirts sticking to their backs as they pushed and pushed.

At last, James collapsed onto the ground, gasping for breath. "I give," he panted. "You win, man."

Ben dropped beside him, chest heaving. For a long moment, they lay there, staring up at the sky.

Silence settled between them like an old friend. Then, finally, Ben spoke. "I like Florence."

James blinked. "Huh?"

"I like her. Florence, I mean." He rubbed the back of his neck, avoiding James's eyes. "Didn't think much of it at first. I assumed, with you being... well, you know... that you two were friends."

James let out a sharp laugh. "Well, I'm glad you got there, genius."

Ben turned his head, frowning. "I didn't mean any disrespect, but if you don't like Florence, why did you pursue her?"

James sighed before replying. "Our parents set us up. I thought she seemed like someone I could settle down with. Even if I didn't love her, I'd treat her well, and she'd want for nothing. We could be good friends. It didn't have to be love."

Ben glanced at James, his face a mix of restraint and regret.

James waved a hand, still chuckling. "Relax, man. It's fine." He sighed, folding his arms behind his head. "Truth is, I made peace a long time ago that my life's going to look a little different than I want. The world isn't kind to people like me, Ben. Not yet, anyway." His voice softened. "But Florence is still my friend."

Ben nodded. "Alright."

Then James smiled. "So... how long?"

Ben groaned, running a hand over his face. "God, don't do this."

"Oh, I'm doing this," James teased. "How long have you liked her?"

Ben exhaled, rubbing his jaw. "I don't know... for a while."

James grinned. "Why?"

Ben thought about it—really thought about it.

"She has depth. More than people give her credit for," he admitted. "She deserves so much more than she's been given. She's smart. Funny. She doesn't take my crap. She actually listens, and she—" He hesitated, then shrugged. "I don't know. She's beguiling."

James hummed knowingly. "You're in trouble."

Ben gave him a look. "Yeah, I figured."

"Speaking of trouble…" James sat up, eyeing him. "You do realize, because she's colored, this is going to be the hardest road you ever walk, right? Legally, socially?"

Ben's stomach tightened. He knew it wouldn't be easy. He wasn't naïve. He wanted to be everything for her. He had even gone to the library and done research on the subject, just as Mama Benard had suggested. "I know," Ben said.

James studied him for a long moment, then nodded slightly. "Alright then."

James stretched with a groan. "So, what's next?"

Ben hesitated, then admitted, "I'm going to New York with her. Just the two of us."

James grinned, his eyes glinting. "Ohhh. This just got interesting."

Ben rolled his eyes, but a small, nervous smile tugged at his lips. For the first time in a long while, he felt hopeful. And for now, that was enough. He rose from the ground, helping James up.

"You should come to the conference too."

"Wouldn't that be awkward?" James said. "My firm isn't usually invited to such fancy events," he teased. "You want me to be your wingman," he added, crossing his arms.

"It's not just that. It would help your firm too," Ben replied, his gaze intent. "I'll put you on my team so no one will question it."

"Can I think about it?" James groaned.

Ben stared at him until James finally relented. "Ugh, I'm going to regret this. I already feel it."

Ben smiled and slung an arm around his shoulder. "Great. Pack your bags, my friend."

***

The next day, Florence sat on her bedroom floor, carefully bandaging her knee from the fall in Ben's office. Her mind wandered. She couldn't stop thinking about the New York trip alone with him. The thought made her stomach flutter, but she pushed it away.

He's my boss, nothing more, she told herself.

A sharp knock at the door interrupted her thoughts. Denise strolled in, already talking before the door closed.

"Alright, girl, spill. You're going to New York with Ben Mayfield? Just the two of you?" Denise flopped onto the bed with a dramatic sigh. "What a girl wouldn't give to be you! I've seen him in the newspaper. White or not, that man is handsome, Florence," she said plainly.

Florence picked up the bandage wrappers and tossed them in the trash. "It's a work trip, Jackie. Strictly business."

Denise raised an eyebrow, unconvinced. "Uh huh. And how do you feel about that?"

Florence hesitated, crossing her arms. "I don't know," she admitted. "Maybe I like him. A little."

Denise sat up straight. "A little?"

Florence sighed. "It doesn't matter."

"Why not?" Denise asked.

"Because white men don't love colored women, Denise!" Florence snapped before she could stop herself. Silence hung in the air between them. Florence swallowed, looking away. "They like us for a time," she said quietly. "They whisper pretty things, steal moments in the dark, but they don't keep us. They don't marry us. And even if they did, what kind of life would that be? Look at the world we live in." She shook her head. "I always imagined my future, my family, with a colored husband and colored children... with a man who understands."

Denise sighed, her expression softening. "I get it, Flo. I do. But listen, don't go deciding how a man feels before he's even had the chance to tell you. Have a little confidence in yourself." She smiled. "You're beautiful."

Florence scoffed. "Oh, please."

"I'm serious!" Denise planted her hands on her hips. "Men—white or Black—don't pass you by because you're not worth loving, Florence. They pass you by because society has told them to. That's their failure, not yours."

Florence bit her lip, staring at the floor.

Denise grinned. "Besides, this trip is the perfect opportunity."

Florence blinked. "For what?"

Denise wiggled her eyebrows. "To feel him out a little. See where he stands. Maybe even… seduce him a bit."

Florence's jaw dropped. "Denise!"

"What?" Denise laughed. "Girl, you're grown! A woman has needs." She clapped her hands. "Come on, let's pick out your outfits. If nothing else, you deserve to look good while you're in the big city."

Florence groaned but let Denise drag her to the closet. An hour later, her bed was covered in dresses, blouses, and skirts. Denise held up a sleek, fitted dress with a deep neckline. "This. For dinner."

Florence snatched it from her. "I am not seducing my boss, Denise."

"Of course not. You're dressing well."

Florence sighed, giving in. "Fine. But nothing crazy."

Denise held up her hands in mock innocence. "Wouldn't dream of it."

As Florence packed, Denise slipped a lacy piece of lingerie from her own bag into Florence's suitcase while she wasn't looking.

If nothing happened, fine. But if it did, Florence would be prepared.

Florence sat at the edge of the bed, staring at the packed suitcase as though it might answer for her. Could she do this? Could she trust a white man with more than her time—her heart, her future? Trust was the root of it. It wasn't just Ben standing in the balance; it was every bruise history had ever left on her skin, her family, her people. White hands had built too many walls, drawn too many lines, crushed too many dreams. Why should his be any different?

Her fingers curled tight in her lap. No one had love for colored women—not the kind that lasted, not the kind that didn't come with a price. If she let herself believe otherwise, she'd be a fool.

And yet… there it was. That dangerous spark. A reckless little ember inside her, warming what she had worked so hard to keep cold. For the first time in years, she almost wanted to believe.

CHAPTER 14:
POISON SEEPS INTO US ALL

The week passed quickly, and Florence was filled with nothing but excitement—perhaps too much. One afternoon over lunch with Mr. Anderson, she found herself smiling at nothing in particular as she stirred her soup.

"You've been glowing all week, Florence," he remarked, setting down his fork. "Care to share the reason?"

She tried to play it off but couldn't hide her grin. "The trip to New York. I can hardly think of anything else."

"Ah, the Big Apple," he said with a knowing smile. "It has a way of capturing a person's imagination. But tell me: Are you more excited for the city itself or the company you'll be keeping?"

Florence gasped, her head snapping up to look at him. "W-What do you mean?"

He leaned back in his chair, amusement softening his eyes. "I know many things, Miss Witkins."

Her blush deepened, and she dropped her gaze to her plate, fumbling for composure. What she didn't know was that a few weeks ago, Ben had quietly confided in Mr. Anderson, admitting his interest in her among his plans. But long before that, Mr. Anderson had watched the two of them toe carefully around the truth, circling one another with hesitant steps neither seemed brave enough to complete.

Florence paused mid-bite, her cheeks warming. "It's just… the city," she answered quickly, though her voice wavered. She lowered her gaze, focusing intently on her plate. "It's only work," she insisted softly, though even she didn't sound convinced. And she wasn't sure if she was trying to convince him or herself.

Mr. Anderson studied her for a moment, then offered a small, knowing smile. "New York will offer you much, Florence. New sights, new opportunities. Sometimes it's worth being open to experiences you hadn't planned for."

She nodded, her spoon still in hand, though she'd long forgotten the soup. His words lingered, threading themselves into her excitement and planting something softer— something more uncertain—in its midst.

***

Back at the office, Florence was so lost in her thoughts she didn't hear his question. She only realized it when she noticed him staring at her. Ben tapped her lightly on the head with his pencil.

"Focus," he said.

Florence winced. "Ouch! What was that for?"

"If you had been paying attention, you would have known," Ben replied.

"What's on that pretty little mind of yours, anyway?" he asked.

"The trip to New York," she said, cheeks warming until they glowed a soft pink.

"Yes? What about the trip?" His tone turned teasing. "Have you packed already?"

"I have," Florence replied.

"I'm sure you'll look beautiful in anything."

This time, she averted her eyes. "I'm sorry for not focusing."

Ben stood and stretched, then held out his hand toward her. "Let's take a walk."

Her breath caught the moment his fingers brushed

hers.

Her heart pounded so loudly she feared he might hear it. A sudden chill crept through her fingertips, icy and electric where they touched his warm skin. Vulnerability swelled inside her like a fragile wave—a mixture of fear and curiosity twisting in her chest. She was scared: scared of what this might mean, scared of the power her boss held over her, and scared of the risk in saying no. But beneath the fear, a dangerous curiosity pulled her forward.

"Where are we going?" she asked softly, still holding his hand but barely meeting his gaze.

"Are you nervous I'll take you and keep you as mine?" he teased, a playful grin lighting his face.

"Yes, a little," she admitted, her voice barely above a whisper.

Ben laughed, the sound warm and easy. "I guess you'll have to trust me."

Her body responded in ways she couldn't fully control—the slight quickening of her breath, the way her skin tingled where his hand enveloped hers. Even as uncertainty clouded her thoughts, she didn't pull away.

Florence finally stood, taking Ben's hand. They walked around the building and down an empty path she'd never taken before. She hesitated, glancing back, unsure where this was going but curious all the same.

When they reached the bottom floor, they stepped into what seemed to be an abandoned part of the building. For a fleeting second, Florence thought he might kill her—and right before New York, too. What unfortunate timing, she thought.

He opened a door, sending up a cloud of dust that she waved away with her hands. The air smelled of paper and time—thick, still, and untouched.

"Ben, where are—"

Before she could finish, the lights flicked on, and she gasped. It was the largest collection of books she had ever seen. She walked forward, mouth slightly open in awe.

"What is this place?" she asked.

"Do you like it?" he asked, tilting his head.

"I love it, but why is it hidden?" Florence wondered.

"When my father first bought this building, it was a library. My mother adored books in her younger years. Back then, my father, when he still had a touch of romance about him, gave her the gift of unlimited pages: an entire world at her fingertips. I can hardly imagine such a gesture from him now. After she passed, he had this section walled over and built what you see today."

Florence nodded, listening intently. Ben had never spoken to her about anything personal before. She stood with her fingers laced together, her body angled forward as though drawn closer by his words.

Ben paused, his gaze distant for a moment. He didn't say it outright, but somewhere deep down, he felt the weight of those books was meant for something—or someone. He wasn't sure how or why before, but now, looking at Florence, a steady certainty stirred within him that maybe these books had been waiting for her... just as he had.

"You're welcome to come here anytime, sweetheart," he said, his voice softer than she'd ever heard it. "Though it needs some cleaning. I can arrange that if you intend to use it."

She looked up at him, surprised by the offer.

"I've noticed you always bring a book with you when you go to lunch," Ben continued. "I don't read much anymore, unless it's for work," he admitted, "but I'd love for someone to use these books."

Florence's heart leapt. She was so excited that she didn't care what his motives were. She stepped farther into the room. Tall shelves held forgotten stories, and an old chair with a blanket draped across it suggested someone had once spent hours here, lost in another world. She brushed her fingers along the arm of the chair, imagining herself sitting there, reading for hours. It felt like being wrapped in warm hugs. That was what books were—an escape, a place to belong when reality grew too heavy.

Ben lingered near the doorway, watching her with quiet admiration. He had no true connection to this room, but he could admit it was a remarkable collection. At this moment, it was only a backdrop. She was the real masterpiece. Sunlight streamed in, catching the swirling dust, making her glow. In her yellow dress, she looked like the tallest sunflower in a garden.

She reached out and plucked a worn hardcover from the shelf. He stepped closer as she turned it over in her hands.

"You have a first edition of *Pride and Prejudice*," she said, her mouth falling open.

"A fan of romance, I see?" he murmured, peering over her shoulder.

Florence spun around, clutching the book to her chest. "Are you serious? Why do you have first editions collecting dust?"

Ben chuckled. "Will you take care of them for me?" His voice was low, almost teasing, his head tilting slightly.

She had been too captivated by the books to notice how close he had come. Now, as she turned to face him, she found herself only inches away.

"I most certainly—" Florence began, but the words dissolved on her tongue. The air between them thickened, charged and electric, brushing against her skin and stealing her breath. Ben's gaze flicked to her lips. When he spoke, his voice trembled with restraint, and words from *Pride and Prejudice* slipped from his mouth.

"In vain have I struggled. It will not do. My feelings will not be repressed."

The quote struck her like a thunderclap—not just for its meaning but also for the way he said it, as though the confession had lived too long behind locked ribs.

"No," Ben whispered, his fingers brushing her waist with quiet insistence. "You still don't see."

Her pulse quickened. "See what?"

His hand rose to her jaw, his thumb tracing her skin as if coaxing truth from silence. His mouth hovered near hers, his breath warm enough to make her dizzy.

"You must allow me to tell you how ardently I admire and love you," he said softly.

Florence's world tilted. She finally understood how Elizabeth had felt. Her fingers loosened, and the book slipped from her hands, landing with a muted thud between them.

Her heart pounded, and for the first time, though Ben had been quoting a novel, it felt as if he were speaking only to her.

Ben exhaled slowly, his fingers twitching as if he were fighting a silent battle within himself. When his knuckles brushed her jaw, a shiver rippled through her, betraying every layer of armor she carried. She had never let herself fall like this, never craved with such intensity. Yet her body answered him in a language she hardly recognized—raw and urgent, beneath her control.

Her breath came shallow as he tilted her head, his thumb tracing the curve of her cheek with a tenderness that felt like both discovery and devotion. The heat of him pressed close, stirring something fierce and unspoken— close enough to spark, yet holding just short of flame. His eyes searched hers for hesitation, for doubt, for any reason to stop. But she held his gaze, caught between surrender and the faintest thread of resistance.

She had none. She wanted this kiss.

He leaned forward, pressing his lips to hers. There was no going back. Her heart drummed in her chest at their nearness, at the way his body molded against hers. He pressed her back against the shelves, and a low groan escaped him as their lips met. He kissed her—not hurried, not harsh—exactly as it should have been.

Desire, long restrained, broke loose. His hands framed her face, drawing her in, and she responded with equal hunger. Her fingers gripped his shirt, clinging as though it were the only steady thing left. The world tilted, narrowing to the heat between them.

Ben groaned against her lips, and the sound sent warmth curling low in her stomach. He tasted like something forbidden, something impossible—and yet, here he was. Here they were.

The kiss deepened, hands exploring with a hunger that left them both breathless. She forgot how to breathe, each inhale filled only with him, every exhale lost to the fire between them. Their pulses synced in a rhythm older than words, hearts beating in tandem beneath trembling fingertips.

Every touch spoke louder than any confession; every shiver a secret shared. Time folded in on itself, paying back every stolen glance, every unspoken word, every moment they had believed this could never happen.

When they finally parted, gasping for air, their foreheads rested together, grounding them. Florence's knees wavered beneath her, weak from the storm of sensation.

Ben's thumb traced the corner of her mouth, his voice low and rough, thick with breath and feeling. Florence let out a shaky laugh, her heart hammering—wild, alive, undone. She had never imagined herself here, in his arms. And yet, for the first time, she wanted to be nowhere else. She wanted this. She wanted him.

Florence let her head rest against his chest before abruptly pushing him away. Panic rushed in. Thinking those words—wanting them—filled her with fear, wrapping around her ribs like a vice. She turned on her heel, heart racing, and strode out of the library without looking back.

Ben stood frozen, his pulse still thrumming from the kiss—from her. He raked a hand through his hair, his gaze falling to the book she had dropped. It lay forgotten, much like the restraint he had once clung to. He had crossed a line today, opened a door neither of them could close again. He turned toward the doors, half a second from chasing her. He wanted to say something, anything—but she was already gone. For the first time, he felt more nervous about this than any trial he had ever faced.

***

Florence hurried home, her pulse still rattling in her chest. Thank God the workday was done. She tossed her things onto the couch without a glance and cut straight across the yard to Denise's porch.

Her knock was anything but gentle; it was the kind that demanded to be answered.

When the door swung open, Denise froze. Her eyes locked on Florence's face, drawn and shaken, carrying something too heavy for words. That look alone wiped the smile from her lips.

"What's wrong, love?" Denise asked, stepping aside.

"I kissed him… well, he kissed me… we kissed," Florence blurted out as she stepped into her friend's home.

Denise squealed. "I knew it! I knew he liked you. Oh, yes, I have to meet him," she exclaimed.

"Meet him? I can't believe what happened, and you want to meet him?" Florence said, her frustration sharpening each word.

"Well, what happened after the kiss?"

"I stormed out," Florence replied, crossing her arms tightly.

"What do you mean?" Denise stared at her, puzzled.

"I just… left," Florence admitted, cheeks flushed as she avoided her gaze.

Denise shook her head. It was like trying to reason with a stubborn teenager. "Why did you storm out? Did you not enjoy the kiss?"

"No, the kiss was fine," Florence mumbled.

"Just fine?" Denise asked, one brow arched.

"What do you want me to say? Fine. Good. It was the best kiss I've ever had. Does that matter?" Florence snapped, her voice rising with irritation.

Denise laughed. "I see someone's all worked up."

Florence's glare could have set the pillow between them aflame.

"Alright, alright, I'm saying this as a friend." She clasped Florence's hands, her grip warm but insistent. "I know you're nervous, but the worst that can happen is it doesn't work out. As long as you keep it between yourselves, no one has to know. Give him a chance. He's handsome, tall, and comes from money—an heir to a law firm, which means he has sense as well as connections. You don't have any other suitors lined up, so why not? Besides…" She gave Florence a sly smile. "A little time away might just help you loosen up where it counts."

Florence gasped. "First of all, I do have other prospects. I have James," she said firmly.

Denise waved a hand as if swatting away a bothersome idea.

"Mm-hm," she murmured, her tone laced with doubt. "Considering you've always said you never felt a thing for him, I don't see that going anywhere. And besides—" her grin widened "—you're still floating from that kiss with Ben."

Florence lifted her chin. "And secondly, I am not uptight."

Denise's laughter rang out. "Oh, darling, you absolutely are. I just can't decide if it's because you haven't been properly kissed in years or if it's simply your nature. I'm leaning toward the latter; it's far more entertaining."

Florence snatched a pillow and tossed it at her, knocking Denise back onto the couch. "I'm leaving," she said with mock dignity. "Glad I could provide tonight's entertainment."

"Awww, don't pout, Florence," Denise called after her, still laughing. "I was teasing! Give the man a chance!"

Her voice followed Florence to the door, but the only reply was the firm click of it closing.

CHAPTER 15:
ALL THE MORE

Ben and Florence were not seated together on the plane, so Florence took the opportunity to sleep. She had avoided him in the airport and intended to keep her distance for the rest of the trip if she could.

Ben was fuming. He distinctly remembered asking Charlotte to book their seats side by side. Somehow, this was the moment she chose to make a mistake. He refused to dwell on it. Florence was avoiding him, so he would sleep. He only hoped the rest of the trip would run more smoothly.

After retrieving their luggage, they headed to the hotel. Ben carried Florence's bags, even though she gave him grief for helping her. James was scheduled to fly in tomorrow and would meet them once he arrived, though Ben had yet to share that detail with Florence. He had not even managed a proper conversation with her.

***

After Florence swept out of the library, Ben went straight home to tell Mama Benard what had happened. He hesitated, but finally admitted, "She's colored."

Before the words had even settled in the air, Mrs. Benard reached over and gave him a sharp smack on the back of his head.

"Boy, what is wrong with you?" she scolded, her voice

sharp but steady. "Why would you stir that pot at your workplace of all places? Do you have any idea what you've just dropped in that girl's lap?"

Ben opened his mouth, but Mama Benard's look stopped him cold.

"You're the one who told me to go after her," Ben said tightly. "I finally do, and this is what I get? Glad to know I have your blessing."

"Benjamin Mayfield," she began, her tone rich with the kind of authority only a mother could carry, "I have stood in your corner since the day you took your first breath. If there's a soul on this earth who supports you, it's me. But I also know what it is to have a white man suddenly decide he's in love with you. As a colored woman—your boss's colored employee, no less—that is not some light, sweet thing. That is a storm, and storms can wreck a woman if she isn't ready."

She fixed him with a look that left no room for argument. "You should have spoken with her first—made sure she knew what she was stepping into—before you let your hormones take the lead. That's all I'll say."

Then her expression softened, and she reached up, cupping his cheek as she had when he was a boy. "Still, I'm glad you've found someone who's worth all this trouble."

Ben's mouth twitched into a smile, and he leaned down to kiss her cheek.

"Don't you go and ruin it," she warned, a sly glint in her eye. "I want grandbabies before I'm too old to remember their names."

Ben gave a slow shake of his head, a half-smile tugging at his lips. "At this rate, you'll be waiting a long while. I'm lucky if she doesn't slam the door in my face next time."

"Give her time. Be patient. Try to see the world through her eyes. You've been used to getting what you want—and yes, I've spoiled you, no question. But this isn't something you can push or charm your way into. She's likely had to fight for every inch of her life, with nothing coming easy. Earning her trust—trust in you and in herself—will be a battle she has to wage inside. Don't make that harder for her."

"It sounds like you're speaking from experience," Ben said.

Mama Benard waved her spoon like a weapon. "Go on, get out of my kitchen." She swung again, and he caught her wrist, kissed her cheek, and bolted down the hall. Collapsing onto his bed, he loosened his tie, her words echoing in his mind. Maybe he had moved too fast with Florence—but Lord, she had a way of making a man lose his good sense. He had not relieved himself in far too long, and it was making it impossible to think straight. Perhaps tending to that before the trip would keep him from acting a fool around her.

Ben had been working out, trying to ease the tension coiling inside him, but it wasn't enough. Not anymore. The kiss had sent him reeling. It stirred something deep he could no longer ignore. Ben prided himself on his self-control, but right now, a trip to the gym would not satisfy the need gnawing at him.

He made his way to the bathroom and turned the water as cold as it would go. Maybe the chill would shock some sense into him. Stepping under the icy spray, he let it run down his overheated skin, but it only made him shudder—and not from the cold. His mind had already drifted elsewhere, lost in the thought of Florence.

He pictured her soft hands gliding over his abdomen. Her warm, sweet scent, with its hint of vanilla, wrapped around him. He could almost feel her lips against his, soft and eager, as he pressed her against the shower wall. Water would trail down every curve of her body, making her glisten, making him tremble with the effort of restraint.

Her lips would be swollen from his kisses, her breath ragged from his touch. He would whisper her name, pleading for her, needing her.

"Florence…"

His hand wrapped around himself, already throbbing and impatient, the fantasy consuming him. He imagined it was her touch, her fingers teasing him, driving him to madness. It had been too long, and his body was desperate. The pleasure coiled deep in his spine, his stomach tightening with the sensation.

He braced one hand against the shower wall. With the other, he thrust into his grip, breath ragged as he fought to contain his moans. The image of her—Florence beneath him, Florence wrapped around him—was too much.

A few more strokes and he was gone, his release stolen by the water as it washed away every trace of his longing. Chest heaving, he let his head fall forward, eyes shut against the rush of sensation.

It wasn't enough. It would never be enough.

***

"Uh, yes, ma'am, it should be under Benjamin Mayfield and Florence Witkins," Ben said, his tone firm yet polite.

The desk clerk checked her ledger, then looked up with a faint, puzzled smile. "Sir, we only have a reservation for one—Mr. Mayfield."

Florence's mouth fell open, and Ben's shoulders stiffened. Heat rose in him, not from embarrassment but from the certainty that this was no accident. Charlotte didn't make mistakes—certainly not two on the same booking. The suspicion that this had been done deliberately coiled tight in his gut.

Ben smoothed his expression. "Then please book another room for me immediately," he said evenly.

The clerk's gaze lingered a moment too long, her smile syrup-thick. When her eyes shifted to Florence, the warmth faded, replaced with a polite coolness that pushed her to the margins. The woman's glance skimmed over her as though she were a detail best ignored.

"I'm sorry, sir," the clerk replied, leaning forward just enough for the gesture to feel deliberate. "The only available room is the adjoining presidential suite. You requested that no one be placed beside you, so we assigned both rooms to you."

Ben noted how her fingers toyed with her pen, the subtle lowering of her lashes. It made her look desperate, even foolish. And, in truth, the arrangement suited him perfectly.

"That's fine, ma'am," he said smoothly. "I'll keep the room, and my partner can stay in the presidential suite."

Florence's lips parted as if to protest, but Ben was already collecting the keys. "Let's go," he said, a grin forming as they headed for the elevator.

Once on the top floor, he handed her the key. "You didn't have to share your block of rooms. I could've found another hotel."

"Don't be ridiculous. I need you nearby."

She blinked at him, startled. "So we can go over the case, of course," he added with a boyish grin.

Florence gave a slow nod. "Alright, then. I'll see you tomorrow."

She took the keys, her fingers brushing his for a moment too long, and stepped inside her room. Leaning against the door, heart racing, she asked herself: Was he Ben—the man who had shielded her more than once, who had just secured a suite for her—or was he Mr. Mayfield, the exacting boss she was meant to keep at arm's length?

She couldn't tell when the lines began to blur, but now they were tangled, and she wasn't sure she wanted to untangle them. Still, she reminded herself: *He is your boss.*

With a weary sigh meant to clear her head, she rolled her suitcase further in. The room was enormous, but all she could think about was the man next door.

The presidential suite radiated luxury: mid-century style fused with old New York charm. Plush, jewel-toned furnishings dominated the living area—a deep emerald velvet sofa flanked by two sleek armchairs in rich cognac leather. A marble coffee table held a crystal decanter of whiskey and matching tumblers. Gold-and-cream damask wallpaper reflected the soft gleam of ornate light fixtures suspended like art pieces.

A grand mahogany writing desk stood by the window, adorned with a gold-plated rotary phone and thick, leather-bound stationery bearing the hotel's insignia. Heavy champagne brocade drapes cascaded from ceiling to floor, framing the vast windows that looked out over Manhattan's sparkling skyline.

Beyond the sitting area, the bedroom was indulgence itself: a king-sized bed with a tufted headboard, crisp white linens, and a fur throw. A record player sat on a sleek console, with a stack of vinyl—Frank Sinatra, Ella Fitzgerald, jazz that perfectly captured the city's rhythm.

The en-suite bath was a study in opulence: black-and-white marble tiles, gold fixtures, a deep soaking tub large enough to swallow her whole. A silver tray held fine French soaps and crystal vials of lavender and vanilla perfume.

The suite whispered of power and old money. Every choice—every finish—spoke of a world where bourbon sealed deals and whispered conversations shaped futures. Florence traced her fingertips along the smooth mahogany desk, its surface cool and commanding. It was exquisite. Yet beneath the beauty, a tightness pressed in her chest. Rooms like this reminded her she was still a guest in a world that rarely made space for her.

After a quick shower, she flopped onto the bed. One problem: Sleep wouldn't come, not with Mr. Mayfield so close. Her mind kept replaying the kiss. She squeezed her legs together, exhaling softly into the pillow. It was going to be a long night.

By seven the next morning, Florence stepped out into the corridor to find Mr. Mayfield already waiting. He wore a charcoal three-piece suit with a silk tie, and for a heartbeat, she forgot to breathe. Her gaze skimmed over him before she could stop it—the vest framing his lean torso, the crisp sleeves hinting at strength beneath, the long legs commanding the space with ease. He looked as though he'd stepped straight from the pages of Esquire.

Before she could recover, he leaned in close.

"It wouldn't kill you to say something nice," he murmured near her ear. "From the way you've been looking at me, I can only assume you've found something worth admiring."

Florence lifted her chin, schooling her expression even as warmth crept up her neck. "You must be imagining things," she said, moving toward the elevator.

"You look quite lovely yourself this morning, Miss Witkins." He followed at her side.

Her sky-blue dress, paired with a matching cape coat and white pumps, made her every bit the polished professional, though the gloss on her lips and her high ponytail lent her a softer charm.

"Thank you for the compliment," she replied, stepping into the elevator—only for her heel to catch between the closing doors. She gasped, tugging at it as panic flickered across her face.

Before she could free herself, Ben caught her arm, pulling her back. He crouched, retrieving the trapped shoe with a frown as he noticed the scuff along its side.

"Thank you," she murmured, a little embarrassed. "They're the only pair I brought. I would've been stranded without them."

He gave the heel one last glance before handing it back. When the doors closed, he stepped closer, the elevator suddenly smaller. With one hand, he tilted her chin until their eyes met.

"Why have you been avoiding me, Miss Witkins?" His voice was low, edged with something she couldn't quite name.

"I—I haven't," she said quickly, though her voice betrayed her.

"Oh, but you have, darling," he countered, his palm resting lightly against the back of her neck, her new hairstyle giving him easy access.

"Mr. Mayfield…" she whispered, cheeks flushing. "What if someone comes in?"

He wanted to taste her lips—soft, full, maddeningly defiant. They cushioned every ounce of her stubbornness, daring him to tame it. But he held back. They were nearly at the lobby.

When the doors slid open, it was none other than James waiting. He raised an eyebrow, his expression catching the charge between them.

"How's it going, Ben… my lady," he said. Florence straightened quickly, still flushed.

"We're heading to breakfast before the meeting. Care to join us?" Ben asked.

"That'd be swell," James said. "Just give me a few minutes to drop my things."

"Sure thing. We'll wait," Ben replied.

When James left, Florence crossed her arms, fixing Ben with a slow, smoldering look—just enough pout to be dangerous.

"Yes, Miss Witkins? Something you'd like to say?" he teased.

"You never told me James was coming to the conference," she said, her lower lip jutting forward like a challenge.

"If you hadn't been giving me the cold shoulder, I could've told you," Ben replied, leaning into the challenge.

Florence gave a small, deliberate huff, tilting her head so her hair fell just so.

When James returned, she rose gracefully and took his arm, her defiance still evident. As they walked out, Ben laughed under his breath and shook his head.

As they stepped through the lobby doors, Ben leaned close, his breath warm against her ear.

"You can sass me all you like, darling… I've got the stamina to keep up."

The sound of silverware clinking on fine china echoed through the grand dining hall. Chandeliers cast a warm, golden glow over the elegantly dressed guests. Lawyers, politicians, and businessmen filled the room with their morning chatter over coffee and eggs Benedict. This lively backdrop set the stage for the quiet battle brewing at their small, private table.

Florence sat between Ben and James, her smile bright. She leaned a bit too close to James, laughing at something he said—laughter intended more to irritate Ben than to amuse herself. She didn't mind the curious stares from the men around her.

"James," she said, swirling her spoon in her coffee, "I've never been in such fine company this early."

She glanced at Ben. His face was unreadable as he cut into his toast with care.

James, ever the amused spectator, chuckled as he buttered his roll. "Is that so, Florence? And here I thought you were accustomed to men like Ben wining and dining you."

Ben didn't rise to the bait. He took a slow sip of his coffee, eyes scanning the dining hall as though the conversation held no interest for him. Florence brushed an invisible speck from James's sleeve and gave him a dazzling smile.

Ben finally spoke, his voice cool as the marble beneath their feet. "You're playing a dangerous game early in the morning, Miss Witkins."

She blinked at him, feigning innocence. "Whatever do you mean, Mr. Mayfield?"

James chuckled into his cup. "Oh, you know exactly what he means."

Florence huffed and took a small bite of her croissant. It frustrated her that her attempts to provoke Ben only made him smile with that infuriating calm. She wanted to unsettle him, to make him crack—but the man had the patience of a saint when it came to her antics. Still, Florence had no intention of giving up. She would see this through until Ben's fascination finally faded.

Ben, however, found this side of her almost endearing. She was spirited, almost playful.

By the time they reached the lawyer's conference, the

air between them carried a tension neither was ready to name. Inside, the hall buzzed with talk of politics, rulings, and the restless tide of civil unrest sweeping the nation.

Ben, immaculate in his three-piece suit, delivered his speeches with measured poise. Florence, attentive as ever, filled her notebook with neat, slanted script. James mingled effortlessly, laughing and shaking hands with practiced ease.

But Ben's thoughts drifted. The panels and debates blurred into background noise behind the weight of what lay ahead: networking rituals, false smiles, and the unspoken hierarchies among men who had known his father for decades.

The conference ended without incident, a small mercy. But the inevitable followed: an evening reception in the adjoining ballroom. Beneath the chandeliers, men in tailored suits lingered over bourbon and champagne, swapping favors and debts like currency. Ben played his role—shaking hands, nodding politely, enduring the echo of his father's presence in every corner.

Florence had been at James's side not long ago; now she was nowhere to be seen. Ben told himself she would return soon, yet his gaze kept flicking toward the entrance.

Then he saw him—Lance Davis—spinning his polished charm on his next mark. Tonight, that mark was Florence. Ben's shoulders stiffened. Lance, catching his eye, sauntered over to her with the same smug air that had made him intolerable since their school days.

"Well, well," he drawled, glancing at Florence before turning to Ben, who was already walking toward them, "didn't expect to see you here. And I certainly didn't expect you to bring someone so... stunning with you."

Florence blinked, startled, as Lance turned his full attention to her.

"You must be Miss Witkins," he said smoothly, taking her hand. "Ben always had an eye for the exceptional."

Ben's jaw tightened as Florence gave Lance a polite, wary smile. "You flatter me, Mr. Davis."

"Call me Lance," he insisted, holding her hand just a moment too long before she withdrew it.

Lance's laugh was low and knowing. "I must say, Miss Witkins, you don't seem the type to waste your time at these stiff legal gatherings. What exactly do you do for our dear Benjamin?"

Florence straightened, her chin lifting slightly. "I work with him," she replied evenly.

Ben's lips curved faintly. Pride—and something warmer—stirred in his chest.

If Lance noticed, he ignored it. He leaned in, his tone dropping to something slick and suggestive. "I can only imagine what that work involves."

Ben's hands flexed at his sides.

Florence's polite smile thinned, her body angling away. But Lance stepped closer, his fingers grazing her arm with deliberate disrespect.

"Some men," he murmured for her alone, "prefer their… companions to be seen, not heard. Kept out of sight, away from eyes that wouldn't understand."

The words dripped with implication—race, class, and the sort of cruelty whispered in corridors.

Without waiting for a response, he pressed his lips to her cheek and slipped a card into her hand. His room number sprawled across the back like a dare.

"What'd you bring her here for, if not to share?" Lance said, his eyes raking over Florence. "A colored girl like that—isn't she meant for all of us?" His laugh was sharp and ugly, drawing a few uneasy chuckles from nearby men.

Ben's jaw clenched until it ached.

That was enough.

The crack of his fist against Lance's jaw cut through the ballroom like a gunshot. Lance reeled, crashing into a passing waiter. Gasps erupted; champagne flutes shattered across marble.

Lance staggered upright, clutching his face. "Christ, Ben! Are you out of your mind?"

Ben loomed over him, fury burning in his eyes. "Disrespect her again, and you'll leave here on a stretcher." He struck him again, and before James—or someone else—could intervene, a strong hand seized his arm.

From the crowd, a sharp, commanding voice rang out. "Benjamin."

Ben turned. His father stood there, lips tight, eyes flashing. He stepped forward, shaking his head with cold disapproval.

"Do you have any idea how ridiculous you look?" his father hissed. "Lance's father is our largest client, and you're making a scene over..." He gestured dismissively toward Florence. "One of your office girls?"

Ben's nostrils flared. "She works with me."

His father's voice cracked like a whip. "Do you know what you've just done? In front of half the people who keep this family's name in business?"

The elder Mayfield stepped closer, looming like a shadow. "You think you can stomp around making scenes? You think our reputation is yours to gamble with? One day you'll learn this world runs on alliances and appearances, not emotions."

Ben stood tall, his voice sharp as glass. "I'm not apologizing."

His father's jaw clenched, the muscle twitching. "You will."

A heavy silence swept the room, broken only by the ripple of whispers. Florence stood frozen, her pulse hammering. The stares pressed in like a weight.

She couldn't stay. Not here. Not now. Turning, she left, her skirt brushing against her legs in frantic swishes.

Ben cursed and followed, calling her name as he reached the door. "Florence, wait!"

She didn't stop.

He caught her just outside, his hand closing around her wrist. She spun to face him, eyes blazing. "What the hell was that, Ben?"

His grip tightened slightly. "He touched you."

"And so you punched him? In front of everyone?" Her voice trembled between disbelief and anger.

"I don't regret it," Ben said quietly. "Not now, not ever. I'd do it again if it meant protecting you."

Florence searched his face. And in that moment, she saw it——this wasn't about Lance. It never had been.

CHAPTER 16:
MORE STIRRING

"Ben," Florence whispered, breathless, as they stood in front of his hotel room.

"We can't do this," she said, her voice shaky as she turned her head. Ben leaned in closer, his presence intense.

"I know," he admitted, his voice low and rough. "But I can't stay away from you. You're in every thought I have, the muse of every dream—whether I'm asleep or awake. Every choice I make now comes with the same question: How can I make her life easier? Even though you aren't mine yet… Florence, I want to give you the world."

"This world doesn't love me, Ben." Her hands pressed gently against his chest, barely resisting as he hovered over her. Ben's breath hitched, his expression flickering with hurt.

"Then I'll create a new world for you—a world where all you know is love," he vowed, his gaze unwavering.

Florence rolled her eyes, but as she looked away, Ben tilted her chin up and captured her lips in a searing kiss. For a moment, the world fell away.

"Are you crazy?" she gasped, cheeks flushed. "You can't do this out in the open."

"I'm crazy about you," he replied with a cheeky grin.

With a frustrated sigh, Florence snatched his keycard and slid it into the door. The room was nearly identical to hers, but somehow, it felt different. It smelled like him, warm and inviting, almost like a hug. She shook her head; someone had to be strong here, and it clearly wasn't going to be Ben. Florence had to get things under control.

"Ben, why can't I get rid of you?" she muttered, running her fingers through her hair. "You can't keep doing things like this—your reputation will suffer. You could put both of us in danger…"

Her words cut off with a sharp breath. Ben pulled her close from behind, kissing the sensitive skin of her neck. A deep groan rumbled in his chest as he kissed her, his hands gripping her waist.

"Why do you smell so good?" he murmured against her skin. "Your presence drives me insane. I can feel you even when you're not near me, and the slightest whiff of your scent makes me tremble."

Florence giggled. "Oh, does it?"

Ben pulled back enough to meet her gaze, his lips curling slowly. "What? Are you doubting me?"

"You're melodramatic," she teased.

Ben's eyes darkened with playful mischief as he began to tickle her. Florence squealed, trying to escape his embrace, laughter spilling from her lips.

"I'm sorry! I'm sorry! Please stop!" she pleaded between giggles.

She bolted, but Ben was faster. He caught her easily, lifted her over his shoulder, and tossed her onto the bed.

Florence's breath caught. This time, as their eyes met, something shifted. His gaze was desperate and full of restraint, as though he were holding back for her sake, afraid to scare her away.

But she didn't run.

Instead, she pulled him toward her, pressing her lips to his in a kiss that left no room for hesitation. She wrapped her arms around his neck and her legs around his waist, pulling him closer to feel his warmth, his need, everything he was.

For once, she didn't think about the consequences.

Ben deepened the kiss, his grip tightening as if she might slip away. They lingered in the kiss for what felt like forever. Lost in each other, Ben finally pulled away, breathing hard. His forehead rested against hers, his breath uneven.

He stared at her, uncertain. The realization of how desperately his hips pressed into hers sent a wave of embarrassment through him. Gritting his teeth, he tried to shift his weight off her, but every fiber of his being resisted the effort.

"We should stop… while I still can," he muttered, his voice thick with restraint.

Florence tilted her head, eyes dark and inviting—a silent challenge.

"Florence," he warned, his voice low, almost a growl. "Stop looking at me like that."

"Like what, Ben?" she teased, her tone soft, almost daring.

She followed him as he sat at the edge of the bed, wrapping her arms around his shoulders. She kissed the side of his neck, noticing his jaw clench and his muscles tighten. That didn't stop his cheeks from burning red.

Her hands slid down his chest, tracing the lines of his torso. But before she could go further, he caught her hands in his, stopping her.

"Florence," he murmured, his voice raw. "I don't want to disrespect you. I need you to know I'm not pursuing you for this." His thumb brushed over her knuckles, his grip firm but gentle. "If we do this, there's no going back. You will be mine—body and soul—and I will be yours. I'll crave you, need you, and worship at your altar."

Florence took a deep breath, her heart pounding in her ears.

Ben's eyes searched hers for reassurance. "If you want to wait until marriage, we can. You have every option with me. The world is yours—you begin and end with it." His voice dropped to a whisper. "I will never force you into anything. But right now, you're dancing on a very thin line."

His grip tightened. His control was slipping.

Florence smiled, her lips brushing his ear as she whispered, "I like dancing on the edge. It seems like you like it too." Her hand slid to the obvious bulge in his slacks.

Ben's eyes narrowed as he studied her. "When did you become so confident? A few months ago, you couldn't even make eye contact with me." His body moved on instinct.

Before Florence could respond, she was on her back, sinking into the plush pillow beneath her. A gasp left her lips as Ben hovered over her, his warmth pressing into her. His lips moved to her neck, trailing slow kisses down to her collarbone. Each kiss sent shivers through her body.

"I need you to tell me, sweetheart," he murmured against her skin. "I need to hear the words from your mouth."

Florence's only response was a soft moan, her head tilting back to grant him more access.

And then, he stopped.

Her eyes fluttered open in confusion. "Why did you stop?"

Ben chuckled, placing a feather-light kiss on her jaw. "I want to hear it."

She huffed, pouting as she turned her face away, her fingers curling into the sheets.

"Ben, I want… you to… you know," she mumbled, cheeks flushing. "Why must I say it?" she grumbled.

"Say it," he warned, a playful edge in his tone, "or I'll leave both of us very unhappy."

She sucked in a breath, biting her lip before finally whispering, "Ben… I want you to fuck me."

His eyes darkened, and a wicked grin spread across his face. "Such filthy words from such a sweet girl. I'll fuck you," he whispered in her ear.

Ben undressed her with a tenderness she couldn't quite describe. His hands moved with reverence, his touch giving her no time to overthink. He traced every curve, every mole of her body as if trying to engrave her into his memory.

He groaned when the last piece of clothing fell to the floor. His gaze lingered on her chest as he kissed and gently bit her skin. His big hands kneaded her breasts as though he couldn't decide which to worship first.

She pressed against him, helpless in her surrender.

"Beautiful," he murmured, his eyes fixed on her breasts.

To prove it, he took a nipple into his mouth, sucking gently. Florence gasped, her back arching, and Ben whimpered at the sight of her writhing beneath him. She moaned his name, fingers threading through his hair, making him purr.

He gave each one equal attention, his tongue and lips teasing and worshipping.

I'd love to fuck these tits too, he thought, his arousal throbbing for attention. With reluctance, he released her breasts and pressed soft kisses down her stomach, moving lower until he reached the spot he had longed to taste.

When he finally arrived, he paused, looking up at her one last time for confirmation. Florence met his gaze with the same intensity, granting him permission.

Ben parted her with his tongue, savoring her wetness as he drank her in. Delicious. He lingered there, his mouth working her until she trembled. Then his tongue flicked over the spot that made her body jolt—teasing, circling, tormenting her with slow strokes before quickening, faster, hungrier. Florence gasped and rose from the bed, unable to resist the storm he was pulling from her.

She buried her hands in his hair, pressing against him, craving more friction.

He cooed at her, his voice low and soothing. "I know, baby, I know."

She grew impatient, hands wandering downward, trying to take control, but Ben wasn't having it. With one hand, he caught both of her wrists, holding her still.

"Please, Ben," she whined, her voice trembling. "I need to…"

Focusing on her, he finally slid a finger inside, his jaw tightening at how her walls clenched around him.

Fuck, so tight.

His self-control wavered. He'd waited so long to have her, and he wanted to savor every second, but his body had other plans. He wanted to take her right then, to bury himself inside her heat and never leave. But he had promised to go slow, to worship her.

Forgive me. I know I said I'd go slow, but she's a goddess.

Florence adapted quickly. Soon, he added a second finger, curling them just so, finding the spot that made her hips jerk.

"Ben!" she cried out, her voice breaking.

He pressed deeper, his mouth humming against her, sending shivers through her core. Every vibration tore another gasp from her lips. His lips and tongue were drenched in her, and still he devoured her like he was starving. Her taste, her scent—she was the only drug he craved, and he was already addicted.

He switched from teasing licks to deep sucking. He latched onto her clit, making her moan louder than ever.

He let go of her wrists and used one hand to tease her nipple, the other pushing her closer to the edge.

He felt it when she began to tremble, the telltale signs of her climax building. The more she moaned, the harder he ground against the bed, desperate for relief.

"Ben, I can't… I'm going to…"

Florence gasped, her body tensing. "I'm—I'm going to…"

He locked eyes with her, watching her fall apart, and it was the most beautiful thing he had ever seen. A few more flicks of his tongue, and she shattered, crying out his name. It was the sweetest sound he had ever heard.

Her orgasm pulsed through her, and Ben didn't stop until every last tremor faded. Finally, he let out a satisfied hum, placed one last kiss between her folds, and moved back up her body.

"You're incredible," he murmured against her lips, his voice thick with need as he gazed down at her, flushed and breathless.

Florence matched his breathing, trying to recover from the most intense orgasm of her life.

As she caught her breath, she tried to pull Ben into a kiss, wrapping her legs around him, but he didn't move. Confused, she followed his gaze—only to see the unmistakable stain on his pants. A slow, teasing smile spread across her lips before laughter bubbled out of her.

"You came while eating me out?" she teased, arching a brow.

Ben groaned, burying his face in her neck. "I couldn't help it," he admitted, his voice tinged with embarrassment. Then, looking up with a faint blush, he added, "In my defense, it's been a long time. Honestly, just licking my neck might have been enough to undo me. Don't worry, I'll be hard again soon."

Florence giggled, though Ben wasn't entirely joking, which only made her laugh harder.

Still grinning, she began unbuttoning his shirt. With each button that popped open, his toned chest came into view. Broad shoulders, sculpted muscles—his body was made for strength and pleasure. She slid the shirt down his arms, her hands gliding over his torso. She kissed along his skin, delighting in how his body reacted to her touch. It didn't take long before his pants strained against him again.

Wanting to take care of him too, she unbuckled his belt, pressing soft kisses to his lips as she worked. Her fingers slipped under the waistband of his boxers, but before she could go further, he caught her hand.

"I'd love for you to touch every inch of me," he said, a blush creeping over his cheeks, "but I don't think I can last long like this." He kissed her hand, licked her palm, then removed the rest of his clothes.

When he stood bare before her, Florence's eyes widened.

There had to be some mistake. Weren't white guys supposed to be... small? So why was he so big?

Florence palmed his length, giving him a tender stroke. His entire body tensed as he hissed. *No way I can take him in my mouth*, she thought, licking her lips anyway.

Ben, however, wasn't having it. With a firm but gentle grip, he caught her ankle and pulled her back beneath him, pinning her in place.

"Don't worry, sweetheart. I don't expect you to. I'd rather be inside you," he murmured, pressing a reassuring kiss to her shoulder. "I'd never hurt you."

She wanted to call him a liar, but the tenderness in his voice steadied her nerves. His lips met hers again, his fingers sliding between her thighs, coaxing her body to ease. Ben kissed her neck, his tongue tracing the curve of her ear. He whispered, "I should've asked this earlier, but... is this your first time?"

"No, but it's been a few years," she admitted.

He nodded, taking his time with her. He praised her beauty, her body, and everything that made her Florence. His mouth closed around her breast again as he tried to distract her when he pushed inside.

The sensation was intense. Ben was hard, almost unyielding, but his gentle kisses and soft murmurs reassured her that he was being careful. His lips trembled against her skin as he moaned, feeling her wrap around him, the tightness sending a shudder through his body.

"God, baby," he panted. "You feel so good."

He was only halfway in, yet her body already clutched him like a vice. She writhed beneath him, discomfort and pleasure warring in her features, but he needed her to stay still. He pressed a hand to her stomach to steady her, then kissed her deeply. His other hand found the tender spot between her thighs.

Her moans climbed higher, her body beginning to yield

to the pleasure. Every muscle in Ben's body fought to hold back, to savor her, but she was unraveling him. As she finally relaxed and let him in, a mutual moan filled the air.

"My sweet Florence," he breathed against her neck, rolling his hips in slow, deliberate strokes.

"You feel so good," she whimpered, her brows drawn.

Ben cursed under his breath, determined to ease her tension. His lips trailed over her chest, kissing her breasts as his fingers worked their rhythm. He shifted his hips slightly, seeking the angle that would make her gasp—and when she did, clinging to him with nails pressed into his back, he didn't relent.

There it was.

He kept moving, focused entirely on her pleasure.

Florence moaned his name, her legs trembling as the sensation coiled tighter within her. Ben hooked her legs over his shoulders, his pace quickening as beads of sweat slid down his spine. His jaw clenched, his breath uneven.

"Florence, baby, I need you to cum for me," he rasped, his fingers and mouth relentless on her most sensitive places. They worked her over until she broke.

Her whole body tensed, then unraveled around him. Florence's eyes rolled back as she bit her lip, her body arching from the mattress. The sight nearly undid him. She clung to his neck as waves of pleasure overtook her, and that was enough—Ben gave in, his release tearing through him as he groaned her name into the hollow of her neck. He gave her everything, matching her rhythm with a few more slow thrusts before stilling, utterly spent.

His muscles finally eased. With a satisfied sigh, he lowered her legs, pressing a lingering kiss to her temple. When he pulled back, she was already slipping into sleep, her body spent and warm against his.

A lazy smile tugged at his lips. He rested his head on her chest, listening to the steady thrum of her heartbeat.

"Mine," he whispered, brushing her forehead with a kiss.

When his breathing evened out, he rose and went to the bathroom. He wet a towel with warm water, wrung it out, and returned to gently clean her before pulling the blanket over her. The sight of her, soft and bare beneath the sheets, stirred him again, but he shook the thought away. There would be time for that.

Snuggling beside her, he let his eyes close. Tomorrow, he'd show her around New York—unless the fiasco from yesterday called him back to the office. Either way, tomorrow could wait. Tonight, he was exactly where he wanted to be.

CHAPTER 17:
STIRRING THE CAULDRON

When Ben woke, he saw Florence breathing peacefully beside him. The blankets had slipped down her body, and the morning sun gave her skin a golden glow. She was beautiful. It was nearly eight, and as much as he loved watching her sleep, they needed to get up. Both needed a shower, and he had to face whatever mayhem awaited him.

He pressed soft kisses to her face and called her name, careful not to get too close; his morning breath was hardly pleasant. She stirred, stretching slowly before her eyes opened and found him watching her.

"Good morning," Florence murmured, her voice still heavy with sleep.

"Good morning, beautiful," Ben replied, his voice rough and deep—sexier than it had been last night, she thought.

"I ordered breakfast. I figured by the time we showered, it would be here," he said, kissing her forehead. "How are you feeling, love?"

"I'm… satisfied." Florence flushed deeply. "Thank you for asking. Well, I should go shower."

Ben pouted. "I thought we'd shower together."

"Why? So you can grope me a bit more?" she teased.

"As appealing as that sounds, sweetheart, I want to give you a little massage—make sure your body isn't too tense. I promise there won't be any funny business." He looked at her with pleading eyes.

Florence sighed, already suspecting she'd regret it. "Fine. Let me grab my shower cap. My hair is all sweated out from last night, and I didn't wear a scarf to sleep."

Ben tilted his head. "You need something over your hair to sleep?"

Florence nodded. "Any type of silk to cover my head, or silk pillowcases and sheets, works too."

He made a mental note. "Well, I don't have that. I'll get it for next time, but I do have shower caps," he said, kissing her cheek as she shielded herself with the sheets. "If there's anything else you need, just tell me. I'll get it for you."

With a mischievous grin, Ben tugged the sheet away. Florence yelped, her nakedness fully revealed.

"Ben." Her voice carried a warning.

"I know, I know. I wasn't going to try anything—I was just looking." He sighed. He would have loved to take her in the shower this morning, but the day ahead was already planned.

True to his word, he massaged her gently as the warm water cascaded over her, his lips brushing the marks he had left the night before. "My pretty girl," he whispered, his voice full of admiration. The affection was almost too much; it made her cheeks warm with embarrassment.

After the shower, Ben retrieved their breakfast. Florence, wrapped in a robe, gasped when he revealed the spread.

"Did you order the whole menu?" she asked.

"Well, I wasn't sure what you liked, so I got a variety," he replied.

Florence chose a bowl of fruit, pancakes, and bacon. Ben, his plate heavier with protein, watched her eat with a grin.

"You know we're going to have to talk about last night," she said.

"I know." He sipped his coffee. "Let me enjoy you to-day. We'll worry about the rest later, okay?" His smile was disarming.

Florence shook her head. "Okay."

"Before I can spend the day spoiling you, I need to meet with the board, my father, and James. I'm going to give you some cash. Explore the city if you like. I'd give you my card, but I don't want questions if someone challenges you while I'm not there. Cash is safer. Let's meet back here by three," Ben said, pulling on his shirt.

Florence stuffed another bite into her mouth. "What if I want to lie in bed all day?"

"I hope it's your bed, because I already called room service to change mine," he said with a smug grin. Florence would have thrown something at him if her hands weren't full.

He was back to his charming, slightly cocky self—and somehow, it was beginning to grow on her.

By the time she finished eating, Ben was dressed. She stood, ready to head to her room, but he caught her by the waist.

"Wow, not even a goodbye? No 'have a great day at work, babe'?" he teased.

"You'll manage," she shot back, her tone dry.

"I thought I handled that attitude last night," he murmured in her ear.

She wriggled free of his grip. "Go to work, pervert."

"Pervert? That's hurtful," he said, feigning offense.

He pulled out his wallet and left three thousand dollars on the desk.

She gasped. "I—I don't need that much money. Who could even spend this much in a day?"

"Even if you don't, keep it. Shop for whatever you want."

Ben kissed her one last time before leaving. Florence stood in the middle of his room, dumbfounded.

He must be nuts, she thought. *I've fallen for a crazy white man. This is the last time I listen to Denise.*

She returned to her own room to dress while he was gone, her mind spinning from the night before. A sigh escaped her. She realized she had dug herself into a deep hole.

***

When Ben reached the first floor, James was leaning against the wall, waiting for him. "Well, good morning, sunshine," James said with a chuckle. "You look like you slept well."

Ben kept a cool expression, though his face heated against his will. "What's the damage?" he asked, trying to change the subject.

"Oh, don't think I'll let you off so easily, Mr. Mayfield. But for now, I'll let it go. We have trouble coming. After you stormed out of the ball, you became the talk of the conference. Your father is upset, and the board members are confused about why you would stand up for a young colored woman."

Ben shot James a look.

"Their words, not mine. They want an apology, and the committee wants a meeting to assess your behavior. Your father also wants to chew you out."

Ben ran a hand through his hair. "Of course he does."

He planned to apologize to everyone else, but not to Lance. *I need to set aside my pride. If I want to take over the firm, I need the board's support. But Lance? He's lucky I'm holding back my anger. No, I'll apologize to him in front of everyone and deal with him later. Yes, that's the route I'll take.*

Ben and James left the hotel, heading toward the board meeting.

Later, Ben sat at the long mahogany table in the conference room, facing a panel of stern, disapproving faces: the firm's senior partners and leading lawyers of Mayfield Company. His father was among them, which only heightened the tension. The weight of his actions pressed down on him, and though he felt no regret, he understood the consequences.

He took a deep breath and stood, his voice calm and steady. "I owe each of you an apology," he began, scanning the room. "Not for my actions but for the burden they placed on this firm, for the shadow they cast over all of you."

Murmurs rippled through the room, but he continued.

"I have always believed in justice, in standing up for those who cannot defend themselves. That belief is what makes me one of the best lawyers among you. But beyond that, as a man, I protect those under my leadership. Miss Witkins works for me, and that alone warrants my intervention." His jaw tightened. "I will never stand idly by while someone abuses their power."

One of the older partners scoffed. "You're a lawyer, Ben, not a damn hero. Some things are bigger than your personal crusade. Your little stunt made our firm look like a group of nigger lovers."

Ben's eyes darkened. He wanted to lash out, but he needed to think of Florence. "If the firm doesn't support its employees—no matter their race—it may need to rethink its standards."

A heavy silence followed. His father still hadn't spoken, but Ben could feel his gaze burning into him. The real reckoning would come later.

***

As the meeting ended, James, who had been eavesdropping, fell into step beside him. "You sure know how to stir the pot," he said. "But I have to say, you look... different."

Ben exhaled, dragging a hand through his hair. "Different how?"

"Less tense," James said with a knowing look. "Lighter."

Ben shook his head, though a reluctant smile tugged at his mouth.

James's chuckle was low. "You finally cracked that case, huh?"

Ben shot him a warning glance, but James only grinned.

"Hey, man. I was talking about getting Florence to warm up to you. Didn't think you'd make her warmer than you planned."

Ben's smile faded. "It's not like that," he said after a pause, his voice softer now, almost vulnerable. "I love her. I want to give her everything."

The humor drained from James's face. His expression turned serious. "That's not how this world works, Ben. The moment you claim her as yours, nobody's going to care about your name, your title, any of it. The man you are to-day—that man won't exist anymore. You know that, don't you?"

Ben nodded. "I know. That's why I have to give her the world before they try to strip it from us."

James sighed, rubbing the back of his neck. "They won't accept it, Ben. Not your father's name. Not your money. Not even what you've built. They'll shut you out."

Ben held his gaze, steady. "Then I'll build something new. Stronger. I'll take this firm from my father and place it in her hands, as my wedding gift."

James let out a long, low whistle. "You really don't do anything halfway, do you?"

Ben only smiled.

James shook his head, the weight of his words lingering. "Good luck, brother."

***

The private meeting with his father was inevitable. As Ben entered the hotel room, he barely had time to close the door before an ornate paperweight flew at him. He dodged, but not fast enough. The sharp corner clipped his brow, and a warm trickle of blood slid down the side of his face.

"You ungrateful little bastard!" his father roared. "I built this firm from the ground up, and you've thrown it away for some nigger girl?"

Ben clenched his fists but stayed calm. He knew any reply would only make things worse. His father sneered, pacing behind his desk. "You think this is about love? About some goddamn romance? This is about your future, about everything I handed you on a silver platter!"

Ben wiped the blood from his brow, his voice cold and even. "If my future means standing by while men like Lance do as they please, then I don't want it."

His father slammed his fist against the desk. "If this gets in the way of the case, I will fire you. Do you hear me? You may be my son, but I won't hesitate to cut you loose. From now on, I will have eyes on you in this firm. Tread carefully."

Ben didn't flinch. "If you're done, I have somewhere to be."

His father's face twisted in disgust. "Get out."

Still seething, Ben left the office, his pulse hammering in his ears. As he walked down the hall, he spotted Lance lingering near the elevators, smug as ever.

Ben strode up to him, standing close enough to make him flinch. "If you ever put your hands on Florence again, I will bury you and your father."

Ben was aware of the consequences his words would have, but when it came to Florence, he didn't seem to care.

Lance's smirk faltered.

Ben leaned in, voice low and steady. "And trust me, no one will come looking for either of you."

Lance swallowed hard, but before he could respond, Ben turned and walked away.

***

Ben had been missing Florence all day. He was willing to take the verbal beating and the harsh stares if it meant that, at the end of the day, she would be waiting for him.

Back at the hotel, Florence stood in front of the mirror. She adjusted her dress, a faint excitement buzzing under her skin. Tonight would be special. Ben had promised to show her around New York, and James would join them.

But when the door opened and she turned to greet him, her smile faded. His shirt hung open at the collar, sleeves rolled up, and a thin line of dried blood trailed from his brow.

"Ben," she gasped, hurrying toward him. "What happened?"

He caught her hand, pressing a kiss to her palm. "Nothing that matters."

She frowned, unconvinced. "Ben…"

He silenced her with a soft kiss, pulling her into his arms. "Tonight is for us to relax. I don't want to worry about anyone else," he murmured. "I promised you a night out, and I intend to keep that promise."

Florence studied his face, searching for the truth behind his words. Finally, she sighed and rested her forehead against his. "Alright. But you're telling me everything later."

He chuckled. "I wouldn't dare keep anything from you."

Ben sat on the edge of the hotel desk, one arm braced behind him, the other resting in his lap. They were about to head out, but Florence insisted on cleaning his wound. He thought it would be good practice for when he made her his wife. Besides, being doted on by such a beautiful woman was no punishment.

A fresh cut ran across his right eyebrow. He winced as Florence dabbed at it with a damp cloth, the sharp scent of antiseptic filling the air between them.

"You're lucky this isn't worse," she muttered, pressing a little harder than necessary.

Ben sucked in a sharp breath. "Ah, gentle, sweetheart. Are you trying to fix me up or finish me off?"

She didn't meet his eyes. "If you told me what happened, I wouldn't be so rough. And if you stopped getting into fights, I wouldn't be patching you up now."

His grin turned her scolding into a game. "You're cute when you scold me," he said, pouting slightly. "This time it really wasn't my fault. Honest."

Florence shot him a look. "Ben."

"What?" he drawled, lips tilting into a smile. "You're so close. It smells nice, all warm and…"

Her hand landed flat against his chest, pushing him back. "You're bleeding."

He shrugged, unfazed. "And yet, I'm still in the mood to misbehave."

She let out a dramatic sigh and reached for the bandage. "I swear, you're impossible."

"The word you're looking for is charming."

She ignored him, peeling open the small gauze pad. She leaned in to cover the cut. His hands found her waist, fingers tracing slow circles along her dress.

"Benjamin."

"Yes, ma'am?"

"Keep your hands to yourself."

He tsked, shook his head, but obeyed.

Florence pressed the bandage down firmly, making him flinch. "I'm glad to see you can behave when you're told."

Ben huffed a soft laugh. "I'll do anything you tell me," he said, looking up at her with wide, innocent eyes.

Florence would have swatted him if he weren't already bleeding. "Mr. Mayfield, I do believe you're close to earning another wound if you don't stop."

His eyes dropped to her lips. "You sure you don't want to kiss it better?"

She rolled her eyes, sitting back with her arms crossed. "I should have let you bleed."

She stared at him for a long moment, then, shaking her head, patted his cheek—right next to the wound.

Ben yelped. "Oof. Florence!"

"That's what you get," she said, standing up and brushing off her hands. "Now, keep that bandage on and stay out of trouble."

After collecting her things, she leaned down and gave

Ben a quick kiss on the cheek.

Ben watched her walk away, her hips swaying with a rhythm that stole his breath. He shook his head with a grin. "God, you're going to ruin me in the best way."

They finally made it out of the hotel. The neon lights of Times Square flickered against the wet pavement. Florence, James, and Ben walked down the crowded street, blending into the restless energy of New York City. The air smelled of roasted peanuts, exhaust fumes, and the promise of adventure.

The night was cold, and though Florence looked stunning, she was shivering. Ben draped his jacket over her shoulders. He took her hand, but she pulled back quickly, glancing at James with unease.

Ben noticed her hesitation, but rather than address it, he pressed on. As Florence walked ahead, James and Ben exchanged knowing looks.

"Where would you like to go for dinner this evening, pretty girl?" Ben asked smoothly.

Before she could answer, he leaned closer, his breath brushing her ear. But Florence pushed him back with a firm hand against his chest.

"Ben, stop." Her voice held an edge, and her eyes darted toward James. "What are you doing? Why are you acting this way out here?" she muttered, giving him a sharp look that meant business.

James, walking beside them, finally stopped and let out a small sigh.

"Florence, it's fine," James said calmly.

She turned to him, guilt written all over her face.

"James, it's not like that... I'm so sorry. It happened suddenly, but Ben shouldn't act this way in public," she scolded. "What if someone reports you? And James, I should have told you..."

James waved a hand, cutting her off with a wry smile. "It would never have worked out anyway."

Florence's brow furrowed. "What do you mean?"

James shifted his weight. In a rare moment of honesty, he said, "I've always liked people who look like Ben."

Florence's mouth fell open. "You mean you like white women?" she asked, tilting her head.

Ben burst out laughing. "Not quite, darling," he said, shaking his head.

She turned to Ben, who gave a small, knowing nod before letting out another laugh. "Oh, come on, sweetheart. I thought you were sharper than that."

Florence looked between them for a second. "Ohhh, you mean…" She blushed at her own misunderstanding.

The tension broke, and Florence let out a stunned chuckle. "I can't believe this."

James shrugged, hands in his pockets. "Guess we both have some secrets."

The rest of the evening passed with light conversation, street hot dogs, and easy laughter. James watched Ben the whole time, noticing how his eyes rarely left Florence. It made him smile.

As the night deepened, Ben's persistence returned. He turned to Florence as they strolled back toward the hotel.

"You know," he began, "there's no reason we can't be together, Florence."

Florence rolled her eyes. "Ben, you're moving too fast, and let's be realistic. A colored woman and a white man, in this country, in this era? It's impossible. It's asking for trouble."

"Impossible?" he scoffed. "Florence Witkins, I don't believe that word exists in your vocabulary."

She sighed. "It's reality."

"Why are you so against us, Miss Witkins?" he asked quietly. His heart ached a little at her resistance.

"Because I know the consequences of the choice you're making, Ben," Florence replied.

Ben grinned. "Fine. You want reality? Let's debate this properly."

Florence raised a brow. "Debate?"

"Like lawyers."

James chuckled. "Oh, this I have to see."

Back in the hotel room, they set up their makeshift courtroom. James, the senior partner, took his seat as the judge behind the small writing desk, exuding authority. Ben, a senior partner and Florence's superior at the firm, announced he would lead the prosecution. Florence, the determined associate, acted as her own defense.

James cleared his throat with mock gravity. "Court is now in session. The matter before us: whether a colored woman and a white man can truly stand as partners in 1968."

Florence stood tall, her voice firm. "Your Honor, the simple truth is that society does not accept couples like us. We would face discrimination, hostility, even danger. People would judge me; they would target me. Our lives would not be easy. It would not only change my life but also the lives of my partners. It may be legal now, but it is still not accepted."

Ben paced like an attorney before a jury, his expression sincere. "But, Your Honor, love has never been easy. If we give in to fear, to what society expects, then what's the point of anything? Shouldn't we be the ones to decide our future?"

Florence folded her arms. "And what about children? Mixed-race kids, stuck between two worlds, never fully belonging to either?"

Ben stopped and turned to her, softening. "Or they could belong to both."

Florence exhaled. "And do you believe society would let them? This isn't about you and me, Ben. This is about the world we would be bringing them into."

Ben leaned back slightly, a faint smile tugging at the corner of his lips. "Do you know who the best attorneys are?"

Florence shook her head.

"The ones who don't have to take their case to trial,"

he said, eyes locking on hers. "They settle things before it ever gets messy, because they know the evidence, they know the strategy—and they know when to fight and when to protect what matters most."

He leaned closer, lowering his voice. "For us... for you, Florence, I wouldn't just hold a trial. I'd argue every point, precedent every piece of evidence, examine every angle—and if necessary, appeal, retrial, whatever it takes... because you're worth every motion, every objection, every step of the process."

For a moment, they forgot James was there, completely caught up in their own argument. James cleared his throat, hands raised. "Okay, settle down, attorneys."

Ben gave a wry shrug, then turned back to her, serious again. "Even though the world might see us differently it doesn't change the merits of our case. And right now, Florence, I am arguing, in every way that counts, that we deserve a verdict together."

Ben's lips curled into a sly smile. "Or is the real question whether Miss Witkins does not want a white man as her husband at all?"

A silence fell over the room as James tapped his fingers against the desk. "Counsel raises an interesting point," he mused. "Miss Witkins, is your opposition based on societal constraints or personal preference?"

Florence hesitated, the weight of the question sinking in. "I don't know," she finally admitted. "It's both."

James leaned back, considering the arguments. "I have to say, this is a compelling case."

Florence sighed, rubbing her temples. "Ben, you make everything sound so easy."

Ben tilted his head. "And you make everything sound so hard. It's okay to want something different... something scary... to want me."

They stared at each other for a moment before James finally stood. "Court is adjourned."

Ben clapped his hands together. "Great! That means I

win."

Florence huffed. "You did not win."

James shook his head with a grin. "I'm not sure there's a winner in this case. Just two very stubborn people."

Ben leaned in toward Florence. "Which means this discussion is… ongoing?"

She let out a soft laugh. "Yeah, I suppose it is. But not tonight. I would like to sleep before our flight tomorrow."

"Are you sleeping with me tonight?" Ben asked, looking a little unsure.

"Yes, as long as you only plan on sleeping," she said. Florence pressed a soft kiss against his lips. Ben tried to deepen the kiss, but Florence refused with James still around.

***

They all returned to their hotels, the day finally coming to an end.

Florence showered, then Ben did. When she finished lotioning her body, she found Ben staring appreciatively. She asked him to look in her suitcase and hand her the bonnet she had brought. When he opened her bag to find it, he noticed more than just a bonnet. Ben let out a chuckle and a tsk.

"Miss Witkins, what, pray tell, is this piece of clothing—or should I say, this lack thereof?" he teased.

Florence's jaw dropped when she saw the sheer lingerie in her suitcase. "T-That's not mine," she said hurriedly. *Ugh, I will have to kill Denise.*

"Did you plan on wearing this for someone else or for me?" he asked, his eyes darkening.

"Neither!" she retorted.

"Get my bonnet and come back," she said, now embarrassed.

He grabbed her bonnet, and she put it on, rolling away from him, but Ben would have none of it. "Florence," he pleaded, kissing her shoulder, "will you wear it for me sometime?"

"Not in your lifetime," Florence responded, making Ben chuckle before they both drifted off to sleep.

CHAPTER 18:
CAULDRON OF WITCHES
BREW

When Ben and Florence returned home, it felt as though their trip had been erased, as if it had never happened at all. Ben threw himself into work, leaving Florence to navigate the days alone. That gave Charlotte free rein to target her. This time, when Florence walked through the door, Charlotte's disdain was sharper than usual—palpable, almost deliberate.

"How was the trip? I hope nothing went wrong," Charlotte said, her tone almost gleeful.

"Everything turned out fine. Thank you for asking," Florence replied.

Charlotte, clearly dissatisfied, stomped away in a huff. The truth was, she had orchestrated the airplane seat fiasco and the trouble at the hotel, yet her schemes had backfired—everything had unfolded in Florence's favor.

Ben hadn't spoken to Florence since their return. His case consumed every hour. Soft light glowed over stacks of legal papers spread across the polished mahogany table. Ben sat at its head, sleeves rolled and tie loosened, his sharp eyes scanning the pages as if daring them to hold a mistake. This case could make or break him, and he intended for it to be the former. There was no room for errors.

"No, no, no!" His voice cut through the room like a

whip. He slammed a file shut and glared at the young paralegal standing stiffly at the far end of the table. "You didn't verify the employer's records with the state labor board? Do you understand what that omission could do to our case? Without that verification, we're left with nothing but circumstantial evidence!"

The paralegal flinched, their face pale. "I—I thought the documentation was enough…"

"You thought?" Ben scoffed, shaking his head. "Next time, don't think—know. We can't afford sloppy work." He rubbed his temples, the strain showing as his temper flared.

Florence watched quietly, lips pressed together. She had seen this side of Ben before: cold, demanding, relentless. Everyone resented him when he was in this mode. Whispers trailed through the office whenever his long hours stretched on.

"God, I hate working with him when he's like this," one associate murmured near the doorway.

"You'd think he was the only one losing sleep over this case," another replied. "If he snaps at me one more time, I'm filing a complaint."

Florence sat still, her expression unreadable. She reminded herself it wasn't her problem. Ben was a fling she had in another state—nothing more. At least, that was what she told herself.

***

Ben exhaled sharply and leaned back in his chair. "Let's take five," he muttered. The room cleared quickly, everyone eager to escape his presence. As Florence gathered her papers, she hesitated. For a moment, she considered saying something—anything—to acknowledge the weight he carried.

Weeks passed, and her concern grew, though she hated to admit it. Ben wasn't eating well, barely slept, and pushed himself to the brink. One evening, when he was still at his office, Florence stayed late too. She had found something in an old case file that could change everything.

Clutching the folder, she knocked on his office door. The desk lamp cast long shadows of his hunched figure on the glass walls.

"What?" he called, his voice rough with exhaustion.

"I found something," she said, placing the folder on his desk. "I was cross-referencing internal memos with hiring records, and I came across this."

Ben rubbed his eyes and opened the folder. By the third page, his jaw had tightened. At the last, he froze: a typed directive from 1967, blunt and deliberate—"Filter out certain candidates without drawing attention." He exhaled, the breath heavy in his chest.

"This…" he murmured, flipping through the pages again. "This could be it."

Florence nodded. "And that's not all. I found references to *Henderson v. United States* in an old case file. That case proved that so-called 'separate but equal' policies were discriminatory. Henderson wasn't allowed in the train's dining car. The policy appeared neutral, but its purpose was to exclude colored passengers. The Supreme Court ruled it was a violation of federal law."

Ben frowned, intrigued. "And you think we can use that here?"

"Yes," Florence said, pointing to a marked page. "The company's internal policy mirrors the same logic. They claim neutrality, but the system was designed to keep certain people out. If we cite Henderson, we can argue precedent is already on our side. This isn't just unethical—it's illegal."

Ben set the papers down and pressed his fingers to his temples. "Good work, Miss Witkins."

For a moment, the weight of it hung between them. Then, as if snapped awake, Ben grabbed a pen. "We need to draft a motion tonight. This goes before the judge first thing tomorrow. We're not just building a case anymore, Florence—we're about to dismantle theirs."

Florence allowed herself the smallest smile. "I thought you'd say that."

The office was empty now. Florence was about to leave when Ben caught her arm and pulled her close, his hands settling at her waist.

"What are you doing? What if someone sees?" she gasped.

"Everyone's gone," he murmured, his voice rough with fatigue. "Please... let me stay like this. I'm sorry I've neglected you. That's no excuse, I—"

"You don't have to apologize. We're not in a relationship. It was just a fling."

Ben's arms tightened around her. "Don't provoke me with that word."

She yelped softly as his hands held her firmly.

"I've been unclear, and I've been too consumed with this case," he admitted. "I don't know what gave you the idea this was only a fling, but I can show you it's far more than that, my love."

She shifted, trying to pull away, but his grip stayed firm.

"I'm not done memorizing you," he murmured with a mischievous glint.

Her eyes widened.

He laughed softly. "I meant your face... beautiful."

"Every move I've made has been to protect you, Florence," he said. It was true—his father had threatened them both, and Ben had been maneuvering ever since. The focus that consumed him had kept her safe, even as it kept them apart.

His words sent a chill through her. His hands brushed her thighs, his breath warm at her neck.

"You should go home and rest," she whispered, trying to break the moment.

"But I've missed you. I'm sorry."

His mumbling continued, barely coherent, his exhaustion showing.

Florence studied him. The green in his eyes was dulled by dark circles. His skin had lost its glow. She tried to remind herself this wasn't her burden.

"I'll make it up to you," Ben said quietly. "Do you have plans this weekend?"

"Not really," she answered.

"Good. Then let me take the lead for our first real date—if you'll allow me, pretty girl."

She blushed. "What could we possibly do out in the open?"

"Don't worry about that. I'd never put you in harm's way. Just trust me," he said, a faint smile tugging at his lips.

"Fine," she said, shaking her head. "Can we go home now?"

His first genuine smile in weeks appeared. "Wait—one more thing."

Before she could ask, he pulled her in, kissing her deeply. One hand cupped the back of her neck, the other traced slow circles at the small of her back. Florence swayed into him.

"I need more of you," Ben whispered against her shoulder.

"Of course. Your bed is feeling lonely, hm?" she teased.

"I'm lonely without you, no matter where I am. I don't just want your touch. I want your thoughts, your time… you."

She stood on her toes and kissed him lightly, just enough for him to chase her lips again.

"No," she said, wagging her finger. "We need to go. I don't want to drive home in the dark."

He reluctantly let her go and followed her to the elevator, carrying her purse and lunch pail. When he reached for her hand, she didn't pull away.

"I never thanked you, Ben."

"For what?"

"For the new fridges on every floor," she said, watching him carefully.

He cleared his throat. "Oh, that wasn't me. The firm—" He stopped when he caught her look.

"Well, I couldn't let you keep going down to that basement. I should've fixed it sooner." He kissed her hand gently.

"I'll thank you properly this weekend," she replied.

The elevator chimed, and they stepped out.

"I'll walk you to your car, ma'am," Ben said, kissing her cheek. The lot was empty as usual. He opened her door, tucked her things in the back seat, and pressed a kiss to her forehead.

"Get home safe," he murmured.

When Ben got home, Mama Benard wasted no time teasing him.

"I told ya to take it slow in New York," she said, smacking him lightly with a cooking spoon.

"Ow!" he grunted. "I tried, but things just… happened."

She grimaced. "Well, now that you've gone and startled the poor girl, when are you bringing her over?"

"Fine. If you promise not to embarrass me."

"Embarrass ya? I don't have to. You do enough of that yourself."

Ben sighed, finishing his dinner. "Thank you, Mama Benard," he said, kissing her cheek. "I'll bring her to meet you when the time is right—and when she wants to."

Mama Benard nodded and turned back to the dishes.

***

The rest of the week passed quickly, and Florence found herself nervous about their first date.

"Miss Witkins," Ben's voice finally reached her.

"I apologize, sir. What did you ask?"

"I asked what has you thinking so heavily over there."

"I was wondering what to wear for our date. I only have one pair of heels, and I'm not sure where you're taking me, so I don't know how to dress."

"Don't worry about that," Ben said, setting his book aside and fixing his gaze on her. "You look beautiful in anything."

Florence blushed.

"Close the door," he said, his tone unreadable. A small wave of nerves crept up her spine, but she did as he asked.

When she stepped closer, he kissed her, softer this time. His lips were light as feathers, a stark contrast to the usual urgency in his kisses. It was as though he were savoring the moment.

"Aren't we supposed to be working?" she scolded.

Ben laughed, rich and amused. "Way to ruin the romance." He reached behind his desk, retrieving a sleek box and placing it between them. "Actually, I called you in here for this."

Florence hesitated, then lifted the lid. Inside lay a stunning black cocktail dress that shimmered under the office light, its fabric clearly expensive. Beneath it, wrapped in soft tissue paper, was a pair of designer heels—straight out of a fashion magazine. She recognized both labels immediately, each a luxury brand.

"Ben, no. I can't accept this." She stepped back as though distance could strengthen her resolve. "It's too much."

Ben shrugged, unfazed. "You should have more than one pair of heels, Florence." His tone was casual, but his eyes held intensity. "And before you start arguing, I don't care what you wear. You could walk in here in a paper bag, and I'd still think you're the most beautiful woman in the room."

Her lips parted, but he continued.

"I didn't want you worrying or feeling that what you had wasn't enough. So, I picked these up for you." He produced a string of real pearls. "Now, this one might be a little overboard."

Florence's mouth dropped open. Ben stepped closer, his voice softening. "Please accept them. Don't say it's too much, because for me, it isn't enough."

Florence sighed. "You know I can never repay you for

this. Not in this lifetime."

Ben chuckled. "You can repay me by wearing it."

"Do you think you can buy my love?" she teased.

He shook his head, a small smile tugging at his lips. "No, Florence. I don't want to buy your love. I want to earn it." His voice grew warm. "I'll earn it by hearing you, even when you don't say much at all. By noticing what you need before you have to ask, and doing the little things that make your days easier. I'll hold you when the world feels heavy, until you remember you're not carrying it alone. I'll tell you, again and again, how much you mean to me—because you'll never have to guess. And most of all… I'll show up, every single time. Not just when it's easy but when it's hard, when it's quiet, when it's forever. The gifts are just a bonus."

It was true. Ben seemed to know what she needed without her saying a word. It felt good. Florence had never been spoiled before, not like this. The gesture unsettled her, but he had gone to such lengths that refusing felt almost ungrateful.

She accepted the gifts, asking if Ben could bring them to her car before they left.

That evening, she twirled in her living room, wearing the dress, the heels, and the pearls. It all felt too grand for her, yet their beauty silenced the doubt whispering in her mind.

Saturday arrived, and the night began. Ben came to pick her up, but he couldn't drive his usual car into her neighborhood—it would draw too much attention. He chose one of his "normal" ones, though even that was a little extravagant.

When she opened the door, Ben stood waiting, his jaw slackening at the sight of her. Florence was the picture of elegance: her hair cascading over her shoulders, her legs long and poised in the heels, her curves tracing the dress as though it had been made for her. Ben silently thanked his shopper.

As she stepped out, he tried to peek inside her house,

but she gently pushed him back.

"Why can't I see your home?" he asked, feigning a pout.

"Another time. It's messy," she said briskly.

He opened the car door for her, buckling her in.

"Will you finally tell me where we're going?"

Ben smiled. "You wouldn't know it even if I said the name."

"Oh, right—because I don't frequent the fancy places you do?"

"No," he said, pausing. "Because this place is… how shall I put it… a secret."

The car fell into a comfortable quiet. Florence bit her lip, and the small motion tightened something in Ben's chest.

She was so at ease she eventually drifted off. When they arrived, Ben opened her door, brushing his lips lightly against her face until she stirred.

"Hello, sleeping beauty. We've arrived," he murmured with a genuine smile.

Florence smiled back. "I'm sorry, I must have dozed off."

"It's all right. I'm glad you feel comfortable enough to."

She gazed at him, dreamy-eyed. "You look very handsome tonight."

He offered his hand, helping her out of the car.

"This is where we're eating?" she asked, frowning at the empty parking lot. *Oh no, has he brought me here to kill me and dump my body?*

She stiffened.

"Relax, my dear. I'm not here to kill you," Ben chuckled. "I thought if we went to a normal restaurant, some fool might seat us apart, or we'd have to endure stares. I didn't want that. So I brought you somewhere better—a place where we can sit together, where I can admire you without interruption."

Florence giggled and let him lead her. "How did you find this place?"

After a pause, her eyes widened. "No… you own this place?"

"Guilty," he said with a soft laugh. "It hasn't opened yet. There's been… resistance, because I intend to keep it desegregated. But the chef agreed to cook for us tonight."

Florence was speechless as he led her inside. The dining room was dimly lit, a few candles flickering on an elegantly set table for two.

"Ben," she whispered, "this is… beautiful."

He squeezed her hand, pulling out her chair. "I wanted tonight to be special."

They talked easily as they ate. Florence was surprised at how natural it felt—how easy it was to laugh with him, how closely he listened.

"So, tell me," she said after a sip of wine, "why did you become a lawyer?"

Ben exhaled, tracing the rim of his glass. "I was trained for it. My father was a lawyer. I resented him, but law was all I knew. It was either follow that path or be lost, and I wasn't prepared to be lost." His green eyes flicked to hers. "Turns out, I'm good at it. Even if I hate parts of it."

"And you?" he asked. "What made you choose law?"

"My school was segregated until I left for college, so my opportunities were limited. I saw how my mother lived, how harsh the world could be, and I wanted more. I didn't want to be barefoot and pregnant. I wanted my own choices. Plus, my father said I had a knack for arguing." Florence laughed softly.

"That you do, Miss Witkins," Ben teased. "What made you move here?"

She hesitated, eyes on her plate. "My mother. My father left us, and I knew if I stayed in Oklahoma, I'd never become more than what the world allowed. I wanted more than scraping by and being taken care of. I wanted a life where I could dream beyond survival."

Ben reached across the table, covering her hand with his.

"Ben... I need to say this." Her voice faltered. "I'm scared. Scared to be loved by you. By... you know."

He said nothing, letting her continue.

"Nobody respects colored women. White men see us as trophies or as something to use. Colored men don't see us as equals either. They see us as mothers, caretakers—but not as partners. I've never been just a woman in someone's eyes, Ben."

His grip tightened. "You are to me, Florence. You can be whatever you want with me. I'll shape a world where you can be yourself."

"That was very corny," she chuckled, but her fingers stayed in his.

"Why are you pursuing this—us—knowing how hard it will be?"

"Because you're worth it. Worth being pursued, loved, and cherished. You don't have to earn that. It's what you deserve. You make me want to fight harder. And because I can't imagine looking at anyone else."

Her eyes flickered with emotion.

"I don't mean to push," he said gently, "but you brought it up earlier. Do you want children?"

Florence let out a soft, almost bitter laugh. "One day. But not now. I want a career. I want more."

"Then that's what you should have," Ben said, with admiration in his voice.

He brushed her cheek with his thumb. "I don't care what the world expects of you. I care about what you want."

Tears pricked her eyes, but she blinked them away with a small smile.

The night unfolded with laughter, whispered truths, and quiet glances. For the first time in a long while, Florence felt seen. And for the first time, she let herself believe she could be loved, too.

"Florence, if you're not too tired, I know a place with

the best desserts."

"Sure."

Ben was elated. The evening had gone perfectly. But as he drove, Florence grew puzzled.

"Ben, this is your house!"

"Don't panic," he soothed, rubbing her wrist. "My mother made dessert for us, and she's eager to meet you."

"Ben, you can't spring your mother on me on our first date!"

"It's not my parents, just my mother—and technically, she's my adoptive mother."

"You were adopted?"

Ben chuckled. "Come in, and you'll see."

***

While Ben and Florence enjoyed their night, on the other side of town, Charlotte paced her bedroom floor. Her anger simmered as the memory replayed in her mind.

It had been an exhausting week, but she had stayed late, determined to get ahead on work. She assumed the building was empty until she heard Mr. Mayfield's voice. Just as she was about to step into the room, she saw them.

Florence sat on Ben's lap, her arm draped casually around his shoulders. Their voices were low, their smiles warm and intimate. The look he gave her—like she was something rare and treasured—made Charlotte's stomach knot with fury.

Charlotte's breath grew sharp and shallow. Peering through the narrow crack of the office door, she froze. How could he possibly be interested in a woman like her? She barely managed to retreat into the shadows, unnoticed.

Her fists tightened at her sides as she slipped away, rage churning in her chest. She must be trying to sleep her way to the top. There was no other explanation. Ben was intelligent, powerful; a man like him would not choose someone like that unless he was being manipulated.

Charlotte stalked down the hall, her mind racing. This

had to stop.

Then fate handed her a chance. She remembered that Ben's father had asked her just a week before to keep an eye on him, to watch that girl and report anything useful.

A slow, calculated smile spread across her lips. This would certainly be useful.

She stepped into her home office and shut the door behind her. Snatching the phone, her fingers trembled with barely restrained fury. The line rang once, twice, before a deep, commanding voice answered.

"Mayfield speaking."

Charlotte drew in a steadying breath. "Sir, I thought you should know…"

Her tone was cool, deliberate now. But beneath it, jealousy and a dark satisfaction coiled tight. She was going to end this—one way or another.

CHAPTER 19:
BREW THE TEST

When Florence stepped into Ben's house, her entire body trembled. His family would never accept a colored woman at his side, and she hadn't even spoken to him about what they were—or if they were anything at all.

Ben squeezed her hand and guided her toward the stairs.

"Wait," she whispered, pulling back. Her voice quivered. "Ben, are you sure? Your family… they're rich, white, and proud. They won't want you with me. I'm just—" she faltered "—a colored girl from Oklahoma. My folks work in a factory."

Ben turned to face her, a soft smile tugging at his lips. "Florence, stop," he said, his voice low and steady. "I'm a grown man. I don't need their permission. And you're not 'just' anything. You're… you."

She tried to argue, but he lifted her hand and kissed it lightly. "Besides," he added with a glint of mischief, "it's too late to run. She's already coming down."

When Mama Benard entered the kitchen, she offered a warm, genuine smile. "Ben, stop teasing the poor girl."

Florence, caught off guard, stared for a moment before realizing her silence bordered on rudeness. She reached out her hand. "Hello, my name is Florence. It's lovely to meet you."

"Don't be nervous, girl. Take a seat," Mama Benard said.

Florence sat at the bar with Ben, who looked at her with quiet admiration before explaining, "Mama Benard raised me when I was younger. I left my parents' house at sixteen, and she came with me. She's been by my side ever since. So, for all intents and purposes, she is and always has been my mother."

Florence studied him with curiosity, seeing a side of him that was tender, almost glowing. She smiled before catching herself staring.

"Would you like some dessert, Florence?" Ben asked.

"Yes, that would be lovely," she replied.

Mama Benard began preparing bowls of ice cream. Florence, eager to know more about Ben, asked, "What was he like as a kid?"

Mama Benard chuckled without turning around. "The same as he is now—stubborn, persistent, loving. Back then, though, he had quite the temper and was a little rebellious. Very spoiled as an only child, but he worked hard too."

Florence laughed. "You were so sweet, Ben… what happened?" she teased.

They were served their ice cream, and Mama Benard pinched his cheek. "He stopped listening to me. That's what happened."

The three of them sat and talked for the next hour, sharing stories. Florence found herself seeing Ben in a new light, a man of quiet commitment beneath the polished surface.

When the bowls were empty, Florence rose to wash them, but Mama Benard stopped her. "Don't worry about it. This one here never cleans."

"Thanks, Ma," he said.

"Well, it's the truth! How about you give her a tour of the house? I'm going to wash these and go to bed. It's past my bedtime," she said with a smile.

Ben kissed her cheek, and she whispered, "You did

good," before leaving them for the night.

He led Florence through his condo, showing her the gym, the entertainment room, the den with his expensive liquor, and several guest rooms.

So, this is what it feels like to be rich, Florence thought. *This is the biggest place I've ever seen—let alone an apartment.*

Ben paused in a mostly empty dining room. The large table sat unused, the space cold and distant.

"We never use this room," he said, clearing his throat. "I don't have company. Or family."

His eyes carried a quiet sadness. Florence touched his cheek instinctively before he kissed her palm. She quickly withdrew her hand and busied herself admiring the china. The tea set gleamed with real silver and gold.

"This place would be beautiful for a brunch or event," she murmured.

As she leaned over the table, arms wrapped around her waist.

"Ben, what are you doing?"

"I'm hugging you," he said, resting his head in the crook of her neck.

Florence ignored the press of his body against hers. She wouldn't sleep with him while Mama Benard was in the house.

"Ben, whatever you're thinking, forget about it."

She turned to meet his gaze, and mischief danced in his eyes.

"Is it a crime to admire my girlfriend?" he asked.

"Who said I'm your girlfriend?" she retorted with a raised eyebrow.

"I did," he replied matter-of-factly.

She whispered, "You still have one more room to show me."

He took her hand and led her upstairs, past the kitchen and down the hall to his room.

As soon as they entered, Florence was surrounded by his scent—warm, familiar, almost comforting, like the office had been. She barely had time to take in his clean, orderly space before her back pressed against the door, his lips on hers, urgent and hungry.

"Ben," she hissed, "there is no way we're doing this with your mother in the house."

"She's on a different floor, and she's asleep. I promise she won't hear a thing. And even if she did, she's been begging me for grandkids."

"Are you crazy?" Florence whispered, covering her mouth.

Ben laughed—a real laugh. In that moment, she saw how young he still was beneath the serious exterior his job demanded.

She smiled, brushing her lips against his. He deepened the kiss, pressing her against the door, one leg between hers. Florence placed her hands on his chest, feeling his muscles beneath the open button of his shirt.

He towered over her, but the way he was asking—pleading—softened him. It made her laugh. Her fingers traced the outline of his body before her gaze fell lower, catching the strain in his pants.

"Florence," Ben murmured, kissing her neck, "please, stay over. Please let me."

His hand moved between her thighs, and Florence snapped her legs closed.

"Let you what, Ben?" Florence asked, tilting her head at him. "I need to know what you want in order to give it to you." This time, she wanted to beat him at his own game. She was taking the lead.

Before she could get an answer, Ben dropped to his knees. "What do you want, sweet girl? I'll give you anything you want: money, a ring, a house, a baby, a title to rule over all your enemies—anything. Please, let me taste you." He gripped her thighs, pushing her legs apart as he kissed along them. Her dress slid up before she could respond.

Florence's knees nearly gave out at his submission. "Ben, w—wait."

"No more waiting," he groaned.

Before she could react, he slid her panties down her leg, balled them in his hand, and took a deep inhale. Florence was too stunned to speak. When he looked back up at her, his eyes were wild, starved. Her heart pounded.

Ben's mind was in overdrive. The only thing he could think of was being inside her again. She felt like a goddess, and though she tried to act tough, her resolve faded with every dirty thing he did. When Ben slid his fingers between her wet folds, she shivered; her knees buckled. He lifted one leg over his shoulder, bracing her with the other. She couldn't collapse—he had barely started.

Florence trembled as Ben's breath brushed against her. He licked a slow stripe between her folds, making her jolt, then paused.

"Look at me. I want you to recognize who is between your legs right now and who's about to make you cum." He flashed a smile before sucking her clit.

The sounds leaving her throat surprised her, but she couldn't help it. Ben devoured her like a man starved. His eyes were half-lidded, almost lost in a trance. He moaned against her, the vibrations making her shake. Then, just before she could reach her peak, he pulled away, and she cried out.

"Please," she begged.

Ben chuckled. "Don't worry, sweetheart. I'm not stopping until you're dripping down my chin."

She didn't have time to chastise his filthy words. His fingers dipped inside her, his mouth resuming its work. When he felt her ready, he added another finger, twirling his tongue over her clit. He searched for that spot while watching her face. She tried to hold back but gripped his hair, pulling him closer. He was rutting against her, leaking through his boxers.

When he finally found her spot, the sound that tore from her lips was one he had never heard before. Her essence coated his fingers as his eyes rolled back. He had to stay focused. Curling his fingers, he sucked her harder.

"Give it to me, Florence. I want to see you come undone, baby."

Her breathing turned ragged. If he kept this up, she wouldn't last. She tried to push his head, but he wouldn't budge. Her moans climbed higher; the familiar tingling climbed her spine.

"Ben," she pleaded, unsure what for.

He scraped his teeth lightly against her clit, and she cried out, her body jolting as her climax ripped through her. Ben drank her in, groaning as her tremors pulsed around him. She shivered, overwhelmed, as he lapped at every drop.

When he finally stood, she watched him suck his fingers clean. Her body sagged, ready to collapse, but he scooped her up and carried her to bed.

She smiled faintly, floating.

"I can't believe you did that—with your mom downstairs," she said, blushing and covering her face.

"I can't believe you thought I wouldn't," he replied, almost cocky.

He removed her dress and unclasped her bra, staring until she covered herself.

"Don't hide from me. You're perfect," he murmured, kissing her shoulders and neck. "I'm sorry, baby. I'm at my limit."

He stripped the rest of his clothes. His tip glistened with precum.

"Do you want me to help you?" Florence asked, wrapping her hand around him.

Ben grunted. "As much as I'd love that, my beloved, I want to be inside you. If I'm going to cum, I'd rather it be here," he said, dipping his fingers into her again, his intent clear.

Contrary to his words, he was patient and gentle. He slid into her slowly, groaning as her warmth wrapped around him. He paused, eyes shut, forcing himself to go slow.

This time, he didn't rush. He explored her—kissing, licking, tracing her curves, his mouth lingering on her breasts, his teeth grazing her ears. Her body clung to him, possessive, almost as if she wanted everything he could give—including a child. The thought made him throb harder, but he fought for control.

He changed positions, flipping her onto her stomach and pushing back in. Leaning over her, he pressed her into the pillow, her back arched.

"You feel so good."

He focused on her, determined to make her finish first.

"You take me so well, princess."

She whimpered; this angle hit her deep, a mix of pain and pleasure.

"Ben… Ben," she moaned, trying to get his attention.

He reached between them, kissing her back, his fingers teasing her clit.

"Come on, pretty girl, don't fight it. Give me what your body craves. Make us cum, Florence."

It was the first time he had used her full name during sex, and the way he growled it made her unravel. His hand and hips worked in perfect rhythm until she shattered around him.

"God, you're such a good girl," he groaned, twitching deep inside her as he spilled into her. Her body accepted everything he gave.

He kissed her shoulders, catching his breath. Then, with instinctive possessiveness, he pushed his release back inside her.

"Ben, please. I'm tired."

"I know, baby. I'm sorry." He kissed her forehead, his tone soft again.

He cleaned her carefully, massaged her shoulders until she drifted off, then slipped a shirt over her. Sliding into bed beside her, he watched her sleep with a quiet resolve: he would never let her go.

When morning came, she woke up first. He was still

asleep, his face soft, boyish almost. Mischief sparked in her chest. She climbed on top, kissed him, and began to grind against him.

"Ben," she whispered against his ear, biting gently.

His hips rutted up, his hands gripping her.

"If you want a different morning than last night, stop," he rasped. "My mother's awake."

But she didn't stop. Her hand covered his mouth to muffle his moans. His breathing deepened, his body tense beneath her. He grabbed her hips, guiding her against him, their heat building slowly, deliberately, until tension broke with a shuddering release between them.

"Well, good morning to you too, beautiful," he murmured, hugging her. "Let's shower. She's probably making breakfast already."

When Florence stepped into the bathroom, her eyes widened—it was larger than most hotel suites.

"I don't have—"

"A shower cap?" Ben interrupted, pulling one from the drawer.

Florence laughed. "Well, look at you... did you plan this?"

Ben chuckled. "I hoped, and I prepared."

She narrowed her eyes playfully. "Also, I wanted to ask: Have you always slept with silk sheets?"

Ben blushed. "No. I got those for you too. I also got washcloths and a loofah."

Florence placed a kiss on his lips. "Good job. That was very considerate. Let's shower."

Ben and Florence made out under the hot, steamy water. Ben pulled back, trying to control himself, but she wasn't making it easy. First, he watched her wash her body— slow, deliberate, teasing. Then, as she rinsed off, she parted her legs, giving him a full view. He deserved an award for restraint; most men wouldn't have lasted this long without touching her.

"Florence," he murmured, pushing her gently away as

she kissed him, "I can't. I won't be able to stop."

Florence smiled, her expression mischievous. "That's fine," she said, turning and bending over to put her loofah back.

Ben groaned, grabbed her by the waist, and pressed himself between her thighs.

"I can't keep coming inside you without protection. It's risky," he muttered.

He rubbed between her thighs, teasing her sensitive bud until they were both satisfied a second time, the hot water washing away the evidence. "I'm sorry, love. If I make love to you this morning, we won't get anything done."

After the shower, Ben had clothes ready for her—an entire stockpile he'd stored in his closet. Florence wasn't sure if it was sweet or a little unsettling, but she had clean clothes and underwear, so she didn't complain.

When they came downstairs, Ben's mother had already laid out breakfast. They sat at the bar, eating quietly.

"How was last night?" Mama Benard asked.

Ben nearly choked, his cheeks flushing. "W-What do you mean?"

"The tour," she said casually.

"Oh. The tour was fine," he replied quickly.

"I could ask about the hanky-panky you two were up to, but I think you're embarrassed enough," she teased.

Florence blushed. "I am so sorry, ma'am. I wasn't—"

"Don't be," Mama Benard cut in. "It's about time Ben stopped being uptight."

"Oh God, please, kill me now. Mama Benard, I'd appreciate it if we didn't talk about my sex life," Ben groaned.

"And I'd appreciate a few grandkids," she snapped back. "If you're doing your job, hopefully that will be soon."

Ben's eyes went wide, and now Florence choked on her food. He patted her back as her cheeks turned crimson.

"Mama!" he barked. Clearing his throat, he added, "I'll be taking Florence home after she finishes eating."

Florence giggled. "It's okay, Ben. It's funny seeing this

side of you. Also, I'd like kids too—one day," she said, continuing to eat.

Ben's eyes darkened for a moment before he finished his meal.

When they headed out to the car, Ben carried her things—some outfits for work and a few purses. He placed them in the back seat, opened her door, then climbed in on the driver's side. After buckling her seatbelt, he kissed her hard, pulling away only when his cheeks flushed.

"When do you want kids?" he asked, his gaze almost black.

Florence laughed, pushing him back. "Did you miss the part where I said someday?"

"It can be whenever you want," Ben replied.

"Who said I'm having kids with you?" she teased.

"Oh, you're having our kids, Miss Witkins."

"You'll be waiting a while for that, buddy."

"I'll wait forever," Ben said softly.

He dropped Florence off at her house. He had driven what he called his undercover car so no one could see inside.

"I'll see you Monday, darling. I hope you enjoyed our first date."

Florence kissed him. "I look forward to our second one."

When she got home, Florence flopped onto her bed, exhausted. She unpacked her bags, placing the clothes into drawers. At the bottom, she found his blazer from the day he saved her. She set it aside—she'd have to return it soon.

She caught her reflection in the mirror, her body sore and marked. *What is he, an animal?* she thought. At least none of the marks would show at work.

Denise had fed Mooni the night before. The little cat whined and yelped, annoyed at her absence, and Florence gave him extra treats and cuddles. Before she could grab her phone, Denise burst through the door, a smirk on her face.

"Well, well, well, look who decided to show up."

"Please stop," Florence groaned.

"So, when should I plan the wedding?"

Florence rolled her eyes and put Mooni down. "Thank you for taking care of him," she said, hugging her friend.

"Tell me everything!"

Florence recounted the date, the dinner, meeting his mom—leaving out the evening and morning escapades. "It was nice. I think… I like him."

Denise cackled. "Of course you do!"

Florence leaned against the kitchen counter, a nervous smile tugging at her lips as she stirred her tea. Denise raised an eyebrow from across the room. She could tell something was brewing.

"I've fallen for him," Florence admitted softly, eyes distant but glowing. "Ben."

Denise froze, then turned, eyes wide. "Oh?"

Florence nodded, a small laugh escaping. "Yeah. And I think… I'm going to tell him. I don't know what'll happen, but I want to go where I'm loved, you know? Even if it's not easy. Even if people judge us. He's white, and I know what that means, but I can't let fear be louder than love."

Denise crossed her arms, her tone teasing but warm. "That's exactly what I told you. But do you listen to me? Nooo. I'm just the friend with all the sense."

They both laughed, the tension easing like steam from Florence's cup.

"I don't know. I feel safe with him. It's easy. I haven't had nightmares since I met him. The field I always see in my dreams isn't full of storm clouds anymore—there's sunshine now."

Denise smiled and hugged her. "Aww, I'm proud of you. You can introduce me to one of his friends."

Then she straightened, her eyes sparkling. "Okay, my turn. I've got news too."

Florence raised her brows. "Oh no. What did you do?"

"I passed the bar," Denise said, grinning like a kid with a secret. "And I'm applying to work at your firm. We could actually work together."

Florence squealed and hugged her tightly. "Denise! Are you serious?"

"Dead serious," Denise said. "So, now you've got to confess your love and polish your desk, because I'm moving in."

They held each other for a moment, both women beaming—proud, a little scared, but ready for what lay ahead.

Part III:
Clear Skies

CHAPTER 20: SERENDIPITOUS MEETING

As the months passed, Florence and Ben focused entirely on their upcoming case. Florence felt their partnership had grown stronger, their teamwork sharper. They had filed motions and attended mediation, and neither side had settled. Court was coming soon. Florence would witness every step of the proceedings, and for the first time, she felt like a true lawyer. Working with the best had that effect.

Their office romance, however, was its own whirlwind. Ben was insatiable to the point where she often had to scold him. He had locked his office door to pull her onto his desk, cornered her in the conference room, even stolen moments in the library with books tumbling around them. She also learned he could be jealous. Whenever she mentioned plans with Mr. Anderson, his expression darkened. If she teased him about it, he pouted, and if she ignored him, he grew sullen.

The media had finally quieted around the case, so their dates at the park had become both an escape and, at times, an extension of work. The sunlight stretched across the grass, dappled by tall oaks. Laughter carried through the air as James, Florence, and Ben exchanged stories about how hectic life had become.

Florence sat cross-legged beneath a tree, holding the trial notes steady. Ben leaned over her, hair falling into his eyes.

"Okay," Ben said, tapping the page with his pencil. He began pacing in front of her. "We start with the history of segregation in the company's hiring practices. Then we line up the testimonies—workers passed over for promotions, denied equal pay, retaliated against."

He turned to her, eyes sharp with purpose. "And then we hit them with the data: pay scales, personnel files, patterns they won't be able to deny."

Florence raised an eyebrow. "And that's when you say your favorite word?"

Ben grinned. "Checkmate."

She chuckled. "You love saying 'checkmate' like you're auditioning for a courtroom drama."

He shrugged. "I'm painting the picture for you."

She nudged him lightly. "Paint away, Perry Mason. But remember, you're up against a colored man in 1968 who's trying to show that just standing in that courtroom is a step toward justice."

Ben's grin softened. "I haven't forgotten," he said firmly. "Not for a second."

Just then, James ran back, arms outstretched, holding a crumpled, colorful crown. "For Lady Florence of Justice!" he declared proudly. A handmade flower crown of clovers and wild daisies rested on his head.

Florence laughed, eyes crinkling as she bowed to accept it. "Why, thank you, Sir James. I will wear it in honor of the truth."

Ben leaned back against the bench, watching her. The way her eyes sparkled as James clung to her arm, the way she patiently explained the difference between evidence and assumption—she was radiant. Barefoot in the grass, folders of witness statements scattered like petals at her feet.

"That's enough touching," Ben muttered, mock-jealous, sliding between them. They both burst into laughter.

"Who would've guessed today's the day I'd see Ben Mayfield jealous?" Florence teased.

"You're lovesick, brother. I can't blame you. She's beautiful," James added, kissing her hand while glaring playfully at Ben.

Ben's jaw tightened, but he said nothing. Instead, he rested his head on her shoulder, eyes wide with mock innocence until she kissed him when James wasn't looking.

The three of them sat in the warm afternoon light—Florence with her flower crown tilting, Ben scribbling notes, James humming over his notepad. For a moment, time stilled. The world felt safe. Full of promise.

***

Their peace didn't last. By Monday, they were back at work. Florence occasionally sensed eyes on her but dismissed it. After all, no one had ever paid her much attention before. This time, she was wrong. Charlotte was watching.

Whenever Charlotte burst into Ben's office unannounced, he barely looked up from his files. He had become a relentless machine, his commanding trial voice echoing through the halls. "Objection. Invalid precedent. Rephrase that." She hated how attractive it made him.

And Florence—always composed, always professional. Too perfect. Too calm. Charlotte found no notes, no smudged lipstick, not even a lingering glance to betray them.

But her gut told her they would slip. And when they did, she would be ready. Ben would thank her for it one day.

It happened sooner than she expected. A Tuesday night. Rain drummed against the window like impatient fingers. Charlotte returned to the office, claiming she had forgotten her umbrella. In truth, she was following her instincts. The halls were dark, except for the faint glow of the conference room.

Inside, Ben and Florence sat close. The work had long ended. Florence laughed at something he said, and then he touched her face—a soft graze of his thumb across her cheek. A pause. Then he kissed her. Slowly. Like a language meant only for her. He pressed her back against the table, wanting more.

Charlotte didn't move. She didn't breathe. Her heart pounded with fury and vindication. She slipped away, heels clicking like a clock counting down. Lucky for her, she knew the security cameras would have caught everything. Only a few people had access to them. Ben's father was one of them.

***

Thursday morning, Ben's father stormed into the office. His voice struck like a thunderclap. "Everybody out. Now."

Ben stood in the center of his office, his back straight. The door slammed shut behind his father.

"Did you think I wouldn't find out?" his father spat. "Having a fling is one thing! Hell, I've done it myself. But actually falling for a nigger girl? Ben, that's a mistake that will cost not only you but everything I've built."

Ben's jaw tightened. "Don't call her that. And what are you talking about?"

"I'll call her whatever I please! You've humiliated me. Sleeping with some girl who has nothing and no one."

"She's smarter than most people in this office, and twice the lawyer you ever were! How do you even know—"

"Security cameras, Ben. Did you forget about them? They look straight into that little conference room, where you disgraced yourself and our family."

Florence had been walking toward the office with coffee when she heard the shouting. She froze, every word burning into her spine.

"She's a stain on our name. On everything I've built."

"Yeah, yeah. She's a disgrace…" Florence only heard this part before running away from the door. Ben finished his words: "She's a disgrace, I'm a disgrace, Mom was a disgrace. Everyone is a disgrace to someone who can't take accountability!

"I love her regardless of how you feel, Father."

But Florence missed the full statement—she was already gone. She walked quickly, head down. No one stopped her.

Charlotte had heard every word Ben said, and it only made her angrier.

Ben searched for Florence after hearing she had left work early. Surely it was because of his father's tirade. He tried to call her for days, with no answer. When he went to her house, she wouldn't open the door, so he left a note. What he didn't know was that after everything, Florence decided to stay with Denise.

Ben was panicked and restless. Mana Benard found him pacing in the living room one night, his eyes red, his voice raw. "You have to give her time," she said gently. "When someone like her has been hurt her whole life, even love can feel like a lie."

He nodded, but it didn't soothe him. He couldn't sit still. Instead, he turned his energy toward the truth: Who had gone behind his back? His father never checked those cameras. Someone had tipped him off.

Two weeks later, Florence found herself in a situation she never imagined. She sat across from Ben's father, her back straight, hands folded in her lap, every inch of her betraying that she knew this wasn't a friendly meeting.

Without preamble, he reached into his jacket and placed a check on the table between them. "Take it," he said smoothly, as if offering a favor. "It's more than enough to make you comfortable. All I ask is that you stay away from my son. Permanently."

Florence glanced at the slip of paper, then back at him. Her chin lifted, sharp with resolve. "You think you can buy me off like I'm nothing?" Her voice didn't waver. "I don't want your money. I want nothing from you or your son."

For the first time, something in his expression hardened. He had expected resistance, but not such firm defiance—it reminded him of young Ben in a way. Slowly, he tucked the check back into his pocket, the gesture deliberate, final.

"Very well," he said, his voice low. "If you won't take it, then you leave me no choice. You'll learn soon enough that without money, without position, my son has nothing to offer you. And when he's stripped of it all, you'll walk away on your own. When he crumbles, you'll see what kind of man he really is."

"Why are you going to such lengths?" Florence asked.

Later that week, whispers drifted through the office like a slow leak of gas: invisible but suffocating.

As Florence battled Ben's father, Ben was at home battling his mind. He pieced it together. Who had the motive? Who had been watching?

He finally found Florence sitting outside her old neighborhood library, arms crossed, eyes sharp.

"Florence," he breathed. "Do you... do you know who told my father?"

Ben looked exhausted, as if he hadn't slept. A part of her heart ached, but she knew letting him go was for the best. She looked at him like he was a stranger. "It's right in your face—or should I say right in your office door, peeking in."

He blinked. "Charlotte?"

Her eyes filled with tears. "You didn't want to believe it. Because you still don't get it. You don't get what it's like being me in your world. You think love fixes everything, but it doesn't fix this. I warned you, Ben, and look what happened."

He tried to speak, but she cut him off.

"I gave you my heart, Ben. But I never stopped wondering when it would be used against me. You... you don't love me. Not the way I need to be loved. You can't love me, Ben."

"Florence, please..."

"No." Her voice cracked. "Don't come find me again."

She stood up and walked away. Ben stood there, shattered.

The office buzzed with low murmurs and stiff postures the morning the letter arrived.

Ben stood in the conference room, holding a legal notice signed by his father. It was a formal motion to remove the workplace discrimination case from his docket, effective immediately.

Florence looked up from her desk, alarmed. "What is it?"

Ben's jaw clenched, veins standing out at his temples. "My father filed to reassign the case, citing a conflict of interest. He's trying to gut me from the inside. I'll make sure it doesn't go through."

Charlotte stormed into the room, eyes wide. "Have you seen this, Ben?" He ignored her. "Your father is freezing access to the firm's resources tied to your account. You're locked out of the budget."

Ben turned, already calculating. "Fine. If he wants war, he can have one. I'll fund the rest with personal assets."

"Ben," Florence said, conflicted, "are you sure you want to do that?"

"It's done." That was the end of their discussion.

"She forged it, you know," Florence heard a voice whisper as she walked past the copier. "I always wondered how she rose so fast. She never even made the shortlist."

Florence paused, confused, until she saw the memo tacked to the break room corkboard. A red circle marked her winning law essay. A crude stamp read: Forgery Alleged.

Her stomach dropped. She ripped it down.

Ben burst into the break room seconds later, snatching the paper from her hands, eyes blazing. "It's my father. He's saying your memo submission was forged. That you lied to win the competition. I'm so sorry. I'll address everyone."

Florence stood frozen, pain in her voice. "No! Don't. They're calling me a fraud, saying I slept my way to the top. Let them think that. After this case is over, I'll transfer to a new law firm anyway."

Ben's eyes darkened with hurt. He turned away silently.

He went straight to find Mr. Anderson, the dam he had built to block his emotions finally breaking.

Ben sat hunched forward, his elbows on his knees, his hands running through his hair as if the motion could untangle the chaos inside him. His voice cracked when he finally spoke.

"Mr. Anderson, I don't know what to do. Florence said she's transferring firms after the trial. I love her. I've loved her this whole damn time. And now… now I've lost her. I tried everything, but she keeps walking away. My father is coming after us—after her. And she doesn't deserve any of it. I was going to propose, you know?" His voice broke, and he laughed bitterly. "I had the ring. I was ready. But now… everything's ruined."

The old man let him finish, nodding slowly, his weathered hands folded in his lap. He studied Ben for a long moment before speaking, his tone steady, like a hammer striking iron.

"Son," Mr. Anderson said, "you can't fight for her if you're already digging your own grave. Right now you're standing knee-deep in mud, and every tear you shed is only making the ground denser around your feet. You want to clear a path to her? Then clear it. Make it so she's got no way back but straight to you. But you can't do that with your head all twisted in grief."

Ben looked up, his chest tight, his eyes burning.

Mr. Anderson leaned forward, his voice softer now, almost fatherly. "I know you're hurting. And you've got every right to hurt. But being hurt alone won't win her back. You've got to stand, boy. Strong, steady. Not just for yourself, but for her, too. If she's the woman you say she is, she's worth building a road wide enough for both of you to walk on. But you can't build it with broken hands. Get your head on straight first. Then fight."

***

Ben stormed into his father's house, needing to look him in

the eyes when he told him the motion had failed. His father sat in his study, glasses perched on the bridge of his nose.

Ben slapped the paper on the desk. "Your motion has been denied."

His father stood, fuming. "You won't win. Taking on this case will only destroy you!"

"Listen well, because I won't repeat myself. I've been patient, restrained, even obedient. The only reason I haven't gutted you already is because I've been playing chess, not checkers. But make no mistake, your castle will fall, and when it does, I'll be standing in the wreckage. If it weren't for her, and the life I want to give her, you would've been discarded the moment you threatened her."

***

Florence's hands trembled as she gathered her things. She was doing this for Ben. Her mother had been right: She wasn't cut out to be around these people. It was easier to break things off now before he realized that himself.

Ben waited until the office thinned out that evening. Then he stepped into the waiting room, his voice like ice.

"Charlotte. My office. Now."

She rose from her desk, chin lifted, trying to appear unbothered. "Yes, sir?"

He didn't sit. He didn't blink. "You told him. My father. About Florence."

Charlotte's eyes flickered. "I don't know what you—"

"You tipped him off. I don't know how you got your proof, and I don't care. You did it out of spite. You put her in danger." His voice lowered, colder than she had ever heard it. "You may think you hurt her. But you'll learn what happens when you betray me."

Charlotte stiffened. "I did what I thought was right. You should be with someone like me. You're ruining your legacy for some—"

"Stop." His voice cracked through the air like a whip. "Don't utter her name. You don't have the right."

She faltered, stunned by his fury.

"I'm terminating your position. You have sixty days to find something new. That's more than you deserve."

His eyes burned through her. No rage now, just disgust.

Charlotte turned to leave and saw Florence standing in the hallway. Frozen, having heard everything. She didn't step in. She just watched.

Ben saw Florence too late. She walked out, numb from what she'd witnessed.

Ben ran after her, catching her by the arm. Desperation cracked his voice. "Florence, I need you to understand how I feel—"

She shook her head, cutting him off before he could finish, her defenses locking into place like always. "No, Ben. You don't get it. We can't be together. I've told you this. You're white; I'm colored. That's not love, that's a fight— and I'm tired of fighting just to exist. People like me don't get to dream about happy endings with people like you. We rarely dream of happy endings at all. We dream of surviving. And with you, Ben, that's not possible."

For a moment, silence stretched between them, the air so heavy it felt like it might crack. Then Ben exhaled, sharp, almost like surrender. "You know what? You're right."

Florence blinked, startled, searching his face for mockery.

But Ben's voice grew steadier, heavier. He stepped closer. "You're right. We aren't equal. You're stronger than me in every way. And I won't stand here and promise you a life without hardship. God knows with me, you might face even worse ones. But Florence, if you only see yourself as 'colored,' then that's all you'll ever be. I see so much more. I see a woman who bends before no one, who terrifies men twice her size, who carries the weight of the world and still keeps walking. I see you. All of you. And I can't walk away from that. You can have a happy ending if you just allow yourself to."

His words burned now, searing like a mirror of her fears and a vow he might never get the chance to keep. "I'll stand with you through every storm. I'll be the first to rise for you, the last to sit down. If anyone dares raise an arm against you," his jaw tightened, "I'll raise an army to take their arms off. And when you're ready to face the storm, I'll walk into the sun with you."

Ben's voice softened. "Do you hear me, Florence? Do you hear what I'm saying?"

She heard him. Every word cut through her defenses, ached in her chest, but it didn't change the truth she clung to. Her hand slipped from his grip, her eyes fixed anywhere but his face. If she looked at him, she knew she'd break.

"It doesn't make a difference, Ben," she whispered, her voice splintering. "Let's just get through this trial and go our separate ways."

Ben's hand fell helplessly to his side as Florence turned and walked away. It felt as if she were walking out of his life forever.

The office was fractured in the days that followed. People avoided Florence's eyes. Some files went missing. Doors closed when she walked past.

Ben gave her space but watched from afar, torn apart by guilt and fury.

James held things together where he could, trying to talk to Florence and checking in on her at Ben's request. Mr. Anderson also tried when he saw her.

Ben and Florence worked long hours in silence—preparing opening statements, coordinating witness schedules, and sorting affidavits. Every breath felt heavier. The weight of the world, of history, pressed on all of them. Ben funded everything himself, fighting his father's machine with his own dime. In a way, he felt freer. This would be his first case untouched by others. His loss or his win.

And still, the date on the calendar crept closer. Monday. Trial begins. The storm wasn't coming anymore. They were already in it.

CHAPTER 21:
MEETING THE MONTH
OF MAY

This was Florence's first trial. When she and Ben entered the courtroom to meet the judge, she could not say the man looked eager to see her. That indifference weighed on her, but heavier still was the silence she had kept with Ben since the confrontation with his father. She continued to do the work, preparing the case with precision. But when he reached for anything beyond strategy, she met him with a cold and steady distance.

She wanted this trial to prove something—not just to the court but also to Ben and to his father. She would show them both how wrong they had been about her. Ben had mistaken her for a fragile girl who needed rescuing. She admitted there had been a thrill in his attention, but she had always known better. She was no stranger to standing on her own.

Ben, meanwhile, could barely endure what had unraveled. His father's venom and his own failure to speak the truth haunted him. He told himself his silence had been to shield her. She had endured more than her share of hardship already, and he believed more challenges still lay ahead. He wanted to ease them, to give her peace, to fill her days with something gentler than struggle. Even if he could not give her everything, he longed to soften her world.

He admitted as much to James one evening in his study, his voice low, his hands restless. Florence had already heard enough of his missteps and enough of his father's contempt. Ben feared she would never forgive him. Yet he clung to the belief that change was possible—that a man could unlearn the poison of the world he had been born into. And if anyone deserved to witness that change, it was Florence. She deserved more than survival, and more than scraps. She deserved the fullness of love, free of shadows cast by the color of her skin.

"Ben, you speak of Florence as if she were a child you have to protect. She is a grown woman. I understand the instinct and the primal urge to lock her away so nothing can harm her, but that's not how life works. Doing that isn't allowing her to grow nor your relationship. She has to find herself before she can ever accept your love, and you have to allow her to do that if you love her."

James looked up at him with a knowing expression. Ben's face turned red, and he cleared his throat.

"Don't worry," James said. "Give her time. This is also your first relationship, and taking a step back will be good for both of you."

Ben sighed, running his fingers through his hair. James rose from his seat. "Focus on the trial. You'll do great. And when the trial is over, I'm sure you will have figured things out. Also, your best friend will be there to cheer you on."

"You're my only friend," Ben grumbled, and James slapped him on the shoulder.

"Exactly. That's why I'm so special."

"Thanks, man," Ben said.

When Ben got into bed that night, his sheets no longer smelled like Florence. They had been cleaned, leaving no trace of her except their smoothness. He missed her—the way she pouted in her sleep, how she clung to him when she was cold. Ben took a deep look into his life and how far he'd come, but the one thing that always held him back was his father.

Ben wanted many things. He dreamed of being a father, a husband, a caregiver. He also craved adventure. But he wanted all these things with Florence. He had been alone his whole life, yet he wasn't bitter. He was content because his patience had led him to her. Patience is what I need right now. He rolled over, set his alarm early—they would be in the courtroom tomorrow—and then went to sleep.

Florence arrived at court first. News reporters swarmed her with questions. Ben showed up seconds later, grabbing her and shielding her from the reporters. Once inside, Florence held her head high, eyes steady—a picture of resolve.

Her navy-blue skirt suit hugged her form perfectly, tailored to move with her, not against her. The jacket cinched at the waist, accentuating her strength without sacrificing femininity. Her pencil skirt fell to the knee. It drew attention but didn't invite judgment. She wore heels—not too high, not too modest—and the shine on them spoke volumes. These were the clothes and shoes Ben had bought her. Confidence radiated from her like light on polished glass. She looked like a woman who knew exactly who she was.

When Ben looked up, his heart nearly stopped. She was the most beautiful he'd ever seen—not because of the clothes, not even the way she carried herself. It was the fire in her eyes. A glow, almost supernatural, surrounded her. She hadn't come to this courtroom to cry or beg. She had come to fight. He felt agitated at all the people crowding her, but he kept his cool. He couldn't afford to get worked up before they even went inside.

When their eyes met, the air seemed to crackle. It wasn't longing. It was something older and sharper: pain, betrayal, and unfinished words.

Florence couldn't help but notice how handsome Ben looked in his suit, though his eyes appeared tired. She wondered if he had stayed up all night preparing for court. That would not have surprised her.

The courtroom buzzed with excitement. The smell of

varnished wood and coffee lingered in the air, like tension before a storm. It was the first day of a three-day trial that had already divided the town long before the gavel fell.

They took their seats at the plaintiff's table. Ben, lead counsel, shuffled through papers. Florence sat beside him, composed, notepad ready. Sometimes, she leaned in to whisper a correction or a suggestion. Other times, she slid over a written note that displayed her expertise. Ben was proud of her; she had come a long way.

Ben wasn't warm. He wasn't charming. He wasn't even liked in the courtroom. Court was not the place to make friends. It was the place where enemies were made, and Ben was known for having a multitude of them.

He earned his reputation the hard way, through intensity, brutal precision, and an unflinching command of the law. He was tough and ruthless. His cross-examinations shattered seasoned witnesses like dry twigs. Juries didn't always love him, but they listened. Judges dreaded his motions. Opposing counsel prepared harder when they saw his name on the docket.

What he lacked in gentleness, he made up for with sheer precision. He did not argue cases so much as dismantle them, stripping them down page by page, statute by statute, until the truth had nowhere left to run. His eyes had been on the defense attorney for months, and he used every skeleton in their closet. His delivery was cool, almost icy—unsettling to anyone who faced him. Yet once he hit his stride, the room fell still, every breath caught in his grip. It was why Florence stayed quiet and sharp beside him. Though she could have walked away, she knew that would only hurt her career. Contrary to their personal struggles, when it came to the law, Ben was the best—and she knew it. She wasn't there to outshine him. She was there to amplify him and to learn.

The defense team sat across from them: white, well-fed, and smug. It included Briarstone Textiles and their lawyer, Franklin Curville. He looked as though he'd been born in a courtroom and fed bias with a silver spoon. He adjusted his cufflinks and smiled at the gallery.

Judge Jefferson, an aging relic in a black robe, could not hide his discomfort whenever Florence spoke or whispered to Ben. So, she tried to stay in the shadows.

"The record will show that the plaintiff's assistant will be sitting in on this case," he said, not looking at Florence. "Mr. Mayfield, you may proceed."

Florence's jaw tightened. She was not an assistant.

"Counsel, you may proceed with your argument." The judge continued.

Ben stood, addressing the court:

"This is not a case about wages or unfair treatment. It is a case about being denied work because of the color of your skin. About doors closed—not by a lack of skill, effort, or resources but by design."

"Your Honor, members of the jury.

"I represent the plaintiff in this case—a man who has endured unequal treatment and professional harm, not for any failing of his own but solely for asserting his right to fair and equal opportunity. The defendant subjected him to unjust conditions, undermining both his career and his dignity.

"This conduct violates the Equal Protection Clause of the Fourteenth Amendment, which is clear: No person within the jurisdiction of the United States shall be denied the equal protection of the laws. This case is not about sympathy; it is about justice. It is about whether the law will protect those who are entitled to it or whether discriminatory treatment will be allowed to stand unchecked.

"As you examine the evidence, I ask you to look closely at the facts: the actions of the defendant, the impact on the plaintiff's professional and personal life, and the clear principle that every individual is entitled to fair and equal treatment under the law. At the close of this trial, I trust you will find that the plaintiff's rights have been infringed and that justice calls for a verdict in his favor."

As he spoke, Florence watched the jury. Eight white

faces. Two racially ambiguous. A middle-aged woman with guarded eyes watched her closely. Her gaze was cold and judgmental.

The defense countered with venom cloaked in civility. "Briarstone Textile has never discriminated. If these individuals didn't meet company standards, that is their own failure, not ours."

Their witnesses painted the plaintiffs as "unreliable," "late," and "not qualified." A white former supervisor, wearing a mischievous grin, said, "We had to keep standards up. It's not about race; it's about culture. Some folks just... don't fit in."

The room didn't gasp. It nodded. Ben's stomach turned. Florence scribbled quickly, lips tight, eyes darker than before. She whispered sharply, "He coded 'colored' as defective. You need to tear that apart."

Each time Ben tried to involve Florence, the judge cut in. "The court will hear from counsel only."

By 3:00 p.m., the momentum had shifted. The jury wasn't with them. Not yet. Right now, the courtroom was favoring the defendant. The defense used subtle but effective language, painting Mr. Caldwell as a troublemaker in a "good town." Racism was treated like a shadow, not a monster. The gavel struck.

"We will recess until tomorrow morning," Judge Jefferson said.

As the courtroom cleared, Ben turned to Florence. "I thought we had more than this—evidence, witnesses. We didn't move them."

Florence was already packing her notes. "We moved them, just not in the direction we had hoped."

He touched her arm. "Can we talk?"

She pulled away. "Not now." *Maybe not ever,* she thought.

She stepped out, back straight, head high. The click of her heels echoed like punctuation.

Ben stayed seated. Rage simmered under his collar.

In the gallery, his father crossed his arms.

"Didn't think you'd win this one. Should've stuck to something safer. Something cleaner."

Ben snapped. "You know what? After this trial, you and I are done. Forever. You don't get to ride my failures like a prize bull. You're a coward with a legacy built on silent racism and greed. You even chose it over my mother and let her die by herself," Ben bellowed loud enough for everyone to hear.

Gasps rippled through the courtroom. Florence paused in the hallway, listening, but didn't turn around.

Ben stood alone, angry and hurt but determined. Tomorrow would be different. It had to be.

Florence returned home and collapsed onto her bed. The day had been grueling, and it was only the first. She hurt from the look in Ben's eyes, but she had to keep her focus on the case. She would visit her mother afterward. She was ready to let go of the pain she had carried. She was ready for a new chapter. No matter what happened with Ben, he had taught her an important lesson—one she should have learned much earlier.

Florence didn't have to earn love; she was worthy of it without lifting a finger. She wished her mother had taught her that, but it was okay. The storm clouds in her heart were almost gone. She loved herself and valued the person she had become—with or without a career, a man, or a mother. Mooni jumped up, purring. She smiled and said, "Hello, Mooni!" and then kissed him on the head.

The second day opened with a different atmosphere. Ben's suit was still pressed, his notes still neat, but the sharp edge of restraint was gone. Today, he wasn't just a lawyer. He was a blade—sharp, controlled, ready to cut deep and make the jury feel it. Florence noticed it as soon as he stood. He didn't approach the bench; he prowled toward it, eyes fixed on the jury as if they were already in his grasp.

"Your Honor, I would like to call Mr. Thomas Caldwell to the stand."

Thomas was tall and wiry, with a head full of silver hair and a voice that sounded like gravel and gospel. He took his oath slowly, as though each word had to travel through the bones of his past to come out true.

Ben began. "Mr. Caldwell, what does it do to a man's dignity to show up day after day at Briarstone Textiles, knowing your work is undervalued, your voice ignored, and your name dragged through the dirt simply because of the color of your skin?"

Mr. Caldwell smiled, but not the happy kind—the kind worn after swallowing injustice for so long it became routine. "I was born in 1906. I fought in Korea. I paid every tax, never stole a dime. And still, the minute I asked for a job where I wasn't mopping spit off the floor, they looked at me like I was nothing."

He paused, voice cracking. "You know how it feels to be told you're a problem for wantin' better? Then working for years like a dog for the company only to be fired because of my color? After I fought for this country, I was promised the American dream that I haven't seen. I was away from my family, I aided America and heeded their plea, but when I needed help, I was left out to die."

Mr. Caldwell wiped a bead of sweat from his forehead. "Being colored is the only sin I've committed here. The law is supposed to protect me, and it didn't. Now people sit in this court to bash and complain when I am the exact product of the injustice you've inflicted."

Silence swept the room. Even the defense lawyer shifted uncomfortably.

"I got attacked outside the corner store last week. Didn't even fight back. Just lay there bleedin', all 'cause someone said I was tryin' to bring 'colored trouble' into a white business. I don't want trouble. I want justice."

Ben turned to the jury. "And if that's trouble, then maybe we need to ask what kind of peace we've built in this country."

Then Ben did something he hadn't planned. He

pointed to Florence.

"Let me ask you: Do you believe discrimination doesn't exist at every level? Look at the woman beside me. Florence Witkins. Graduate degree in political science, highest honors. Passed the bar, but not allowed to work as the lowest level of lawyers. Instead, she is working as an assistant."

Florence clenched her jaw; though he wasn't technically wrong, it still irked her. She had helped build this case, shaped every word he spoke, but the judge wouldn't let her speak, she wouldn't get credit, and she wasn't even guaranteed to advance in her position.

Judge Jefferson bristled. "Mr. Mayfield, it is inappropriate…"

"I am speaking," Ben said, louder. "And I'm speaking the truth."

He turned back to the jury. "She earned her seat beside me, but still, she's silenced. Not because of competence. Not because of law. But because of perception. Because of race. You might think I'm odd for critiquing my own firm, but that's who I am. I'm a lawyer who speaks the truth, no matter what happens next." Ben played this card, but in reality, it helped him set a trap to take his father's firm from under him. Image was everything to his father, and that was a card Ben couldn't pass up.

His voice lowered, more dangerous now. "In 1896, the Supreme Court ruled in *Plessy v. Ferguson* that 'separate but equal' was acceptable. You know what Homer Plessy did to get arrested? He sat on a train car he wasn't 'meant' for. That's it. He wanted dignity. Today, Thomas Caldwell wants to be compensated for his distress. Miss Witkins wants to be heard. Martin Luther King wanted equality. Different situations, same wall."

Gasps from the gallery. Judge Jefferson's gavel banged, but the sound was drowned out by something louder: a shift.

At this comment, even Florence shifted; no one had

dared to bring up MLK given that he had passed a few months ago. It wasn't unheard of, but it might paint Ben as a colored sympathizer. It made Florence nervous.

"Defendant, you may now question the plaintiff," the judge stated. After what felt like an eternity of grueling questions. Tommy stepped down from the stand. Ben clasped his hand. For the first time, the jury looked at them not with suspicion but with recognition. The tide in the courtroom was turning in their favor.

Across the courtroom, Mr. Curville sat still. His jaw was tight. His fingers drummed on the chair's arm like a ticking bomb.

As they left the courtroom, Florence touched Ben's sleeve. "You didn't have to do that. It was dangerous for your reputation."

"I did," he said. "I wanted to. Do you think I care about my reputation or my status, as you so put it?" he said, tilting his head slightly.

That night, Florence agreed to meet Ben at a hotel lounge, finally giving him a moment. Though Ben had sworn he'd made his last plea, the truth was, he could never stop trying with her.

"You've been different lately," she said. "I heard what your father said. I heard how you didn't defend me."

Ben's face paled with shock, and then understanding. "Did you stay for the entire conversation, Florence?"

"Well, after hearing how I was a disgrace, I thought it would be time for me to leave."

Ben nodded. "I did defend you. If you had stayed for the rest of the conversation, you would've heard— Ben was cut off mid-sentence.

"Would it have mattered what I heard?"

Silence.

"Florence…" he said, voice thick, "I would move mountains if it meant you could see the sun shine better. I would pull you back from the darkest parts of your soul to see you shine again, Florence. I will show you your worth every day until you believe it, even if I receive nothing other than to be by your side."

Her eyes glistened.

"I love you. That's what I told my father. I didn't say it to you before, because I thought it would just tangle things up—and I thought it might have been too soon for you. But it's the only thing that makes sense to me anymore."

"You don't love me, Ben. You only think you do because you don't have any other options right now. You'll meet another girl."

"How can you say that when you never even gave me the chance? And listen to me, Florence. You're not an option. You're the only choice. There isn't another girl, because I don't need a girl. I need a woman. And that woman is you."

She turned away, breath caught between fear and fire.

"You don't have to say you love me, because I already know," Ben said. "I just wanted you to understand my feelings."

Then, gently, he leaned in and pressed his lips to her cheek, soft and reverent, like a vow.

Her heart pounded in her throat. And before she could speak, he whispered, "Trust me. One more day. Then everything changes."

He walked away, leaving her at the edge of the storm and the promise of something more.

Florence went home, head spinning. She called Denise to ask her to watch Mooni after the trial. She was going to visit her mother and promised to share everything when she returned. Denise agreed without any questions.

At 4 a.m., a knock jolted her from her restless thoughts. She cursed under her breath; she had barely slept. Her mind had churned all night with arguments, case points, Ben's words, and her own heartbreak. Court was in less than four hours, and someone was disturbing her peace.

She opened the door with a sharp, "What—" but stopped.

No one was there. Only a matte-black box tied with a white satin ribbon. Inside lay a tailored white suit: sleek pants, a button-up vest with subtle pearl details along the seams, matching designer heels, and a delicate string of pearls draped across the vest's collar like soft punctuation. Her fingers brushed the note pinned to the lapel:

Every princess deserves a set of pearls.
—Ben

Her throat tightened, and she held back the tears. Tomorrow, when she walked into the courtroom, she wouldn't be Florence Witkins. She would be the storm that turned the tide.

Ben stood with Mr. Anderson in the hallway outside the courthouse. His shoulders were tight, his jaw clenched.

"You've been carrying a lot, son," Mr. Anderson said quietly, resting a reassuring hand on his shoulder. "Courtrooms have a way of weighing men down, and I know something else has been too." His eyes flicked knowingly toward the distance between Ben and Florence.

Ben's voice dropped. "I'm not sure we'll still be a team after this. I think I've already lost her."

Mr. Anderson gave his shoulder a firm squeeze. "Then take another look, Ben."

As those words left him, Ben turned, and there was Florence, walking toward them. For a moment, everything else fell away.

She caught the last of Mr. Anderson's words and offered him a soft smile. He clasped both their hands. "Whatever the verdict ends up being, it doesn't change who you are. It doesn't change what you mean to one another. Don't let a gavel decide more than it's meant to."

"Thank you, Mr. Anderson," Ben said.

"Yes… thank you, Henry," Florence added warmly.

Ben blinked. "Wait a minute… Henry? Why does she get to call you Henry? You still make me call you Mr. Anderson!"

"We have a special relationship," Mr. Anderson said with a wink.

"What does that mea—"

Before Ben could finish, Florence tugged him along. "Not the time," she said, grinning, though warmth lingered in her eyes.

Before they made it to the courtroom, Ben pulled her aside.

"Ben! We have to get ready to go in," she whispered.

But when she truly looked at him, her heart stuttered. He stood at the top of the courthouse stairs in a crisp, perfectly tailored white suit. She flushed. The symbolism was unmistakable: they were a united front.

Ben's heart raced when he saw her in her suit. The vest hugged her waist perfectly. The light made her skin glow. From behind, the slope of her back shifted with each breath. He grumbled inwardly. This was not the time for desire.

But God, he missed her—her laugh, her warmth, her mind. He stared at her and, with fierce clarity, vowed, *I'll marry this woman. I'll give her everything. She deserves to be and have whatever she desires.*

He bit his lip. He wanted nothing more than to put a ring on her finger and fill their home with children. He wouldn't mind if she still wanted to work. He'd take care of the kids. He'd do anything she asked.

A hand on his shoulder broke the thought.

"That's a dangerous look, my man," Mr. Anderson said, catching them after returning from the restroom.

"I see our talk about going for what you want had a different kind of effect," he added casually.

Ben chuckled. "I'm not sure what you mean."

Mr. Anderson pointed at him. "Ben Mayfield, I suggest you focus on the court case if you want whatever you were thinking about to happen."

"It will happen with or without the court case," Ben said firmly.

Mr. Anderson laughed and shook his head. "I like that

confidence. This is the Ben I know." He slapped Ben lightly on the back. "Good luck."

Ben breathed in, steadying himself.

He and Florence finally walked into the courtroom side by side.

***

Everything would be decided today. The courtroom was tense. Ben opened, then stepped aside. He had a different plan. Florence stood.

For the first time in the trial, the room fell silent. The colored woman stood tall and didn't ask for permission. Even the judge seemed taken aback.

"Please allow my partner to take the lead today. Ms. Witkins will be providing the closing statement," Ben said, emphasizing partner.

"My name is Florence Witkins. I have lived the life of every plaintiff in this case and more. I have sat by for three days while people debated whether our pain was real. But I need you to hear me today. Understand me fully.

"Do you know what it's like to work harder than anyone else in the room and still be called unqualified?

"To know your skin causes people to see your intelligence as a threat?

"To be told you're too angry while you're still bleeding from the wounds the world has left on you—it's a cruelty all its own.

"You want to talk about standards? Lynching was only officially outlawed in this country a few months ago—in 1968. This year. In America.

"We've sat through this trial listening to veiled racism disguised as professionalism: 'He's not a team player, doesn't take direction well, needs to be more professional, not a good fit, doesn't seem polished.' Do you think it's a coincidence who those words are aimed at?

"We are here today because being colored in this country means we have to beg for humanity again and again. And the trauma of being told 'no' by people who refuse to see you creates a second prison, one inside the mind.

"And the question is, are you willing to let that continue because it makes you comfortable?"

A hush. The gallery had gone utterly still.

Ben rose slowly, never taking his eyes off her. His voice was softer than usual, but resolute.

"You've witnessed someone fighting for more than justice. That was a plea for dignity. We may not understand her resolve, but we can bear witness, and we can have compassion. This case isn't about numbers. It's about the right to exist in a space without being made to feel small.

"Our client, Mr. Caldwell, asked for a job—not special treatment. He was spit on in the street for filing this suit. Attacked while walking home. Not because he stole or hurt anyone, but because he dared to say, 'I deserve to be treated equally.'

"You know who else said that? Addie Wyatt. Recy Taylor. Thurgood Marshall. Rosa Parks. Bayard Rustin. They weren't saints—they were citizens. Citizens who demanded their full rights.

"This isn't new. This isn't a misunderstanding. One spoke out against the jobs that paid us less. The other had to beg the courts to see her humanity after the men who raped her walked free. She got no justice. Addie had to fight twice as hard to stand where a white man could stroll. Our people have watched without sympathy or care. Injustice has torn apart their communities.

"And now, the weight is on you to decide what justice looks like in your town. Don't let fear tip the scales."

The room stood still as a gavel.

The judge cleared his throat, stunned.

"We will recess to deliberate."

Ben and Florence sat side by side, hands barely touching, breath shallow.

When the jury returned, time stopped.

The foreman stood. "In the matter of *Briarstone Textile*

v. Thomas Caldwell… we find in favor of the plaintiff."

Gasps. Then tears. Florence covered her mouth. Ben exhaled for the first time in hours. The courtroom erupted.

Ben's father, seated in the back, rose, his face like stone. Furious.

Ben turned slowly, smiled, and hugged Florence.

He didn't wait for his father's response. He walked out.

Outside, reporters swarmed—flashbulbs popping, pens scratching.

"Miss Witkins, what makes a secretary qualified to argue in court?"

"Who gave you permission to speak like that today?"

"Are you in a relationship with Mr. Mayfield?"

"Don't you think colored people should be grateful for how far they've come?"

It was a storm. Florence barely heard the words, but she felt their intent: to break her, to belittle her, to remind her where they thought she belonged.

Ben pushed through the crowd, eyes cold. "That's enough," he snapped. "Get out of her face."

The reporters faltered.

"You want a quote?" His voice dropped. "Write this down. This win was Florence Witkins's. Her courage, her mind, her voice won this case. Her career as a lawyer is just beginning. Every word she spoke was the truth—and the truth tends to hurt."

He paused. "If you're uncomfortable, good. That means you're listening."

He glanced down at the stenographers. "If anyone spreads another false rumor about her—about her relationships, her looks, her status—I'll have a lawsuit on your editor's desk by Monday."

The flashbulbs slowed.

He slid an arm around Florence's shoulders and led her out.

"They were ready to bury me," she whispered.

"Did you believe I'd let them near you?" he murmured.

"They'd have to kill me first."

Outside, under the afternoon light, Florence finally spoke. She told Ben she needed to find herself before she could accept him.

"Be patient," she said, echoing his words.

She shared that she would visit her mother for the rest of the month. Ben nodded, his heart aching.

He took her hand, led her beneath a shaded tree, and pressed her gently back against it.

"Ben! I'm wearing white," she gasped.

"I'll buy you a new one," he whispered, his lips brushing hers.

"You did well, pretty girl," he said, breaking the kiss too soon. She reached for him, and he smiled, deepening the kiss.

A throat cleared. "Ahem," James said, shaking his head. "That was some trial, huh?"

Florence covered her face. Ben dropped his head to her shoulder with a laugh.

"Let's go, Beautiful."

"Way to ruin the moment," Ben muttered.

James laughed. "I had to stop you from doing something indecent to that poor tree."

"I have class," Ben said, holding Florence's hand.

"Really? I've never seen it," James quipped, earning an eye roll from Ben.

When Florence left, Ben stayed to make sure no reporters followed her.

Then he got into his car. The battle was won. The war had just begun.

CHAPTER 22:
MAY YOUR FLOWERS BLOOM

The trial had ended, but the backlash had begun. Ben was seen as a sympathizer. He didn't mind. As long as Florence was away, he could handle the negative press. There was no one around to harass her. Reporters followed him everywhere—at work, in restaurants, even at his condo. It had reached the point where he preferred to stay inside. Luckily, he had already laid the groundwork for taking down his father. All that remained was to hammer the final nail in the coffin.

He had devised a plan months ago: phone calls, gentle dinners, slipped memos, and confidential numbers.

Ben had spent years being underestimated by his father. It wasn't surprising. Most of the time, he worked behind the scenes, aiming to be the perfect son his father wanted others to see. While his father schmoozed the old guard, Ben courted the future: young partners, ambitious clerks, women and colored lawyers with degrees but no platform. He listened, sought them out, and promised something his father never would: opportunity. He couldn't promise they would change or that life would be fair, but he could offer them a chance. Then came the buyout scheme.

Ben was no fool. He focused on younger generations for the future, but he also needed the board, made up of conservative old white men, on his side. Without their support, the plan would fail. Luckily, many had grown tired of his father's antics and conquest for title and power. Ben relied on shell companies and silent investors. Mr. Anderson gathered previous business partners to support Ben. James had civil rights contacts from the East Coast. Other allies were clever lawyers who believed in change. He bought the firm's shares through proxies, and one by one, the board turned.

The final blow came at the annual partners' dinner. He had been fitted for a suit months ago, and although he usually hated these events, he looked forward to this one.

Ben walked in, handsome and tall, radiating a different kind of confidence. Calm in his pressed charcoal suit, he handed his father a sealed envelope.

"What's this?" his father barked, annoyed.

"A courtesy," Ben said coolly. "Before the vote."

The room fell silent as the board filed in. When they stood—every single one of them—Ben's father's face twisted.

"Effective immediately," Ben announced, "Mayfield Law Firm is under new leadership. The firm is now majority-owned by me and my partners. The old practices, the old culture—they end tonight."

"You all voted for this!" his father shouted, glaring at them. They had gone to an empty conference room at the hotel where the dinner took place.

"I made them offers they couldn't refuse. You've grown content, Sir. Times are changing, and you weren't willing to change with them. I made the board some offers, and they accepted. Think of it this way," Ben continued. "You can now live out your days knowing you were the best. How about spending time with your family and retiring?" He smiled, wrapping up the meeting, eager for dinner.

Later, in the corner office that had once been a throne, Ben found his father pacing like a caged wolf.

"You smug little bastard," his father growled. "You'd destroy your own legacy, my legacy, for that... that negro girl?"

Ben shut the door, teeth clenching.

"I didn't destroy anything," he said. "You did. By believing you were the only one worthy to lead. By treating people like tools. By treating me like a ghost. I never once wanted your legacy. All I wanted was a father. But you cared more about your work than your own family, and it's gotten you where you are today: alone, miserable, and tormented."

His father slammed his fist on the desk.

"I built this from nothing! You have no idea what I've been through. What I've sacrificed."

"That's where you're wrong," Ben stated. "I know all too well what you've sacrificed, and I won't make the same mistakes. You built a cage for everyone, including yourself, and it's time I broke out of it."

The older man's voice dropped, bitter and trembling. He began to throw things off his desk, flipping chairs as his chest heaved. "You think you're so different from me, son, but you're not. Take a hard look in the mirror, and you'll see my reflection. I created you. That girl you think loves you so much will leave you. I know she will. Your relationship won't work, and you will be filled with anger and torment; you'll become like me. Your story is closer to home than you think. You are my son—"

Ben froze. "What are you talking about?"

His father's jaw tightened.

"I should've never let that woman into my house. I should've never let her raise you. Now you're a nigger lover all thanks to her." He spat.

"Who? Miss Benard? This has nothing to do with her. She taught me that love can come from anyone willing to give and receive it, no matter your color. She isn't the problem," Ben told him.

"Oh, but she is. She is exactly why you became this cruel version of me," he almost sobbed.

"You are willing to make everyone else the problem instead of taking accountability for your own actions." Ben seethed. How could he blame his issues on the woman who raised him?

"That woman has been a pain since she came into my life," his father said, raking his fingers through his hair. He looked older than his sixty years. Stress had taken its toll. His sad, lonely soul seemed worn down. Unfortunately, Ben had no sympathy left.

"I knew her, son. I knew her more intimately than you ever will. That woman—the woman you think you know—Mama Benard is not the woman you think she is."

"No," Ben said. "Regardless of what you say about her or your history, there's a fundamental difference between you two. She saw me—not as Ben Mayfield, the second heir to an empire, but as Ben, regardless of who I became. She is my family. You were nothing more than a lesson, sir." Ben walked out of his father's disheveled office.

"You're making a mistake. Winning this trial made you more enemies. Facing them alone is a foolish mission," his father yelled as Ben shut the door.

"I'm not alone, though." Ben smiled and walked out of the building.

He made a mental note to ask Mama Benard about what his father had been referring to earlier.

His father collapsed into the leather chair, defeated. The office was no longer his. The legacy, the power, the name—it was gone.

All that remained was the shell of a man who had built everything but never learned how to love anyone.

Ben walked the halls not as a shadow or a son but as a leader. He carried the name of the woman who had taught him to be true to himself.

All that was left was to patch things up with Florence. Though they had left on good terms, Ben still had to earn her back. He debated whether it was too early to propose, but he supposed it was. He would earn her attention first, then give her the world.

***

On the other side of the world, in Tulsa, Oklahoma, Florence had touched down to visit home. When she stepped on the soil, red as clay, her heart felt lighter. She saw her past struggles as growing pains. Now, she felt like she had blossomed into her most beautiful self. Nightmares were rare, and when they came, they were nothing but wet flowers left by previous storms. It was cloudy, not quite clear, but a single ray of sun shone in the background. Florence knew only good things were ahead—even though she was jobless at the moment.

The front door creaked open. The smell hit her like a ghost: burnt starch, rose talc, stale silence.

"Florence?" her mother's voice called from the kitchen, sharp as ever. "Well, it's about time."

Florence stepped into the dining room, clutching her coat like armor. The table was set perfectly. China plates shone, forks gleamed, and the food... she was certain her mother hadn't made it. Everything was arranged for the performance. Nothing had changed.

Her mother's eyes swept over her from head to toe.

"You look too skinny," she said instantly. "And that skin—dull. What happened to the glow you used to have? Honestly, how do you expect to find a man looking like that?"

Florence took a deep breath and let the words fall off her like dust.

"I didn't come here to be criticized, Mama."

"Well, I made pot roast. You used to like it before you moved up north and started eating that white people's food."

They sat. Florence picked at her plate while her mother poured herself a drink and told Florence she could help herself. After a long pause, Florence said softly, "The food is delicious."

"I'm sure. So after all these years of you avoiding me, what made you come back so suddenly? Life isn't working out just like I told you it wouldn't," her mother said.

"I came to tell you something. I forgive you." Florence continued ignoring her mother's comments.

Her mother blinked, confused. "Forgive me? For what?"

"For all of it. For never being there. For making me feel like I had to earn every scrap of your affection. You taught me to be ashamed of softness, success, and authenticity. For loving your image more than your child."

Her mother scoffed, waving a hand dismissively. "Oh, please, Florence. Cut the crap with all the philosophy talk. I did the best I could. You're ungrateful. There was nothing wrong with how I raised you. You had clothes, didn't you? You went to school. And now look—you're a lawyer, aren't you? You're welcome."

Florence used to flinch at that tone, to shrink, to argue, to beg. But not tonight.

"I'm not angry," Florence said. "Not anymore. I finally understand… you gave me what you could, but it wasn't love. I spent too long thinking I had to earn it, perform for it, be perfect for it. But I don't anymore. I know you can't love because you have never truly felt it, and that's okay. If anything, I feel sorry for you."

Her mother squinted. "What are you going on about now?"

Florence smiled—sad, but strong. "I love myself now. And I'm proud of who I've become. Not because of you but despite you."

The room was silent for a beat. Then her mother sniffed, raising her wine glass. "If that's how you feel and you've washed your hands of me, why are you here? Just to tell me how horrible a mother I've been? How you loved your father more?"

"You're the only mother I have, so you're the only one I've loved, like he was the only father I had. You both made mistakes. I don't resent either of you. There is no measurement of love."

"Well, I'm glad you feel that way. Since you're here, I've arranged a few dates for you while you're in town. Good men. Doctors. One's in real estate. You'll thank me later."

"There's no need," Florence said. "I've already met the man I'm going to marry… if he'll still have me." She thought it might be a bit early to consider marriage.

Her mother froze. "You—what? You met someone?"

Florence nodded. "I love him."

"Well? What's he doing?"

"He's a lawyer too. Brilliant. Kind."

"And he's colored?"

"No," Florence said. "He's white."

The wine glass hit the table too hard. "A white man? Florence, are you out of your mind? After everything I taught you, all my warnings—this is what you chose?"

"I didn't choose love, Mama. It found me."

Her mother stood, voice rising. "You've become some white man's slave, is that it? What will the neighbors say? What will our family say? You're going to let that man ruin your reputation?"

"No one ruined me," Florence said, standing taller now, her voice clear and rooted. "You did that. You broke me down for years. You taught me love had to be earned, that I had to be silent, smaller, obedient, pretty—but never enough. You wanted me to fear everything: white people, men, love, and myself."

Her mother looked shocked, as if Florence had spoken a language she didn't know.

"I came here to tell you something," Florence continued, eyes burning. "You can accept me as I am or not. Either way, I will not be your mirror anymore. I will not twist myself just to make you feel comfortable."

"Florence…"

"This is the last time I shrink for you. I forgive you, but I won't be less to keep your love. I don't need it anymore."

Her mother said nothing. Florence picked up her coat. Her hands trembled, but she held her head high.

"I'm happy now. I love who I am. And if that makes you ashamed… that's not my burden anymore."

Florence turned toward the door.

"I'll be staying at a hotel nearby if you decide you want to start a new relationship—one built on trust and respect. Come find me. I'll be here until Sunday."

Florence walked out. This time, she used her visit as a vacation. She also looked through the newspapers she had brought for potential jobs. She could ask James, but she wanted to see her options first.

By the time Florence had reacquainted herself with the town, she was glad she had left. There was nothing but racism and drama here, though she did visit some family. She hadn't expected her mother to budge, but at least she had given her an opportunity.

The week passed, and Saturday arrived. Florence felt relaxed; she needed this week to do nothing. That night, as she got ready for bed, there was a knock on her hotel door. Peeking through the peephole, she saw her mother.

Florence opened the door, allowing her mother to enter, head held high. "Mother," Florence said.

Her mother stood in the dining room. One hand rested on the table for balance, the other wiped something invisible from her eye.

"I don't… know how to say things like you do," she muttered. "Not with all your pretty words. I'm not saying I agree with all that mess you said about me or with you marrying a white man."

Florence stayed still, not expecting more—but something inside her held its breath. Her mother cleared her throat and stared at the floral placemat instead of her daughter. "But I know I wasn't the mother you needed. I was angry a lot. Scared more than I let on. Too proud to ever say it."

Florence blinked. Her heart hammered. "I didn't know

how to raise a girl like you," her mother continued. "You were always… reaching. Wanting more. I didn't know what to do with that. I learned to stay in my place."

"I was wrong." Florence turned fully, absorbing her mother's words.

"I don't know how to be different overnight," her mother added, voice shaky but real. "But if… if you meant what you said about trust and starting over—"

"I did," Florence whispered.

Her mother nodded slowly. "Then… maybe we can try. I don't want to be shut out of your life, Florence. I know I've already missed too much, but I'd like a chance, even if I don't deserve one."

Florence's eyes filled with tears. For a moment, she was ten again, aching for her mother to see her.

"We'll have to set some ground rules, Mother, some boundaries."

"I'll do my best," her mother said.

Florence stepped forward, cautiously.

Then, her mother opened her arms. Not wide, not graceful, but open.

Florence hesitated, then stepped forward and fell into them.

For the first time, they held each other not as mother and daughter but as the women they had become.

She turned toward home. Toward Detroit. Her steps were steady, guided by familiar streets and memories. She was ready.

When Florence finally laid her head down, she no longer felt storm clouds pressing on her horizon. The sky above was wide and open—a clear expanse where light could pour through. The field she stood in stretched endlessly, golden and quiet, no longer heavy with rain.

Far in the distance, a figure stood—too far to see clearly but close enough to know she wasn't alone.

***

Ben sat in bed, the room dim around him, wondering what Florence was up to. He had been planning nonstop for her return. Earlier that week, he had met with Denise, devising a plan between the two of them. Florence was stressed and kept emphasizing how she needed to find a job. Although Florence claimed she didn't have a job, she was insane if she thought Ben would let her leave his side. He would pretend to give her space, but he was preparing her new position. After a vote, Florence would work as a junior associate. He could have given her a higher position, but he knew she wouldn't accept it. He wanted to do things right, to make sure she couldn't accuse him of giving her the job unfairly. Florence had earned this, and Ben wanted her to know— without a doubt—that it was fair and square.

Ben hired Denise as a paralegal. They agreed to keep it a secret from Florence so they could start on the same day. Ben also evaluated everyone else and hired additional staff. He took care of some tasks himself, since he no longer had an assistant, knowing Florence would expect him to be on top of things quickly. When she returned home, he asked Denise for a house key. He wanted to set up a romantic evening for the two of them.

Ben placed flowers all over Florence's house and created a petal walkway. He set a tablecloth, candles, wine, and a meal. He arranged to be dropped off so his car wouldn't be noticed. He had considered running her a bath, but he wasn't sure how long the taxi would take to arrive. Mama Benard helped prepare the meal. While he waited, Ben looked around her house—not snooping but taking in her world. It smelled of her, and he missed her. He found his coat in one of her bottom drawers and wondered why she hadn't returned it.

Ben smiled, thinking about the day they had met. He decided not to propose today; he would wait. Still, he wanted to spoil her a little and had bought her a new set of jewelry. He wanted today to mark the day they officially started dating, if she would let him. Mooni seemed to accept him as well, rubbing against his legs as he tried to walk. When Ben sat down, Mooni purred in his lap. He had always wanted a pet, but his parents never allowed one. Mooni was clingy but would bite Ben when he petted him too much—somewhat resembling Florence, which made Ben laugh.

***

The apartment was dimly lit; the soft flicker of candlelight bounced off the walls. The air was thick with the scent of roasted garlic, butter, and something sweet. A jazz record hummed softly in the background, warm, romantic, and nostalgic. She figured Denise wouldn't be over—it was well past Mooni's feeding time. When she turned the corner, she gasped at the flowers and candles. Ben pulled her by the waist and placed a soft kiss on her lips as he held her in his arms..

"Hello, my beloved." He held her close, lips still warm from the kiss, eyes shining with a boyish heat. "I've waited for you patiently," he whispered into her neck.

Florence laughed. "It seems you have. Good boy."

"For you, I am."

CHAPTER 23:
BLOOM THE COLORS OF
YOUR SOUL

Florence lingered in the doorway, overwhelmed by the flowers, the warmth of the room, the way everything seemed to hum with intention. It was all for her—she felt it. She hadn't realized how much she missed Ben until now.

"You did all this?"

He shrugged modestly, trying—and failing—not to look too proud. "Denise helped. But the idea… that was all me."

He walked toward her, his hand reaching out slowly, reverently, and taking hers. Her fingers melted into his. He brought them to his lips and kissed her knuckles.

The weight of her hand in his—familiar, warm, grounding—settled something inside him, like gravity finding home. "Come, sit. You must be tired."

He pulled out her chair, helped her sit, then began preparing her plate. The care in every movement spoke volumes in its silence. He poured her wine, sat beside her, and watched with awe as she took her first bite.

Ben ate quickly, like he always did, but even that didn't stop him from glancing at her between bites. When he was done, he leaned back in his chair, hand propping up his chin, drinking her in like the last light of day.

She caught him staring.

"Is there something I can help you with?"

Ben smiled. "Is it a crime to bask in your presence?"

It is when you're staring at me while I'm trying to chew.

She laughed and shook her head. The candlelight caught her skin, giving her a glow that felt almost celestial. Ben smiled, but there was an untold ache in it. Her laughter wrapped around his ribs, warm and dangerous.

She finished her meal, set her fork down, and stared back at him. He reached out and caressed her cheek, and this time, she didn't flinch. She leaned into it. His thumb brushed beneath her eye, reverent. "How did you manage to do all this?"

He grinned. "Denise has a soft spot for a man who wants to win a woman's heart. This is especially true if that woman is her best friend."

"Well, thank you. It's lovely. Actually… I brought you something too," Florence said.

She stood, and Ben's eyes followed her. She took his hand again and led him gently toward the bedroom.

"I like where this is going already," Ben said playfully.

Florence giggled. "You've got a dirty mind, Mr. Mayfield. That's not your gift."

She knelt by her suitcase, unzipped it, and took out two shopping bags. One had a floral print for Denise; the other was deep navy blue. From it, she carefully retrieved a small box wrapped in silver paper. She stood and held it out to him with both hands. *I'm trusting you with this.*

Ben's smile softened. He unwrapped the paper and opened the box. Inside was a small star-shaped pin, carved from pale, smooth moonstone with silver-trimmed edges. On the back, there was an engraving: *"You are the Perseus to my Andromeda."*

It was the star of Andromeda. Ben recognized it but was still a little confused.

"You helped clear away my storm clouds, Ben, when I didn't even know storms weren't normal. You were there, ready to jump in. I am grateful to you."

"You rescued me. You became my Perseus," Florence whispered, a little embarrassed at how corny it sounded. It had actually been a pin her father gifted her long ago. When she returned home, she had picked it up to give to him.

Florence stood facing Ben. "Now, it's my turn to fight for you, to tell you I'm not going anywhere."

Her breath trembled as she finally spoke, eyes avoiding his at first. "Ben… all this time, I pushed you away because I was afraid. Not just of you but of myself. Being a colored woman, I've always had to be strong. Always had to protect myself. Always had to stand tall, even when inside I was breaking. Society has only ever seen me as that—a colored woman. A label. A burden. Never simply… Florence. And when you came along…" Her voice cracked. "…you saw me. You looked past all of that, past what the world said I was, and you treated me like I was more. And that terrified me."

Her gaze finally rose to meet his, wet with unshed tears. "I didn't know how to love myself, Ben… not really. So, how could I trust myself to love anyone else? Every time I hurt you, it wasn't because I didn't care. It was because I cared too much. Loving you felt like stepping into sunlight after living in the shadows, and I was so sure that one day it would burn me."

Her voice broke, her hand pressing against her chest as if to steady her heart. "But I loved you, Ben. I loved you the whole time. I was just too scared to believe it could last. And I'm so, so sorry for every moment I made you doubt me, for every time I walked away when all I wanted was to run into your arms."

She took a step closer, vulnerability trembling in every word. "But if you'll still have me—if you can still accept me, even after everything—I'm finally ready. Ready to stop running, ready to stop hiding, ready to love you the way you've always deserved."

His thumb brushed over the cool stone of the table

beside him as he searched for words. He didn't speak—not right away.

"Florence…"

She held her breath, her heart pounding in the silence between them.

Finally, a slow smile broke across his face. "It's about damn time," he whispered before pulling her into his arms. His lips found hers in a kiss that carried every unspoken word he hadn't said.

With a laugh breaking through his joy, he lifted her clean off the ground, spinning her around the room. Florence's laughter mingled with his, the sound ringing out like the answer to every doubt that had once stood between them.

Ben closed the box carefully, then stepped closer. His arms wrapped around her, not with hunger, but with tenderness: the kind of hug that said, *I've waited. I'll always wait.* She melted into him. *I'll keep it with me. Always.*

They embraced in the warm glow of candlelight. The scent of home filled the air. Laughter echoed around them. They shared a promise: love, though hard to find, was here to stay.

Ben and Florence sat on the couch, talking contentedly as Florence leaned her body against his. He spoke of his father. She shared her story about her mother. Finally, she realized she was ready to love herself. That, in turn, meant she could love Ben, even if it wasn't always easy.

"Well, I can buy you whatever you want. I can transfer the condo to your name. I can build you a new one if you don't like mine. You don't even have to take my last name."

Florence giggled. "Who said I'd take your last name? You're already thinking about marriage?"

"Well, of course I am. I want to marry you, Florence. I want to win with you; struggle with you; laugh, cry, live, and die with you."

"Is that your proposal?" Florence replied sarcastically, though she smiled at the sentiment.

Ben laughed. "Does that mean you'd say yes if it was?" He arched his eyebrow. "Don't worry, when it's time for me to propose, you'll know." He kissed the side of her head.

"What about work? What happened to Charlotte? Have you found another assistant?"

"You can be my assistant," Ben said cheekily, snuggling up to Florence.

She grimaced. "So you can force me to dote on you all day?"

"It was just a suggestion," Ben pouted.

"I don't know what I'm going to do about work," she admitted, laying her head on his shoulder.

"You don't have to work if you don't want to. I work hard so we can enjoy life—and I've saved for this. Let me take care of you. I want to."

Florence rolled her eyes. "Then when we go broke, it will be my fault."

Ben scoffed. "You think you could spend all my money, sweetheart? I'd love to see you try." He chuckled, cocky and amused.

Their eyes locked in a heated stare. Florence blushed and turned her head, steadying her breath.

Ben shook himself out of it. "Princess, I'd be more impressed than angry if you were actually able to spend all my money. But okay, you can go back to work. Which brings me to my present."

Ben stood up and handed her a key.

Florence looked down at it. "You want me to move in with you?"

Ben laughed. "That's not a bad idea; we'll circle back to that. But no, this key is to your office—at the firm, as a junior associate."

Florence gasped. "Ben, I can't... people will think that I—"

Her sentence was cut short by Ben. "I knew you'd think that, so I had the board take a vote. They were impressed with you at the trial, so they all agreed that you have a promising future. This one wasn't on me. You earned this yourself."

Tears welled in Florence's eyes. "Thank you so much," she said, hugging Ben.

Florence knew her life was about to change for the better. She had done it—stuck it out—and her hard work had finally paid off.

"Actually, there's something I've been wanting to ask you, but I didn't want it to seem like I was asking for favors. You know my friend Denise? She just completed her degree and passed the bar. She's looking for somewhere to gain experience.

Ben rubbed the back of his head, a bit nervous. "Yeah, sure. I'll look into it."

Florence didn't know that Ben had already given Denise a job. They were just waiting for her to return to work to surprise her.

Mooni jumped onto Ben's lap, curling up right between them.

"He likes you," Florence said. "He's the most important boy in my life. Isn't that right, Mooni?" She kissed his head. Ben let the statement go.

"Are you staying the night?" Florence asked shyly.

Ben stood, much to Mooni's discomfort. He reached over, pulling Florence back flush against him and kissed her neck. "Are you offering?"

"I am offering to let you sleep here. Just sleep," Florence clarified.

"That's fine. Being in your presence is more than enough. I missed you," Ben said, finally capturing her lips.

Florence wanted to be with Ben, but she wished to take it slow. She didn't want to rush into sex right away, she wanted to tease him a little. She showered while Ben waited for her to come to bed. When she got in, Ben cuddled her all night as if he were afraid she might be nothing but a dream.

The next morning, Florence woke first. She brushed

her teeth and made breakfast. When she returned to check on Ben, he had already brushed and was looking for her. She smiled warmly, fixed their breakfast, and they sat at the table.

"What are you doing today? How are you getting home?" Florence asked.

"Well, we can do whatever you want. I planned on having my driver pick me up. We need to move somewhere we don't have to hide to see each other," Ben pouted.

"I know, but it's hard to find that fast unless we build our own house in the country," Florence said half-jokingly. Ben thought it wasn't a bad idea.

They moved to the couch and played with Mooni until he got annoyed and left. Ben stared at Florence until she looked away, uncomfortable. He tilted her chin up.

"Can I kiss you, please?" He would've begged for more, but a kiss was enough for now. She nodded, and he captured her lips. The kiss was chaste, her lips tasting faintly of the pancakes they had shared. He was melting.

He turned to deepen the kiss, pushing her back against the couch. His tongue tickled her lips, asking for access, and when she granted it, he took full advantage. He kissed her deeply. His chest rose and fell quickly. He felt her hands on him—not pushing him away but holding on. He wanted more. Her legs wrapped around him. He pressed his hips against hers. His hand touched her waist.

Just then, Florence's front door flung open, interrupting them. Both Ben and Florence immediately straightened, faces flushed, chests heaving. They looked as guilty as they felt.

Denise shook her head with a hint of embarrassment.

"Well, good morning to you guys as well. I'd love to know what was going on here."

Florence responded, "It wasn't like that," fixing herself as she stood to hug Denise. "How have you been?"

Ben clenched his teeth. *Something might have been happening if she hadn't barged in*, he thought.

"Obviously not better than you. I actually approve of your boyfriend here," Denise said.

"Nice to see you again, Denise."

"Likewise," she said with a raised eyebrow.

"When you're free, Florence, let's catch up," Denise winked as she exited Florence's house.

Florence didn't return to work right away. She took at least two weeks off to recover and get ready for her new role. As the days passed, her routine became filled with Ben. Once he got off work, he came straight to her house. On weekends, she stayed at his place. Mooni was invited, too, though he liked the flat less than she did.

Ben bought cat towers. Florence said they were unnecessary because they didn't live there. When she was with Ben, she wanted for nothing. He spoiled her more than anyone ever had. This began to feel natural. He told her his money was hers. She could buy anything she wanted, but Florence felt guilty spending it. So, he brought her gifts or took her shopping to see what she liked or what he liked. This was how she gathered enough jewelry for a dowry, lingerie sets meant more for Ben, and a brand-new wardrobe.

The light was soft, almost golden, casting shadows against the faded wallpaper. The scent of garlic and simmering broth filled the kitchen. Florence sat on a stool, nervously twirling the bracelet on her wrist while Mama Benard stirred the pot. Ben leaned against the counter, sleeves rolled up, watching the two women talk.

"Mama Benard?" Florence asked softly.

"Yes, baby?" came the reply.

Florence glanced at Ben before continuing, hesitant. "Do you think Ben will be okay with the backlash he's facing at work? I know there've been troubles, but he won't tell me much. Every time I ask, he just smiles and says it's fine. I'm worried. I don't want him to suffer because of me."

Ben started to speak, but Mama Benard held up her hand. She set the spoon down and turned to face them both. Her eyes were far away, heavy with something unsaid.

"Sit," she said gently.

They obeyed, taking seats across from her at the kitchen table. Mama Benard folded her hands together, staring at them as though the truth were etched into her skin. When she finally spoke, her voice was low but steady:

"There's something I've never told you, Ben. It's been buried for a long time. But you both need to know."

Ben's brows furrowed. "What is it?"

She took a breath, her voice seeming to carry her back through time.

***

"I was fourteen when I came to work for the Mayfield family, cleaning, cooking, folding linens. That's when he started noticing me—your father, Ben. Not the way a boss notices the help but the way a boy notices a girl.

We stole little moments—a hand brushing mine in the hallway, a laugh shared in the greenhouse. He gave me small things: an orange, a ribbon, a book of poetry. For a while, I believed it was real—that love could ignore color and class."

Her voice tightened. "But when I found out I was pregnant, everything changed. Your grandfather, the elder Mayfield, found out. He paid me off to leave, said it was the only way to save your father's future. I didn't want to go, but I knew if I stayed, it would destroy us both. So, I walked away, carrying his child alone."

Her eyes glistened, but she didn't stop. "I raised that boy myself. He was mine. My son. My joy. But when your grandfather discovered him years later, he had him killed. Snuffed out like he was nothing but a stain to be erased."

Florence's hand flew to her mouth. Ben froze, his face pale, his breath caught between disbelief and grief.

Ms. Benard's jaw tightened. "Your father thought I'd abandoned him. Thought I'd left because I chose to. He believed I betrayed him. He was angry, but once he found out about his son and that your grandfather had him killed, there was no more light left in him. He grew hard that day; cold.

He hated me for it. And in time, that hatred spilled over to you—and to people in general, but especially to colored people. The bitterness ate him alive. It turned into the cruelty you grew up under."

She paused, her expression softening. "But there was a time, before it all turned to ashes, when your father tried to give me a piece of the world. You already know the law firm was a library before it became what it is today."

Ben blinked, startled. "Yeah… he gifted it to my mother?"

She shook her head slowly. "No, Ben. He gifted it to me. It was ours. Your father bought it for me in secret—a place we could hide away from the eyes of the world. No one knew. Not his family, not the town. Just the two of us. We'd sit among the dusty shelves, reading, laughing, pretending we were free. It was our little secret."

Her lips trembled into a sad smile. "I never thought anyone else would step foot in there again. But you—without knowing—turned that place into something new. A place of law, of voice, of power. You gave life back to what was once a shelter for me."

She reached across the table and took Ben's hand, firm and steady.

"But you, Ben—you were different. Even as a little boy, you'd sit with me while I cooked, asking how I was feeling. You cried when I cried. Nobody taught you that. That was your own heart. You became my son too—the only one I had left. And when you asked me to come with you, I didn't hesitate."

Her eyes flicked to Florence. "And now you've found love of your own. Real love. The kind his father never had the courage to keep. Don't let the world poison it. They'll glare, whisper, maybe worse. Ben won't suffer because of you, Florence—he'll suffer for you. But together, you can survive it."

Tears blurred Ben's vision. He swallowed hard, his voice rough. "Why didn't you ever tell me the little boy…

was my brother?"

Mama Benard's grip tightened. "Because I didn't want my pain to be your pain. I didn't want you to resent your father or grandfather because of me. But you're a man now. You deserve the truth."

The three of them sat there in the soft light, the weight of the past heavy between them. And suddenly, Ben understood: The walls of his firm held more than law books and files. They carried a secret history of forbidden love, loss, and survival—one that now lived inside him too.

After they finished, Ben's mother told them she was going to lay down.

"Ben, you have a keeper," she whispered to him.

Ben smiled. "I know."

***

"I'm putting some earplugs in, so make all the noise you want," she said, patting Ben on the back. He nearly choked and turned completely red.

"Mom, that's not—"

She waved him off before he could finish. "Good night."

Ben smiled, apologizing for her. Florence laughed, finding their relationship adorable.

"Well, I have been thinking..." Ben looked up from his plate, taking her hand in his.

"What have you been thinking, darling?" he asked her.

"Well, we've been dating for a couple of weeks since I got back, and it's safe to say we both missed each other. If you wanted to, we could—"

Before she could finish her sentence, Ben had already scooped her up from her chair. She squealed.

"Ben! Put me down. I'm so embarrassed right now."

"You shouldn't be embarrassed to let your husband love you," he said, looking right at Florence.

She didn't argue with his statement; she ducked her head against his chest. He carried her to their bedroom, placing her feet on the ground before closing the door. He pushed her gently against it, his hips insistent as he whispered how much he'd missed her. Every kiss made him whine. Florence had never seen him this needy. It was almost exciting.

Florence pushed against his chest, sending him back onto the bed where he looked at her with begging eyes. She climbed on top of him, sealing his lips with hers. He breathed her intoxicating scent, every hair on his body standing on end. He was so aware of her that he almost felt like he was drowning in her—and he wasn't complaining.

"Did you miss me, Ben?" she asked seductively, seeing how badly he was hanging on. His pants were so tight he started rubbing against her to get any friction at all.

"I did, Florence. I did. I need you so bad, baby. Please."

"Did you touch yourself while I was gone?"

Ben blushed, his eyes averting hers. She pulled his chin up so he could look her in the eyes.

"I'm sorry," he said, like he might get in trouble for touching himself. Florence found his eagerness endearing and decided to push him further.

"Can you show me?"

Ben looked at her in silence.

"Show me how you touch yourself, love," she whispered in his ear, licking a slow stripe up his neck before sucking on it. Ben shivered. He might have felt embarrassed, but he wanted her so much he was ready to do anything she asked.

She slid his shirt off his shoulders, kissing his collarbone as she moved down his chest. Each kiss sent a tremor through him. Ben's breath caught. His chest rose and fell with anticipation, like he was bracing for a wave.

When she reached his stomach, her lips lingered at the line where skin met waistband. His pants were already tented with want. Florence looked up at him, her eyes locked on his as her fingers found his belt. She unbuckled it slowly, teasingly, tugging the zipper down with the same aching pace.

Her palm pressed gently against him through the fabric of his boxers. Ben let out a low, helpless groan, his head falling back slightly as he tried to hold himself together. She smiled softly at the sound of him unraveling.

But then, she withdrew.

Florence sat back on her knees in front of him, her eyes glowing with curiosity and power. "Show me," she whispered.

Ben blinked, surprised by the command, his breath shallow. But he didn't hesitate this time—not with her.

His hand slipped down, wrapping around himself with a shaky breath. Florence watched intently, her lips parted, her gaze dark with desire. Each slow stroke felt like a confession, showing his longing, his restraint, his reverence—everything laid bare for her.

Tension clung to the room like heat. The only sounds were their heavy breaths and the weak noises he made with each move. Candlelight flickered on the walls, casting wild shadows across his body, glinting on the sweat at his brow.

Ben's jaw clenched, his eyes fluttering closed for a moment as he muttered her name like a prayer. He opened them again, needing to see her. "Come here," he said, his voice husky and raw. "I want you."

Ben felt more desperate with each stroke. When Florence noticed his brows drawn together and his jaw tightened, she realized he was close. She stood up and stopped his hand, replacing it with hers to keep him from finishing. Ben whimpered, almost a cry, as his head fell against her shoulder.

"Why did you stop?" he growled, his body shaking with desperate need. She wanted to laugh. He was so cute; she couldn't help it. Florence pushed him back onto the bed and climbed up after him.

"Because if you're going to finish, I want it to be in me," Florence said, biting his lip.

Those words flipped something in Ben. He lost all his patience. He dragged her body up to his awaiting mouth.

"Wait, wait," she told him.

"No more waiting," he growled.

Ben's mouth was on Florence before she had time to think. She gripped the headboard for balance as her hips moved on their own accord. The pleasure he gave her made her legs shake. She worried he might be crushed, but when she looked down, he seemed drunk with pleasure—she knew he was fine.

He grunted and groaned into her, circling her sensitive clit, trying to push her over. Ben needed to see her come undone for him. He had been so patient—he deserved this. He deserved to have her cover him in her very essence. He wouldn't complain. In fact, he'd want to come back for more. But the throbbing between his legs made him doubt he could last that long.

She tasted so good, Ben feared he might become addicted. She was beautiful—her skin flushed deep red, her moans spilling out recklessly. The sound of her pleasure made it impossible for him to hold back. He slowed his rhythm as her legs tightened around his head. His hands smoothed over her thighs, grounding her. "Breathe," he murmured against her skin, coaxing her to relax. She was so close—and he wanted her to feel every second of it.

"Ben, you have to stop. I'm going to…"

Ben doubled his efforts, gripping her legs so she couldn't escape. He was desperate for it. He sucked her most sensitive spot, and Florence cried out his name. She gripped his hair as her body shook. He basked in everything she gave before her body slumped forward and the trembles stopped. When Ben lifted her from that position, she saw his satisfied expression as he licked his lips.

"You enjoyed that a little too much," she teased him.

"You're right," he responded unabashedly.

"Florence, I can't wait any longer."

After her climax, Florence's mind had blanked for a

second and she had forgotten about Ben. His tip was an angry red, dripping down his shaft. Ben moved her hips down his body.

"Can I?" he asked with such a pleading tone.

"How could I tell you no?"

Ben huffed at her statement, happy to finally get the approval he wanted. He didn't take it slow like she expected. He lined her hips up and slammed into her to the hilt. Florence gasped, biting her lip at the unexpected pace.

"I'm so sorry, baby. You feel too good," Ben groaned. He couldn't stop his hips from doing what they wanted, what they needed. As Florence cried out, Ben tried to muffle her with a kiss. He was sure he wouldn't last long, and he wanted her to enjoy it too.

"Florence. Touch yourself."

Ben wasn't asking—he was commanding. The whiny, submissive man she knew a moment ago was gone, replaced by someone fueled on nothing but desire. He grabbed her hips, making sure to hit her sweet spot, but he was trembling. Florence did as he said, touching herself, making sure to look him straight in the eyes as she did.

She wanted him to see that she was no longer embarrassed. No longer afraid of who she was. Now, she wasn't scared to show how much she wanted him too. Every time Ben looked at Florence, his restraint wavered. Watching her made it almost unbearable to wait. His eyes rolled back as his hips never faltered. Ben, teetering on the edge, pushed Florence's hands away and did it for her. Luckily, it only took a slight flick for her to come undone.

He cried out, "Florence..." as her walls closed in on him. He bit his lip, trying to hold back the fall into the inevitable abyss.

"It's okay, Ben. Cum for me," she whispered, biting his ear. That was his undoing; he couldn't hold back even if he wanted to. Ben moaned her name as it spilled from his lips, feeling as though gravity itself had shifted. He was floating. He wanted her pregnant. The thought of Florence round with his child sent a sharp pulse through him. He growled, his hips starting up again as he flipped her beneath him.

"What are you doing?" she whined.

"One more time. I promise," he murmured, kissing her lips.

Ben didn't keep that promise. He kept her up for half the night.

The next morning, guilt tugged at him as he watched her stir. She was finally going back to work today. It was Monday, and they both had to be in the office. Ben woke her with soft, gentle kisses.

She looked at him, a little pouty, still sleepy from the night before.

"I'm sorry, sweetheart. I know you're tired, but you need to eat, so you have to get up."

Florence wiped the sleep from her eyes and began getting ready. She chose one of the outfits Ben had already stocked for her. As they dressed, she asked, "Did you look at Denise's résumé?"

"Oh, I feel like she needs a bit more experience before she can start working," Ben said, trying to sound casual. In truth, Denise was already on her way to the office.

"More experience?" Florence frowned. "That makes no sense. She needs a job to gain it. But you won't hire her because she doesn't have one?"

Silence stretched between them.

"If you or your company don't want to hire her, just say that. Don't make up excuses," Florence said firmly.

"That's not it," Ben replied, running his hands through his hair.

He tried to explain, but Florence turned away.

"It's fine," she said, moving to the kitchen to eat her breakfast.

The car ride to work was silent. Ben knew she was upset, but he hoped it wouldn't last.

When they arrived, Florence didn't even let him carry her things. The coldness stung.

"Have a good day!" he called after her.

"You too," she answered without looking back.

Ben felt the weight of their argument long after she disappeared through the doors.

When Florence entered her new office, a giant bouquet of flowers sat on her desk—so big she couldn't see behind it. She smiled, already knowing who had sent them. Guilt softened her irritation, but the wound was familiar. She'd been told the same thing once: that she needed experience but couldn't get it because no one would hire her. She thought Ben understood that better than anyone.

As she stepped closer to pull out the card, a figure popped up from behind the desk, making her scream—until she realized it was Denise. They both squealed and hugged tightly.

"What are you doing here?" Florence gasped.

"Your man hired me as a paralegal! I don't have a fancy office like you, but I'm in the building."

Florence grinned, relieved and genuinely happy.

"Ben is quite the guy. I like him. I'm happy for you, Flo," Denise said warmly.

They hugged again, then Florence stepped back.

"I actually have to go somewhere."

"A little office romance?" Denise teased.

"Something like that," Florence replied with a grin.

She made her way to the top floor, now only three floors above hers, and knocked on Ben's office door.

"Come in," he called.

He stood as she entered, and she wrapped her arms around him.

"I'm so sorry about this morning."

Ben pouted. "Yeah, you were cold to me."

She smiled. "The flowers were beautiful. And thank you for hiring Denise. How can I make it up to you?"

"Well," Ben said, "I have a few ideas."

He pulled her into his lap and kissed her. Their lips moved in perfect sync, the room spinning around the heat between them. Her arms wrapped around his neck, his hands tracing the hem of her skirt.

Then came a knock. Florence gasped and slipped off his lap.

"Come in," Ben said, his voice a touch too rough. He cleared his throat, adjusted his collar, and forced a neutral expression. Florence ducked under his desk just as the door opened.

A tall man in a navy suit stepped in with a clipboard. "Mr. Mayfield," he greeted warmly. "Sorry to interrupt. We're about to start the new hire orientation and wanted your input."

As Ben spoke with him, Florence, feeling mischievous, pressed her hands against his thighs. He stuttered. She giggled silently, unzipping his pants.

Ben straightened in his seat, fighting to keep composed. His fists tightened as he tried to push her away discreetly, but she didn't budge.

"The new group looks promising," the man continued. "One of them reminds me of that young associate you worked with last spring—what was her name? Tall, sharp, intense..."

"Uh—yes. Florence," Ben said, his jaw tight.

"Yes! That's it. She handled that trial like a pro," the man said, scanning his clipboard.

Florence teased him further, her lips and hands working skillfully until he began to tremble.

Ben nodded stiffly, gripping the armrest. "They, uh, seem like a strong class."

The man went on, oblivious to Ben's struggle.

"Well, I'll let you get back to it," he said at last. "Just thought I'd check in."

Before Ben could reply, Florence flicked her tongue around him, and he accidentally let out a low groan.

"Appreciated," Ben said quickly. "Have a good afternoon."

"You too, sir."

The door shut with a click.

Silence.

Ben exhaled hard, loosening his tie and leaning back with a sigh. "You are going to be the death of me," he muttered toward the desk.

From beneath, Florence's muffled laughter rose. "You started it," she whispered.

Ben chuckled low, rubbing a hand over his face. "We can continue," he murmured, pulling her up onto the desk and pressing against her.

Florence chuckled. "That was just an apology. If you want more of that, maybe lock your door next time."

She kissed him lightly, then stepped away. "Later. I have to go to orientation."

EPILOGUE

Ben and Florence married on a hot August afternoon in Virginia, one of the few states that issued interracial marriage certificates. The heat clung to every breath that day.

"I thought we were just going to say we'd gotten married," Florence said lightly, her voice carrying the lazy ease of summer. She tilted back the bottle of cold lemonade in her hand, condensation dripping onto her fingers. "I didn't know we were actually driving to get the license."

Ben's hands tightened on the steering wheel. His eyes stayed ahead for a moment before he glanced at her. "Florence, I can't believe you. I thought you wanted a ceremony. It doesn't have to be big—just friends and family." His voice softened, a tremor beneath the words. "I want everyone to know we belong to each other, not just in words, but in the way the law sees it. I want the world to understand that you're mine, and I'm yours."

The sunlight caught in his eyes, making them shine with something deeper than the day's reflection—a plea that went straight to her heart.

Her defenses crumbled; nothing remained to shield her from him. She loved him.

Their wedding was simple. It took place at the courthouse. Only a few cars were parked out front, and a small group of trusted friends and family attended. Denise, Florence's best friend, helped her prepare, brushing the soft curls from her face before whispering that she had always known this moment would come. Mr. Anderson, now a friend to both Florence and Ben, guided her down the narrow aisle, past wooden benches, until she reached Ben, waiting.

James stood as Ben's best man. Ben's mother attended, and so did Florence's—an appearance that surprised everyone. Florence's mother sat stiffly, her mouth tight with tension. Her presence was something, though not approval. Still, Florence no longer needed permission. She chose herself. She chose to love this man openly, knowing it meant facing the world's hostility head-on.

They returned to Detroit to begin married life, and for a brief moment, peace followed them. But two months later, a newspaper headline shattered that illusion: The owner of Mayfield Law Firm had married a colored woman. One sentence ignited the firestorm they had both been bracing for.

The backlash was relentless. They were stared at, whispered about. Anonymous letters arrived with threats. Protesters loitered near Ben's penthouse, shouting slurs and throwing objects when Florence entered the building. Her reserved parking spot became a battleground. Ben offered her a different entrance, but she refused. Some places, even painful ones, become your own.

Ben carried his burden with quiet strength, though the strain showed in his jaw and the slump of his shoulders at night. He didn't care about their hatred—he cared about Florence's safety.

He worked tirelessly, running through papers late into the night, determined to find a way to hand over his company to Florence. She had become his partner in every sense, yet the law refused to recognize her—she couldn't hold shares simply because she was a woman.

So, he devised a plan. After long talks with Florence, they agreed to entrust the company temporarily to someone they both trusted. Mr. Anderson came out of retirement to act as their stand-in—the steady hand who would carry their vision while Ben stepped down. Anderson spoke on their behalf, guarding their wishes until the courts could be challenged.

Still, it ate at Ben. He wanted Florence to have everything—not just the company but also the recognition, the respect, the place at the head of the table she had earned ten times over. Yet the world barred her path, not only because she was a woman but because she was a colored woman.

But that didn't matter. If the world wouldn't open its doors, Ben would work in the shadows, pulling every string, breaking every wall, until Florence could stand in the light— not as a hidden partner but as the rightful leader she was born to be. He never doubted her ability to succeed on her own. But she was his wife, and he wanted nothing more than to see her win. If he could help her get there, all the better.

In time, they moved to the outskirts of Detroit, where they built a house—hoping for relief and seclusion. Ben still traveled for business, delegating much of his practice to James. The hate never vanished, but it became more manageable. They built their home with their own hands, hammering out their grief one board at a time.

One afternoon, Florence was outside decorating her new vehicle. Ben had offered her an Aston Martin, but she preferred something more practical—a family SUV. She leaned against the hood when he came up behind her.

"Need my help? I'm pretty good with my hands," he murmured, pressing a kiss to her neck.

"I know you are," she replied with a sly smile. "Maybe if you weren't so good with your hands—among other things—I wouldn't have this belly."

"I happen to like this belly and the pretty lady sporting it," he said, splaying his fingers over her baby bump and kissing her cheek.

Florence had become pregnant a year after they married. When she told Ben, she watched the realization ripple across his face—first shock, then pure, unfiltered joy.

"We're going to have a baby?" he whispered, his voice cracking.

Florence nodded, though her smile was hesitant. She had only just begun her career. She had worked too hard to step back now.

"I'm scared, Ben," she admitted one night, hands folded over her belly. "What if this… derails everything I've worked for?"

He cupped her face gently. "Then I'll stay home," he said without hesitation. "Let them think I disappeared for a while. It's not like I can't afford it. Let me do this—for us."

And he did. Ben stepped back from the spotlight, determined to protect Florence from the pressures of motherhood and public judgment. She rose through the ranks, becoming the first colored woman to lead a legal department.

Ben doted on her throughout the pregnancy. "You shouldn't stay on your feet all day," he pouted as he rubbed her swollen ankles before bed.

"Maybe it's time you stepped back from work for a bit," Ben suggested.

Florence hated the idea, but she didn't mind the thought of having him to herself before the baby came.

"Okay," she responded.

"Okay? That's it?" Ben smiled, surprised she agreed so quickly.

He kissed her foot, then began trailing kisses slowly up her leg.

"Ben Mayfield, don't even think about it," Florence hissed.

"Please?" He looked up at her, pleading, as he climbed beside her. "Lie on your side. I'll be gentle, my love," he whispered, kissing her lips, his hand resting over her belly.

Florence rolled her eyes with a smile and reluctantly gave him the intimacy he sought.

She had feared becoming a parent. She worried she wouldn't be a good mother because she had no parental mentors. But Ben watched those fears dissolve as she became the best mother to their babies. She cried when she had to return to work and fretted over every detail, but to Ben, it was endearing.

Years passed, and their son was followed by a daughter. Ben had been worried when their first child was born. Florence was miserable during her pregnancy—her feet swollen, her stomach unsettled, plagued by cravings she couldn't fulfill. Ben cared for her as best he could, rubbing her feet and back, hoping to reassure her that she wasn't alone. Her second pregnancy was easier, and so was her last.

"Ben!" Florence called from their bedroom.

"We can't keep doing this," she said, holding up the results from the doctor's office.

Ben smirked. "I can."

Florence swatted his arm.

Ben couldn't help himself; she looked so beautiful pregnant. It reminded him that there was a permanent mark of their love. He would have had ten children if she wanted that or could handle it. But he knew it would harm her health, so he settled for three. He loved being a husband and a father, and Mama Benard loved the babies even more than anyone else.

"I'm serious," she pouted. "This is the last one."

And it was. Their baby girl was born in early spring when the daffodils lined the driveway. Ben had wanted a girl for so long that he was content with three children.

Around that time, Ben received a call: his father was dying. He hadn't spoken to the old man in years—not since the wedding, not since the silence had made its position clear.

"I'm not going," Ben said flatly, cradling their newborn.

Florence placed a gentle hand over his. "You don't have to go for him," she said softly. "But maybe... go for yourself. Let him see who you've become."

Reluctantly, Ben agreed. He brought the baby girl with

him, wrapped in a soft white blanket. The house smelled of dust, old wood, and antiseptic. A colored nurse—young and poised—greeted him at the door. Ben had chosen her deliberately, a quiet act of defiance.

His father lay motionless, sunken into the bed, too weak to feed or dress himself. The nurse adjusted his pillows as Ben stepped closer.

"I wanted you to see what became of everything you fought so hard to keep," Ben said, his voice low. "And if you wanted Florence to have our money so badly, you could have just asked me to give it to her instead of wasting your precious breath. You didn't even visit Mom when she was sick, but here I am, taking care of you. I even got you a nurse. I'm the perfect son you taught me to be."

Ben beamed at the tiny bundle in his arms. "This is one of many of your grandchildren. They will inherit everything."

The old man's lips twisted, his voice thin and rasping. "You won't give a dime to that negro family you've got." His words dissolved into a hacking cough that rattled through his frail frame.

Ben straightened, meeting his father's gaze with cold finality. "I wasn't asking."

He kissed his daughter's forehead, gave the nurse a nod, and walked out without looking back.

Florence and Ben built a life as strong as the home they made together. It stood outside of town, far from the city but close to their loved ones. The house had Florence's favorite bay window and a garden full of wildflowers. It was their fortress.

Florence had become a partner at her firm. At meetings, she was introduced with reverence. She wore her power well: unapologetic and elegant. Denise, now a junior associate at Ben's company, visited often with her daughter. James and his partner Kevin—whom he had met at the New York conference—had built a happy life together. Coincidentally, Kevin was the same man who had once held Ben back before he could reduce Lance to nothing. Though James and Kevin weren't legally married, they had built a home of their own, and Florence and Ben visited them every Christmas.

Their love lasted not because the world changed, but because they grew strong in the right places and stayed gentle where it mattered. Their children—a blend of their looks and spirits—grew up hearing stories. These tales were not about hate but about resistance and love that was stronger than prejudice.

One evening, Florence stood on their porch, watching the sunset melt into gold. Ben came up behind her, wrapping his arms around her waist.

"You remember when you told me you didn't need a man?" he murmured, kissing her cheek.

She smiled. "Still true, but I do love my husband."

He laughed. "My wife saying she loves me?" He pretended to be shocked.

"I guess that's all I need. I love you more."

***

The Storm is Over Now

The water danced upon the leaves, and Florence expected the storm to begin as usual. A few droplets hinted at what was ahead, but today their rhythm changed. They fell slowly, no longer harsh. The sound no longer carried chaos, nor did it echo abandonment. As the droplets landed on the petals, the sound wasn't perfect—still, it was beautiful.

For the first time, Florence heard serenity. The life she had been given once made her heart thrive on instability, so much so that chaos became her normal. But now, this rhythm felt different. The old beat was forgotten, lost in the past.

This time, she wasn't alone. A figure stood in the field. She knew him well. Ben watched her from across the grass. He joined her, and their souls locked on each other. With

Ben, there was silence and stillness.

If Florence had called out, the only sound would have been his answer. But she didn't—not this time. She didn't scream for help. The tears didn't fall. The storm never came. The fields lay clear, the sun shining in bright rays.

Florence lay in the grass with a smile, taking Ben's hand—his smile mirroring her own. They leaned back and closed their eyes. In that moment, she was certain they were of one mind. She had finally achieved it.

Irehide.

ACKNOWLEDGMENTS

First and foremost, I thank God for all that I am: the gift of creativity, the strength to persevere, and the grace to complete this work. Without His guidance, none of this would have been possible.

I am deeply grateful to the MoveWrite School of Creative and Erika Roman Saint-Pierre, whose insight and instruction helped me grow in both confidence and craft. A heartfelt thank you as well to the writing groups I connected with on Discord—your encouragement, honest critiques, and sense of community sustained me through every stage of this process.

To my coworkers and friends who generously offered your time, opinions, and support whenever I needed a second pair of eyes, thank you. Your input added depth and clarity I could not have achieved alone.

To my PR team at BMRPR, thank you for your professionalism, dedication, and care in bringing this project to life. Your expertise in navigating the promotional journey has been invaluable.

To my family, thank you for being my constant source of love, strength, and grounding. Your belief in me, even in moments of doubt, carried me through. Your unwavering support, prayers, and encouragement gave me the courage to keep going.

Finally, to my grandmother, who first introduced me to the art of storytelling and nurtured my love for words, thank you for being my earliest inspiration. Your influence continues to shape the writer I am becoming.